## SHE THOUGHT ~~HE WAS THE~~ MAN
## SHE LOVED . . . .

He raised her hand to his lips and pressed a kiss to her palm.
Marguerite gasped. While other men had kissed her hand, it
had been nothing more than a courtly gesture, a brief touch of
cool, dry lips on the back of her hand. This was far different.
His lips were warm and moist, lingering in the sensitive center
of her palm. Just as a pebble tossed into a river caused ripples
to spread to both shores, so too did his caress send waves of
delight through her veins. And yet, although ripples grew fainter
the farther they spread, the pleasure his kiss wrought grew ever
stronger as it coursed nearer her heart.

If this was only a prelude, as she suspected it was, what
delights would the marriage bed bring?

"In truth, I begin to believe in Fate," she said as he continued
his gentle assault on her hand. " 'Twas surely Fate that brought
you to my home. Now we must find a way to keep you here."

"I assure you I've no intention of leaving," he promised in
his husky whisper. He slid one arm around her waist and drew
her close to him.

Marguerite raised her hands, wanting to touch his face, to
draw him even closer. As she did, she pushed back the dark
hood that had kept his face shadowed.

"You!"

The man who had brought her such pleasure was not
Lancelot. It was his brother.

# CRITICAL ACCLAIM FOR *SILVER THORNS*

# SILVER THORNS

## AMANDA HARTE

**PINNACLE BOOKS**
**KENSINGTON PUBLISHING CORP.**

PINNACLE BOOKS are published by

Kensington Publishing Corp.
850 Third Avenue
New York, NY 10022

First Printing: September, 1996

Printed in the United States of America
10  9  8  7  6  5  4  3  2  1

*For Donna —*
*I hope you enjoy*
*this trip to the Middle*
*Ages.*

For Don—my husband, my best friend, and, yes, my knight in shining armor. Who ever thought that the Ides of March and a Roman camp would be the beginning of the adventure we call love?

*Best Wishes,*

*Amanda Harte*
*9/19/96*

## Principal Characters in Order of Appearance

Alain de Jarnac, the Silver Knight
Marguerite de Mirail, chatelaine of Mirail
Louise, companion of Marguerite
Jean, younger brother of Louise
Guillaume de Mirail, lord of Mirail, father of Marguerite
Janelle, mother of Alain de Jarnac
Charles, brother of Alain de Jarnac
Henri de Bleufontaine, neighbor of Marguerite, enemy of Alain
Gerard, son of Albert the cobbler of Bleufontaine, lover of
   Louise
Diane de Lilis, betrothed to Charles (Alain's brother)
Honore, lady of Poitiers, friend of Alain
Robert, father of Alain
Philippe, friend of Robert and Guillaume, second husband of
   Janelle, and father of Charles

# Chapter One

At least it wasn't raining. Normally he wouldn't mind it. In fact, he preferred rain when going into battle. Unfortunately, today he wasn't waging war, nor was he facing an opponent at the other end of a lance. Lord knew, it would have been easier if he were.

The knight on the silver gray destrier let the reins slacken as he looked around him. Though the wheat field could not compare to the raw magnificence of Outremer, there was no denying its beauty. It spoke of fertile ground, of centuries of tradition, of home. This morn it also reminded Alain de Jarnac of the obligation awaiting him.

He cursed roundly, not caring who heard him. Sweet Mary in heaven, he needed no reminder of the fate which was now mere minutes away. And yet, despite everything, his pulse quickened. It was a familiar sensation, the normal precursor to a battle. Yet today he faced no battle, no adversary save a chit of a girl with eyes that the troubadours claimed outshone the heavens. Troubadours, Alain reminded himself firmly, were known to exaggerate. He took a deep breath and willed his pulse to slow. The Silver Knight had won more dangerous skirmishes than this one.

" 'Tis a good omen. I know it is." Marguerite de Mirail gestured toward the narrow window. "This is the perfect day for Lancelot to come."

Her companion smiled. It was a beautiful morning; there was no denying that. The sun was shining, there wasn't a cloud in the sky, and a soft breeze kept the May day from being too warm. But had the dawn brought torrential winds and rains, Louise knew Marguerite would have found them propitious. That was simply her mistress's way.

Marguerite pirouetted as she stepped back into the room. The soft folds of her gown swirled around her ankles, and her golden braids swung rhythmically. Today even the most glib-tongued of troubadours would have searched in vain for words to describe Marguerite de Mirail. On an ordinary day she was beautiful, but today anticipation had given her a new radiance. The sparkle in her eyes owed nothing to the reflected beauty of her sapphire bliaut, and the smile which spoke of happiness transformed her face so even a jaded courtier could not ignore it. Though she had yet to meet the man of her dreams, Marguerite was a woman in love.

"Your gown is beautiful," Louise said with only a touch of envy that she would never own so fine a garment. "Lancelot will be sure to fall in love with you when he sees it." In truth, she doubted the man would consider the gown anything more than an impediment, something which prevented him from enjoying a full view of the chatelaine of Mirail's charms.

What male would care that Marguerite and Louise had spent days embroidering an intricate design of flowers around the hem or that the flowers held a special significance? If Louise knew men at all, the one thing that was certain was that their interest lay in what the gown concealed. Lancelot would be no different, for all that he was one of Richard the Lionheart's most trusted knights. He was still a man, wasn't he? Yet Louise knew that Marguerite was unwilling to accept the coarser realities of her approaching betrothal, and so she did not voice her thoughts.

"Come! You must come!" A woman burst into the room, her normally stolid features flushed with exertion, her words shattering the serenity which had filled the small chamber.

"What is it, Clothilde?" Marguerite forced herself to speak in the low voice that rarely failed to calm her people, even though a knot of apprehension began to settle in her stomach. Oh, Lord, not today! If Clothilde had raced up the staircase, something must be dreadfully wrong. The portly woman rarely stirred from the serving chambers, and she never, ever moved more quickly than the garden snails.

"What's wrong?" Marguerite repeated the question. The chill sweeping over her was not brought by the light breeze that chased a piece of yarn across the stone floor. For a moment the only sound in the luxuriously appointed room was Clothilde's rough breathing.

" 'Tis Jean." The older woman's tone left no doubt of the gravity of the situation. "Jean's hurt."

Louise blanched and grabbed a chair for support.

"Fetch my basket, and be quick about it." Marguerite shook her head impatiently. The last thing she needed was to have Louise fainting or, worse yet, caterwauling while she tried to heal her brother. Tall and thin almost to the point of gauntness, Louise was an eminently practical woman . . . except when her younger brother was concerned.

The harsh words met their mark. Though Louise bit her lip to keep from crying, she moved swiftly across the chamber. A moment later she trailed Marguerite and Clothilde down the long stairway, the basket clutched in her hand.

When they reached the bailey, Marguerite needed no directions. The gathering of men and women who should have been working told her where Jean lay. The leaves on the tall poplars rustled; a songbird warbled; but in the courtyard no one spoke. Marguerite could feel their eyes on her, could hear their wordless pleas.

The boy was in pain. That much was obvious, though he made no sound. His face contorted in a grimace, and while he tried to force his lips into a smile, mindful that someone who had reached the exalted age of ten could no longer shed a tear, Jean was unable to conceal either the fear shining from his eyes or the blood which dripped from his arm.

Marguerite laid a comforting hand on his forehead and murmured soft words as she tried to assess his injury. Though the amount of blood was alarming, the steady drip was far less dangerous than a pulsing spurt. Sweet Mary, she prayed, let me help him.

The sun which an hour before had seemed pleasantly warm now beat uncomfortably on Marguerite's back, and waves of heat radiated from the ground. She brushed a tendril of hair from her face, then turned to Jean.

"What happened?" she asked. She watched him carefully, searching for a sign that her optimism was well founded and she'd not be forced to use a hot knife. As she wiped the gash again, she noted that the blood no longer dripped from it. Marguerite raised her eyes to the heavens. Thank you, she breathed silently. Her prayer had been answered, and it would not be necessary to cauterize the wound.

"I was chopping wood." As if he sensed her relief, Jean found his voice. "The ax slipped."

Marguerite followed his eyes as they moved to the left. There, embedded in the earth, was the head of an ax. The handle, a shred of leather thong still clinging to one end, lay several feet away.

Louise gasped, and Marguerite could hear her swallow deeply before she spoke. "How could you be so clumsy, today of all days?" Annoyance mingled with concern, making Louise's normally sweet voice strident. The boy stiffened but made no reply.

Marguerite bent her head to conceal her smile. Perhaps Louise would be less of a hindrance than she'd feared. "I hardly think he planned to cut his arm," she said. Marguerite leaned closer to Jean and added in a loud whisper, "Father René tells us our sisters are a blessing."

"Not this one." For the first time, Jean managed a smile.

"You're a fine one to talk!" Louise retorted. "You never could stay out of trouble."

When Clothilde returned with the flagon of wine, Marguerite's mind continued to whirl. If only she could keep Jean and Louise sparring, it might lessen the pain the boy felt.

"Father René never told us brothers were a blessing," she said, moving Jean's arm to fully expose the gash.

Louise placed a hand on her brother's head and carefully averted her eyes from the gaping wound. "Indeed, they're not. They were placed on earth to teach us patience."

"A lesson you've yet to learn," Jean quipped in a voice which came dangerously close to breaking. "Mère says you'll never learn to wait."

With one hand Marguerite held Jean's arm steady as she poured wine onto the wound. Though it would burn, the discomfort was necessary if she were to keep his flesh from festering. The boy gasped.

"Will you tell me a story?" Jean's lips pursed as he tried to master the pain.

"Of course." Marguerite laid his arm on a clean piece of linen, then tipped her head to the side, considering. When she'd started treating the barony's ailments, she'd discovered that her patients seemed less aware of their suffering if she kept their minds occupied with other thoughts. At first she'd related tales the troubadours had brought to the castle; then she'd begun reciting the adventures of Aeneas and Ulysses. The men seemed to relish the accounts of battles so different from the ones they'd seen, and the women sighed each time Marguerite described Penelope's fidelity to her long absent husband. Today, though, there was only one story Marguerite wished to recount.

"It was on the fairest day of summer," she began, "a day as beautiful as today, that Guinevere first met Lancelot."

Jean's pain-darkened eyes widened with something akin to incredulity. "You believe that nonsense, too! I thought it was only my feather-headed sister." He turned his head and glared at Louise.

Marguerite raised an eyebrow. " 'Tis not nonsense," she said in the voice she normally reserved for disobedient serfs.

"I should say it's not!" Louise frowned at her brother. "You're just too much of a dolt to appreciate true chivalry."

"Better a dolt than a fool," he retorted.

"Better a fool than someone with less sense than a quintain."

The color rose to Jean's cheeks, and Marguerite could feel his pulse begin to throb. It appeared his sister's presence no longer held any therapeutic effects.

"I need fresh comfrey for Jean's wound," Marguerite told Louise. "Will you fetch me some? You'll find it by the stream. Remember, 'tis the plant with the lance-shaped leaves."

Louise gave her brother a parting glance. "I couldn't forget that," she said with a grin. "I'll just think of *Lance*lot."

The crowd began to disperse, reassured by the smiles which lit both Marguerite's and Louise's faces, knowing there was much work to complete ere the visitors arrived.

"Will I be all right?" Jean asked when his sister could no longer hear him.

"You'll dance at my wedding."

"Wedding." Jean paled. "Sweet Mary, I forgot. Today's the day he's coming." The boy stared at Marguerite, and the pain she'd seen reflected in his eyes was replaced with fear. "Mère will flay my hide when she finds out I made you late."

Before Marguerite could reassure him that he'd face no punishment, the sound of trumpets cut through the clear air.

"They're here!" Jean said with a whimper. "You've got to go."

"They'll wait," Marguerite replied.

"My people and I welcome you to Mirail." Guillaume de Mirail stood proudly as he greeted his guests, his crimson tunic and matching hose clearly chosen to honor them. Behind him half a dozen knights nodded their heads in welcome, while the serfs who had clustered in the courtyard, anxious for a glimpse of the visitors, bowed.

As he dipped his lance in greeting, Alain studied his host. The baron appeared older than Alain had expected, with gray liberally streaking the blond hair, but his eyes were as blue as

Janelle had said. Like an August sky, she had told him, and she had not exaggerated. Nor had she been wrong in predicting that a man would quickly forget Guillaume's handicap, for Guillaume himself appeared oblivious to his missing arm.

Motioning his brother to his side, Alain nodded to his men to dismount. "We thank you for your hospitality," he said, his eyes searching Guillaume de Mirail's face. The words were mere formality, of little significance. What mattered was the expression in the baron's eyes. For the briefest of instants they widened. Though Guillaume caught himself so quickly that another man might have missed that momentary shock, Alain did not. It was what he'd expected, what he had feared. As the stab of recognition twisted his bowels, Alain fixed a slightly amused smile onto his face and let his eyes wander through the crowd.

There was a quiet murmur as the people of Mirail stared at the two knights, both tall and blond and yet so different. For while Charles's hair was golden, Alain's was so pale it appeared almost silver, and his shoulders were far broader than his younger brother's.

"You must be Charles," he heard the baron say.

His brother laughed. "None other. A legacy of the crusade, I've been told."

Indeed! Alain willed himself to show not the slightest reaction. Guillaume's laugh matched Charles's, and soon Alain's men joined in the mirth, not seeming to notice that their leader's smile had faded.

For a moment longer Alain scanned the crowd. There were several women richly dressed and obviously of noble birth, some comely enough to tempt a hungry man, yet none matched the troubadours' fulsome praise. Where was she? Alain turned to Guillaume, one raised eyebrow the only sign of his question.

As Guillaume met Alain's gaze, a flush stained his cheeks. "You seek my daughter," he said in a voice that held more than a tinge of shame. "I fear Marguerite has been delayed."

Delayed, when their visit had been planned for weeks? Alain raised both brows in a gesture his men recognized as the precursor to a display of fury. The delay was rudeness personified, undoubtedly the whim of a senseless chit.

"It's no . . ."

Alain cut off Charles's words. "You know women," he said with a laugh that did naught to hide his rancor. "She's probably searching for ribbons to match her gown. Come," he said to Guillaume. "I would like to see your castle."

Mayhap Jean was right. Mayhap it was all romantic nonsense, though Marguerite wanted desperately to believe it was not. The tales of King Arthur's court had touched her heart as nothing else had done, not the stories of bravery she'd read nor the songs the troubadours had brought from the Crusades. That was why she'd so painstakingly embroidered a border of special blossoms on her bliaut and why she and Louise had searched the countryside for the same flowers Guinevere had worn the day she met Lancelot.

Today was the day Marguerite would meet her Lancelot. Today was the day Alain de Jarnac would reach Mirail, and she would first see the man to whom she'd been promised since birth. It was to have been a day of magic, as she and her betrothed discovered the love which would unite them throughout the ages. Though her gown was ruined and her flowers gone, Marguerite wanted to believe it still would be. A true Lancelot would love her even though she wore her second-best gown and had naught but ribbons to decorate her hair.

He was alone, his back turned, when she entered the Great Hall. For a moment she stood silently, staring at the stranger. Tall and muscular, he wore a tight-fitting tunic that revealed broad shoulders. Even the traveler's coarse hose could not hide a pair of well-shaped legs. His hair was golden blond, the tilt of his head telling her this was a man who was confident of himself.

"Lancelot," she breathed. The troubadours had not lied. The man who was soon to be her husband was indeed a knight worthy of the Round Table.

He turned, and a flush of embarrassment stained Marguerite's cheeks as she realized she'd spoken aloud. The stranger stared at her for a moment, confusion clouding his eyes, before he grinned in sudden comprehension.

" 'Tis my pleasure to make your acquaintance, Lady Guinevere." He bowed low, his hand sweeping the rushes on the floor in a gallant gesture. "I knew from the perfect weather and the warm reception that I was in Camelot, but even the minstrels' tales did not prepare me for you. Your beauty makes the day pale."

Marguerite's hand flew to her throat as she tried to regain her composure. It had happened! Her dreams had come true. He was tall, muscular, so virile—the perfect knight. Though others might call him Alain de Jarnac, Marguerite knew this was Lancelot. She drew in a deep breath as she looked at him. His unlined face bore no scars from battles or tournaments. His nose and chin were firm, and his brown eyes sparkled as they met hers, then moved to complete his own study of her.

"You're the most beautiful woman I've ever seen," he said reverently, when his gaze had moved slowly back from her toes to her face, lingering ever so slightly over the lush curves that her gown did little to disguise. "I never dreamed there was anyone like you."

With a blush from the effusive praise staining her cheeks, Marguerite managed a few words as she extended her hand in greeting. "Welcome to Mirail." She paused a moment before adding, "Lancelot." For a little while longer she'd continue the pretense, turning her own home into Camelot and Richard's knight into the man of legends. When Father arrived she'd begin to call him Alain.

Where was Father? Marguerite looked around the hall. It wasn't like him to leave a guest unescorted. For that matter, where were all the servants? They should be preparing the evening meal. Later; she'd worry about them later.

"Has Merlin been to court recently?" Lancelot asked, joining the game. As he pressed her hand between both of his, Marguerite felt tiny shivers of excitement race up her arm. This was what the troubadours had foretold. If the real Lancelot had been half as wonderful as this man, it was no wonder Guinevere had sacrificed Arthur and Camelot for him.

Marguerite tried to mask her feelings, and her joking tone gave no hint of the inner turmoil this tall stranger was creating. "No," she said, "but we expect him tomorrow for dinner. We're having a hunt in two days, and you know how he enjoys them."

"Ah, yes, falcons always caught his fancy, didn't they?"

So intent was she on the fantasy she and Lancelot were creating that Marguerite did not hear the footsteps behind her.

"I see you've met Charles."

Marguerite spun around and stared at her father. Charles? What did Father mean? And who was the stranger at his side? The man wore an expression that could only be called grim.

Her eyes narrowed at the wariness she saw on her father's face. Though his lips were lifted in a smile, the mirth did not extend to his eyes. Something was amiss.

She looked at the man she knew as Lancelot, seeking an answer to the puzzle but finding only the friendly grin that had warmed her heart so recently.

"At your service, my lady," he said with another low bow.

Almost against her volition, Marguerite's eyes were drawn to the other man. Like Lancelot he was dressed in the coarse tunic and sturdy hose that traveling demanded, but while Lancelot wore the warm shades of the earth, this man's clothing was dismal gray, unrelieved by any color.

He was taller than her knight and more powerfully built, with shoulders that bore witness to hours of practice throwing a spear. While other women might find his size attractive, his height and breadth seemed overpowering to Marguerite, a grotesque exaggeration of Lancelot's perfection. His hair was silver blond, a pale imitation of the other man's radiant golden beauty. And his eyes! The stranger looked at her with icy blue eyes which bore no resemblance to Lancelot's warm brown orbs.

Marguerite noted that the big man's face was bronzed, as though he rarely wore his helmet. A jagged scar, its whiteness contrasting vividly with the brown of his face, ran across the stranger's forehead and confirmed her supposition that the man did not wear a helmet regularly, even in battle. Lancelot would not be so foolish.

Her eyes darted to the other knight's unblemished beauty. Here was the man of her dreams, the one the troubadours had described. This was the man she was destined to marry.

Her father's words drew her back.

"Marguerite," he said, putting his hand on the stranger's shoulder. "This is Alain de Jarnac."

# Chapter Two

Alain? Father must be mistaken. But the sinking feeling deep in her stomach told Marguerite it was no error, not even a feeble attempt at a joke. Somehow, though the knight who stood next to her appeared to be Lancelot, he was not Alain de Jarnac.

"I see you've met my brother." The big man's voice was harsh, with none of the gentle speech and smiles a courtier usually employed toward women. He did not bow, nor in any way greet her save to stare at her, his eyes coldly assessing. Though his rudeness was unexpected, it was the import of his words rather than their tone which sent a shiver down Marguerite's arm.

Alain's brother? She'd listened carefully to the tales the troubadours had sung of the Silver Knight's prowess in battle. She'd managed not to blush at the reports her servants had whispered when they'd thought her too engrossed in Mirail's accounts to hear them, tales of amatory exploits which made his military successes fade into seeming insignificance. Yet not once had she heard that Alain de Jarnac had a brother.

" 'Tis not such an unusual occurrence, you know." His voice held more than a hint of mockery. "Brothers are the natural result when a man and a woman . . .'' He broke off abruptly, his blue eyes apparently serious as he studied her. ''Perhaps I should demonstrate rather than explain.''

Marguerite felt the blood rush to her face. How could the man be so crude? If another visiting knight had treated her with such disrespect, her father would have challenged him to a joust, once more showing the world that though his left arm might end at the elbow, he could still hold a shield and, more importantly, could still defend his daughter's honor. Today, though, there was a wistful expression on Father's face that she'd never before seen, and he did naught but smile at the big man as though unaware of his rudeness. It was almost as if Father were under a spell.

Marguerite's eyes moved quickly from the tall man to his brother and back to her father. Something was definitely amiss when Father looked and acted so strangely.

Reminding herself of her duties as chatelaine, Marguerite fixed a smile on her face. Though one of her guests appeared to lack the most rudimentary knowledge of chivalrous behavior, she would not embarrass her father. She'd provide full hospitality to the travelers, and then she and Father would talk.

She turned to the golden-haired knight. ''I suppose I can't continue calling you Lancelot,'' she said softly. Somehow she would recapture the magic of the day, the wonderful moments they had shared before Father and that man had intruded.

''My name is Charles,'' he said. ''But a beautiful woman like you can call me Mordred if she wishes.''

As though she'd ever confuse him with the villain of Camelot!

His melodic voice continued, ''Just having you speak to me is like seeing the sun after a fortnight of rain.''

Watching the exchange, Alain felt a glimmer of recognition. It was what he had expected. This was the mindless banter he had heard at the court, the only conversation Honore and the other women seemed capable of conducting. His fiancée, it seemed, was no better than his mistress. Women! They were all the same. They craved pretty faces and pretty words and were too shallow to know there was only emptiness behind them.

She was beautiful; there was no denying that. When he had entered the Great Hall, Alain had seen a woman deep in conversation with his brother. She stood with one shoulder toward him, revealing only her profile, yet that was enough to tell him the minstrels had not exaggerated.

Alain had been prepared for a tall woman with golden hair and blue eyes. The troubadours had told him that much. What they had not told him was that Marguerite was so fragile. She was slender, almost to the point of being thin. Undoubtedly as weak in the body as she was in the mind. Oh, Janelle, why did you do this to me? Surely the bonds of friendship, no matter how they were forged, did not require such a sacrifice.

Marguerite's eyes were as blue as her father's, yet they bore no welcoming smile. Instead she regarded him as though he were some loathsome insect that had crawled out from under a rock. That was far from the normal reaction women had to his presence. Fluttering eyelashes, blushes, simpering words— even bold caresses—Alain had learned to deal with them all. But antipathy, that was a novelty. It was almost as if Marguerite shared his reluctance for this betrothal, and that was distinctly unexpected.

Though he felt no mirth, Alain forced a laugh. "I fear my brother has spent far too much time with the court jesters," he said. "That must be where he learned such senseless speech."

Guillaume chuckled.

As Charles flushed with embarrassment over the unmistakable barb, Marguerite came to his defense. "I suppose you prefer the coarse language of battle to the gentle words of courtly love."

"Most assuredly. At least a battle cry is honest, not a form of deception."

Of course he'd feel that way! Marguerite's blue eyes flashed. "Then I pity the woman you'll marry, for she'll never hear a soft word from you."

The moment the words were out of her mouth, Marguerite

realized her error. *She* was the woman Alain de Jarnac was to marry.

What changes a few minutes had wrought. An hour ago, she had been eager to meet the man to whom she'd been promised since birth. For years she'd taken pride in the tales of his exploits, and if she'd wondered why the man she was to marry had never once in all those years come to Mirail to meet her, why he had never acknowledged her existence with so much as a message or a token of his regard, she'd pushed those concerns to the background. The Silver Knight, she'd assured herself, was a true chevalier, sacrificing his own happiness for the greater cause of God and country.

It was all a lie. She'd built her dreams on a poor foundation, and like a castle set on sand, her illusions had crumbled with the first storm. A noble chevalier. What a jest! The man who stood next to her was no gentle knight, merely a crude warrior. Far from being the hero of her dreams, he was an apparition from a half-remembered nightmare. Unfortunately, he was also the man her father expected her to marry.

She smiled the polite, meaningless smile she'd been taught since early childhood, her lips curving sweetly though her eyes flashed with anger.

Alain, however, appeared impervious to her mood. "I fear your pity is misplaced. My wife will be the most fortunate of creatures, for she'll have an honest husband. She will know that I speak the truth," he explained, "not meaningless platitudes, designed to make even the ugliest of women believe she is a beauty." His eyes moved slowly from the top of Marguerite's head to her velvet-clad feet, coldly assessing her features and her clothing, as though trying to determine to which category she belonged.

While her father continued to chuckle, apparently finding some humor in the man's crude speech, Charles let out a gasp. "Please excuse my brother," he said quickly. "As you surmised, he learned the language and manners of battle, not those of chivalry." Charles's brown eyes met Marguerite's, and his smile reassured her. "You must know I wasn't speaking platitudes," he said. "I meant everything I told you."

Marguerite returned the smile, and this time it was a genuine one. Here was the knight of her dreams. "I'll treasure each word," she assured Charles.

The snort of impatience could only have come from the big man. Charles was right, Marguerite reflected. His brother had spent so much time in battle that he'd even begun to sound like his horses.

"I thought we would dine outside today," she told her father when he gently reminded her of her duties. Though it required more effort from the kitchen staff than serving a meal in the Great Hall, Marguerite had planned to honor Lancelot's arrival with the intimacy of a meal alfresco. Tomorrow would be soon enough for a formal banquet.

Using dinner preparations as an excuse to leave the Great Hall, Marguerite walked quickly toward the kitchens. She needed time to think, to plot her strategy. For the expression on Father's face had told her this was no skirmish to be easily won. For some reason, he was determined she would wed Alain, regardless of the man's obvious flaws.

But the kitchens brought no respite. Though a dozen women worked, aided by three young boys who were responsible for keeping the immense fireplace filled with wood, the usual bustling activity was absent. In place of briskly moving hands and feet, Marguerite found wagging tongues. She stood in the doorway, for once unnoticed by the people whose livelihood, indeed whose very lives, depended on her.

"They're both so handsome," Louise said with a dramatic sigh. She was perched on a high stool, and from the way her fingers played with the end of her dark brown braid, Marguerite surmised she'd been there for some time. It was no wonder the Great Hall was empty, if everyone at Mirail was more concerned with speculation about the men from Jarnac than in their assigned tasks.

"For myself," Cook announced as she sliced an eel, "I prefer Sir Alain. He's one fine figure of a man." She turned to a woman who was kneading bread. "Did you see the size of his hands, Belinde? I'd wager all of him's that big."

"Enough to split a woman, if you ask me," the baker's

assistant announced. "You can have him. I'll take the younger one. He looks like he'd be gentle with a woman."

"They're like the sun and the moon," Louise interjected. "One so golden, the other silver. I couldn't decide who was more handsome."

Marguerite raised an eyebrow. Alain handsome? Oh, she had to admit, he exuded a certain virility which some women might consider attractive. But handsome? Definitely not. On the other hand, Charles was beautiful—there was no other word for it—and more than that, he was gallant. His courtly words reverberated in her mind.

Charles was everything a maiden could want. Alain . . . the very thought was enough to destroy even a healthy appetite. But Father, for some inexplicable reason, was oblivious to his flaws. 'Twould be a challenge indeed to convince Father that Alain was unsuited to be her husband.

The scent of newly mowed grass drifted upwards as Marguerite led her guests to dinner. She had ordered the meal served in the orchard. There, at one of the highest spots within the barony, the diners could overlook the castle walls and see the swiftly flowing river.

As a child Marguerite had spent happy hours perched on a limb of her favorite apple tree, dreaming of the day a knight would claim her. That day had come. It was now her responsibility to ensure that the story had a happy ending.

She had made her plans carefully. Today there would be no high table for the honored knights. Instead their table was set a short distance from the ones where Alain's and Charles's retinue and the Mirail knights would eat. Snowy linens covered the table, and a silken canopy protected them from the more unpleasant aspects of having birds overhead.

As two pages pulled out the long bench, Marguerite took a seat between Charles and Alain, indicating that her father should sit on Alain's other side. It was, she reflected, an ideal arrangement. Father would be pleased that Alain had the place of honor on her right. More importantly, he'd keep the big man engaged in conversation, leaving Marguerite to devote herself to Charles. Unfortunately the plan had one flaw. It was almost as if

Guillaume had divined her ploy, for each time Marguerite turned to Charles, her father managed to address a question to him, deftly forestalling the private conversations she had envisioned. Instead she had to content herself with gazing at the handsome knight who sat on her left. He had washed the travel dust away and was now clad in a tunic of forest green which highlighted his golden beauty.

The man on her right had also bathed, for Marguerite had heard the ribald comments of the women who had assisted him, but other than the finer fabric, his garments appeared identical to the ones he had worn earlier. Gray, it seemed, was his favorite color. How appropriate. Dull clothes for a dull man.

As Guillaume helped himself to a plate of stewed eels, he fixed his gaze on Charles. "You're closer to the duke and duchess than I am," he said. "Do you think this rift with Henry is permanent?"

Though the troubadours were never loath to embellish a tale, there had been no need to embroider the English court's latest scandal. Ever since Eleanor of Aquitaine and her son Richard had fled England, the courtiers could speak of little else. The woman who had once been Queen of France and who had divorced the sainted King Louis to marry England's Henry and become Queen of England was now once again on French soil, back in her native Aquitaine.

Would Henry try to force her to return? Would Eleanor seek Louis's forgiveness and refuge in the French court? Would England and France go to war over this woman who seemed to provoke controversy wherever she went? The speculation was endless.

Charles leaned forward to look at Guillaume. "I fear I'm not privy to the inner workings of the court," he said.

Marguerite felt a stab of disappointment. She had hoped that Alain, with his close ties to Richard the Lionheart, would be able to satisfy her curiosity about Eleanor. It had taken only a few minutes to realize that Alain was the last person who would know—or care—about court politics. But surely Charles had been part of the inner circle.

Alain snorted, and once again Marguerite was reminded of his affinity to his equine companions.

"What Charles means," he said, staring directly at Marguerite, "is that he's so anxious to discover what lies beneath the ladies' skirts that he has no time to learn what's in their heads."

Though Marguerite could sense Charles's anger, he said nothing in his own defense. Perhaps he was accustomed to Alain's unprovoked attacks. She was not.

"Am I to surmise that you have conducted an extensive study of the ladies' minds?" she asked Alain.

She must have raised her voice more than she had realized, for there was a sudden silence at the next table as the Mirail knights and those from Jarnac strained to hear whatever it was that had so inflamed the young mistress.

"A most extensive study," Alain agreed. "Would you be interested in learning the results?" Without waiting for her reply, Alain continued. "The conclusion is inescapable. My brother has shown remarkable sagacity in exploring only certain portions of the female anatomy." Alain's gesture erased any doubt his dinner companions might have had about his meaning. "At least a man can find pleasure there. Exploring a woman's head, I have found, is a futile exercise. There's naught to explore, for it is totally empty."

The sound of barely muffled laughter drifted across the orchard.

"I must defer to your superior judgment," Marguerite said in a deceptively sweet voice. "After all, I'm but a poor, ignorant female. Yet it seems to me that having an empty head must be preferable to having one filled with nothing more important than lust."

Once again she felt Charles's swift intake of breath. He laid a hand on her arm, as though to caution her, but this time Marguerite was immune to his touch.

"Lust, it seems to me," she continued, "is the only thing a knight knows. Lust for power, lust for land, lust for women. The result is war, pillage and rape." She stared at Alain, daring him to disagree. "Yet women with their empty heads are the ones who keep the peace, defend the demesne and bear children. Surely that's preferable to man's destruction.''

She dismissed the page who offered her a plate of roast pork. This was not the time to eat. Once again her rude guest had managed to destroy her desire for food.

Alain's appetite, however, did not appear diminished. He piled his trencher with pork, then turned toward Guillaume. ''It appears your daughter has never heard, 'Silence gives the proper grace to women.' ''

''If you want to quote Sophocles,'' Marguerite said before her father could interrupt, ''you might consider, 'Men of ill judgment oft ignore the good that lies within their hands, till they have lost it.' For myself, I find Demosthenes's wisdom more appropriate. Perhaps you recall his words, 'You cannot have a proud and chivalrous spirit if your conduct is mean and paltry; for whatever a man's actions are, such must be his spirit.' ''

Alain stared at her for a long moment, his blue eyes sober, his hand no longer reaching for food. Was he shocked, Marguerite wondered, at her knowledge of the Greek philosophers? Father had warned her against displaying her education, occasionally cursing his weakness in indulging her craving for learning. Then Alain's face softened, and as his lips curved Marguerite saw a fleeting resemblance to Charles. Alain was not handsome, of course, but for an instant he seemed . . . human.

Seconds later she realized it was only an illusion, for Alain spoke not a word to her. Instead, he turned to Guillaume. ''Janelle was right. She predicted your daughter would be both beautiful and spirited, a rose complete with thorns for the unwary.''

Marguerite felt the blood rush to her cheeks. Not only had the man not had the courtesy to respond to her last question, but now he was discussing her as though she were not present. She was no feather-brained court lady, good for only one purpose, and she would make certain Alain de Jarnac recognized that.

The angry retort died on Marguerite's lips as she glanced past Alain at her father. He was smiling, yet his eyes bore an odd expression. It reminded her of the persimmon she'd once eaten: sweet but tart at the same time. Marguerite felt a twinge of fear. It had not been her imagination. Something about Alain de Jarnac's visit was affecting her father deeply.

Guillaume shook his head slightly, and Marguerite had the impression he was trying to bring himself back to the present. "What is the situation in Poitiers? Is Eleanor determined to remain there?"

Lifting his goblet, Alain took a swallow of wine before he replied. When he spoke, it was slowly, as though he were considering each word. "Eleanor is a proud woman. Even if she wants to return to England, I doubt she'll be satisfied until Henry begs for pardon. And, knowing Henry, that'll never happen. If it's possible, he's even prouder than his wife."

"Now you see the truth of my words. Henry's lust may lead to war." Marguerite had no intention of allowing Alain to continue ignoring her. "It appears that the king is misguided enough to share your opinion of women. He must have believed his wife was either stupid or had no pride. Only a witless woman would not have realized what was happening, and Eleanor is far from witless. Besides, even if she no longer loved him, she could not countenance his dalliance with Rosamund. No woman with any pride could." Marguerite fixed her eyes on Alain, willing him to understand her point of view. "Eleanor was right to leave Henry."

Above them two birds twittered as though discussing the royal separation.

"Was Eleanor right to turn Henry's sons against him?" Alain asked in a soft voice. "For that's what she's done. Richard is now pitted against his father."

Before she could reply, Charles placed his hand on Marguerite's and said soothingly, "You shouldn't worry about men's affairs. That's our responsibility."

Alain laughed, and the soft spring breeze ruffled his hair as he shook his head. "I think you missed the point, dear brother. We weren't discussing men's affairs but, rather, those between a man and a woman. After all, isn't that what caused the rift between Eleanor and Henry?"

"But, Alain." Charles's voice left no doubt that he disagreed with his brother. "A knight's duty is to protect his lady. She shouldn't have to worry about affairs of the court."

"A knight should provide physical protection," Marguerite agreed. "However, not all women are empty headed." She softened her words as she spoke to Charles. It was apparent he had listened to his brother once too often and had started espousing his opinions. "Hasn't Eleanor shown the world women aren't as weak as you'd like to believe? After all, she's been queen of both France and England and, in each case she was an equal partner with her husband—not a mindless puppet."

Though Marguerite did not agree with Eleanor's politics, there was no denying that she was living proof that women were equal to men.

"You're right about Eleanor," Guillaume agreed. "She has had a glorious past." His face bore a wistful expression as he said, "I don't think I'll ever forget how she led her ladies on the crusade. But look where she is now. The only court she presides over is a court of love."

It truly was a day of surprises. First Father's strange reaction to the visitors and now his reference to the crusade. That was most unusual, for he rarely mentioned the crusade. In the past when Marguerite had questioned him about the pilgrimage, his answers had always been curt. And then from the day when, with his face contorted with pain, he had told Marguerite that he had lost far more than his arm during the fateful ambush, she had ceased to press him for information. Now he was introducing the topic. Strange, indeed.

A page moved between Charles and Marguerite, offering them a platter of peacock. Her appetite once more restored, she allowed the boy to serve her. As she lifted a piece of the meat toward her lips, Charles spoke. "A royal bird for the Queen of Hearts," he murmured. "I envy the peacock," Charles continued in a low voice, "for it has touched your lips, while I must only gaze at them from afar."

Though the troubadours' songs had told of knights extolling their ladies' graces in just such phrases, Charles was the first

man to woo Marguerite with words. Even Henri de Bleufontaine, who made no secret of his desire to marry her, had
never courted her this eloquently. Marguerite smiled. Perhaps
Camelot had indeed come to Mirail.

Before she could reply, her father spoke, asking about the
hunt she had arranged. Though the conversation remained
impersonal for the rest of the meal, Marguerite was intensely
aware of Charles seated next to her. This was the man of her
dreams—handsome, gentle and so romantic as his hand reached
over to grasp her fingers. It was the lightest of touches, and
yet it sent a shiver of pleasure up Marguerite's arm, a pleasure
which died as Alain swiveled his head to glare at his brother.

Perhaps it was naught but chance, but it appeared the man
had some inner sense that told him of Charles's movement.
Cheeks flushed with chagrin, Charles dropped Marguerite's
hand and made no further attempt to touch her.

As the sun set, Guillaume led his guests back to the castle,
asking his daughter to show the guests to their room.

"I trust you'll find everything you need," Marguerite said,
holding back the tapestry which covered the doorway. The
room she had given the knights was the finest Mirail had to
offer. Situated at the end of the corridor, it boasted windows
on two sides and provided a magnificent panorama of the surrounding countryside. All was in readiness, for Marguerite had
arranged for fresh rushes on the floor, and the bed linens had
been aired that morning.

"I shall never rest tonight knowing you're so close." Charles
bent over Marguerite's hand and kissed it reverently.

When Charles released her, Alain took a step closer, a sardonic grin on his face. "Never fear, my dear lady. I shall sleep
soundly."

Without warning, his arms reached out for Marguerite. One
firm hand cupped her chin and tipped her head toward his while
the other encircled her waist, pulling her close so that his lips
could mold themselves to hers.

This was not the gentle homage Charles had paid her. It was
a brand, a statement of ownership rather than a caress. There
was no softness, only a harsh urgency as Alain's mouth moved

over hers and forced her lips to part. For a moment Marguerite remained inert, too shocked to move. Then Alain's tongue invaded the sweet recesses of her mouth.

"No!" she cried and pulled away from him, her face flushed with outrage. It had been better—far better—when he had ignored her.

As Marguerite drew a deep breath, Charles closed the distance between them. He stood at her side, facing his brother. "You owe Marguerite an apology."

Alain's laugh was a short, mirthless explosion of sound. "An apology? Why?"

"That should be obvious." Charles gave Marguerite a reassuring glance. "No chivalrous knight would conduct himself in such a fashion."

"Perhaps not," Alain agreed smoothly. "But we've already established that you're the chivalrous one, not I. You should know by now that I do what I want." His eyes moved from Charles to Marguerite. "I suspect that I have merely confirmed my fiancée's opinion of the male species and its preoccupation with ... " He paused, a faint smile crossing his face as he looked at Marguerite. "I believe the word you used so often was *lust.*"

Marguerite left the room with the sound of Alain's laughter ringing in her ears.

# Chapter Three

"Scum!" The knight's hazel eyes darkened with rage. "You have one simple task, and you cannot perform even that properly." He took a step forward, his hand clenched into a fist. "Or was it deliberate? Did you think perhaps to shame me in front of my men?"

The moonlight spilled through the window onto the only floor in the château which boasted a covering other than rushes. A few feet away, his worn boots touching no more than the fringe of the Turkish carpet, a smaller man stood silently. Mindful not to trespass on the forbidden warmth, his brown eyes nonetheless dared to meet his master's.

"I'll teach you to leave my mail tarnished." With a swift movement, the knight swung his arm backward, then struck his servant. It was a fierce blow, far more severe than the misdemeanor warranted. The man's head jerked from the force of Henri de Bleufontaine's hand, yet he made no sound, merely raised his head and once more stared at his master.

Henri lifted his hand for another blow, then winced as he tried to clench his fingers. "One day you'll step too far," he said, "and then nothing will protect you. Not you or the devil's spawn you call a sister."

Other than a rapid blink, Gerard, son of Albert the cobbler of Bleufontaine, made no sign that the words had met their mark.

For a long moment the two men glared at each other. Henri was the first to lower his eyes. Picking up the coat of mail, he tossed it at Gerard. "Clean it, you oaf!" As Gerard bent to retrieve the finely tooled armor he'd polished so painstakingly, an expression of pure lust crossed Henri's face. "There's much to be gained from this journey. Much, indeed."

For the first time Gerard spoke. "Yes, m'lord." His voice was harsh and guttural, the words almost incomprehensible to someone unaccustomed to his speech.

"Things will be different when I'm master of Mirail." Henri squared his shoulders and strutted across the carpet. "They'll envy me then. Not a knight in the realm will have what I will— those rich lands and the lovely Marguerite spreading her thighs for me each night." The sound of his mirth echoed from the stone walls. "Perhaps she won't want to wait for darkness," he said with a chuckle. "From what I've seen, she's a lusty wench."

"Yes, m'lord." As Gerard left the room he said a silent prayer that the saints would guard Marguerite de Mirail. The good Lord knew that if Henri de Bleufontaine had his way, she'd need more protection than mere mortals could provide.

"Mayhap the troubadours were right." Louise drew the silver comb through her mistress's long tresses. "They said a maiden's visage would change when she met the man she was destined to love." Her fingers moved swiftly as she spoke. "I thought it was naught but a tale, yet you look different than you did this morn."

Marguerite willed her face to remain impassive. It was true; she could feel the change in herself. The softness, the sense of melting inside were surely caused by Lancelot's arrival at Mirail. They could not possibly owe their origins to that crude kiss Alain had inflicted on her. Nay, that would bring only lines of strain to a maiden's face.

"If I look different, it must be from the excitement of the day," Marguerite suggested. "We've never had such a day as this at Mirail."

" 'Tis true. All anyone can talk about are those two handsome knights. Father René tells us that envy is a fearsome sin, and I fear I am risking extra time in purgatory, but I vow today I wish I had even one man vying for my hand."

Marguerite smiled. Louise's parents had long rued the day their daughter had become Marguerite's personal servant, for they blamed her reluctance to marry on her mistress's peculiar ideas. Love and romance, Adele had told her daughter, were luxuries not granted to serfs.

"What of Jean-Claude?" Marguerite asked. "He's offered to marry you so many times I've lost count."

"Jean-Claude!" Louise's sniff left no doubt of her opinion. "He's not a man. He's a greedy little creature who can talk of naught but the dower he wants my father to arrange. I'll remain a spinster rather than marry a man like that." Her hands stilled, and Marguerite felt her expel another breath. "Oh, Marguerite, I want to be loved for myself, not because I bring a flock of sheep with me."

It was, Marguerite reflected, no more than any woman would wish, no less than she should expect. Charles, she was certain, offered her such a love. As for Alain, the man appeared not to know the meaning of the word. For him, the wealth of Mirail and the opportunity to extend his lands were likely the only reasons he sought her hand. That and a promise made more than two decades ago.

"Charles is so courtly." Marguerite's lips curved into a smile as she thought of his compliments and the gentle touch of his hands.

"It's like the tales of Camelot," Louise agreed. "I only pray that the ending is different, for no man is worth the risk of being burned at the stake." She drew the comb through Marguerite's hair. " 'Tis a pity you love, and yet you're both promised to others."

Marguerite's head turned so swiftly that the comb tangled in her hair. "What did you say?" she demanded.

In the pale moonlight, Marguerite could see a flush rise in Louise's cheeks. "Perhaps 'tis only a rumor," the dark haired woman said. "You know how people embroider a tale."

But Marguerite was not to be dissuaded. Servants' gossip, she had learned, was frequently more accurate than her father believed. "Tell me the story," she insisted. "I'll judge its truth."

Louise spoke slowly, as though each word were painful. "Clothilde heard it from one of the squires," she said. "They told her the knights would journey to Lilis before they returned to Jarnac."

Lilis was several days' travel from Mirail, and unlike Jarnac, which was located to the west of Mirail, it was due east. Though it was not uncommon to combine visits to several demesnes on a single journey, a lengthy trip like the one to Lilis was rarely undertaken without a purpose. Sometimes it was to renew ties of kinship or to strengthen the oath of fealty. Yet the barony of Lilis was not allied with the Jarnac family by either kinship or homage. The journey must have another purpose.

With a sinking feeling in her stomach, Marguerite asked the question whose answer she had already divined.

"Did Clothilde learn why they're going to Lilis?"

Once again Louise appeared hesitant. "It may not be true," she prefaced her words. "Clothilde could be mistaken."

Marguerite shook her head impatiently, urging Louise to confirm what she surmised.

"They say that Charles is to be betrothed to Diane de Lilis."

While his brother may have found the proximity of a beautiful woman disturbing to his sleep, Alain de Jarnac did not. He wakened with the early dawn feeling rested and, yes, eager for the day. It was an unexpected sense of anticipation which surely had nothing to do with the chatelaine of Mirail. It was, Alain told himself, due solely to the fact that his business here would soon be concluded and he'd be free to return to Poitiers and Honore. Unlike some women he could name whose tongues spewed forth bitter words, Honore knew that the way to please a man was through actions rather than words. She had also developed a high level of skill in the most pleasurable of those actions.

With a brief glance at his brother's sleeping form, Alain drew on his hose and tunic, then strode from the chamber. Judging from the pale hue of the sky, it would be nigh onto an hour before the other inhabitants of the castle wakened.

Wandering the perimeter of the bailey, Alain looked closely at the castle walls. As other travelers had recounted, they were rounded, built following a style Guillaume had seen in Outremer. The Saracens claimed that the curves prevented besieging armies from scaling them, but the French were plainly skeptical. Was this another Eastern trick, designed to lull them into false security? Everyone knew that walls should be square. How else would they have sufficient strength to withstand an attack? Guillaume, it appeared, was wagering his life and those of his serfs on the validity of the Saracens' claims. The castle of Mirail was yet another legacy of the Second Crusade.

With a snort of disgust, Alain quickened his step. He needed no more reminders of that particular holy war. While it may have been waged for the purest of reasons, to Alain it was a symbol of only one thing: the perfidy of women. Yet here he was, within walls that would constantly remind him of the East and all that had occurred there, soon to lose his freedom because of a vow that had been made in the heat of battle.

He turned his gaze toward the castle, wondering which window led to Marguerite's chamber. Was she still asleep on her virgin pallet, dreaming of Charles's embrace?

The woman was an enigma. How could she have smiled when Charles plied her with those meaningless compliments? Surely she had seen the absurdity of his words. Alain knew his brother fancied himself an expert at wooing a woman, yet how could he have uttered such inanities? Imagine wishing to be a dead peacock! How foolish could a man be? Yet, far from being insulted by the banal sentiments, Marguerite seemed to admire them. She was as empty-headed as the women of Eleanor's court.

Not once had Honore or the other women of his acquaintance

offered an opinion on anything other than fashions, jewels and
the troubadours' rhymes. Alain was not certain whether they
lacked the thoughts or simply feared to express them to him.
In either case, it mattered not a whit. Women were created to
provide physical pleasure. When he craved intellectual stimula-
tion, he sought the company of the learned monks.

And yet, Marguerite seemed to be different. She had challenged him when he'd given his assessment of the court ladies,
and she'd been remarkably well informed about Eleanor. Far
from being subservient and bowing to his superior experience
and intelligence, she had parried his ideas as skillfully as he
himself did a warrior's lance.

Feather-brained or scholarly. Frivolous or serious. The question was, which was the real Marguerite?

Marguerite hummed softly as she returned from the riverbank. It was the most glorious of mornings. The sun's warmth
had evaporated the last drops of dew from the grass, leaving
her slippers unmarred by dampness; she had heard a cardinal
calling to his mate; and her basket was nearly overflowing with
freshly picked herbs. Yet those were only the sugared almonds
on top of the gâteau. What made the day special was Charles.
Marguerite's optimism had risen with the dawn, dispelling her
fears that Father would force her to marry Alain. It wouldn't
happen. It couldn't! Father was a just man, known throughout
the land for his fairness to his people. Surely he would accord
his own daughter the same opportunity to plead her case that
he gave his lowliest serf.

"I pity the dawn."

As Marguerite turned at the familiar voice, she made no
effort to contain her pleasure. Charles had sought her company
before he had broken bread. It was the best of signs, a gesture
worthy of the troubadours' tales.

"Why do you pity the dawn?" she asked, sliding the basket
onto one arm as she extended the other hand to Charles. "I
must confess it's my favorite time of the day. The world seems
fresh and new, and the sky is such a rosy hue."

He bent low to press a kiss on her fingertips. "Ah, now I understand why it happens." As he raised his eyes to meet hers, Charles smiled. "The dawn must flee each day, because it cannot compete with your radiance."

Marguerite felt a warmth rise from her fingertips along the length of her arm as Charles held her hand between both of his. "I trust you rested well," she said.

He clasped her hand a little tighter and nodded. "Though I had feared sleeplessness, my senses were drugged by your nearness."

"Then you won't need any of my potions." Marguerite glanced down at her basket.

"Does your basket contain something to restore a man's common sense?"

He had come from behind, his footsteps silent on the soft grass. A flush rose to Marguerite's cheeks as she looked at the intruder. Him again! How dare the man interrupt her moment with Charles?

Without waiting for her reply, Alain continued. "It would appear my brother is in sore need of such a remedy." He paused for a moment, a frown etching furrows in his face as he fixed his gaze on Charles. "Your squire was searching the bailey for you. It seems you were in such a hurry for your assignation that you neglected to tell him which tunic you wanted prepared."

Though Charles's lips tightened, he said nothing. Instead he raised Marguerite's hand to his lips and pressed another kiss on it. "I shall count the minutes until I see you again," he said. With obvious reluctance he released her hand and began to walk toward the castle.

Marguerite smiled.

Alain's eyes narrowed as they moved from the woman he was to marry to his brother, and realization hit him with the force of an angry Saracen's blade. The chit was besotted with Charles; she actually believed his drivel. As he considered the consequences, Alain de Jarnac, the man who had taught the French army the meaning of courage, was seized with dread. He could not allow it to happen. Cursing himself for agreeing to combine the journey to Mirail with Charles's betrothal in Lilis, Alain searched for a way to avert disaster.

"Don't let me interfere," he said in a voice that was reassuringly normal.

For a second she stared at him, her blue eyes wide with something akin to surprise. Then Marguerite spoke. "How kind of you to permit me to pursue my duties." While her voice had been gentle and melodic when she'd spoken to Charles, it was now harsh with anger.

"Perhaps I've been away from France too long," Alain retorted. "I was unaware that a chatelaine's duties included dallying with senseless knights."

Her eyes met his, and Alain could feel her anger, though she said not a word. When she spoke, her voice was low and controlled, as though she had decided not to give the slightest hint of her emotions.

"Anyone with even a modicum of . . ." Marguerite paused, then stressed the next word, ". . . sense . . . knows that one of a chatelaine's most important duties is to make her guests feel welcome."

She had courage. He'd grant her that much. Another woman would have cringed at his obvious sarcasm, but not Marguerite. No, she'd taken his words and flung them back at him much as an angry knight would have tossed his gauntlet.

Her skirts swayed softly as she walked across the ground, and, try though he might, Alain could not stop his eyes from following her. By all rights she should have a graceless gait to match her acid tongue. Yet instead of that, Marguerite's movements were fluid, her hips undulating in a motion that was all the more seductive for its obvious innocence. She was walking, nothing more, and yet it was the most provocative thing Alain had seen in years.

He followed a few steps behind her. A man might as well enjoy the view she provided, for engaging her in conversation was as dangerous as thrusting an arm into a viper's nest.

Though he had expected her to follow Charles back to the manor house, she turned, propped open the door to a small hut, then stepped inside.

"How is your arm?" he heard her ask, and once again her voice was soft and soothing.

"It doesn't hurt. Not a bit." The words held more than a hint of bravado, the high tenor telling Alain it was a child who spoke.

Curiosity propelled him into the hut. Was Marguerite fulfilling her duties as Mirail's chatelaine by visiting an injured serf? That was certainly preferable to dallying with his brother.

Alain paused in the doorway.

"Who are you?" The child's voice was steadier this time.

As Alain waited for his eyes to adjust to the darkness, he replied, "I'm Alain de Jarnac. Who are you?"

Once he moved from the doorway, Alain could see that the building consisted of a single sparsely furnished room. Three pallets lined one wall. Opposite it a crudely hewn bench stood in front of the fireplace that provided both warmth and cooking. It was here that Marguerite stood, unwrapping a cloth from a young boy's arm. Alain raised one eyebrow. Marguerite, it appeared, was doing far more than consoling an ailing servant. Once again she had managed to surprise him.

Her head was bent, and Alain noticed the graceful curve of her neck. She was indeed a lovely woman, albeit one of the most infuriating he'd ever met. For to his annoyance, she kept her eyes on her task, never so much as acknowledging his presence.

The boy, however, was quick to react, his gasp audible, his expression frightened. "Does he know that I'm the one?"

"What one?" Though knights throughout France had a healthy respect for his prowess and the Infidel had quickly learned to fear the Silver Knight's sword, Alain was not accustomed to frightening children. Yet it appeared the mere mention of his name was enough to rouse terror in this boy. Alain found that disturbed him almost as much as Marguerite's refusal to look at him.

" 'Tis all right." Marguerite's voice was low and soothing. She made a reassuring clucking sound. "Your arm's much better," she said. "Look at the color."

But the boy was not to be distracted. "Does he know?" he demanded.

Marguerite drew a handful of leaves from her basket and laid on the child's arm with an assurance that told Alain she had done this many times before. "He won't hurt you," she said.

Alain took a step closer to the bench. "I assure you I make it a practice never to harm injured men."

As he had hoped, the child seized on the word 'men' and managed a small smile. "Even if I caused Marguerite to be late?" Clearly he was still doubtful. He touched the forearm which Marguerite had finished binding. "It was an accident, you know."

Alain smiled. "I should hope so. A man needs to keep his sword arm safe." He turned to Marguerite, determined to make her acknowledge his presence. "I suppose that's why you weren't in the bailey to greet me yesterday."

This time she raised her eyes to his. "Did you think I was searching for ribbons to match my gown?"

"The thought did occur to me," he admitted, surprised that she had been able to guess his reaction so accurately.

This time there was no doubt of her anger. Though her voice was low, it seethed with barely controlled fury. "I fear I must question your extensive study of women," she said. "It appears to have left you with many wrongful notions." She gave the boy a quick pat on the shoulder. "Now, if you don't mind, Jean needs to rest."

Slinging her basket over her arm, Marguerite walked quickly out of the house.

Alain gave the child a rueful glance. "Women!"


Guillaume was alone in the small room off the Great Hall, his head bent low over the table as his hand traced the words on the parchment.

"Can I help you?" Marguerite asked, suppressing her smile. It was the second good omen of the day, a chance to set the mood and turn it to her advantage. For if there was one thing her father hated, it was recording the demesne's accounts. Another man would have hired a clerk or used the priest's services, but Guillaume de Mirail was not another man. At the same time that he had been taught to read and write as a small boy, he had also heard tales of dishonest clerks and, yes, thieving priests, and he had vowed that no one else would control such a vital part of his estate. He alone would inscribe the records.

It was a task he detested. Though he was one of the few men of his acquaintance who could read, he still lacked the facility with the written word that Father René displayed. For him reading was a burden and writing a tribulation to be borne.

All that had changed when Marguerite had shown first a curiosity and then an aptitude for scholarly pursuits. Though Father René had protested, telling Guillaume a female had no need for such learning, the baron had remained adamant. His daughter would master reading and writing, not to set her apart from other women, but so that she could relieve him of one burden.

He raised his head and grinned. "Your timing is impeccable, my dear."

It'll get better, Marguerite promised herself. She pulled a bench next to her father and bent her head to the task. Half an hour later when she had untangled the accounts, she stretched her hands in front of her, spreading her fingers wide to ease the cramps.

"I must confess that I'm relieved," her father told her. "Though it suited me well, I had feared that teaching you to read and cipher was an error I would regret." His smile was indulgent as his eyes moved from the neatly penned accounts to the daughter who had completed them. "I had almost begun to believe Father René's dire prophesies that 'twould be considered unmaidenly. But now it appears your husband will value those talents."

Alain! She cared not a whit what he thought. Charles was the one whose opinion mattered. Though she hadn't expected her father to broach the topic, this was the opening Marguerite sought.

"I wanted to talk to you about my betrothal," she said, pushing the account ledger across the table.

Guillaume beamed. "He's far more suitable than I had dared to hope. Oh," he said, that remote expression she'd seen the previous day once again crossing his face, "I knew Janelle's son would be valiant, but I didn't dare dream he'd be the perfect mate for you."

Perfect! How could Father be so misled? Marguerite was not one to believe in spells, yet there was no escaping the fact that ever since the Jarnac knights had arrived, her father's behavior had been peculiar.

"Please, Father." Marguerite fingered the ink well, a not so subtle reminder of the service she'd just provided. "You must see that he's all wrong for me. He cares only for military matters, not those of the barony, and he's open in his scorn for women. Being wed to such a man would bring me only strife and unhappiness." Marguerite fixed her eyes on her father's face. "I cannot marry Alain de Jarnac."

Guillaume turned startled eyes on his daughter. "I fear I do not understand. You know your betrothal was planned even before you were born."

She had heard the story scores of times, and in the past it had always seemed romantic. Surely the troubadours could not have invented a more stirring tale than a promise made on the battlefields of the crusades, where two men had vowed that should they survive the infidel's swords, they would strengthen their friendship through the ties of matrimony. Guillaume's first-born daughter would be betrothed to Robert and Janelle's son Alain.

"But, Father, that was before we knew what he was like." Marguerite's voice rose in protest. "Surely now that you've seen him, you can't wish me to marry him."

Guillaume began to pace the small chamber. It was not, Marguerite knew from experience, a good omen.

"To the contrary, Alain de Jarnac is everything I would wish for in your husband. He's a valiant knight and an honorable man. Moreover, he'll be a good, strong mate for you." Guillaume sighed. "I fear Father René was correct. Perhaps I have been too indulgent. Nay, Marguerite, don't try to sway me in this. Alain is the man for you.''

"He's crude." Marguerite shuddered slightly at the memory of both the big knight's words and his rough embrace. How could Father find him a suitable mate for her? Either he had not noticed Alain's lack of manners or somehow it had not offended him.

Guillaume shook his head. "My dear, you're wrong about him. Mayhap you've spent so much time reading and listening to the troubadours that you've been unable to learn about real men. In this matter you'll have to trust my judgment. Alain de Jarnac is not crude; he's strong. 'Tis a most important difference."

Marguerite rose and faced her father. It appeared he was impervious to her logic, his eyes somehow so clouded that he mistook flaws for strengths. She'd have to turn her arguments in another direction.

There was one thing she knew Father would not overlook, though he had been careful not to allude to it in front of the Jarnac knights.

"Alain is part of the traitors' court." Marguerite enunciated each damning syllable clearly.

For a long moment there was no sound, and she knew her words had hit their mark. During the Second Crusade, Guillaume, Robert and their friend Philippe had been loyal to the French King Louis, fighting at his side on the long, perilous journey to recapture Jerusalem from the infidel.

Though Guillaume and Philippe had been bachelors, Robert's wife Janelle had accompanied them as a member of Eleanor's court. That had been the last time they had all been united. Following Robert's death on the crusade, Janelle had wed Philippe, and the bonds of friendship had been strained. For while Guillaume's loyalty to Louis had never wavered, Janelle had remained part of Eleanor's court. When Eleanor had divorced Louis to marry England's Henry, Janelle and Philippe had declared allegiance to the English king and Eleanor, placing Guillaume and his dearest friends on opposite sides of the royal rift.

Guillaume's face was serious as he resumed his pacing. "Be that as it may," he said slowly, "Alain is still Janelle's son, and the vow we made remains. Though both Janelle and Robert are gone, I will not renege on our promises."

There was one possibility left. Perhaps it was one Father had not considered.

"Charles is also Janelle's son," Marguerite pointed out. "If I married him, you would not have broken a vow."

Outside the narrow window a bird trilled its contentment with the spring morning as Marguerite searched her father's face for a sign that he would reconsider.

"My dear, you know the terms of our agreement. My first-born daughter would marry Robert and Janelle's firstborn son." The lines which etched Guillaume's forehead added years to his age. "A man's word is his honor." He pronounced each syllable carefully, as though speaking to a half wit. "If a knight were to break his promise, he would have nothing left to distinguish him from the animals."

As he looked at Marguerite, the sadness in her father's eyes made her want to weep.

"Marguerite, there is no choice. You will marry Alain de Jarnac."

# Chapter Four

It should be no more difficult than capturing a castle. After all, the strategy was the same. Discover the weakest spot, then use it to enter and conquer. While there were hundreds of variations, the underlying tactic was consistent, and the results were always the same, at least when it was the Silver Knight who planned and executed the strategy. Victory was assured, as both the Saracen infidels and his own unruly vassals had learned to their detriment.

How different could it be to win a woman's heart?

Alain shook his head slightly. The siege must not be prolonged. Not only were he and Charles expected at Lilis within the fortnight, but soon Richard would need his services. Even now there were rumors that the newly crowned Duke of Aquitaine would require force to obtain his vassals' fealty. A smile crossed Alain's face. Richard might be named Lionheart, but he was still a boy, one who could benefit from Alain's years of experience. Yes, the campaign to win Marguerite's heart, or at least her willingness to marry, would have to be a short one. There were other, more important, demands to be met.

The question was, how was she most vulnerable? Oh, there was that unfortunate attraction she appeared to feel toward

Charles, but that was a weakness Alain could not exploit. To the contrary, that was an obstacle to be overcome. There had to be something else, some other way to woo her.

Wooing women was not an area where Alain de Jarnac had vast experience. If the truth were told, it was one where he was sorely lacking. For, as Charles had pointed out, he had been more concerned with winning battles than women. Not that he had lacked for victories in the latter category. It was simply that he had not had to wage campaigns.

Flowers. That was it. Alain remembered that she had entwined flowers of some sort in her hair, and there had been a few fragrant blooms in the basket of herbs she had picked yesterday. And hadn't Honore mentioned that women liked the scent of flowers?

He strode through the bailey, pausing only briefly to glance at the gardens. The plants growing there were obviously designed to be useful, not ornamental. When he reached the riverbank, Alain stopped, attracted by a sweet fragrance. It was light and yet it teased the senses, reminding Alain more than a little of the woman who was his reluctant fiancée. If he could find the source of that scent, he would take it to Marguerite.

Feeling a bit like the hounds who helped track game, Alain sniffed the air again. A few minutes later, his hands filled with delicate purple flowers, he headed back toward the castle. If this were any indication, the siege of Marguerite would be as easy as he had hoped.

She was seated in the solar, her golden head bent as her fingers plied needle and thread. Perhaps it was because the room was smaller than the solar at Jarnac that it seemed warmer, more inviting. Perhaps it was because the tapestries covering the walls were of brighter hues. Perhaps it was the presence of well-padded chairs that enticed a man to sit and linger. It was most assuredly not the viper-tongued female who made the room feel like the welcome ending to a long and arduous journey.

She sat, silent for once, intent on her sewing. Alain glanced at the fabric in her lap. It looked much like his dark blue mantle.

A closer look told him it was his mantle. Somehow she had discovered the small rent that had been there for months.

"I thank you for your kindness," he said.

She raised her head. If she was startled by his presence, she gave no sign. " 'Tis naught." Her voice was as cool as the river that wended its way next to the castle. "I would be shirking my duties, were I to allow you to leave Mirail with your raiment in tatters."

Alain stiffened at the implied insult to his squire's abilities. One could hardly call the cloak tattered when the rip was no more than a meter long. Remembering the object of his visit, he drew the bouquet from behind his back.

"I brought these for you," he told her, offering her the fragrant purple blooms. "When I saw them, they reminded me of you." The words, so carefully rehearsed, came stiffly. Had he been giving them to Honore, he would have said no more than, "Put them in water before they wilt." But Marguerite was not Honore. He could not buy her favors; instead, he had to win them.

Her fingers stilled. Though her eyes widened as she looked at the flowers, she made no move to accept them. It made no sense, yet she seemed to recoil ever so slightly.

"Marguerite," Alain said again, "the flowers are for you."

She hesitated, then asked, "Was there a reason you chose these blooms?"

So that was it. No man had given her flowers before, and she was as unaccustomed to receiving such gifts as he was to offering them. Alain smiled. What kind of inane response would Charles make? "Indeed there was," he confirmed. "First the scent and then the beauty reminded me of you. It was as though the flowers spoke your name." Good lord, were those words really coming from his lips? Never in his life had he uttered such platitudes.

"I fear I must refuse your humble offering," she said. This time there was no doubt about it. Though her words were polite, her tone was coldly angry, as if she were somehow offended. But how could she be? All he had done was bring her a few damned flowers.

The sound of footsteps rang out on the stone floor. As Charles entered the solar, Alain cursed. The last thing he needed was his brother.

"My lady," he said bowing deeply, "my heart rejoices at the very sight of you. I beg you permit me to remain in your company."

Alain cursed again. If language like that was what it took to win a woman, there was the possibility that this battle might last longer than he wished. The Silver Knight was adept at mastering new weapons, but some—like the use of meaningless phrases—required more practice than others.

"Don't you have something else to do?" Alain demanded of his brother.

Charles sank into one of the comfortable chairs, giving every indication that he intended to remain. "There is naught I'd prefer than to be here with the beautiful chatelaine of Mirail." His eyes moved quickly between Alain and Marguerite, pausing when they noted the flowers in Alain's hand.

"What are those?" he asked.

Marguerite spoke, and this time there was a hint of humor in her voice. "Your brother chose them specially for me. He claimed they reminded him of me. Lavender," she said, and her upper lip curled ever so slightly.

Charles's laugh was a short explosion of mirth. "Oh, Alain, you should have enlisted my aid. Lavender!"

Marguerite joined in the laughter, her silver peals mingling with Charles's guffaws.

Alain tossed the flowers onto the floor. Standing with his legs braced as though expecting an attack, he loomed over his brother and Marguerite. "By all the saints above, what is the matter with you two? All I did was bring her some damned flowers."

They exchanged a wordless glance. When Marguerite opened her mouth to speak, Charles shook his head. In a voice that was surprisingly gentle, he explained, "You, my brother, have much to learn about the language of flowers."

Language of flowers? Was the man daft? People spoke;

animals might communicate in some form, but flowers most assuredly did not talk. Even a fool knew that.

"'Tis true," Charles explained. "Mayhap you should have asked my advice. I would have told you to bring Marguerite a cedar leaf or a fern, but never a piece of lavender."

Alain grimaced. Apparently this wooing business was not going to be as easy as he had hoped. It was beginning to seem as fraught with perils as crossing the wilds of Outremer. "Explain this to me," he ordered, still mystified. Why would anyone prefer a cedar leaf over a fragrant purple flower, no matter what it was called?

"As any *preux chevalier* should know," Charles said, "each flower and plant has a meaning. When you give a lady a flower, you give her more than petals and leaves. There's a message, too."

Picking up one of the massive chairs as easily as if it were constructed of straw, Alain positioned it facing Marguerite. "Am I to suppose there was something wrong with the message my flowers carried?" he demanded.

"Perhaps not," she said. "Perhaps you truly intended to tell me that you distrusted me."

Distrusted her? Of course not. "All I wanted to do was give you something that smelled and looked good," he retorted. "It appears I made a tactical error. I should have brought something ugly like the leaves Charles suggested." Alain made no effort to disguise his annoyance.

"The cedar leaf carries the message, 'I live for thee,' and the fern speaks of fascination," Charles explained.

Alain turned to Marguerite. "And I suppose you would have preferred either of those to something with a scent that fills the air with gladness and lingers even when it's out of sight."

"Of course she would."

"Charles." It was a single word but so filled with menace that Charles could not mistake his brother's intent.

Alain fixed his gaze on Marguerite. "Is it possible that less than a day ago you scoffed when I claimed ladies' minds were filled with naught of importance? As I recall, you were swift to challenge my judgment. And, now it appears that you care for naught but superficialities.'' His eyes moved from Marguerite's face to Charles and back again, daring her to make the connection between his words and his glance. '' 'Tis wondrous, is it not, what the human mind can conjure, how it can turn illusion into reality?'' He paused for an instant, then continued. ''Since you are so fond of Demosthenes, perhaps you recall his words, 'Nothing is easier than self-deceit. For what each man wishes, that he also believes to be true.' ''

Marguerite drew a quick breath. Though she would not have thought it possible, it appeared that the big man had been hurt by her response to the lavender. Perhaps he truly had had no idea of the flowers' significance and had not meant to insult her. Perhaps she had misconstrued his intent. His voice had sounded so sincere that perhaps he was telling the truth and had indeed chosen the lavender for its scent alone.

Marguerite felt the flush of embarrassment stain her cheeks. No matter what she thought of the man and his abysmal lack of courtly manners, she should not have caused him pain. In doing so, she was no better than he.

''Mayhap you're right. I have always believed Aristotle when he said, 'In all things of nature there is something of the marvelous.' ''

''I wish you two would stop talking about those Romans.'' It was not simply Charles's petulant tone which surprised Marguerite but the import of his words.

''Aristotle and Demosthenes were Greeks,'' she said quietly.

''Greek, Roman, they're all the same to me. I never did see much value in memorizing the words of people who've been dead a long time.''

Alain laughed. ''My dear brother,'' he said, mimicking Charles's own words, ''you have much to learn about the language of wise men.''

''It is I who am to blame.'' Guillaume's eyes were fixed on the horizon as he spoke. He and Alain had reached the point in the castle's walls where the river bent sharply to the right. From their vantage point they could see the extent of the barony, its fertile fields where the serfs toiled and the forests whose game kept Guillaume and his guests well fed.

"Father René advised me to remarry or, at the least, send Marguerite to another barony where she would have the company of women."

As Guillaume turned to face him, Alain saw the sorrow on the older man's face. Was it for his daughter's lost childhood or something else, something more sinister? Alain had spent the past hour with Marguerite's father, ostensibly examining the castle's fortifications but actually trying to learn the truth behind the man's frequently wistful looks. He had discovered much about the barony but little about the baron. Though the man spoke freely on other subjects, he ventured few personal details. Indeed, it had taken careful questioning just to bring him to this point. Now, however, he seemed to have turned garrulous.

"Janelle went even further and offered to raise Marguerite as her own daughter."

The remark had been made in all innocence. Alain was certain of that. Not only would Guillaume have had no way of knowing just how painful Alain would find that particular revelation, but from what Alain had observed, he was not a man who took pleasure in inflicting pain. Still, there was no denying the regret Guillaume's words had unleashed.

Guillaume leaned against the wall, cupping the stub of his left arm in his right hand. "I've often wondered if I should have taken their advice, but the prospect of giving up my daughter was too repugnant. At the time I felt I had lost too much, and so I was selfish. I kept Marguerite with me and indulged her whims. You've seen the result." Guillaume grinned. "Thank God she's only quoted philosophers to you. Somehow she found a copy of Ovid's more sensational poetry when she was naught but a child and memorized the most scandalous passages. I never knew when she would decide to recite them or to whom . . . even Father René."

Though the words were rueful, Alain did not miss the pride in his voice. Guillaume might have been an indulgent father, but he was also a devoted one. Perhaps his apparent sadness was caused by nothing more than the prospect of losing her when she married. It was what Alain wanted to believe, the easy answer. Unfortunately, Alain had never been one to delude himself with easy answers. The truth, he feared, was far different and far more dangerous.

"I've heard that Charles is to wed Diane de Lilis. Is it true?"

Alain nodded. "My mother and Philippe thought it would be a good alliance, since Charles will not inherit Jarnac." He watched Guillaume's face carefully, but this time there was not even a momentary flinch. Instead the older man continued to speak.

"Charles looks so much like your mother that it's almost uncanny. For a moment when I first saw him, I thought I was seeing Janelle again." Guillaume's smile was wistful as he began to walk slowly around the perimeter of his castle. "Did your mother ever tell you of the time Eleanor decided all of her ladies should don coats of armor and pretend they were warriors?"

Alain shook his head. There was no need to tell Guillaume that the Second Crusade was a topic rarely discussed in their household.

"Your father, Philippe and I had been bathing in a stream. When we returned, we found Janelle and Eleanor in mock combat." The sadness returned to Guillaume's face. "Isn't it odd what tricks memory can play? I had almost forgotten that day, but when I saw Charles dismount, it was as though it had all happened only yesterday."

The explanation was plausible, the alternative almost unthinkable. Watching the play of emotions on the older man's face, Alain could not ignore Guillaume's apparent vulnerability. Though none would have dared call the Silver Knight a coward, this was one time when he was loath to attack, to take advantage of an opponent's weakness. For the question he had to ask would cause naught but pain, reopening wounds that appeared to be only half healed.

There was an alternative. If Alain were careful and kept to the course he had set for himself, there would be no need to ask the question. For if there was one thing he had learned, it was that one's own pain would not be diminished by inflicting it on another. There were times when the greatest victory was the battle not fought.

"Be careful." Louise handed her mistress a carefully rolled piece of parchment. Her thin face pursed with concern, she continued, "His servant bade me give you this when no one else was near. In truth, Marguerite, I fear you two are courting danger."

Marguerite, however, did not share Louise's pessimism. She smiled, knowing that the missive had come from Charles, then unrolled the parchment and read the carefully penned plea. "Yes." She nodded her response. "Tell him I agree."

Her knight, it appeared, was as frustrated as she, for each time they had managed to be alone together, Alain had appeared within mere moments, leaving them the chance to exchange no more than a few words.

Though Louise continued to predict doom, to Marguerite it was like the tales of Camelot. She and Lancelot were forced into a clandestine rendezvous so that Arthur would not learn of their love. And yet there was a difference, for Guinevere had once loved Arthur, while she Marguerite felt naught but scorn for Alain. Oh, she had to admit that he was well read, having gone beyond the trivium and the quadrivium, and that he seemed to share her love of the Greek philosophers. But learning and a quick repartee could not compensate for the lack of courtly manners. And lack them he did.

"Father," she said an hour later, "I wish to speak with you."

Guillaume raised his eyes from the mail he was polishing. Though Mirail had a full complement of servants who could have performed the task as well as the master, Guillaume would permit no one else to touch his coat of chain mail. Marguerite had long suspected it was a matter of pride, that Guillaume needed to prove that though he might lack an arm, he was still able to perform knightly duties.

Today his eyes narrowed slightly, as if trying to decide why

Marguerite had interrupted him at a time when he preferred to be alone.

"If it's Alain you wish to discuss, I beg you spare your breath. The marriage will take place."

Marguerite shook her head, setting her golden braids to bouncing. " 'Tis not that," she said. "I would simply ask you not to announce our betrothal at tomorrow's hunt." It was a delaying tactic, but if luck were with her, Father would not recognize it as such.

"Why not, my child? It would seem an appropriate time, since many of our vassals will be here."

A week ago she would have agreed, but a week ago she had not met Alain de Jarnac.

"Oh, Father, a woman is betrothed only once. The ceremony should be a special occasion, not shared with anything else. Having it part of the hunt would seem to diminish its importance." Her eyes misted as she thought of how wonderful it would be if the betrothal were to Lancelot and not his crude brother.

Guillaume was silent, and for a moment Marguerite feared that her ploy had been unsuccessful. "All right, Marguerite," he said at last. "We will delay the betrothal, but only for a few weeks. I will ask Alain to return here after his journey to Lilis, so that we can have a proper celebration."

Carefully schooling her features so they would not reveal her satisfaction, Marguerite left the hall, feeling like a prisoner who had won a reprieve.

Later that day as she walked along the perimeter of the bailey, exchanging greetings with the people of Mirail and mediating small disputes, her heart was heavy. This was her life, and all too soon it would be taken from her.

She had always known that when she married she would have to leave Mirail for part of the year and live in one of her husband's castles. In the past the thought had brought only a modicum of pain, for not only had the parting seemed to be in the distant future, but it had been closely woven with her dreams of courtly love. When she left Mirail, she had believed, her sadness would be tempered with the joy of being with the man she loved, the knight of her dreams. Reality, she was discovering, did not always resemble dreams.

But tonight at least would be a dream come true. Tonight she would meet Charles, and for a few stolen moments they would pretend their love would have a happy ending.

From one corner of the garden rose the scent of crushed mint, wafted by the gentle night breeze. Marguerite chafed at the warmth of the dark cloak she wore, wishing she could throw back the hood and let the breeze blow through her hair. But she recognized the wisdom of Louise's advice and kept her distinctive golden hair covered. The last thing she and Charles needed was to have Alain discover them together.

"You came!" Charles stepped out from the shadow of the oak tree and grasped both of her hands in his. Unlike Marguerite, he had not covered his hair, and it gleamed in the moonlight. "My lady, the moments that we have been parted have weighed heavily on my heart."

"I, too, have been lonely without you, Lancelot." Indeed she had missed Charles's fine words and his longing glances. If her knight was not so well educated as his brother and did not know the difference between Demosthenes and Virgil, 'twas only the tiniest of flaws, proof that he was a man, not a figment of her imagination or the troubadours' tales.

"I beg your indulgence," Charles said as he drew her to a bench in one corner of the herb garden. "I have written a poem for you. 'Tis merely a rude offering, not worthy of your beauty, but I beg you not to scorn it."

Dropping to his knees in front of her, Charles began to recite.

> Moonlight crowns her golden head.
> As she smiles, my heart is led
> To deeds so brave I proudly claim,
> I do them all in Marg'rite's name!

There were several more stanzas, each extolling one of Marguerite's features and describing the feat of bravery which it had inspired. When Charles finished and bowed his head humbly, there were tears of joy in Marguerite's eyes. "Oh, Charles, it was wonderful. I shall cherish this moment forever."

"May I claim a reward?" he asked as he rose to his feet.

"Anything."

"I would beg a kiss." As Marguerite nodded, he drew her slowly into his arms. With gentle hands, he pushed the hood from her head and gazed into her eyes. "You are truly my lady," he said, his voice husky with emotion. Slowly, as though he wished to prolong the moment, he lowered his lips to hers. They were just a breath apart when a harsh laugh rent the darkness.

"What a touching scene!"

# Chapter Five

" 'Tis all right," she said, though the tears which slid down her cheeks and her red-rimmed eyes gave lie to her words. "You've no cause to worry."

For a moment he stood motionless. Nothing in his training had prepared him for a moment like this. Slowly, awkwardly, he put his arm around her shoulders, remembering a distant time when she had sought to comfort him in the same way.

"Are you ill?" he asked.

"Nay." Her sobs began to subside, though her voice remained thick with tears. " 'Tis naught."

With all the wisdom of his thirteen years, Alain knew his mother was lying. She had never cried, not once, not even when someone would unthinkingly refer to his father and the brutal ambush that had taken Robert's life, leaving Janelle alone, unprotected and carrying his child. If she was crying today, it was because someone had hurt her unbearably. And there was only one person who could have been responsible.

"What have you done to my mother?" Alain's hand reached for his sword but came away empty. He had left his armor in the Great Hall, wanting to surprise his mother with his *unscheduled visit and realizing the clanking would have alerted her to his approach.*

*Philippe met his stare. "I've done naught to your mother,"* he said, his brown eyes cold and unblinking. *"Not that you've any right to challenge me. Janelle is my wife. What occurs between us is our business and only ours."*

*Though he knew the folly of provoking his stepfather, Alain could not contain his anger. "It is my business when you make my mother cry."*

*Philippe shrugged. "If she's weeping, it's her own fault. Don't blame me, for I had naught to do with it." His words were blunt, his tone harsh. A wiser man would have backed away, but where his mother was concerned, Alain had yet to learn wisdom. Despite everything that had happened, he still clung to the illusion that his mother loved him.*

*"I don't believe you, Philippe. You're the only one who could have hurt her." Alain clenched his fist, seeking biblical retribution: pain for pain. "The truth is, my mother would be better off without you, and so would all of Jarnac."*

*His words met their mark. The man moved with an agility honed by years of battle, his arm swinging so swiftly that Alain was unable to dodge the blow. He landed on the rush-strewn floor, twisting his body at the last moment to protect his head.*

*"You know nothing!" Philippe's voice rose to a shout as he stood over Alain. "You speak of the truth, but you know nothing of it. I've protected you from that very truth all these years. By God, I will do it no longer." When Alain tried to rise, Philippe placed a booted foot on his chest. "Listen to me, and listen well, you young cur. Though you ought to know better, you believe your mother to be some kind of saint. The truth," he stressed the word, "is that she's nothing more than a whore."*

*His words were more effective than his blow in knocking the breath from Alain. "You doubt me. I can see that. If you want to know the truth, ask your mother who fathered Charles. It was not Robert."*

The memory had haunted him for years. When he had finally mustered enough courage to question his mother, she had denied

Philippe's accusation, insisting that Charles was indeed Robert's son. And yet the doubts had remained, fed by odd phrases, wistful expressions and the very real fact that he and Charles had more differences than similarities. All of which could be explained if what Alain feared was true.

There was no doubt that Charles was what he claimed to be, a legacy of the Second Crusade. But if he was Guillaume's son as Alain believed, Charles was also Marguerite's half-brother, changing the seemingly harmless flirtation they enjoyed into incest. That was one flower that could not be allowed to bloom.


"Will you allow Charles to wear your favor?" Louise shook the wrinkles from the dark blue bliaut before she handed it to Marguerite.

"I dare not." Poor Charles had experienced the brunt of his brother's anger last night when Alain had discovered them together in the garden. Though Marguerite longed to acknowledge her knight's chivalry publicly, she feared both Alain's and her father's reactions. She would not risk angering Father, for then he might insist on an immediate betrothal.

"No one will wear my favor," she told Louise. "After all, 'tis only a hunt, not a tournament."

A distant horn heralded the arrival of still more guests. While some of the visitors had arrived the previous evening, the majority of Guillaume's vassals had begun to congregate in the bailey and the Great Hall before dawn. Anticipation of the hunt and the revelry which would follow ran high, for there had been few opportunities for the vassals to demonstrate their martial skills over the past year. Peace, Guillaume had once told Marguerite with a smile, was not always valued, particularly by men who craved the excitement of battle. Having met Alain, Marguerite no longer doubted the truth of her father's words.

When she reached the Great Hall, a dark-haired knight detached himself from the crowd. "Marguerite, you grow more beautiful each time I see you."

He was dressed in his usual blue garments, an affectation

that never failed to amuse Marguerite. Even the large stone
that decorated the hilt of his sword was blue, although when
it had belonged to his brother, there had been a blood red ruby
in its place. Kneeling in front of her, he reached for her hand.

"Rise, Henri. It can't be comfortable kneeling in chain
mail." Marguerite touched his shoulder, then removed her hand
quickly, giving him no opportunity to kiss it. Not only did she
know from experience that his mustache would tickle, but after
the bliss of Charles's lips, she craved no other touch.

" 'Tis true. The mail cuts into my legs even through the
chausses." Henri de Bleufontaine rose to his feet and looked
down at her, his hazel eyes intense. "But for you, my dear
Marguerite, I would bear any pain."

Marguerite gave him a quick smile. His words were courte-
ous, almost as eloquent as Charles's, and yet they left her
unmoved. Perhaps it was because she had known Henri for so
long. With lands adjoining Mirail, he was a frequent visitor to
the castle.

Louise had once intimated that Henri viewed himself as
Marguerite's suitor, but she had been quick to dismiss the
notion. Though her betrothal had not been made public, Guillaume had discouraged his vassals from seeking Marguerite's
generous dowry. As for Henri, he had never shown her more
than normal courtesy, although there had been times when she
had caught him staring at her, an enigmatic expression on his
face. Today his eyes seemed to bore into hers, and his lips
were slightly parted, reminding her of the hounds when they
scented a hare.

Forsooth, Marguerite chided herself, the ale must have been
more fermented than usual if she was imagining Henri as a
predator. She smiled again, then took a step away from him as
she turned to scan the gathering of knights, searching for
Lancelot. There were many familiar faces, including that of
the big silver-haired man, but Charles's golden head was not
among them.

"May I have the honor of sharing your trencher at dinner?"
Henri, it appeared, had not understood her attempt to dismiss
him.

"I fear not," she said, and this time she did not accompany her words with a smile. "My father has asked me to give the Jarnac knights the places of honor." Henri should understand that the highest courtesy would be accorded to distant visitors.

As if unwilling to accept her refusal, Henri laid his hand on her shoulder, his fingers splayed wide in a proprietary gesture. Marguerite moved slightly, trying to free her shoulder.

"Then perhaps you will grant me your favor for the hunt." As his eyes moved from the pale blue ribbons she had threaded through her braids to the crimson ones which secured the ends, Henri's fingers moved lower, brushing the top of her breast. Marguerite recoiled from the intimate touch.

"If you want to live another hour, I suggest you let her go."

There was no mistaking the menace in his voice. Henri's hand dropped to his side as Marguerite took a step backward. How had Alain moved so quickly? A moment ago he had been on the other side of the hall speaking to Roland de Grosfleuve. Now he was standing between her and Henri, making no attempt to mask his displeasure. Clad once more in gray, he stood, his hand on his sword in an unmistakable threat, his blue eyes coldly furious.

"Who do you think you are?" Henri demanded.

Before Alain could reply, Marguerite intervened. "This is Alain de Jarnac," she said in as calm a voice as she could manage. No doubt the pounding of her heart was a simple reaction to Henri's loathsome touch. It couldn't be the fierce expression on the big man's face that caused her pulse to race as though she were fleeing an enemy.

"Jarnac. I thought I had heard you'd died in a hospital somewhere in Italy."

"Sorry to disappoint you, but your sources are obviously as poor as your judgment."

Ignoring Alain, Henri turned to Marguerite. "So this is the man who thinks he's going to share your trencher tonight." His words were little more than a sneer.

"I am the man who will share far more than her trencher." Though Alain did not touch her, the look he gave Marguerite left no doubt of his intentions. She felt the blood drain from her face, then rush swiftly back. Marguerite looked around, hoping no one else had overheard the exchange. But the other knights and their squires appeared to be more interested in speculating on the location of the best game than in a dispute over seating arrangements.

Alain glared at Henri. For a second there was silence as the two men measured each other. Then Henri nodded stiffly and walked away.

"One of your father's vassals?" Alain's voice was calm, as though the brief confrontation had had no effect on him.

"His lands adjoin Mirail . . ."

"And he'd like a merger of both lands and bodies."

For the second time a flush stained Marguerite's cheeks. "Henri would never speak so crudely," she said. Somehow the man had to be taught the proper way to address a lady.

"Perhaps not. Perhaps his speech would be courtly. His actions, on the other hand . . ." Alain raised an eyebrow, then looked pointedly at the breast Henri had touched. "It appears he's unaware of our betrothal."

"For the simple reason that there *is* no betrothal." Marguerite was not sure why she defended Henri. Lord knew he deserved no defense. And yet Alain was little better.

"How fortunate that particular problem is easily remedied. I shall speak to your father while we hunt. Your priest can formalize the arrangements tonight."

He spoke as though there were no doubt of the outcome, as though her wishes were of no importance. Deep in her heart Marguerite knew it would be difficult to sway her father, to convince him that she should marry Charles rather than Alain, but she could hope. And until the betrothal occurred, there was always the possibility that Father would relent.

In the meantime there were a few lessons Alain needed to learn. He was a warrior, accustomed to taking what he wanted by force. Moreover, it seemed that the women he knew were spineless creatures, unable or unwilling to defend their rights, all too willing to capitulate to his greater strength. This time it would be different.

"The betrothal will not take place until after your journey

to Lilis." Marguerite allowed herself the pleasure of gloating. "My father has promised me that."

The big man stared at her for a moment, his blue eyes coldly assessing. "If you think the delay will change the outcome, that somehow you will marry my brother, I assure you, you are wrong. You will be my bride ere the year ends."

Marguerite shivered. It was no more than she had feared, yet as he spoke, the words seemed more a threat than a promise. Giving her only a perfunctory nod, he walked quickly to the other side of the room. Marguerite narrowed her eyes. Though the Silver Knight might think otherwise, the battle was not over.

"You must get a message to Charles's squire," Marguerite told Louise when the men had left for the hunt. "I wish him to meet me on the riverbank at midnight." Her servant clucked a warning over the prospect of a clandestine rendezvous. "Tell him to wear a cloak this time so that no one will recognize him," Marguerite continued, "and, if you love me at all, be certain that Alain does not overhear."

There had to be a way to end the betrothal before it took place. Somehow she and Charles would find it. The alternative was unthinkable.


"It was a fine hunt."

The afternoon sun was warm on Marguerite's face as Roland de Grosfleuve bent his head in homage to her. After hours of relative quiet while the men had hunted, the castle was once more filled with the clank of armor, the neighing of horses and, above it all, the sounds of tired but contented men's voices.

Marguerite had seen her father only briefly. He had entered the bailey with Alain at his side, and when he had dismounted, his movements had seemed awkward, as though the hunt had exhausted him. Alain, however, appeared to have suffered no ill effects.

"Roland exaggerates," Henri muttered as he moved to stand at Marguerite's side. "Though I can scarce believe it, it appears that your serfs have been poaching, for we saw no stags. A few miserable hares, that's all we encountered.'' He kept his voice pitched so low that she had to move closer to distinguish the words.

"But I thought that Charles killed a large deer.'' Marguerite smiled, remembering the courtly words with which her Lancelot had announced his success. " 'Twas the only thing that helped me bear the hours we were parted,'' he had assured her. Because there was the ever-present danger that one of Alain's servants might overhear her, she made no mention of their forthcoming meeting. Instead she had smiled sweetly and then turned her attention to other guests.

"It was merely a doe,'' Henri informed her. "The serfs have taken all the stags. Marguerite, your father needs to enforce the law. Once he's hanged a few of those thieving serfs, you can be sure the rest will stop killing the deer.''

Since Henri did not appear to expect a response, Marguerite did not bother to tell him that her father believed a serf's life was worth more than a deer's. After all, the deer did not plant fields or weave cloth.

As Marguerite moved through the Great Hall, greeting the knights and murmuring congratulations when they spoke of their prowess in the hunt, Henri remained at her side. Though he said little, Marguerite noticed that he nodded frequently, as though granting approval to her words. When they walked, he would touch the small of her back, apparently guiding her through the assembly. Both were oddly proprietary gestures which made Marguerite uneasy. It was not like Henri to be so possessive. And yet there had been the incident this morning.

Marguerite moved a few steps to the right. Henri followed. Short of being rude and demanding that he leave, there was nothing Marguerite could do. Her father—and she herself— valued peace among the vassals. She would simply ignore Henri.

But soon it was not so easy.

They were in the center of the hall when he slid his arm around her waist and drew her close to him. Marguerite stiffened. The man had gone beyond the limits. She had not granted him—or any man—the right to hold her. She moved swiftly, twisting out of his grasp.

A second later Alain stood at Marguerite's side.

"I thought I warned you." Though Alain did not touch her, Marguerite could feel the fury emanating from him. The anger he had unleashed on Charles the previous night had been naught compared to this. That had been warm; this was a cold fury, and strangely it seemed far more dangerous.

Alain stared at Henri, silently challenging him. When Henri did not respond, Alain shrugged. "It appears you're a slow learner. Since you obviously require more than a warning, I shall be forced to teach you a lesson."

The friendly conversations which had filled the room stopped abruptly as the knights and their squires realized that something far more interesting than a recital of the hunt was occurring.

"There's naught you can teach me." Henri spat on the floor in front of Alain's feet.

It was an insult designed to provoke the big man's anger. Yet to Marguerite's surprise, Alain showed no sign that he recognized the insult. He merely gestured toward the door. "We'll fight in the bailey," he said. "I would hate to cause Lady Marguerite's servants more work cleaning blood from the floor."

Silence greeted Alain's words as the men waited for Henri's response.

"Full armor, unmounted and naught but swords."

"As you wish." Alain, it appeared, was unaware of Henri's reputation as a swordsman. While his skill on horseback was considerable, it was his ability to wield a sword that had gained Henri de Bleufontaine his reputation as a formidable opponent.

"Can you not settle this peacefully?" Marguerite asked Alain.

He raised his eyebrow in the expression she had learned meant disbelief. "Perhaps I was mistaken," he said, not bothering to hide his scorn, "but I thought it was a knight's duty to protect his lady's honor. And I understood that a lady's greatest desire was to have two warriors vying for her favor. Isn't that the courtly legend that you admire so deeply?"

"I value peace more than aught else." The words came quickly, almost unbidden. It was only when she had spoken them that she realized how true they were. Chivalry and battles fought for a lady's honor had a romantic ring when the troubadours told the tale, but there was no romance in seeing a man's blood on the floor.

"I shall attempt to remember that and will perhaps spare the wretch's life."

"Fear not, my lady." Henri's words were little more than a snarl as Alain's insult hit its mark. "I shall not permit this animal to disgrace Mirail with his presence for even one more hour."

"There will be no blood shed." Guillaume stood between the two men as they faced each other in the center of the bailey. Though he had not been close enough to hear Marguerite's words, her father knew her well enough to know she had no desire for either man to be wounded. Using his position as baron, Guillaume set the rules. It would be a *joute à plaisance,* an exhibition of skill rather than a battle designed to vanquish an enemy. "The first man to fall forfeits his sword to the other. If blood is drawn, the man who caused it is deemed to have fallen."

The crowd's murmurs indicated their approval, for all knew that a bloodless fight required more skill than one with no holds barred. It promised to be an exciting battle between two highly regarded warriors. Many of the men in the bailey had seen Henri in battle and acknowledged his superior abilities, while the Silver Knight's pugilistic skills were legendary. Though Marguerite heard several men wagering, the odds were nearly even. None could say who would win.

Marguerite watched as the two men faced each other, the sun glinting off their chain mail, their differences immediately apparent. Henri stood with his weight balanced on the balls of his feet, his hand gripping his sword. Alain, in contrast, appeared relaxed, his shield leaving his entire right side exposed, his hold on his sword as casual as though he were entering a friendly castle rather than facing a deadly opponent.

"Is he a good fighter?" Charles's question startled Marguerite, for she had not heard his approach.

"Henri?" She nodded. "He's the best warrior of all my father's vassals. Some say he's one of the finest in King Louis's realm."

"Then he's met his match in my brother." There was pride in Charles's voice. "No matter what faults he may have, Alain is unsurpassed on the battlefield. You need not worry about him."

Worry about him? Absurd! Of course she wasn't worrying about the big man. The fight was his idea, after all. He had challenged Henri. There was no need to fear for him.

The courtyard had been cleared, and the two men faced each other. As Guillaume nodded, they turned, each taking six paces. They stood at the edges of the bailey, swords and shields ready.

Marguerite watched her father raise his arm. When he lowered it, the duel would begin.

"No! Wait!" The child's voice was followed by a loud bleat as a large, newly shorn sheep scampered into the middle of the courtyard.

The crowd laughed, its tension dissolved by the sheep which, finding itself surrounded by humans, began to run in circles. When the child had managed to corral the animal and drag it from the bailey, Guillaume raised his arm again, and the crowd settled back, prepared for a long battle.

Henri moved swiftly, covering the distance between him and Alain in three long strides. The crowd gasped, for Alain appeared oblivious to Henri's attack and moved not an inch. He had not yet transferred his shield into battle position, and his sword hung at his side. Marguerite watched a smile of satisfaction light Henri's face. He lunged forward, his sword thrusting at Alain's unprotected right side. The crowd roared its warning, but still Alain did not move. Henri's smile turned into a full-fledged grin as he drove the sword home.

The movement was so deft that afterwards none could say how it happened. All they knew was that Henri landed face down in the dirt, and that somehow his sword had sliced his other hand. What was clear was that he had forfeited the battle on both counts and that the Silver Knight was responsible.

The crowd's shouts turned to laughter.

"I vow, I don't know what was more amusing—the frightened sheep or Sir Henri in the dirt." The man's voice carried clearly, redoubling the crowd's mirth.

As he struggled to his feet and wiped the blood from his hand, Henri's face darkened. "You'll pay for this, Alain de Jarnac," he muttered under his breath. "I promise you that."

# Chapter Six

He was there. As she slipped through the postern, she saw his dark form silhouetted against the lighter gray of the river. He stood facing the swiftly flowing stream, his head bent slightly as though he were contemplating its depths.

"Oh, Lancelot," she cried. "I feared my message might have gone astray or that your brother might have kept you from coming."

At the sound of her voice, he turned, his cloak swirling around his legs. The voluminous hood kept his bright hair hidden from prying eyes and cast shadows over his face.

"Nay, my lady. There was naught that could have kept me from your arms tonight." He spoke in a whisper, as though wary of being overheard. "I have counted the moments since I received your invitation. By all the saints above, never has time seemed to pass so slowly."

As Marguerite took a step toward him, he moved back into the shade of one of the trees which lined the riverbank. It was the movement of a prudent man, for who knew what eyes might be watching? Marguerite moved closer, seeking the same protection. Though it appeared that Charles's departure had escaped his brother's notice, the big man had surprised them altogether too many times for them to take unnecessary chances.

" 'Tis true, and yet I fear time is moving too swiftly. Your visit to Mirail is near its end."

"Let us speak not of endings." He reached for her hand and held it clasped between both of his. The warmth of his palm on hers sent shivers up her arm. "We have a lifetime of beginnings ahead of us."

It was a wonderfully romantic thought, worthy of the troubadours' tales. Unfortunately, it had little foundation in reality. Marguerite shook her head slowly. "I spoke to my father again today," she said. "He's adamant that I marry your brother. 'Twas all I could do to convince him to postpone the betrothal. Oh, Charles, how can I bear to marry that man?"

He tightened his grip on her hand. "We must trust in Fate," he said in the same low whisper. "Oft times she's wiser than we. But come," he said, drawing her closer. " 'Tis not words I crave tonight."

He raised her hand to his lips and pressed a kiss on her palm. Marguerite gasped. While other men had kissed her hand, it had been nothing more than a courtly gesture, a brief touch of cool, dry lips on the back of her hand. This was far different. His lips were warm and moist, lingering on the sensitive center of her palm. Just as a pebble tossed into the river caused ripples to spread to both shores, so too did his caress send waves of delight through her veins. And yet, although the ripples grew fainter the farther they spread, the pleasure his kiss wrought grew ever stronger as it coursed nearer her heart.

His lips parted and Marguerite shivered with delight as his tongue began to trace circles on her palm. The minstrels' songs had promised bliss, but they had been maddeningly vague about the nature of that pleasure. If this was only the prelude, as she suspected it was, what delights would the marriage bed bring?

"In truth, I begin to believe in Fate," she said, her voice trembling as he continued his gentle assault on her hand. Nothing in her experience had ever felt so wondrous. " 'Twas surely Fate that brought you to Mirail. Now we must find a way to keep you here."

"I assure you I've no intention of leaving," he promised in his husky whisper. His mouth was so close to her hand that each breath he took fanned her palm, reminding her of the greater pleasure his lips could bring. "Nor have I any intention of wasting tonight in conversation."

Suiting his actions to his words, he slid one arm around her waist and drew her close to him. With the other, he tipped her head back, then lowered his lips to hers. It started as the softest of caresses, a kiss as gentle as the touch of a flower's petals. And then his mouth parted, nipping gently at her lips, urging her to grant him access. Willingly she opened her mouth, and when his tongue entered it, the pleasure it spread made all else pale. If there was heaven on earth, this was surely it.

Marguerite raised her hands, wanting to touch his face, to draw him even closer. As she did, she pushed back the dark hood that had kept his face shadowed.

"You!"

She recoiled in horror, the heavy thudding of her heart caused by alarm, not the touch of that man's lips. She had feared he would learn of her assignation, that he would interrupt her and Charles or even prevent Charles from coming, but never, not in her worst nightmares, had she dreamed this would happen.

The man who had brought her such pleasure was not Lancelot. It was his brother.

"How could you?" she demanded, trying to break free from his arms.

"How could I what?" He kept his arms around her, drawing her closer until the length of her body touched his. When she tried to move, he only increased the pressure of his arms.

Marguerite noticed that he no longer whispered. What a fool she'd been! She had thought he had kept his voice low so that no one would overhear them. Instead it had been so she would not recognize him. No doubt his move into the tree's shadow had been equally calculating. As for kissing her hand, that, too, had served its purpose. With his face so close to her palm, she had had no opportunity to study his features.

No wonder the man's victories in battle were legendary. He was indeed a cunning adversary.

"Have you no shame?" she asked. The best defense, she had always heard, was a good offense. " 'Twas not you I sought to meet here."

Though the leaves filtered the moonlight, they let through enough illumination that Marguerite could see the glint in Alain's eyes.

"That may be true. But, my dear, I suggest you not forget it is I whom you will wed." This time his voice seemed tinged with amusement. "Surely it would have been inappropriate to have shared such a . . . shall we call it intimate? . . . moment with my brother."

The blood rushed to Marguerite's cheeks as she thought of how she had responded to his kisses and caresses. It should not have happened. Surely she should have realized that it was Alain, not Charles, who kissed her. But sadly, inexplicably, she had not. Her senses, it appeared, were easily tricked.

"How did you learn of my message?" she asked. There should have been no way for him to know she was to meet Charles. She had not trusted the message to writing for fear that it might have been intercepted as Charles's notes to her had been. And, while she had not delivered the invitation herself, Louise had assured her that no one had overheard her when she spoke to Charles's squire.

Alain laughed. "It seems you have made a tactical error, my dear fiancée." He stressed the last word. "You have underestimated your enemy. This afternoon's episode with your overzealous suitor should have shown you that I am accustomed to winning. I suggest you accept the fact that I have no intention of breaking that pattern now. And so, my dear, never doubt that I will get what I want."

Marguerite considered the import of his words. "You say you want me, but I know not why."

"That, my dear, is the question, is it not? Mayhap someday I'll answer it."

When she wakened the next morning, it was to the sound of horses and men milling in the bailey. It was not an unexpected sound, for the knights who had joined Guillaume for the hunt were scheduled to leave this morning. It was still early. Dawn had yet to break. But even that was not unusual, since some of the men had journeyed long distances and would seek to reach home before darkness fell. What was unexpected were Louise's words.

"Hurry, my lady, or you'll miss him."

For a moment Marguerite stared at the other woman, uncomprehending. Sleep had been long in coming. Perhaps that was why Louise's words made no sense.

"They're saddled and ready to leave," Louise said. "I warrant Charles had no part in the decision."

Charles! The thought brushed the last of sleep's cobwebs from Marguerite's brain. He and Alain had planned to remain at Mirail another day. Now something—or someone—had changed the plans. The blood rose to Marguerite's cheeks as she thought of one reason the Jarnac knights might be leaving early.

Without bothering to rebraid her hair, Marguerite raced down the stairs and into the bailey. If Alain de Jarnac thought he was going to steal away in the darkness merely to prevent her from bidding his brother farewell, he was wrong. This was one time when the invincible Silver Knight had underestimated *his* opponent.

"Ah, there you are, my dear." Her father greeted Marguerite as she hurried into the courtyard. The Jarnac entourage was packed, all the men save Alain and Charles mounted. Had she been five minutes later, she would have missed them. "Although Alain insisted I not waken you, I knew you'd want to bid him farewell."

Indeed! Though Father had no way of knowing it, he had just expressed one of her most fervent desires. She would like to bid Alain de Jarnac farewell . . . forever.

The object of her thoughts turned from giving his men orders and walked toward Marguerite. "I explained to your father that, as someone approaching her own betrothal, you would understand Charles's eagerness to reach Lilis and have his betrothal to Diane made formal." His voice was even, and

Marguerite wondered if she were the only one to hear a threat underlying the seemingly innocent words.

"Of course I understand," she said sweetly. "Just as I am sure you'll understand that I wish to bid your brother Godspeed."

Without waiting for his response, she walked toward Charles. The flickering lights of the torches revealed his bittersweet smile.

"I shall never forget the days I have spent in Camelot," he said when she approached him. "They will lighten my heart on this wretched journey."

Ah, yes, Alain was right. Charles was unable to contain his eagerness to leave Mirail and her. That much was evident.

Heedless of Alain's certain disapproval, she extended her hand to Charles. His eyes darted toward his brother then back to Marguerite. Slowly he dropped to his knees in front of her and took her hand in his.

"Good-bye, my love," he said so softly that Marguerite had to strain to hear him. He bent his head and pressed a kiss on her hand.

It was a lovely, courtly gesture, precisely the one a *preux chevalier* should use to bid his lady farewell. If it evoked no stronger feelings than mild pleasure, that was of no account. It was unfair to compare gentle, chivalrous Charles to his brute of a brother. It was unfair to think of how last night's embrace had stirred her blood, for what she had felt then was nothing more than lust. And lust, as Marguerite had once informed Alain, was not one of the higher emotions.

"They laughed at me." He tipped the jug of wine, draining the last of its contents into his mouth. "They acted as if I were a common buffoon, not a knight of the realm."

The room was small and poorly illuminated, but if the walls needed cleaning and the rushes were sorely in need of being changed, neither of them cared. All that mattered were the three jugs of wine they had emptied and the soft mattress they would soon share.

"Fools. They're all fools." The woman's words had begun to slur, but he was beyond noticing. "You're the finest ..." She paused for a moment, searching for another word, "... the bravest knight in all of France."

She reached for the jug. When he upended it, showing her that it was empty, she shrugged and began to unlace her bliaut.

"All his fault." He kicked his shoes into the corner, heedless of the mice whose nest he had disturbed. "They call him the Silver Knight. When I'm done with him, they'll call him the Battered Knight." He laughed at his wit, waiting until the woman joined in his mirth.

As she pulled the bliaut over her head, he grinned. It had been a long ride, but she would make it worthwhile. She always did.

"Next time you'll defeat him. I know you will." Her chemise followed the bliaut. "No one is better with a sword than you."

She stood naked in the center of the room, tossing back her hair so that he could admire her ample curves. "Come here," she said with a grin that was meant to be sultry. "Show me how good a swordsman you are."

For a few moments, Henri de Bleufontaine's thoughts of revenge were forgotten.


"By all the saints above!" Marguerite cursed softly as she broke yet another strand of yarn. Spinning, a task she had once enjoyed, was proving to be an exercise in frustration this morning. Not only was she unable to produce the fine, even thread which was the pride of Mirail, but today she could not even prevent the yarn from fraying.

"Is something wrong?"

The note of concern in Louise's voice made Marguerite pause, letting the spinning wheel slow, then stop. She'd heard her servants discussing her moods, speculating on the reason she, who had been known for her even temper, now snapped at the least annoyance. 'Twas not female problems, she'd heard one assure another, for the mistress never suffered from those ailments. Nay, 'twas something else that bedeviled the chatelaine of Mirail.

Boredom. Though nothing about it had changed, somehow her daily life had lost its zest. It reminded Marguerite of the time the cook had forgotten to add a pinch of cloves to the pork. Although perfectly roasted, the meat had seemed tasteless without that soupçon of spice. Life at Mirail continued, but without the seasoning of Charles's gentle smiles and his courtly compliments, it was bland, leaving Marguerite to long for more.

"By now they should have reached Lilis."

Marguerite nodded. Each day she had estimated the distance the Jarnac entourage would have covered. Today, if she had guessed correctly, they would be at the home of Diane de Lilis. Though Marguerite had never met the woman, she knew that Diane was rumored to be both comely and a great heiress. Her lands, in fact, were greater than those of Mirail itself.

Perhaps Alain would reconsider when he met Diane. As the older son, he should make the better alliance. He could marry Diane, leaving Charles to wed Marguerite. That, however, was a dream with little chance of becoming reality. For some reason, Alain wanted her, Marguerite. It made no sense, for they were clearly unsuited. She was not the spineless, brainless woman Alain preferred, and he was far from the courtly knight of her dreams. Why, then, did he think he wanted to marry her? It was a question that perplexed her during the day and haunted her dreams.

"Everyone agrees, it was just like the tales of Camelot." Louise leaned back against the stone wall, letting her fingers fall idle. The other women had retired to their huts to prepare the morning meal, leaving Marguerite and Louise alone in the spinning shed. "Alain was so brave, defending your honor."

"More likely, he was simply defending his own honor. Henri defied Alain, and that was an insult few knights would ignore." Marguerite set the wheel to spinning again in an attempt to focus her attention on the yarn—on anything other than Alain de Jarnac. "I suspect that when Alain fought Henri, it was to ensure that every man present knew not to challenge the Silver Knight again." Alain's motives were something Marguerite had considered carefully. At first, like Louise, she had viewed the challenge as an act of chivalry. But when she had applied logic, reviewing all the facts at her disposal, she had realized that Alain de Jarnac did nothing for chivalry. His motive was far more mercenary. As he had told her that night on the riverbank, he wanted her, and she suspected that when Alain de Jarnac wanted something, he rarely failed. It was an appalling thought.

The sound of horns heralding visitors broke through the still morning air. Abandoning her spinning wheel once again, Marguerite went to the doorway. The spinning shed was located on the perimeter of the bailey, close to the wall. By taking only a few steps outside, Marguerite could see the approaching visitors. No matter who came, it would be a break in the monotony of her daily life, a chance to forget—if only for a few hours—that she was betrothed not to the man of her dreams but to his crude, overbearing brother.

" 'Tis Henri," Marguerite told Louise as she recognized the blue banners. When he had assumed control of Bleufontaine, Henri had insisted that all of his livery be made of the purest blue cloth available. With a mischievous smile, Marguerite turned to Louise. "I shall wear my blue bliaut," she said, frowning at the forest green one which she had donned only hours before. Henri was not an honored guest, merely one of her father's vassals, but it might relieve the tedium to pretend that he deserved the highest courtesy Mirail could offer.

It might also soothe his bruised ego, for Marguerite had no doubt that Henri's defeat at the hands of Alain de Jarnac had been a bitter one. Though Alain had refused to take Henri's sword or another monetary forfeit, the man's pride had to have suffered. It was not easy being the brunt of a joke, particularly for a man like Henri.

As she greeted Henri and the three squires who accompanied him, Marguerite saw the speculative glint in Henri's eyes. He'd never know whether she had chosen her clothing to honor him, or whether by chance she had already been wearing blue.

"I beg your hospitality and that of your father." Henri dismounted and bowed his head to Marguerite.

"Certainly. We welcome you to Mirail." Marguerite gave Henri her warmest smile as she led him into the Great Hall and offered him a flagon of wine. The man responded with a smile of his own, but mindful of his wandering hands, Marguerite kept a safe distance from him. This was one game that would be played on her terms.

"I bring messages for your father," Henri said. He quaffed deeply of the wine, then wiped his mustache with the back of his hand. "But I must confess that 'tis not only business which brought me to Mirail. I hoped to hear you play the lute again."

His words confirmed what she had surmised from the heavily laden horses he had brought with him, that he intended to stay at Mirail for several days. As for wishing to hear her play the lute, 'twas only an excuse. While Marguerite had many talents, music was not among them. Even to her untrained ears, her own playing was less than pleasing.

"Another suitor," Louise said as she listened to Marguerite's selections of dinner dishes. "Soon your father will have to insist you marry, if only to save Mirail. Entertaining all your suitors will beggar the barony."

"Nonsense." Marguerite dismissed the notion of imminent ruin along with the idea of Henri's courtship. "The man is naught but a visitor, come to discuss politics with my father. I can only pray that he'll bring more interesting tales than the last peddlers." They had had little news of either the royal court in Paris or Eleanor of Aquitaine's newly instituted courts of love. "Now I beg you assist Cook with dinner preparations."

She was almost at the kitchen when it happened. As Louise rounded the last corner, a man entered the narrow corridor. At least she surmised that it was a man, for the legs were distinctly masculine, and the arms which held an immense pile of armor were muscular. Naught else was visible behind the shields and hauberks.

"Careful!" she cried, raising her voice as she pressed her

back to the stone wall. There was simply no way the man could have seen her approaching, and the rattle of the armor he carried would have prevented him from hearing her footsteps.

He stopped abruptly, the huge pile of metal and leather teetering. Louise saw the muscles in his arms ripple with the effort of holding their burden. Slowly, the topmost shield began to slip. The man bent backwards, trying to prevent it from falling, but gravity had begun its work. The result was inevitable.

Instinctively Louise raised her arms and grasped for the shield as it tumbled. Her hands caught one edge, and for a moment she was able to steady it. But the weight was too great, and she could not hold it. With a clang, the metal struck the stone floor.

"Holy Mary in heaven!" The man swore violently as he lowered the rest of his burden to the floor. "There'll be no pleasing him now." His voice was deep and raspy, unlike any Louise had heard, and it took a moment for the words to register. It was almost as though he spoke in another tongue.

He was a man indeed, Louise saw, and had he not been scowling as he surveyed the damage, he might have been a comely one. His hair was brown, perhaps two shades darker than her own, and his eyes—those eyes which now betrayed his fear—were a deep brown. Though his clothing was worn, it bore no stains other than the normal dust from a journey.

" 'Twas my fault," she said as he inspected the shield. The dent in one edge caused the furrows around his mouth to deepen.

"He'll not believe that." The man hunched his shoulders, as though preparing for the inevitable blows. "Not that I'd hide behind a woman's skirts." He pronounced the words slowly, giving Louise's ear a chance to become accustomed to his unusual voice.

She felt a stab of pity. From the way the man spoke, it was obvious that the simple act of forming words brought discomfort, perhaps even pain. Now he was facing more pain because of an act he had not caused. 'Twas her cry which had startled him, sending the armor tumbling.

Louise thought quickly. The man was obviously one of Henri de Bleufontaine's servants, and the anger that he feared was his master's. While it was not unusual for a knight to beat his serfs—indeed, although Guillaume was noted for his fairness, Louise had heard tales that it brought many men great pleasure to show their domination in purely physical ways—she did not wish this man to suffer when the fault was hers.

She studied the shield. The dent was not large. Jean-Claude, the blacksmith, could repair it easily. Oh, it would cost her a kiss, and the queen of heaven knew that Jean-Claude's kisses were far from pleasant. Unlike this man, he felt no need for water to contact either his skin or his clothing. Louise was never certain what stank more, Jean-Claude's breath or his clothing. Yet surely a few moments of being close to the blacksmith was little enough to pay to save this man from a beating.

"Our blacksmith will smooth the dent so skillfully that your master will never know it was damaged," she said. "We will tell Sir Henri that the leather strap appeared worn and that my mistress insisted we replace it."

The furrows disappeared from the man's face, and the corners of his mouth turned up. He was, as she had thought, a most appealing man when he smiled. Indeed, if needed, she would grant Jean-Claude more than one kiss to ensure that this man smiled again. There was something about him, perhaps the fact that he cared for personal cleanliness, which told her this was no ordinary serf, and his plight had touched her heart.

"Somehow I will repay your kindness." His voice crackled, but his brown eyes had begun to sparkle. "What is your name?"

"I am called Louise," she said. "And you?"

He formed the words carefully. "I am Gerard, son of Albert the cobbler. My lord has made me his personal servant."

Once again the man's face darkened, and Louise wondered at the cause. It was an honor to be a knight's servant, an elevation to a status far higher than cobbler, yet the man seemed to consider it a burden rather than a boon.

Gerard bent his knees and reached for the pile of armor. "I must have this cleaned before my lord sups," he said. "But I would thank you again for your kindness." He looked up at her, a smile on his face. "Will you meet me in the bailey tonight?"

Wordlessly Louise nodded. As she hefted the shield, she grinned. Mayhap Marguerite was right. Mayhap Camelot had come to Mirail after all.

# Chapter Seven

"I've heard tales that the king is worried." Henri leaned forward, directing his words to Guillaume. 'Twas most pleasant, indeed, having the fair Marguerite between them as they dined. Though they were the only people seated at the high table, he had shifted his weight so that he was a mere hair's breadth from Marguerite. None could fault him for the accidental brushes against her arm or the occasional contact with those luscious breasts. 'Twas only natural as he moved to face her father. Natural, too, was his body's instinctive reaction to those touches. Mother of heaven, she was a comely wench! Henri's eyes darkened at the thought of her in his bed, those long legs wrapped around him, drawing him ever closer as he feasted on the perfection of her breasts, sinking his . . .

"Is it errant knights that worry him or the queen?" Guillaume's voice held a hint of amusement.

Henri blanched. By all the fires of hell, the man couldn't have guessed his thoughts, could he? Guillaume might be an undemanding lord, but Henri doubted he'd countenance blatantly lascivious thoughts of his daughter.

"The problem is Eleanor." Henri spat the name. How could one woman cause so much trouble? Granted she was beautiful enough to turn even a royal head, witness the fact that she had bewitched two kings, but that was no reason for those men to have given her such power. She was naught but a woman, and had Louis and England's Henry been real men, they would have kept her relegated to a woman's proper place. Instead, look at the trouble she had caused.

Marguerite spoke. "I've heard some of Louis's vassals are leaning toward Eleanor, particularly now that Richard has been crowned." The news that Eleanor had had her son crowned Duke of Aquitaine had spread quickly, with peddlers and troubadours embellishing the story of the coronation in Limoges and Richard's symbolic wedding to Saint Valerie. With each telling, the tale had grown, and by the time it reached Mirail and Bleufontaine, Richard had appeared nothing short of heroic.

"Aquitaine has always been powerful." Guillaume speared a morsel of roast pork with his knife. "For a short while when Eleanor and Louis were married, it seemed that we would have a united France. Now . . ."

Henri watched his liege lord carefully. Though the man had never forsworn his vows of fealty to Louis, there were some who thought he favored Eleanor of Aquitaine's court. For himself, Henri cared little about politics. One lord was much like another. What mattered was which would provide him the greatest opportunities. Be that as it may, it was important to know where Guillaume's loyalties lay, for a wise man could play upon those sympathies and use them for his own purposes. In the contest for the fair Marguerite's hand, Henri needed every advantage he could muster.

While there was no doubt that Marguerite herself was a prize to be won, having her in his bed was only the beginning. For years Henri had realized that as her husband he would gain wealth and power. But now . . . now there was an added reason to woo and win the chatelaine of Mirail: revenge.

"Eleanor has done much damage."

Henri smiled. There was no doubt where Marguerite's loyalties lay. Even more than her words, the rancor in her voice made her opinions clear. He need worry no more, wondering which faction Guillaume supported. Marguerite's simple statement proved that the rumors were untrue, that Guillaume had never wavered in his support of Louis. For she would echo her father's thoughts, and then, when she married, her husband's.

All that remained now was to convince Guillaume that he, Henri, was the right man to become Marguerite's husband. Then he'd have the opportunity he sought. With the wealth of Mirail and its vassals behind him combined with the power of Bleufontaine, Henri would make Alain de Jarnac rue the day he had challenged him.

Victory might be sweet, but the satisfaction of revenge lasted far longer. It was a lesson Henri had learned on a deserted path half a dozen years before and one he vowed he'd never forget. In one act he'd exacted payment for a lifetime of abuses and, oh, how sweet the retribution had been. It was a shame that miserable excuse of a monarch did not appreciate the value of seeing his enemies grovel, for it was indeed one of life's greatest pleasures.

"In truth, I do not understand why the king does not gather his vassals. He could easily defeat Richard's men." Under the guise of reaching for another piece of pork, Henri took the opportunity to rub his hand across Marguerite's breast. Mother of God! He could feel the nub tighten beneath the thin cloth, and his own body hardened in response.

She leaned back, leaving his hand touching only air. Ah, the woman was a tease. She sought to heighten his desire by forcing him to wait as she played the coquette. Another man might have been fooled by her demure airs, but she could not mislead Henri, not when he had seen the warmth in her eyes. It was as he had thought. The lusty wench wanted him as badly as he wanted her.

"Mayhap the king values peace and his vassals' lives more than power." The warmth Henri had seen in her face was reflected in her voice. "Louis is a wise man, and it would seem he's witnessed enough destruction to avoid it."

Henri grinned at the emotion in her voice. It was true. She was as passionate as he had thought, a woman who would share his own appetites. He smiled in anticipation.

* * *

"My sister has her head stuffed with feathers."

Marguerite uncovered Jean's arm and inspected it carefully. She had found the boy once again chopping wood and had insisted that he stop long enough for her to assure herself that his activity was not reopening the gash. Satisfied that the wound was healing properly, she raised her eyes to his. "Feathers? Why do you say that?"

Jean curled his lip in disgust. "All she can talk about is that man Gerard. She gets this silly look on her face, and her voice sounds quivery, like she's scared Mère is going to beat her." With all the wisdom of his ten years, he announced, "Girls! They're so dumb."

"And I suppose boys are smart." Marguerite applied another poultice to Jean's arm, then wrapped a cloth around it. The child's innocent words had solved the puzzle of Louise's inattentiveness. For the past two days, Louise had seemed almost like a stranger. Marguerite had had to remind her about even the most routine tasks, and her eyes had been glassy, as though focused on some other time or place.

When Marguerite had questioned her, she had claimed to be suffering from a digestive ailment, yet she had refused Marguerite's remedy, insisting that rest would cure her. Now it appeared she had been spending her free time with Gerard, whoever he was, and based on Jean's comments, Marguerite doubted the two of them were resting.

"Boys are smart," Jean asserted. "You wouldn't catch Alain de Jarnac acting as silly as Louise. He's got more important things to do."

Alain de Jarnac! The last thing Marguerite wanted was to hear yet another one of her people praise the man. His prowess with the sword, the clever way he had defeated Henri, even the way he cared for Neptune, his destrier. No aspect of the man's life appeared to be outside the scope of Mirail's interest. Since he and Charles had left, it seemed that everywhere she went within the barony's walls, the only topic of conversation was the Silver Knight.

After a glance at the sky assured her that rain was not imminent, Marguerite ordered her palfrey saddled. Perhaps once she was outside Mirail's walls, she would be able to escape Alain de Jarnac's ever growing reputation.

High clouds scudded across the deep blue sky, and the poplar trees bent in the wind. By nightfall the rain would begin. Marguerite smiled as she bent low over the mare's neck, urging her into a gallop. The approaching storm reflected her own mood, dark and tumultuous, but perhaps the aftermath would bring the same cleansing that the storm provided.

She gripped the horse's mane, not caring that her own hair had loosened from its braids and was streaming behind her, a golden mane of its own. All that mattered now was the sense of freedom riding gave her. For a few blessed moments she was no longer Marguerite de Mirail, chatelaine of a large barony with all its concomitant responsibilities. Responsibilities that included betrothal to one overbearing knight. Instead, she was simply a woman reveling in the solitude and grandeur of her world.

As the horse began to tire, Marguerite slowed her pace. In a few minutes she would head back to Mirail, but for now she would enjoy the carefree feeling that only riding seemed to bring her.

She heard the approaching hoofbeats before she saw the horse.

"Father!" she cried, as he reined in his stallion to ride next to her. His face was red with exertion, and the grooves next to his mouth seemed deeper than normal. "Is aught wrong?"

"Can't a man spend some time alone with his daughter?" He spoke slowly, drawing deep breaths. "With all our guests, I have had little opportunity to speak with you."

Marguerite smiled. It was true. In the past she and her father had spent several hours a day conferring over the barony's affairs, making decisions that ranged from which fields to leave fallow to how severe a penalty the cooper's wife should pay for damaging her husband's tools in a fit of anger. Over the last few weeks, there had been little time for discussions of any kind.

They rode together for a few moments, speaking of trivial things. Then Guillaume slowed his horse again and turned to face Marguerite. " 'Twas not the barony's affairs that brought me out here," he admitted, "but yours. Tell me truly, my daughter. Are you unhappy? Is this betrothal that repugnant to you?"

For a moment Marguerite was silent. When she had approached him in the past, Father had been adamant about her marriage and had not wanted to consider her happiness. What had caused him to change?

"I have no wish to marry Alain de Jarnac," she said slowly. "You know that."

Guillaume nodded. Now that the flush had receded from his face, it appeared unnaturally pale. "You heard Henri at dinner last evening. There is discontent among the King's vassals. With no wars and no crusades to occupy them, they have little to do other than stir up trouble amongst themselves." Guillaume's eyes were serious as he looked at Marguerite. " 'Tis not only the King's vassals who are restless. I fear the same malady has spread to our knights and that we may face a rebellion. I overheard several of our vassals when they came to Mirail for the hunt, and there's cause for concern. Some of Roland de Grosfleuve's comments were little short of treason." Guillaume touched Marguerite's hand. "It will take a strong man to keep peace at Mirail."

His touch was cool, but it was his words which sent a shiver along Marguerite's arms. "Mirail has you."

"I'll not always be here." His voice was matter-of-fact. "We need to plan for the future. Alain is a powerful knight, and—more than that—he is wise. He will guard your lands and keep Mirail safe for your children. My dear, I know of no other man who can do that."

What he said was true. There was no disputing that. But surely marriage should be based on more than such practical concerns.

"Mayhap you're right, but I fear Alain's allegiance to Eleanor and her court may endanger Mirail. Is it not likely that

King Louis would look askance at having a barony as rich as Mirail held by one of Eleanor and Richard's knights?''

Once again Guillaume's face was pale. ''Alain is an honorable man. I feel confident he'll do whatever is best for you and Mirail.'' He took a deep breath and leaned back in the saddle. ''I also believe Alain is the man you must marry.''

It was as though a cloud had obscured the sun, leaving only a chill in its wake. Marguerite shivered again. From early childhood she had known it was her duty to protect Mirail. But why, oh why, was duty so painful?

The man was a fool. She was wealthy and not unpleasant to the eye. More than that, she appeared besotted with him. She simpered and blushed when he spoke to her, and her eyes followed him when she thought no one was looking.

Alain rubbed his destrier's flanks, then turned his attention to Neptune's powerful shanks. It was the perfect alliance, one no knight in his right mind would refuse. Yet Charles was being an obdurate fool, persisting in those futile dreams. You'd think his brother would have the common sense the Good Lord had given a horse.

''I must talk to you.''

Alain continued grooming Neptune. ''So, talk.'' He had little doubt what his brother wished to discuss and even less desire to be part of that conversation.

''Not here.''

When Alain raised his eyes, he saw Charles glance around the stable as though expecting servants to materialize from the walls. Alain gave Neptune's hooves a thorough inspection, then followed his brother outside the walls of Lilis. When they were far enough away that their words would not be overheard by the guards who patrolled the outer walls, he stopped.

''What is it you wish to discuss?'' He made no attempt to soften his words, not caring that Charles flinched at the harsh tone.

''I cannot go through with this.'' Charles scuffed his boot

on the dirt, drawing a large *M* with his toe. "I do not love Diane."

The clouds which had obscured the sun since midday darkened, leaving the air thick with moisture. By dusk the storm would arrive, and yet, judging from his brother's face, a storm of a different nature was imminent.

Alain shrugged. "What bearing does love have on marriage? Diane is an heiress; she's pleasing to look at; she's of an age to bear your children. Why, she even has all her teeth. What more could you want?" He was baiting Charles; he knew that, but, by all the saints above, the man deserved it. It was time he faced reality.

"That may be enough for you, but it's not enough for me." Charles glared at Alain, his brown eyes fierce with emotion. "I want more than that. I love Marguerite, and I want to marry her."

From the corner of his eye, Alain saw a woman standing on the castle walls. Though he was too far away to distinguish her features, the saffron garment could belong to only one person. He smiled inwardly. Mayhap there was a way to end this nonsense.

"Marriage to Marguerite, my dear brother, is naught but a foolish dream. Wake up! The reality is that you will celebrate your betrothal to Diane de Lilis on the morrow."

But Charles would not be denied. "Why is it a foolish dream?" he demanded. "You said it yourself. The lands of Lilis are the perfect alliance with Jarnac. Since you're the heir to Jarnac's lands, why don't *you* marry Diane and let me marry Marguerite?"

The logic was compelling in its own perverse way, but the notion of swapping brides was oddly unsettling.

"You know the terms of the agreement between my father and Marguerite's." No sooner were the words out of his mouth than Alain realized what he had said. It was the first time he'd referred to Robert as only his father, not theirs. If God was merciful, Charles would not notice the lapse.

"What difference does it make—one son or the other? We'd still be doing what they wanted."

Alain steeled his face to remain expressionless. Now was not the time to answer Charles's question truthfully. This was one case where honesty would bring only pain and where a small prevarication was justified. "That is not a possibility."

"Why not? It makes perfect sense to me."

Why not, indeed? Such an alliance would only violate the most basic of natural laws.

"No."

Charles clenched his fist. "That's not an explanation. In case it has escaped your notice, I am not a child, Alain, and I'm tired of being treated like one." He took a step forward. "Do you have any idea what it was like growing up in your shadow, hearing how perfect you were, watching you get everything I wanted? Well, brother, this is one time you won't get everything. I won't let you have Marguerite."

Deliberately Alain gave him a smile that was little more than a sneer. "How do you propose to stop me?"

It was all the provocation Charles needed. He lunged forward, knocking his brother to the ground. As the dust swirled, he swung his fists wildly, catching Alain's jaw, then continued pummeling his brother.

For a moment Alain remained motionless, calculating. Then with a groan, he heaved Charles off his chest and onto the ground. Landing a punch to Charles's face, he watched with satisfaction as the blood spurted from his brother's nose. At the sound of a soft rustle, he buried his fist into Charles's ribs.

"Stop! Stop, you brute!"

Two small fists pounded on his back.

Alain swiveled his head then ducked as the heiress to Lilis swung her arm at his face. In her saffron-colored gown, she reminded him of a mother goose, hissing and biting to protect her young, heedless of the fact that her adversary was far larger and more powerful than she. But Charles, of course, was not her child, a fact that made her attack all the more satisfying to Alain.

Quickly Alain rolled out of range of Diane de Lilis's blows. Then, with the dexterity which made him such a formidable foe, he leaped to his feet. A moment later, Diane knelt at

Charles's side. She touched his face gently before she turned to glare at Alain.

"You're no more than an animal." Her hazel eyes sparkled with fury. "How could you hurt your brother?"

Wordlessly Alain returned to the castle. It appeared his plan might work.

"You two are so different," Diane murmured as she wiped the blood from Charles's face. "It's hard to believe you're brothers." She dipped the cloth in water again, and stroked his cheek.

Charles grimaced. "At times, I wish we were not."

His wounds were superficial, not requiring the attention Diane was giving them. While he suspected she was well aware of that, Charles saw no reason to cut short her ministrations. The feeling of those soft hands on his face was distinctly pleasant.

"You were so brave." Diane spread a salve on her fingertips, then spread it over the cuts on his face. Though the salve was cool, the trail her fingers left was as warm as the summer sun.

She put one hand under his chin and tipped his face toward the window. With her head tilted slightly to one side, she studied his features. Her fingers moved gently, almost timidly, as she traced the contours of his face. As she continued her exploration, Charles felt his blood begin to pound.

Sweet Mary in heaven, she was a comely one. Why had he not noticed the way her eyes sparkled? They were neither green nor brown, but an intriguing combination, so much more beautiful than blue. And that hair. Why had he thought blond was attractive? Brown was so much more pleasing. Her face was surely one that would inspire the most passionate of troubadours' songs, and the body encased in that yellow gown was enough to tempt even a monk.

She gave his chin a gentle squeeze, then slowly drew her hand away. When she spoke, her voice was soft. "Oh, Charles, you're the perfect knight."

It was the sweetest of praises, the accolade every chevalier craved. Charles clasped one of her hands between both of his and gazed into her eyes. "I fear I am far from perfect, but there is no one who will dispute me when I say that you are the perfect lady."

———  ——

His lips were sweet and warm, sending ripples of delight along her limbs. His hands ignited fires wherever they touched her, making her ignore the cold stone beneath her back. Though she had once thought the troubadours exaggerated the pleasures of love, in truth, they had touched only the surface.

She felt oddly bereft when he drew his lips from hers. It was always thus. The moments they could spend together were brief and far too few.

"I cannot bear the thought that we'll be parted." Gerard spoke the words so softly that they were little more than a whisper. It was the sword hanging over them, the fact that Henri's visit would soon end.

"Mayhap you need not leave." Louise had spent every waking hour searching for a way to keep Gerard at Mirail. "My lady could ask for you in lieu of your lord's annual duty." She had heard tales of similar arrangements on other fiefs. Though uncommon, they were not unheard of.

Gerard shook his head slowly. "No," he said in that harsh voice which had become so dear to her. "It is not possible."

"I believe my lady would do this for me. She has always been a most generous mistress."

" 'Tis not Lady Marguerite who is the problem. 'Tis my master. He'll never let me go."

"I don't understand." Louise grasped Gerard's hand, seeking the comfort of his warmth. "Why would Henri not agree?"

"That man doesn't need reasons. He simply does what he wishes. But," Gerard said as he drew Louise back to the floor, "let us not worry about the future. Let us enjoy what we can of the present."

* * *

"I saw you with the brown-haired slut." Henri stood in the middle of the visitors' sleeping chamber at Mirail, fingering his sword.

Gerard felt the blood drain from his face then rush back. The man was a demon. Either that, or he had spies everywhere. He and Louise had been so careful, ensuring that no one saw them together, meeting in an unused storeroom, leaving no traces of their rendezvous. How had Henri learned of them?

And how could he call Louise a slut? She was still as pure as the day she was born. They'd shared kisses and caresses, but not once had they lain together as man and woman. It had not been for lack of desire. The Good Lord knew they had burned with the fires of passion, and neither of them had wanted to end those oh, so pleasurable kisses. But they had, for Gerard had no wish to leave Louise with a babe, a child he might never see.

"I see you don't deny it." Henri drew his sword from the scabbard and turned it over, moving it so that the sun glinted off the jeweled hilt. He turned his gaze to Gerard and leered. "See that you use *your* sword wisely." His leer left no doubt of his meaning. "Keep the brown-haired wench happy. When she's limp with pleasure, ask her about her mistress. I want to know everything. What she likes, what she doesn't like, where I can find her alone."

Gerard recoiled in horror. Though he had no illusions about his master, what he had asked him to do was unconscionable.

"You want me to spy."

Henri shrugged and returned the sword to its scabbard. "What of it? 'Tis not a mortal sin, so you'll not burn in hell." His grin was so evil that Gerard wondered if he had somehow stumbled into the nether world. "I'll give you a choice, you miserable excuse for a man. Use the wench to get the information I need or . . ." He paused, as though considering the alternative, ". . . there'll be one less nun at Saint Lazaire."

It was no choice, and Henri knew it.

# Chapter Eight

There was no apparent reason for it. The day was perfect as only early June could be, with songbirds trilling and the scent of flowers filling the air. Not a cloud marred the sky, and the sight of a tiny squirrel stuffing acorns into his cheeks should have made Marguerite smile. Instead, she found herself oddly, inexplicably uneasy. The hairs on the back of her arms prickled, and she felt a sense of foreboding, as though a storm were approaching.

There was no storm, only a feeling of impending danger.

Marguerite pinched a comfrey leaf, then, satisfied with the sap which oozed from it, she plucked several stems.

"He's so wonderful. I never dreamt I could feel like this." Louise knelt in the dirt next to her and held out the basket.

Marguerite blinked rapidly, trying to dismiss the odd sensation that had plagued her since early morning. What was Louise saying? Something about unusual feelings. She listened as the brown-haired woman continued her litany of praise. Gerard, that was the name Jean had mentioned. One of Henri's serfs.

She nodded, and for a few moments everything seemed normal as she noticed the becoming flush which colored Louise's cheeks. Mayhap Louise was right, and love did change a maiden's visage. It had certainly changed Louise. The once-practical woman was now given to smiles and sighs, to tears and trills of laughter. Her moods changed as often as spring weather and were equally unpredictable.

Marguerite rose and crossed the small garden, seeking the mint she knew grew in the corner. Tomorrow she'd speak to Father. Perhaps he could arrange an exchange with Henri. She had heard Henri wax eloquent over the meat pie the second cook made. Mayhap he valued cuisine over whatever service it was Gerard performed and would be willing to trade Gerard for the cook.

"Would that I could be with him!"

"We must . . ."

It caught her unprepared, a pain so sharp it took away her breath. Her chest tightened in agony as the pain spread down her arm, growing in intensity with each inch it traversed. She opened her mouth to scream, but before she could force a sound from her throat, the world went black.

Father!

Marguerite forced her eyes open. Fear, made all the more potent by its simplicity, permeated every pore of her body. Grasping her skirts in both hands, she ran toward the castle. She had to find him.

The Great Hall. He was not there.

The alcove where he was wont to polish his armor. Not there, either.

"Bertrand, have you seen my father?" The old retainer shook his head.

The pain was worse now, like a hot knife thrust deep into her breast, and yet it was cold . . . so very cold.

"Father!" Marguerite cried as fear propelled her through the narrow corridors. "I'm coming!" The only reply was the echo of her own voice. Her feet faltered, and she started to stumble as the cold grew ever stronger.

Hurry. She had to hurry. She had to find him before . . . Deliberately she refused to even think the word. But when she reached the small counting room where they had spent so many hours together, Marguerite knew her deepest fear had been realized.

He lay on the floor, one leg twisted beneath him, his good arm bent at an unnatural angle. Yet, though it appeared an uncomfortable position, there was a faint smile on his face and an expression of ineffable peace.

"No!" Marguerite screamed the word. It couldn't be. And yet it was.

On the desk a piece of parchment fluttered in the light breeze, and dust motes bounced in a ray of sunshine. Everything was the same. Nothing was the same.

With a cry of anguish Marguerite dropped to her knees and made the sign of the cross over the man who had been her father, her mother and her best friend; the man who would never again chide her for her love of books or praise her for keeping the barony's accounts; the man who had been part of her life forever but who was no more.

"Why, sweet Mary, why?" she demanded as tears streamed down her cheeks. " 'Tis too soon." There was no answer. There never would be.

Her cries had alerted the servants, and the once-empty hallways rang with the sound of footsteps. She had only seconds longer to be alone with him. Choking back a sob, she bent to close his eyes and give him one last kiss. As she watched, it seemed that his face was taking on an unnatural pallor and that his familiar, beloved features were somehow changing into a stranger's.

Marguerite shuddered, remembering the ride they had shared only two days before. Father had been unusually pale then. That day he had spoken of the future as though he would not be part of it, as though he had had a premonition that the end was near.

Dear God, how had he known? And how, oh how, had he been able to bear the knowledge?

"My child, you must trust in our dear Lord. He does nothing without a reason." The priest spoke softly but firmly.

Marguerite knew Father René sought to comfort her, but today his words brought naught but a renewal of the pain she longed to extinguish. A week had passed since her father's death, a week in which she had found herself strangely unable to function. Even the simplest of decisions had demanded more energy than she possessed.

She knew her people were worried. There was no ignoring the murmurs which stopped abruptly when she walked by but which she nonetheless overheard. In other times she would have been pleased by her people's loyalty, by the fact that they feared for her as much as for themselves. But these were not other times. She was unable to reassure them, and so the people of Mirail who had depended on Guillaume and Marguerite were left to worry about their future, about who would protect them, who would ensure that Mirail continued to prosper. For there was no doubt that the barony needed a leader.

"The Lord will bring you sustenance." As Father René continued to speak, his voice seemed of little more importance than the droning of the bees in the far corner of the garden. Marguerite heard the sound but paid no heed to it.

Though bright sun streamed through the open window, the room felt cold and dark, and the sound of birds chirping in the distance did not lift her spirits. She rose and walked to the window, hoping the priest would leave her in peace. She needed time to be alone, to hug her memories closer. For memories were all that remained.

At the sound of Father René's departing footsteps, Marguerite began to relax. She leaned forward into the window embrasure, and her nostrils began to twitch. The breeze was wafting a fragrance toward the castle.

Marguerite sniffed deeply as she recognized the scent, and for the first time in days a faint smile crossed her face. Lavender. The image of a big man with a sardonic grin on his face was followed by one of the same face displaying a brief, but touching vulnerability.

Would she ever smell lavender without thinking of Alain de Jarnac, she wondered. Though the man did naught but annoy her, she had to admit he was right about one thing. Lavender was a lovely fragrance. It did indeed haunt the senses. And in the case of Alain, it had done far more, bringing out a side of him Marguerite suspected few had seen. Who would have thought that the man had poetry in him? He'd been almost eloquent in describing the flower.

Feeling oddly comforted, she made her way down to the Great Hall. There she saw Father René conferring with Bertrand, the elderly retainer who had served as factotum for the barony since before Marguerite's birth. At the sound of her footsteps, the two men looked up. It was surely her imagination that Father René appeared chagrined. He murmured something to Bertrand, his voice too low for Marguerite to distinguish the words; then the old man scuttled from the room.

"God grant you peace," the priest said, his eyes failing to meet Marguerite's. Moments later she was once again alone.

"There are travelers coming," Louise announced the following day as she entered the spinning shed where Marguerite was supervising the women's work. "The watchmen have seen their dust."

With a quick smile Marguerite left the women to their work. In truth, they needed encouragement rather than supervision. She had not missed their startled expression when she had entered the shed this morning or the visible relief when she had taken her place among them.

Father had always said that life was for the living and that there was naught more important than safeguarding the people of Mirail. It was time—well past time—that she remembered that. He would not have wanted grief to paralyze her.

" 'Tis Henri de Bleufontaine," the watchman said as Marguerite entered the outer bailey to await her guests. Louise's small gasp of pleasure told Marguerite she was thinking of the servant Gerard. It was Marguerite's turn to sigh. While the Bleufontaine party was visiting, Louise would be of little value.

"My lady." In a courtly gesture Henri dismounted, then knelt in the dust in front of Marguerite. "I came as soon as I heard the grievous news. Your father was a fine man and a

worthy lord, and he will be sorely missed.'' The words came
out smoothly, and if they sounded a bit rehearsed, 'twas only
because Henri—like most men—was unaccustomed to expressing his grief, for his next words were laden with emotion. '' 'Tis
up to us now to ensure that your father's legacy is well cared
for.'' Henri rose and looked around the bailey, his face devoid
of expression, only his eyes revealing the pleasure he derived
from his survey.

When Marguerite had given orders for Henri's men and
horses to be cared for, she led him into the Great Hall.

'' 'Twas kind of you to come to pay your condolences,'' she
told Henri.

'' 'Tis more than that which brought me to Mirail.'' As Henri
stood at Marguerite's side, his hand brushed her thigh. ''I want
to help you. 'Tis no secret that your father's death has left you
unprotected.'' He moved slightly, capturing her hand in his.
''In truth, I could claim that I was doing no more than exercising
my duties as your father's vassal, but I see no reason to dissem-
ble. You must know that I feel far more than mere friendship
for you.'' He turned so that he was facing her and drew her
hand to his lips. His mustache tickled her knuckles, reminding
Marguerite of the brush Louise used to clean her garments.
Pressing a kiss on her palm, Henri continued, ''Marguerite, I
wish to marry you, but before I petition King Louis for permission, I wanted you to know my intentions so that you could
add your petition to mine. It would,'' he said, ''be an admirable
alliance. You would gain protection of your lands, and I . . .''
He smiled and kissed her hand once more. ''I would gain my
heart's desire.''

Marguerite stiffened and tried to pull her hand away. Marry
Henri? Never! 'Twas Charles she wished to wed. However,
mindful of the need to protect Henri's pride, Marguerite spoke
softly. '' 'Tis too soon,'' she said. ''I cannot think of marriage
while I am still mourning my father.''

Henri's face darkened. Then he smiled once more. ''Of
course. It is only natural that you need time to accustom yourself
to the thought that Mirail requires a new lord. I shall await
your pleasure, my lady.''

When he had left, Marguerite drew a deep breath. What she had told Henri was no less than the truth. She did not wish to think of marriage today. But she must. Henri was right about one thing: Mirail needed a baron.

"Send a message to both Lilis and Jarnac," Marguerite told Bertrand moments later. "Tell Charles that I beg him to return to Mirail on a matter of some importance."

It was surely only her imagination that Bertrand seemed uncomfortable with her command.


"I feared I would never see you again." Louise's voice was husky with unshed tears, but for the first time in a week, the tears were ones of joy, not bereavement.

"Hush, my sweet. We're together now, and that's all that matters." Gerard wrapped his arms around Louise and drew her into the shade of an apple tree. As he lowered his lips to hers, he muttered something that sounded like "Forgive me."

" 'Tis wrong to feel joy on such a sad occasion," Louise said a long while later, "but in truth I'm happy to be with you."

Gerard's brown eyes darkened at the thought of the wrong he was about to commit. "How is your mistress?" he asked. Gently he plied Louise with questions, punctuating them with kisses that left both of them breathless and longing for more.

'Twas a sin he'd no doubt pay for in eternity, but if there was one thing Gerard had learned, it was that somehow the strong survived. The weak needed protection.

Marguerite was strong. Marie-Claire was not. That left him no choice.


Boredom. It was the deadliest of enemies, catching a man unaware, weakening him through its insidious powers, leaving him easy prey for other dangers. As a commander, Alain was well aware of boredom's potential, and he took measures to prevent his men from succumbing. Now he himself was the victim.

He should never have agreed to accompany Charles to Lilis. There was naught to do save watch Charles and Diane, two besotted fools who appeared to believe they had invented romance.

Oh, it had been a masterful stroke, arousing Diane's protective instincts. She had turned the very considerable force of her charm on Charles, and the man had capitulated with nary a protest. Since the day he had bloodied Charles's nose, Alain had not heard him mention Marguerite's name. It was what he had wanted, a battle won with the minimum of effort. Why, then, did it bring him no satisfaction? And why was it so irritating to see Diane smile at Charles as though he were the embodiment of every hero ever born?

The image of another face appeared before him, but this one wore no smile. Instead disdain oozed from each pore, and sarcastic words seemed on the verge of pouring forth from those luscious lips. Lips which could, Alain knew, rouse a man to the heights of passion. Just the thought of her uninhibited response on the riverbank made his pulse race.

Women! They were definitely the complicating factors in a less than perfect world. Either they simpered like Diane or flayed a man with their sharp tongues the way Marguerite did. What he needed was a woman who understood a man's desires and could satisfy them. A woman like Honore.

Within an hour, he had saddled Neptune and was on his way to Poitiers. Every comfort a man could want was waiting for him there.

The third night when he grew weary, Alain saw a fire in the distance and realized that he craved human companionship. Riding alone had proven only marginally better than remaining in Lilis. The same boredom had plagued him, accompanied by the same thoughts of the beautiful termagant who would one day be his bride. Even desultory conversation would be an improvement.

Approaching the fire carefully, Alain recognized the tents. 'Twas a band of peddlers he had seen on the road to Jarnac last year.

"You seek aught?" The leader of the band rose to greet

Alain, his eyes shrewdly assessing the value of Alain's armor and his destrier.

"Food, companionship and . . ." The glint of silver caught Alain's eyes. "Mayhap a trinket for a lady." Honore would enjoy some brightly colored beads to twine in her hair.

The leader nodded and offered Alain some of the pork stew that bubbled over the fire. Its savory aroma filled the air, whetting Alain's appetite. When he had eaten his fill and repaid the peddlers' hospitality with two of the oranges he carried for just that purpose, Alain studied the peddlers' wares. He quickly dismissed the ribbons, remembering that he had given Honore a rainbow of ribbons the year before. He moved to the tray of jewelry. As he reached for a strand of multicolored beads, something sharp pricked his hand. Instinctively, Alain grasped the object and laid it in his open palm.

It was a single, perfectly formed rose designed to adorn a lady's gown. Alain turned it over, admiring the craftsmanship. Not a detail had been omitted, from the delicate lines of the petals to the thorns which protected the stem, the same thorns which had pricked Alain's hand. It was so realistic that, had it not been for the silver color, Alain would have brought it to his nostrils to enjoy its scent.

He studied the brooch for a moment, then grinned. The lady liked flowers. That much he knew. Mayhap she'd like this one.

It was only as he approached the river Clain and saw the walls of Poitiers that he realized he'd forgotten to buy the colored beads.


Something was amiss. When she entered the bailey, there was none of the normal morning hubbub. Instead, there was silence broken only by the sounds of animals braying. "Good day." She greeted the blacksmith who stood in front of his shed. Her words, or perhaps her presence, broke the dam of silence, and the courtyard once again filled with human voices. Still, it was peculiar. She had not heard such silence since the day Jean had gashed his arm, the day Alain de Jarnac had come to Mirail.

As she walked through the open area, pausing to greet her people, Marguerite sought the cause of the unusual silence. When she reached the perimeter where the river's current turned the great stones that ground the wheat, she found not silence but sound.

"You oaf! I told you the flour was too coarse!" The sound of flesh striking flesh punctuated Henri's words and galvanized Marguerite as nothing had done since her father's death. She picked up her skirts and ran into the miller's shed.

"Is aught amiss, Henri?" she asked, though her eyes moved quickly to Jacques the miller's face. She gave him a reassuring smile, then turned back to the tall knight.

He flushed. "This man dares to call himself a miller, yet the wheat in last night's bread had chaff in it."

Marguerite raised one shapely brow. "Indeed? I must confess that I found naught wrong with last night's bread. Both Cook and Jacques are skilled artisans. They have served Mirail well for many years."

"Mayhap." Henri turned to glare at the miller. "Then, again, mayhap it is time for a change."

Marguerite felt the blood drain from her face. How dare the man be so presumptuous? Mirail was *her* barony. These were her people, and only she would direct them. It was time Henri understood that he was a guest, naught more.

"Come, m'lord," she said in a voice as cold as the steel of Henri's sword. "Let us discuss this in comfort."

The news of his arrival preceded him, and by the time he reached Honore's chambers, she was standing at the doorway waiting for him.

"Alain! What a wonderful surprise!" She reached her arms up and linked her hands behind his head, pulling his face close to hers and pressing a warm kiss on his lips.

He drew back slightly. How was it he had never noticed how cloying her perfume was? It filled a man's nostrils, leaving him unable to breathe properly.

"Was it a successful journey?" she asked, drawing him into the room.

Alain nodded. "My brother's betrothal is complete."

"And yours?"

He shrugged. "It appears my fiancée is less than eager for this union. I must return to Mirail to formalize the betrothal. But first . . ." His eyes moved from her face to her toes, slowly assessing each part of her body, wordlessly telling Honore what he planned to do.

"First you would like to bathe." Honore chuckled as she directed servants to heat water for the large tub.

Alain grinned. How right he had been to come to Poitiers. Honore knew exactly what he needed. A hot bath, a hot dinner and then an even hotter night in her bed. That scarlet gown would soon come off, and then he could feast on the luscious body it now concealed.

As she helped him disarm and undress, Honore trailed her fingers along his body in a movement that had never failed to arouse him. Today it did. Alain closed his eyes for a second. It appeared he was more tired than he had realized. 'Twould only be a momentary problem, though. As Honore bent her head to remove his chausses, a shaft of sunlight caught her hair. It was odd how memory distorted reality. He had always thought Honore's hair pretty. Why had he not noticed how the color resembled tarnished brass rather than sunshine?

"Come, m'lord. Let us get you ready." Though Honore led him toward the gleaming tub, her glance at his body left no doubt of her meaning. She had more than a bath in store for him.

Eschewing a cloth, she lathered the soap between her hands, then reached for Alain's arm. With careful, sensuous strokes, she moved her hands from his shoulder down to his fingertips and then up again, seeking to do far more than cleanse the dirt from his skin.

"My lady." A man's voice called out as he knocked on the door. "A message for the Silver Knight."

Alain heard Honore's soft curse.

"Later," she said, and her hands continued their sensuous forays along his chest.

Abruptly Alain sat up in the tub and shook his head, unwilling to dismiss the summons so easily. No servant would have interrupted them this soon after his arrival if the message had not been urgent.

"Enter!" he called.

Honore muttered a mild imprecation as the door opened and a man in dusty livery entered the room. She stepped away from the tub, but although her face bore a smile, there was little else in her demeanor to suggest welcome.

"What is it?" she asked sharply.

The man paid her no heed but walked toward Alain. "Guillaume de Mirail has died," he announced, his voice breathless as though he had run from the city gates. "They beg you return immediately."

Guillaume. Though Alain was no stranger to sudden death, the news was so unexpected that it left him momentarily speechless. Old men died in their beds, young men on the battlefields. Men of Guillaume's age lived. Or so Alain had always believed. But now Guillaume was gone and Marguerite was alone.

In one fluid movement Alain rose, heedless of the water splashing onto the floor. "Prepare my horse," he directed.

When the man had left, Honore turned to Alain. "Stay at least the night." Her voice was low and controlled, though her eyes entreated him. "You're weary from the long journey, and I . . ." She laughed softly, seductively. "I have just the cure for your fatigue."

Alain barely heard her. Logic told him that one more night would make little difference, and yet logic had no bearing on the sense of urgency that propelled him toward Mirail and Marguerite.

He was needed, and suddenly the boredom that had plagued him for weeks was gone.


They came in twos and threes, some accompanied by large retinues, the others bringing only a squire and a few servants.

But come they did, the vassals of Mirail, and as they did, Marguerite's uneasiness grew.

"The people are frightened," Louise told her one afternoon as they sat in the solar, embroidering an altar cloth. "They fear a harsh master who will change life and bring war upon us."

War. It was a fear Marguerite shared, though she would not voice it. Only two days earlier she had overheard Roland de Grosfleuve speaking to Henri, telling him they should transfer their fealty to Richard the Lionheart. Another knight had joined them, agreeing that allegiance to the young duke would bring them more wealth and power than King Louis could provide.

"What about Lady Marguerite?" still another knight had asked. "She and her father were always fiercely loyal to the king."

"Lady Marguerite?" Though she could not see his face, Roland's voice left no doubt of his scorn. "She's naught but a woman. What can she do?"

What indeed? The question had haunted her, causing her to pace the floor each night, unable to sleep. She knew she could run the barony as well as her father, for she had handled the daily affairs for years. For as long as she could remember, she had known that at some point Mirail would be hers, and she had prepared herself for that eventuality. Gradually she had taken over more and more of the running of Mirail until there was little her father had done save demand homage from the vassals and renew his own vows of fealty to the king.

Unfortunately those were functions Marguerite was ill-equipped to assume. This was what her father had foreseen, what he, too, had feared. Though Marguerite was intelligent, educated and courageous, none of those qualities bore any weight with the vassals. She was not a knight. Like it or not, Marguerite needed a man to keep her vassals loyal. He need take no part in the daily running of the barony, and indeed Marguerite had no intention of surrendering the reins of Mirail to him or anyone else. All he had to do was grace Mirail with his presence.

When, oh when, would Charles arrive?

# Chapter Nine

He should have been here. Dawn had begun to break, sending rosy tendrils across the dark sky. Birds' songs heralded the coming day, breaking the deep silence of the night. It was a time of peace, the last calm moments before the hectic pace of the day began. It was a time Marguerite had always loved. But today she found no comfort in the red sky's promise of a clear day. Today, as she had for the past seven mornings, she climbed to the top of the ramparts and paced their circumference, her eyes searching the horizon for signs of his approach.

Where was he?

Marguerite forced her feet to move steadily, although her breathing remained ragged. 'Twas not exertion which set her heart to pounding and made her breath short, but apprehension. He had to come, for she needed him more with each passing day. The unrest she had sensed among her vassals continued to grow, fueled by the absence of a male they could call their leader.

It mattered naught that the barony ran as smoothly as it had during her father's life, that the serfs looked to Marguerite for direction. The vassals cared naught for that. They knew only that she was not a warrior.

Then there was Henri. The man was nothing if not persistent. Though he had never again presumed to direct her serfs, he had accompanied her on her daily rounds, as though his presence at her side would help establish him as the seigneur of Mirail. And when they were alone, he was ardent in his courtship, lavishing compliments and small courtesies on her. Each evening without fail he would ask her to marry him, reminding her of the many ways he could help her and of how he cherished her. Each evening she refused.

Last night when they had dined in the Great Hall, he had risen to his feet, raising a silver flagon in a toast. "To the most beautiful woman in the kingdom," he cried. "My lady Marguerite." As the assembled vassals and servants applauded, then joined him in drinking to their lady's health, Henri had gestured to one of his servants. Moments later the man returned bearing a wooden chest.

"For you, my dear," Henri said. In full view of the assembly he knelt at Marguerite's feet to present the chest to her. "A small token of my regard."

The blazing emotion in Henri's eyes sent a shiver down her spine. It was a mixture of greed and lust and something else she could not identify. All she knew was that there was danger in accepting the gift and no way she could refuse. With fingers that were barely steady, Marguerite opened the chest.

" 'Tis lovely," she said as she drew forth a length of finely spun blue silk, holding it so that everyone could admire its beauty. The courtiers applauded, signaling their approval, for even from a distance the sheen of the costly fabric was unmistakable. It was a gift for royalty, an extravagant gesture worthy of the troubadours' tales.

It was also a masterful stroke in the campaign to win her hand in marriage. By presenting the gift so publicly, Henri was assured that Marguerite would not refuse it. And he had gained her people's approval, for who could fault a man who demonstrated his regard for their mistress in so generous a fashion? What Henri did not know was that there was no way she would marry him, for her heart was given to another.

Where is he? Marguerite's slippers slapped against the cold

stone as she continued her circuit of the wall. Why had he delayed so long? As quickly as it had been roused, her anger died, replaced by the chill of fear. If he had not come, the delay was surely not of his volition. Visions of brigands and an ambush rose before her. Please, Sweet Mary, let him be safe. She closed her eyes in silent prayer. When she opened them, a cloud of dust swirled on the horizon. He was coming!

Marguerite narrowed her eyes, trying to identify the travelers. As the dust grew nearer, she frowned. There was only one rider, not the cortege she had expected, and that one rider was coming from the wrong direction. Lilis was east of Mirail, but the man was coming from the west. He was racing, as though his mission were urgent, his horse's hooves fairly flying across the hard-packed dirt. It must be a messenger. But as the man approached, Marguerite saw the sun glint off chain mail. This was no ordinary messenger, but a knight. She narrowed her eyes again, searching for an identifying escutcheon.

He was here! The Jarnac coat of arms was clearly emblazoned on the horse's armor. Even from a distance there was no mistaking the sword entwined with grape vines. Charles was here!

Marguerite raced down the stone stairs and into the bailey. Shouting a command to lower the drawbridge, she ran across it. She would greet him in the relative privacy of the outer courtyard.

Her heart pounding, her mouth dry with anticipation, she straightened her shoulders and raised her head. For the first time since her father's death, she felt truly alive. She was the chatelaine of Mirail, and soon she would be much more: a wife.

"You!" The blood drained from Marguerite's face as the knight reined in his destrier and removed his helmet.

Alain slid to the ground. "Were you expecting someone else?" he asked. His voice was as harsh as she had remembered, devoid of the courtly tones Charles always employed. Though his face bore lines of fatigue, his eyes blazed with anger as he continued. "Were you perhaps awaiting my brother?"

Marguerite stiffened. How like the man to try to put her on the defensive. He was a masterful warrior, no doubt of that.

What he had yet to learn was that she was not a castle to be captured.

"What if I were waiting for Charles? Surely even you can understand that a woman might prefer his company to yours."

Alain took a step closer, his height forcing her to bend her neck backwards to meet his eyes. "I assure you my brother will not be returning to Mirail. He is quite happily ensconced at Lilis with the company he prefers." Alain looked at the sky, as though judging the hour by the sun's position. "At this very moment he is most likely in bed enjoying the fair Diane's favors."

It hurt. She had no armor to deflect his attack, no defense against his words or the unpleasant image they evoked.

"How can you be so crude?" she demanded.

"How can you be so rude?" He parried her thrust, returning one of his own. "Surely even the lowliest peddler receives a warmer welcome than you've shown your future husband."

Marguerite looked around the courtyard, pretending to be searching for someone. "Indeed, my lord, you have wounded me deeply by intimating that I have somehow failed in my duties. But I fear you must be mistaken, for I see no husband—present or future—at Mirail."

A frown crossed the big man's face, deepening the grooves that framed his mouth. "Let us discuss this later." He led Neptune across the drawbridge.

As they entered the bailey, a bevy of servants appeared, followed by Henri. Marguerite suppressed a smile. Henri was not an early riser. He had apparently dressed hastily, for his clothing was askew, and yet he carried his sword, as though expecting an attack.

"Jarnac, what are you doing here?" Henri fingered the hilt of his sword as his eyes moved from Alain to Marguerite and back.

Alain ran his hand through his pale hair. Though there was nothing in the man's posture to indicate it, Marguerite knew he must be exhausted, for he had obviously ridden all night. Still, his voice reflected amusement rather than fatigue. "There must be something in the water here in Mirail. Everyone seems

to ask the same question.'' He turned to Marguerite, his blue
eyes flashing a warning. ''Perhaps you'd like to explain why
I've come. Your summons was so poetic.''

The sun and the long ride must have addled the man's brains.
She had sent him no summons, no message at all. And yet . . .
A niggling suspicion grew. Since he had come from the west,
Alain had clearly not received the message she had sent to
Charles at Lilis, yet he had learned of Guillaume's death more
quickly than he would have from traveling peddlers and troubadours. Someone had notified him, and there were only a few
possibilities. The question was, why would Bertrand have sent
the message to the wrong man?

Alain and Henri looked at Marguerite, waiting for her reply.

'' 'Tis simple,'' she said. ''Alain has come to pay his respects
to my father's memory.''

''And to assure his daughter's future.'' The big man slipped
the comment in so smoothly that it seemed a natural conclusion
to Marguerite's statement.

Henri's hand tightened on his sword, his index finger caressing the large blue stone. ''How were affairs in Poitiers?'' he
asked. ''I've always wondered what it must be like at the
traitors' court.''

''I couldn't tell you. In my experience traitors rarely reveal
themselves openly. They prefer to do their work in underhanded
ways.''

''Then you've had much experience with traitors?''

''From early childhood,'' Alain agreed.

Though the words they spoke were commonplace, Marguerite sensed they held a significance known only to the two men.

''Come,'' she said to Alain. ''Let me offer you some wine
to wash away the travel dust.'' She started to walk toward the
castle. Surely the men would follow her and cease their silly
bickering.

''How kind of you.'' Alain's voice held more than a hint of
mockery, reminding Marguerite how he had accused her of
failing in her duties as a hostess. ''Then we will continue our
discussion.''

Henri moved to Marguerite's side, and he touched her arm

briefly. "I'm sure you will want my counsel in whatever it is Jarnac wishes to discuss, won't you, my dear."

The men were like angry dogs circling, each looking for an opportunity to attack. It was all so absurd, for she was neither a bone for the taking nor a bitch in heat.

When they reached the Great Hall, Alain jerked his head toward the open door, an obvious command that Henri leave. "We neither want nor need your assistance."

"I want to hear that from Marguerite." Henri started to pull the sword from its scabbard.

Men! Did they think only of battle? The slightest disagreement seemed to require force for its resolution. With men at the helm, it was a wonder the human race did not expire.

"I need to speak with Alain privately." Marguerite hoped her words were sufficiently conciliatory that Henri would leave without challenging Alain. It was bad enough that Alain had come rather than Charles. The last thing she needed was the clash of swords as two foolish men argued.

When they were alone, Alain turned to Marguerite, gripping her arm so tightly she was certain she would have bruises. "This charade has gone on long enough. Why were you encouraging him?"

The unexpected attack startled her, and for a moment she could not reply. "Encouraging Henri?" Though the thought was so ludicrous she almost laughed, the intensity on Alain's face told her this was the wrong time for laughter. "I was not encouraging him," she said. "I was simply trying to prevent conflict. Henri is a powerful knight, and I would rather have him as an ally than an enemy." She tried to pull her arm from Alain's grasp. "You probably wouldn't understand that, since you value only martial skills and seem to think a battle will resolve every problem."

Alain tightened his grip, pulling her so that she was only inches from him. She could feel the heat emanating from his body, and his breath fanned the top of her head.

"It may come as a surprise to you," he said, "but I am capable of forming a thought that has naught to do with battle. Yes, I'm a warrior—and a damned good one—so I value martial prowess. But never doubt that there other things I prize more deeply—qualities like loyalty and fidelity." His laugh was short and mirthless. "Not having any firsthand knowledge of them, I wouldn't expect you to understand just how valuable they are. Which leads me back to my original question: why were you encouraging Henri?"

The man had gone too far. How dare he insinuate—even think—that she was disloyal? In a deliberate mockery she flung his words at him. "Which brings me back to my original statement: I was not encouraging him."

Alain glared at her. "It appears we've reached a stalemate, but there's an easy solution." He placed one hand under her chin and forced it up so that she was looking directly at him. "Call your priest. I would have us marry today."

"It would appear your easy solution is not so easy, oh valiant warrior." Marguerite laced her words with heavy sarcasm. "We have a small problem. You say you would have us marry today, while I would not have us marry at all—not today, not ever."

For a long moment his only reaction was the tightening of his lips, that and the look he gave her. Had she once thought his eyes were cold? Today they blazed with a fire so hot it seemed to scorch her.

"Marguerite, let us cease this childish game. You know we must marry—and quickly—to protect your lands."

He made it sound simple, but it was not.

"My lord, you are mistaken. I know I must protect my people and my lands. That much is true. I know that to accomplish that, I must marry. That I will also concede. But, as for the last part . . ." She smiled sweetly as she looked up at him. "I do not know—nor will I agree—that I must marry *you*."

As her words met their mark, his lips thinned with anger. "Who else is there? I've no doubt the line of suitors would stretch the length of France were word to spread that the beautiful heiress to Mirail sought a husband, but choosing one would take time, and that is one thing you cannot afford. And so, my dear, who is there? Henri?"

As Marguerite started to speak, Alain interrupted. "Do not even suggest my brother. You will never, ever marry him."

"Why not? We love each other."

Alain laughed. "Diane de Lilis might beg to differ with you on that subject. My brother's much-vaunted fidelity disappeared more quickly than spring snow when exposed to the warmth of her smile."

They were all lies, the deliberate cruelty of a man who would use any tactic, no matter how base, to achieve his goals.

"I don't believe you."

"Then don't. It matters not. What matters now is that you need a husband, and my esteemed brother is not available for the position."

"I'll manage alone." They were empty words, and both of them knew it.

Alain sank into the large carved chair her father had called his own, and for the first time Marguerite saw signs of fatigue on the big man's face.

"Why are you fighting this?" he asked. "I thought you were a loyal daughter, but it appears I was wrong."

Marguerite stiffened. "What do you mean?"

" 'Tis simple. While he was alive you pretended to be the dutiful daughter, but now that your father is dead, you disregard his wishes. You surely cannot deny that he wanted us to marry."

There was no argument she could mount, for Alain was correct. No matter how she had tried to convince him otherwise, it had been her father's most fervent wish that she marry Alain de Jarnac. He had even spoken of it on that last ride they had taken together. Yes, regrettably, Alain was right. Her father had indeed wanted her to marry him.

If only there were a choice! But Alain was also correct when he assessed her options and found them sadly limited. In her heart she knew what Father would say, that the future of Mirail was more important than her own desires. And yet, it was so hard—so damnably difficult—to watch a dream die.

"You speak of marriage as if it were a battle to be won, a part of some grand military campaign." Her voice was soft and low as she tried to make Alain understand. "I want marriage to be more than a strategic alliance. I want . . ."

Before she could tell him how she longed for love, he interrupted.

"It's time you learned that in this life, what you want is not always what you get. Call your priest, Marguerite."

" 'Tis the most romantic thing I've seen." Louise sighed and wrapped her arms more tightly around Gerard. "There's not been a wedding at Mirail in over fifty years."

They had stolen away to the storeroom, their arms and lips eager for each other. Though Louise would have given most anything to have brought her master back to life, there was one thing she would have been loath to trade: her time with Gerard.

"Is your mistress truly going to marry Alain de Jarnac?" Gerard's hands moved slowly down the length of her body, sending shivers of delight through her veins.

"Aye. It was her father's dearest wish." She told Gerard of the pact Guillaume had made with Robert and Janelle during the crusade.

Gerard closed his eyes lest Louise see the despair in them. "I wish it were not so."

She cradled his face between her hands and kissed his lips gently. "I know. I cannot bear the thought that you must leave. There must be a way that we can remain together. There must." She punctuated her words with kisses, each growing more fierce than the one before.

Sadly Gerard shook his head. "Life does not always bring our heart's desire." It was a lesson he had learned all too well.

The rain began at dawn, a fine mist that dampened the grass and moistened the trees' leaves without turning the dirt into mud.

"Would that it were sunny." Louise glanced at the window as she shook the wrinkles from her mistress's gown.

Marguerite shrugged. Though she knew her people would

be disappointed, for many of the festivities would be curtailed if the rain continued, she could not claim to be surprised. The dreary weather matched her mood. Today was the day she would wed Alain de Jarnac. It was somehow fitting that the heavens wept along with her.

She raised her arms as Louise slid the ornately embroidered gown over her head. That, too, was fitting, for she would be married in the gown she had planned to wear the day Lancelot arrived at Mirail. So much had changed since the first time she had worn the bliaut. The gown had been stained—almost ruined—with blood, but that was naught compared to her dreams. Those dreams, which had been as fresh and new as her dress that morning in May, had shattered, the mere memory of them bringing pain.

The gown had been renewed. Louise had carefully removed the stains, and none but the most discerning eye would know that aught had been amiss. Marguerite's dreams, however, were beyond repair.

It was all a farce. The lovely gown, the fresh flowers that would ring her head, the smile she forced onto her face, the wedding itself. Today she would be like one of the troubadours, playing a part, making her audience believe a lie. She would do it well, for she owed that much to her people and her father's memory. But when the festivities were ended and she and Alain were alone, he would learn just how hollow his victory was.

"I'm so happy for you." Louise settled the gown over Marguerite's hips, then clasped the golden girdle around them. "Your father would have been proud to be here."

Marguerite nodded. Father would indeed be pleased that she had followed the path of duty. 'Twas one of the thoughts that had sustained her during the three days of preparation—that and the image of Alain's face tonight when she told him . . .

A firm knock sounded at the door.

"I would like to see you . . . alone." Alain fixed his dark blue eyes on Marguerite, and the corners of his mouth turned up in the faintest of smiles.

"Yes, my lord," she said, dropping a deep curtsey. Since she had agreed to marry him, she had changed her tactics, treating Alain with supreme courtesy, as though he were a valued guest rather than a despised suitor. There were, he would soon learn, many ways to win a battle.

When Louise had left, Alain handed Marguerite a soft velvet pouch. "I thought you might wear this today."

She wasn't sure what surprised her more, the gift or the air of vulnerability that surrounded Alain. Though he stood as tall and proud as ever, his eyes reflected uncertainty. The man was always so confident of himself and his abilities. Why, then did he seem ill at ease this morning?

Marguerite felt his tension as if it were a living thing, and she found her own fingers trembling as she loosened the cord and reached inside the pouch.

"Oh, Alain!" Marguerite exclaimed in delight. " 'Tis the most beautiful thing I've ever seen." She turned the exquisitely formed rose so that she could see it from every angle. Truly the silver brooch was a work of art. As Marguerite stroked the delicate petals, the heaviness which had lain over her heart began to dissipate. What a wonderfully romantic gift! Mayhap the man did care for things other than battle. Mayhap there was a chance he would become a *preux chevalier*.

She looked up at him and smiled. He returned the smile, and Marguerite was startled by the change in his face. He was no longer so forbidding, and though he was not her idea of a handsome man, there was no doubt some women might consider him attractive, particularly when a smile replaced his customary scowl.

"I fear I did not consult an expert on the language of flowers," he said with a little laugh, reminding them both of the day he had brought her lavender. "I hope the rose does not offend you."

Marguerite felt a swift shaft of disappointment. Of course the man did not know that roses were the symbol of love. Of course the gift was nothing more than it seemed, a beautiful piece of jewelry. But, oh, how wondrous it would have been, had he chosen the gift for its symbolism.

Forcing back her disappointment, she said nothing more than,

" 'Tis a most appropriate gift for a wedding, and I thank you greatly for it.''

Once again he smiled, and once again she was struck by the warmth of his expression. "I thought of you when I saw it. The rose is beautiful, but there are thorns for the unwary.''

"Then you will have to take care not to hold the rose too closely.''

"Or perhaps I shall remove the thorns first.''

Soon it would be over. The priest would pronounce the words, they'd endure the banquet, there would be the wedding night, and then . . . At the thought of the wedding night, Alain paused. That had some potential. As he remembered Marguerite's response the night they had met on the riverbank, Alain grinned. His bride-to-be was a passionate woman; all she needed was someone to unleash her ardor, and he was the man to do it. He would teach his new wife the finer points of passion at night while he spent the days establishing his authority at Mirail.

When she joined him in the chapel, it was all Alain could do to keep a sober mien. By all the saints above, she was beautiful! She had left her hair, that glorious golden mane that begged a man to touch it, unbound, and she had pinned his silver brooch above her heart. Marguerite was wearing some sort of dark gown with gold threads running through it. It covered her completely, leaving only her hands and her neck exposed, and yet somehow it managed to be the most alluring garment he had ever seen, hinting at the delights hidden beneath it. He could hardly wait to remove it. Indeed, the wedding night promised to be an interesting one.

But first there was the celebration. Alain knew that the vassals who had gathered here and all the people of Mirail would be watching carefully, trying to assess their new lord. The opinions they formed this evening would be difficult if not impossible to change, and so it was essential that they gain the correct impression of him.

When the pages had ensured that everyone was served, Alain

rose to his feet, drawing Marguerite with him. "I propose a toast to my bride, the beautiful chatelaine of Mirail. May her life be filled with happiness."

The crowd cheered and downed a glass of ale in Marguerite's honor.

Alain's eyes moved quickly, scanning the assembled guests, watching their reactions. The smiles of approval were universal, or nearly so. At the far end of the first table, Henri de Bleufontaine sat, his eyes fixed on the trencher in front of him, his lips curved into a sullen scowl. Surely the man had not been foolish enough to believe Marguerite would marry him.

Roland de Grosfleuve rose from his seat next to Henri and held his flagon high. "To the new lord," he cried when the room was once again silent. "May he be a worthy successor to Guillaume."

The cheers could not compare to those awarded Marguerite, but Alain was not disappointed. It was a beginning. It would take time to win over all the vassals—particularly Henri—but winning men's loyalty was a skill Alain had developed at a tender age. 'Twas far easier than taming a reluctant bride.

When Alain started to sit, Marguerite tugged on his hand. She put her hand on his arm and addressed her people. "My bridegroom needs no introduction, for I venture to say there is no one in this room—or, indeed, in all of France—who has not heard of Alain de Jarnac's valor. By his very presence the Silver Knight will help me keep Mirail safe, and so I bid you all grant Alain the loyalty you gave my father."

The crowd roared its approval. Marguerite's words were generous, and yet Alain found them puzzling. It was almost as though she expected him to be some sort of figurehead, doing naught but exercise Neptune. The woman had much to learn.


"I must confess, I know not how to ask you this."

Marguerite looked up in surprise as Louise began brushing her hair. The banquet and the entertainment had ended, curtailed by Guillaume's recent death, and the two women had returned to Marguerite's chamber to prepare her for the bedding ceremony.

Marguerite raised an eyebrow. It was unlike Louise to sound so unsure of herself.

"My father always counseled honesty. Mayhap you should simply ask."

Louise drew the brush through Marguerite's long tresses several times before she spoke. "I wondered ... er ... I was concerned ... um ... you never knew your mother ... Did my mother ... ?" Louise's words trailed off.

Marguerite smiled. "Are you worried that I may not be prepared for my wedding night?"

Louise flushed, then nodded.

"I assure you I am well prepared." And indeed she was. Her father had been even more diffident than Louise when he had explained what he called the marriage act, describing in detail what transpired between a man and a woman, what would be expected of Marguerite. At the time, it had sounded awkward and uncomfortable, but bearable. When she had met Charles, Marguerite had revised her opinion, admitting the possibility that some pleasure might be involved. But that was of little import tonight. Tonight there would be no awkwardness, no discomfort. For this would be one wedding night when there would be no blood on the sheets.

Duty dictated that she marry; it did not require her to consummate the marriage.


"My lady awaits you." Louise opened the door to Alain and the men who accompanied him into Marguerite's chamber.

She stood in the center of the room, clad only in her long hair, her posture as proud as if she wore an ermine robe and a jeweled crown. The men murmured appreciatively as Louise lifted the golden tresses, revealing her mistress's body in all its splendor. "She has no blemishes," Louise told them.

Indeed she did not. She was even more beautiful, more perfectly formed than he had dreamed. Alain could feel his body responding. The wedding night promised to be even better than he had expected.

As Roland stripped the robe from Alain, leaving him as naked as his bride, the men's murmurs turned to ribald jokes.

"A true warrior," one said with a coarse laugh. "He keeps his sword ever ready."

"And what a sword. 'Tis no wonder the infidel flees at the sound of his name."

Marguerite said naught, merely smiled as sweetly as though the men were discussing the weather.

At last they were gone, leaving him alone with his bride. His beautiful, desirable bride. The room was dark save for the shaft of moonlight that spilled onto the floor. The soft scent of clean rushes and another fragrance, a sweeter one, filled the air. All was ready, for on the other side of the room, his bride was waiting.

Alain bolted the door, then approached the bed where Marguerite now sat, her perfect body covered by the sheets. Sweet Mary in heaven, she was beautiful!

"You need come no nearer." Her voice was cold, bearing no hint of the passion he himself felt. Alain stopped. What was the woman saying? Her words continued. "You will sleep in the adjoining chamber." To ensure he understood, she gestured toward a small door in the side wall.

She was daft. She must be. The strain of her father's death and the responsibility of running the barony alone must have been too much for her. Alain took another step toward the bed. "Is this some sort of jest?"

She shook her head, and the long tresses fanned out on the pillow. "I assure you 'tis no jest. I may have had to surrender my lands to you, but I will not give you my body."

This time her voice quavered, and Alain smiled as he reassessed the situation. She was frightened. Marguerite was a virgin, a woman raised without a mother or close female guidance. Though she had read Ovid and those damnable tales of Camelot, she had no experience, no woman to tell her how glorious it could be. No wonder she was frightened of the wedding night. 'Twas only natural.

Alain grinned. As any warrior knew, there was more than

one way to win a battle. He would use different tactics to win her.

He climbed into the bed.

"I told you to stay out of here." There was no doubt about it; her voice was quavering. He would have to allay her fears before he could reach his goal.

Though half an arm's length separated them, he could smell her sweet scent and feel the warmth of her body. The moonlight revealed those oh, so tempting curves, setting his blood racing. "I shall do naught but sleep," he said, hoping his soul would not be damned for the lie. " 'Tis necessary if we are to keep Mirail safe." Deliberately, he used her own words. "How would your people feel if the servants told them I spent our wedding night in another room?"

He could see the confusion on her face. At length she nodded. Turning so that her back was toward him, she said, "Good night."

Alain settled under the sheets. Patience, he told himself. Patience. Unfortunately, it was not a virtue with which he had been endowed. "They're wonderful people you have," he said as his hand moved toward her. "Very loyal." He stroked her hair, his fingers glorying in the soft golden strands.

She jerked back as though he had hurt her, drawing her hair close about her.

"It won't work."

"What won't work?"

"Trying to beguile me. I assure you, I will not be seduced."

Forgetting his resolve to wage this battle slowly, Alain pushed himself to a sitting position and glared down at her. "You are my wife, before God and the people of Mirail. Have you forgotten that?"

"To the contrary, I am most mindful of that fact, distasteful as it is."

Distasteful? She found him distasteful?

"You agreed to marry me."

"I had no choice. We both know that." Her voice was once more maddeningly devoid of emotion. "I needed a man's presence to keep Mirail safe, and you were available. As you yourself pointed out, time was of the essence, and I did not have the luxury of auditioning other candidates.''

She pushed herself to a sitting position, tugging the sheets so they covered all but her shoulders.

"But you found me—what was your word?—distasteful."

The blood began to pound in Alain's ears. Why had he thought it would be different this time?

"You know as well as I that you are not the man I wished to marry."

"I suppose you're thinking of my sainted brother, wishing he were here in your bed."

She didn't deny it. "Would it be so dreadful if I were?"

Yes! The word reverberated in his head. Alain's anger and frustration could be ignored no longer.

"You're mine," he told her. "By all the saints above, I vow you will not forget it."

As she faced him, her eyes sparkled with anger. "I am not some castle you can conquer."

"No, you're not," he agreed. "You're a silly woman who doesn't know the difference between dreams and reality. This is reality."

He pressed her into the soft mattress, lowering his lips to hers in a fierce kiss. He had meant to do no more than remind her of the kisses they had shared on the riverbank, but her body was so soft, so alluring. And the sweet scent that filled his nostrils was enough to drive a man crazy. No one save a eunuch could resist Marguerite, and Alain de Jarnac was far from a eunuch.

His hands strayed to her breasts.

"Stop!" she cried and tried to push his hands away.

"Don't fight. I'll make it good."

She twisted, trying to escape his grip, but it was for naught. She had no chance against his superior strength.

"You could not."

She had issued a challenge, but his bride had no way of knowing that no one challenged the Silver Knight and won. He would make her respond, make her share the passion that surged through him.

Using only his lips and his tongue, he caressed her throat, then moved ever lower. At first she twisted, trying to escape his marauding lips, but gradually her struggles subsided, turning into whimpers of pleasure.

It was more than he could bear. With a quick thrust, he plunged into her soft body.

He had won the battle. She was his wife in deed as well as name. Why then did the victory hold no pleasure?

# Chapter Ten

It was shameful, positively shameful. Marguerite slashed at the tough stem, her knife doing little more than fray it. How could she have let it happen? In truth, she had had no control. Though her mind had willed one thing, her body had betrayed her.

How many times had she heard Father René intone the words, "The spirit is willing, but the flesh is weak"? Until last night, those had been only words, an abstract concept. Now she knew the truth behind them. Her flesh was woefully weak, and not merely in a figurative sense. How embarrassing that her knees trembled and grew weak at the thought of what had transpired in her chamber mere hours ago.

She shook the last drops of dew from the deeply toothed leaves, then laid the stem in her basket. The man was masterful; there was no denying it. 'Twas no wonder he had gained such renown as a warrior, able to vanquish even the most valiant of foes with only a modicum of effort. The saints above knew he had had no trouble defeating her. He had found her weak link— her deplorably traitorous body—and had used it, turning her defenses against her.

It should not have happened. Alain was totally unschooled

in courtly graces, and honeyed words were as foreign to his lips as snow in June. Who would have dreamt that the touch of that same man's lips would have been so pleasurable, that the tip of his tongue had set her blood to boil, chasing every rational thought from her body? He was a crude man, skilled only in the martial arts. His hands bore calluses from wielding a sword and lance. Who would have thought that they could wreak such havoc with a maiden's senses, turning her bones to jelly and her blood to rivers of fire?

It was shameful, positively shameful, that she had allowed him to breach her defenses so easily, that the events of the night had not followed her plan. It had been the best of plans. Though she had been unable to avoid marriage, she had vowed to remain chaste, keeping her mind and her body pure for Charles. That vow had crumbled under the strength of Alain's siege, and for far longer than she wanted to admit, she had thought of naught but the knight in her bed, the one who had made her body sing with pleasure.

She could not undo the damage. Marguerite cut another shoot of agrimony. Though there was no way to regain her virginity, she need not compound the wrong. What had happened last night would not be repeated. There was no need to let Alain know how her traitorous body had enjoyed his caresses, and there was most definitely no need to allow her weak flesh to once again dominate her spirit. For the sake of her people, she would pretend to be a happily married woman during the day. What transpired in her chamber at night was something else.

"What is it you gather?"

The knife slid from her grasp. Sweet Mary in Heaven, why did the man have such power to rattle her? The soft ground had hidden the sound of his approach, leaving her once again defenseless against him. She looked up, then quickly lowered her eyes, but it was too late.

He wore a simple tunic of fine black wool that stretched across the expanse of his shoulders. There was nothing unseemly about his clothing. It was merely her memory that flashed the image of how those shoulders had appeared clad only in moonlight, of the silver fur that covered his chest, of the powerful muscles in his thighs. Memories, traitorous memories that made her flush with embarrassment at the same time that they filled her with a deep longing.

Temptation, Father René had preached, could always be resisted, and resist it she would. What she felt was lust, nothing more. Surely that was the easiest of the sins to overcome.

" 'Tis agrimony," Marguerite said, displaying the gray undersides of the leaves. Perhaps if she spoke of ordinary things, she would be able to ignore the lure of the big man's body. "I have found that a decoction is most efficacious as a remedy for digestive ailments, and I fear that the wedding feast may have exacerbated many."

"Then it is not for you?" Was it her imagination, or did his blue eyes hold a hint of amusement? It must surely be the light, for Alain was not noted for his humor.

"Nay. My ills cannot be cured so easily." He stood so close that her nostrils quivered at the scent of him, the same scent that had lingered on her sheets this morning.

"I've heard that unguents will ease the soreness."

Blood rushed to Marguerite's face. " 'Tis not that!" In truth, the night's activities had left a faint soreness, and she had applied a salve to the afflicted areas. That was an admission she would never make to him. The physical aspects of the night, since they would not be repeated, need not be discussed.

"Then why did you leave our bed so easily? 'Tis customary for the bride to remain abed with her groom."

"I fear you must forgive me." Marguerite laced her words with sarcasm. " 'Tis my first experience as a bride, and 'twould appear that I am not fully acquainted with the customs."

Alain took a step closer. Though he did not touch her, he stood so near that every pore of her body seemed to drink in his scent.

"I have no complaints," he said, "for you demonstrated a remarkable aptitude for the more important customs of the marriage bed."

He was laughing at her. The man had the audacity to laugh at her.

"You, my lord, demonstrated a remarkable lack of the more important aspects of chivalry."

He stared at her for a moment, as though trying to determine whether she was serious. Then he laughed.

" 'Tis odd, is it not, that I heard no complaints last night."

It was a low blow.

"I suppose 'tis too much to expect a warrior to understand that the most painful wounds are not always visible."

Oddly Alain flinched. "Is that an accusation? Do you believe me so ignorant that I don't know there is more than one way to wound a man?"

His voice was tinged with anger, and for a second Marguerite was silent, considering his reaction. Somehow, unknowingly, she had touched a sensitive cord. "No," she said at last, "I don't believe that. Indeed, you use psychic blows well. They're simply another weapon in your formidable arsenal."

She met his gaze, remembering how he had won his battle against her without resorting to physical force. "You defeated Henri with humiliation as much as with your physical prowess. To be truthful, I don't know which was more powerful or which injured him more. No, Alain, the problem is not that you're unaware of the wounds you inflict. It's far deeper than that. You see naught but your goal. All that matters to you is winning, and you care not how you achieve that victory or what wounds you leave in your wake."

"The issue is not Henri, is it?"

Marguerite shook her head. "You're not a *preux chevalier* who puts his lady's needs and desires ahead of his own."

"About last night . . ."

She interrupted, her voice sharp with anger. "Let us not speak of last night. What occurred then was regrettable, but it cannot be undone. All that matters now is that it will not be repeated." She would never again allow lust to rule her. If nuns and Knights Templar could abide by their vow of chastity, so could she. Like them, she had taken a vow. This time she would keep it.

The sound of his laughter was so unexpected that Marguerite almost dropped her knife again.

"Never again? I think not." Alain laid his hand on her arm, and when she tried to brush it away, he only tightened his grip and laughed again. "If there is one thing I have learned about you, my dear wife, it is that you are a dutiful woman. Indeed, I might throw your own words back at you and say that you see naught but your duty."

He shrugged, and the fine wool slid easily over his shoulders, reminding Marguerite how his arms had felt wrapped around her. She forced those thoughts away by clenching the handle of her knife so tightly that it hurt her palm. Pain, it appeared, was a suitable antidote for other forms of physical distress.

"Your duty was to keep Mirail safe, and so you married me. Now your duty is to produce an heir for Mirail," Alain continued. "And, unless the laws of nature have changed overnight, there is only one way that will be accomplished."

"You're wrong."

"Indeed? Is there a new method for procreation? I knew you were a scholarly woman, learned in many subjects, but I never realized that you had uncovered one of the mysteries of life. Pray, tell me about it, my sweet. I am woefully ignorant, for I thought there was only one immaculate conception."

He was laughing at her, trying to humiliate her as he had Henri. Alain had yet to learn that she was not as easily vanquished as Henri.

" 'Tis not my sense of duty that is the question here, but rather your singleminded pursuit of goals." She loosened her grip on the knife. "You are correct in your assessment of why I married you. Indeed I made no secret of that, but I said naught about an heir. 'Twould appear that you are the one who established that as a goal, and now you feel you must accomplish it without any consideration for the other people involved, namely me and the child."

"Can you deny that Mirail needs an heir?"

Marguerite let the silence grow. "Eventually," she admitted.

"Were you perhaps hoping that I would be killed on some battlefield and that someone else would sire your heir? Because if you were, I assure you that I have no intention of dying anytime soon."

Marguerite stared at Alain for a long moment. "You're the man with all the questions. Now, answer one of mine. Tell me, oh great warrior, do you want a child for his own sake, or would he merely be a symbol of your virility?"

When Alain did not reply, Marguerite reached for her basket. "I see that I was right." She picked up her knife and pointed it at Alain. "Let me use terms that you will understand. You may have won one battle, my valiant knight, but I assure you that the war is not over."

The sound of sobs rent the air. Marguerite placed the torch in its holder, then knelt next to the woman huddled on her pallet.

"What is wrong?" she asked as she put her arm around Louise's trembling shoulders. "Are you ill?"

Another shudder shook Louise's frame. " 'Tis naught that you can heal." Her voice was thick with tears, her eyes red and swollen.

Marguerite drew her into a sitting position and handed her a cloth. "Wipe your eyes," she said softly. "Then tell me what is amiss."

"He's gone. Gerard is gone." Louise began to sob again. "I don't know how I can bear it."

Marguerite hid her smile. Would that all the world's ills could be so easily remedied. "I shall send a message to Henri, asking him to trade Gerard for the second cook. Though I'll miss those savory meat pies, 'twill be a small price to pay for your happiness." She waited for Louise's cry of delight.

"Nay! You must not." The dark-haired woman blurted out the words, then began to sob in earnest. "He said you must not do that."

"I don't understand. Does he want you to come to Bleufontaine instead? I would dearly hate to lose you, but you must know I would not stand in your way."

Louise shook her head. "Gerard wouldn't explain. When I asked, he just gave me a strange look." She sniffled. "It must be something horrible. Mayhap he doesn't love me. Mayhap he's already married.''

Marguerite nodded. "Men are like that," she agreed, thinking of the fairhaired man whose image she could not banish, no matter how she tried. "They think of naught but a tumble in the hay, and when it's over . . ."

"Gerard's not like that." Louise sprang to his defense. "Oh, I won't deny that he kissed me, but 'twas all he did. He would not lie with me." She sobbed again. "Mayhap he found me ugly."

As Louise wailed, Marguerite shook her head slowly. Where were the happy endings the troubadours had promised?

She was in the small counting room, her golden head bent low over the books, her hand busily inscribing numbers on the parchment.

"Is there aught you wish, my lord?" she asked as he entered the room.

By all the saints above, she was beautiful. His eyes moved quickly from her face to her fingers, remembering how smooth her skin had felt beneath his hands and lips, how her murmurs of pleasure had echoed in his ears, doubling his own pleasure. Was there aught he wished? Indeed, there was, though it was not the reason he had come here.

Never again, she had said. That was where she was wrong. The little spitfire would be lucky if he waited until tonight.

"My lord?"

"I would see your father's books."

An hour later, Alain leaned back in the chair. It had been a difficult hour, trying to concentrate on columns of numbers while she was sitting on the other side of the table, close enough that he could hear her breathing and smell the scent that was hers alone.

"Your father was meticulous in his accounts. 'Tis most unusual to see records kept so well."

She smiled, those luscious lips turning up at the corners,

reminding Alain of how delicious they tasted. It was all he could do to remain on his side of the table.

"I thank you for the compliment, my lord, for you see, 'tis I who keep the accounts at Mirail."

"You?" Though he knew she could read and write, and though he had seen her inscribing numbers in the ledgers, Alain had not expected her to be as accomplished as a monk. "I would not have guessed it."

Her smile faded, and the look she gave him was glacial. "There is no reason for you to have known. After all, who keeps the accounts has no bearing on anything you value."

She pointed to an entry in the ledger that lay open before her. "Perhaps you would like to give me the benefit of your counsel. The land here in the fourth quadrant has not produced well for the last two years."

He stood behind her, bending to look at the entry. She was right, of course. He saw the diminishing returns from that plot and the softness of her hand. Though she worked in the gardens, there were no calluses on her fingers, only soft, sensuous pads which could thicken a man's blood in instants.

"We need to let it lie fallow for at least one season." She was speaking again, not giving him an opportunity to interject a word. "The dilemma is that the serfs depend on the grain from that plot. If we leave it fallow, they will not have enough food to last the winter." As her finger moved from one line to another, Alain remembered how her hands had felt gripping his shoulders when passion had overcome her.

"It seems our only choice is to ration the demesne's own grain this winter and give part of it to the serfs. Do you agree?"

His bride was right, although for the life of him, he could not imagine why she had pretended to seek his counsel. Mayhap she merely wished to demonstrate her competence in yet another area, to prove she was not the frivolous, empty-headed female he had thought her.

"It seems a prudent suggestion," he agreed.

"The land will be more fertile if left fallow."

Her eyes darkened, and Alain knew she was referring to

more than a plot of ground. If this was his wife's reminder that she had no intention of sharing the marriage bed, she had much to learn about him. She was not a field he planned to leave untouched.

"Bertrand mentioned it was time to mete out justice." The bailiff had spoken with Alain in the Great Hall that morning.

"Yes, that was one duty which was delayed by my father's death."

Alain had heard tales of how Marguerite had seemed helpless after Guillaume's death. Seeing her now, it was difficult to believe that anything had kept her from her duty.

"What are the suits?" he asked.

Marguerite counted on her fingers. "There's the theft of two chickens, a dispute over boundaries, a question of paternity." She outlined her proposed judgments, once again surprising him. Marguerite had selected punishments that were not unduly harsh but were still stringent enough to serve as deterrents to future misdemeanors.

"Will you sit by my side?" she asked.

Alain blinked. "I shall, of course, pronounce the sentences," he said. " 'Tis important that the people of Mirail begin to see me as their seigneur."

She bristled, her eyes darkening with passion. "The people of Mirail know that I am their chatelaine and that you are my husband." Though her eyes sparkled with anger, her voice was cold. "You need do naught more than sit by my side and nod your agreement as I announce the punishments."

A figurehead. 'Twas true then that she thought he'd be content to remain on the barony, serving no useful purpose. His bride might be wise in many ways, but she had much to learn about the man she had married.

No doubt there would be a skirmish before she conceded defeat, but there was no question of the eventual outcome. Alain knew the danger of fighting a war on too many fronts. Today he'd let her think she'd won, for there was a far more important battle to win: the marriage bed.

*   *   *

"You bastard! It's your fault!" Henri pulled his sword from its scabbard and lunged at Gerard, swinging the deadly weapon.

The serf feinted to one side, then resumed his position at the edge of the carpet. When Henri was in this mood, he'd do no harm. It was only when his anger had abated, when the flames had turned to smoldering coals, that he would actually strike.

"You should have warned me. I could have prevented it, if only you'd told me." The knight's anger was palpable but still outside the dangerous range.

"I did not know until it was too late." Though it was the truth, he had little hope that Henri would believe it. The man trusted no one and was quick to seize on the worst interpretation.

Gerard had watched his master seethe during the three days of preparation for Lady Marguerite's wedding, saying little, fueling his anger by that very silence. Now that they were back at Bleufontaine, it was time to seek a scapegoat.

"A likely story! You concocted it, you and that harlot. You thought you were so clever that I'd never guess what you'd done. You were wrong. By all the fires of hell, you'll pay for this."

His words sent a shiver along Gerard's spine, evoking images of the fate he feared would soon be his. That he'd be forced to pay for his sins, he had no doubt, but it was not Henri's fury he feared. Instead, 'twas the fires of hell that seemed to loom ever nearer and their master whom he feared. The arch-fiend would exact payment for the lies Gerard had told Louise, and all the good intentions in the world would not mitigate his punishment.

Henri lunged again, the point of his sword ripping the tapestry that hung over one wall.

"It will be more difficult now that she's married. You'll have to get rid of him."

Gerard stood his ground. "I will not murder, not even for you." Perhaps his penance for lying would be only a few centuries in purgatory. If he compounded the sin with murder, his soul would be damned for eternity.

"You will do as I say." Henri spoke the words with certainty. "Perhaps you choose not to act for me, but I know you'll do anything. Anything . . ." He repeated the word for emphasis, ". . . for the nun at Saint Lazaire. After all, I have heard that unfortunate accidents can occur even within convent walls."

Gerard kept his voice low. Though there was no point in provoking Henri's anger with a show of disrespect, he could not let the threat go unanswered. "I swear to you by all the saints above that if anything happens to her, the world will know exactly what happened to Gilbert."

Henri's only reply was silence.

He was such a gentle man, his voice always calm, his face smiling, his words so pleasant. Indeed, he was the perfect knight, the man of her dreams. Marguerite smiled as she drew the brush through her long hair. She had dismissed Louise, wanting a few minutes alone. The saints above knew she needed a brief respite before she resumed the battle with another knight, a less than perfect one. Though dreams had an unpleasant way of turning into nightmares, for just a few moments she would pretend that this one would come true, that she and Charles would find a way to be together.

"Let me help you." It was not Charles's melodic voice that made the offer.

Marguerite did not turn to face Alain. "I'm quite capable of brushing my hair," she said, matching the action to her words.

"I never questioned the fact that you were an extremely capable woman, with talents far beyond simply brushing your hair." There was that same hint of amusement that she had heard in his voice earlier today. Damn the man! Was he laughing at her?

"I know you can do it," he continued, "but I want to."

She swung around to face him. "And what you want, you always get. Isn't that what you told me this morning? Well, then, here you go!" Marguerite hurled the brush at him.

With a deft movement, he caught it in one hand then moved

to stand behind her. It appeared that either her tactic had no effect or he was unwilling to be drawn into a battle. Seeming to ignore her outburst, he began to draw the brush through her hair. For a long moment, he said nothing, merely continued the rhythmic motion.

She would not have believed that something as simple as grooming her hair could be so sensuous. Louise had brushed her hair every night for years, and before that Adele had performed the same duty. Sometimes it had been painful, as the women tried to remove snarls; most times it had been a thoroughly forgettable experience. Never had it been like this.

It was as though the brush were an extension of Alain himself. As the bristles touched her scalp, they sent messages of delight along her nerve endings, reminding her of the far greater pleasure his lips had wrought the night before. When he pulled the brush through the ends of her tresses, it set off sparks. Marguerite closed her eyes, unwilling to be reminded of the sparks his fingers had ignited when he had drawn them slowly, then insistently, from her toes up the length of her legs. It was a tactical error. Closing her eyes only heightened her other senses, tantalizing her nostrils with the scent of his body so close behind her, attuning her ears to each breath he took.

As she forced her eyes open, he spoke, his voice low and intimate. "Your hair is beautiful. I want to feel it wrapped around me."

The image was so vivid it made her gasp in surprise.

"You want it, too, don't you?"

With a jolt, she returned to reality. This was lust, pure and simple, nothing more. Alain was setting temptation before her, but she was strong. She could resist. She had to.

Forcing a lightness she was far from feeling, she laughed. "Oh, Alain, I fear there's no hope for you. Surely you must know that a *preux chevalier* would have used prettier words than that. He would have told me that my hair reminded him of sunshine, or gold or even moonlight. But 'beautiful'? I think not. 'Tis far too ordinary."

She heard the deep intake of breath and knew her words had met their mark.

"Oh, Marguerite, I fear there's no hope for you." He mocked her words. "It appears you're still dreaming. Wake up, little girl. I'm not a *preux chevalier*. I'm not Lancelot. I'm not even my much-esteemed brother." He grabbed her by the hand and pulled her off the stool.

With his body pressed along the length of hers, his arms holding her so close she could scarcely breathe, he spoke again. "What I am is your husband, the only one you have, the only one you'll ever have, and the only man who's going to take you to his bed."

# Chapter Eleven

"We will reach Jarnac tomorrow." Alain reined his destrier in next to Marguerite.

Though his announcement was not unexpected, it brought a smile to her face. Journey's end would be most welcome. The sun was high in the sky, and rays of heat radiated from the ground, seeming to swirl around the horses' legs along with the ever-present dust. Though it had been a mere week since they had left Mirail, Marguerite longed to be free of the constant motion, the flies and the dirt. If there was one thing she appeared not to have inherited from her father, it was a love of travel. Pilgrimages and crusades were not for her.

The word spread quickly through the retinue, and Marguerite heard shouts of joy. It seemed her people were as unsuited for travel as she.

"We have made good time," Alain told her.

It was no wonder, for each day they had broken camp with the dawn and had traveled until the last rays of light. Normally Marguerite loved the long hours of sunlight that accompanied summer. This was one time she did not. When she had tried to protest the arduous schedule, Alain had informed her that he had deliberately curtailed the travel in deference to her and her servants. "My men and I would have gone a third farther each day."

But now, mercifully, the end was near, and she would be able to rest her bruised body. Why had no one warned her that traveling all day on a mule was far more arduous than the short rides she and her father had taken?

The only advantage she had found to travel was that Alain had not joined her in bed since they had left Mirail. It was, she knew, only a temporary respite, for he had made it clear that he would not respect her desire to sleep alone.

While they had been at Mirail, he had been nothing if not persistent. Each night he had found new ways to bring pleasure to her body. Nothing—not even Ovid's most erotic poetry— had prepared Marguerite for the magic Alain was able to conjure with his lips, his tongue, his fingers—even his toes. It had taken every ounce of self-control she possessed to lie there, pretending that she felt nothing, pretending that his caresses did not stir her blood. They did, of course, but it was lust, nothing more, a temptation sent to test her will.

Alain de Jarnac had yet to learn that her will could match or beat his own.

"Will the vassals have gathered?" Marguerite turned to her husband and smiled sweetly. It was part of the charade. During the day they pretended to be the perfect married couple. It was only at night that they revealed the truth. Far from being blissful newlyweds, they were bitter adversaries.

Alain had insisted that they make the journey to Jarnac now, for he shared her father's fears of restive vassals. His marriage, he explained, was a good reason to summon his own vassals. They would be curious about his bride, and while they satisfied their curiosity, he would take the opportunity to have them renew their vows of fealty. It was a wise strategy, but Marguerite expected nothing less of her husband. Where military matters were concerned, there was none who could surpass him.

Alain shook his head in response to her question. "I bade them wait until the new moon. That will give us several days in Jarnac to prepare for their arrival." It was far less time than Marguerite suspected she would need, for the castle had been without a mistress for the eight years since Janelle's death. If she were to provide proper hospitality for the Jarnac vassals, she would need at least a week. There were rooms to air, meals to prepare, rushes to gather for the floors. None of that was impossible if there were properly trained servants, but Alain had been unable to reassure her on that count.

"I feared that you would find days at Jarnac boring." Marguerite's eyes widened. Boring? That was highly improbable. Frantic and exhausting were more likely. "And so I asked Philippe to arrange a tournament."

"How kind of you!" Marguerite made no effort to conceal her sarcasm. A tournament required even more preparation. Though Alain might be well versed in military strategy, he was woefully uniformed about domestic affairs. And this was the man who thought he could help her run Mirail!

"I suppose that since the tournament is only for my pleasure, you will not compete."

Alain looked at her as if she were a half wit. "Naturally I shall compete."

"Naturally," she confirmed. "Fighting is, after all, what you love most."

" 'Tis not a matter of love as much as life. This is what I was trained to do."

And, she suspected, where he felt most comfortable. One day when the rain had fallen in torrents, proscribing all but the most essential outdoor activities, Alain had joined her in her solar. While she had repaired his men's clothing, darning hose and mending rents, he had spoken of the men themselves, describing each one's idiosyncrasies.

Marguerite learned that Pierre was a formidable fighter, so long as he wore his tunic inside out, but should some hapless squire attempt to dress him more conventionally, Philippe would refuse to lift his sword. Jacques prepared meals that Alain claimed rivaled even the royal chefs' until a well-meaning serf had pounded the dents from Jacques's favorite pot. The cook had been so outraged by what he considered the desecration of his tools that it had taken a direct order from Alain before he had agreed to cook another meal.

As he had spoken, Marguerite had heard more than amusing stories. There had been pride in Alain's voice, and she had had the feeling that he was describing more than a band of warriors. This was a family, one where he was the parent. His references to Philippe and Charles had never carried the same warmth.

The seemingly endless journey to Jarnac had given Marguerite a chance to study the man she had married. 'Twas far less distressing than contemplating the reception that awaited her. She noticed that as they rode, Alain's eyes moved constantly, scanning the horizon. It seemed an instinctive movement rather than a conscious one, and she doubted he was even aware of it. The vigilance was simply another aspect of the life to which he had been bred.

"A band of men is approaching." Alain gestured with a gloved hand. The swirl of dust that had attracted his attention was so distant that Marguerite had not noticed it. "It would appear that some of my vassals are so eager to meet my bride that they are coming early."

Though his voice was calm, he kept a firm grip on Neptune's reins as he motioned to his two closest squires.

"Do you recognize the livery?" Marguerite asked.

Alain did not answer immediately. He bent his head slightly, as though he were squinting, trying to distinguish details.

"Brigands!" he shouted. "Take cover!"

The response was instantaneous. Within seconds Alain's men had lowered their visors, raised their shields and drawn their horses closer to Alain, waiting for his command. There was a sense of expectancy but no fear as the knights moved into position.

With a few curt commands, Alain ordered the women to gather in a small knot. He kept his three most trusted lieutenants at his side, then deployed the other knights in a circle surrounding the women.

"Your duty is to keep them safe," he told the men. "Regardless of what happens to me, protect Lady Marguerite and her servants."

Only when he was satisfied did he lower the visor of his helmet and urge Neptune forward. Alain and the three knights rode abreast, their horses so close that their flanks almost touched. They moved slowly, at a stately pace, as though taking part in a triumphal parade rather than facing a hostile band of men.

The bandits were closer now, their horses' hooves pounding the earth and setting up a cloud of dust.

Alain and his men continued forward. As the bandits approached, Alain raised his spear. It was a gesture of greeting rather than a challenge, and Marguerite caught her breath. What was the man doing? The brigands were obviously prepared for battle, yet Alain was behaving as though this were a friendly meeting. As if to underscore his intent, Alain raised his visor and faced the band's leader.

Marguerite counted quickly. The odds were uneven. Not only did the brigands outnumber Alain's men by at least two to one, but they were not handicapped by having women to protect.

But odds, it appeared, meant little to Alain de Jarnac.

"I see you have not brought a priest." His voice betrayed no fear. "If you wish, we can delay the battle until your men have received the Sacrament, for I would not want to be the cause of sending so many men to their deaths unshriven."

It was an audacious claim, designed to weaken the brigands' resolve. Marguerite heard a low murmur as the opposing force considered the import of Alain's words.

"We'll fight," the leader announced. "My men are not cowards."

"Nor are mine," Alain replied. " 'Tis merely that I deplore the shedding of unnecessary blood. What is it you seek from me?"

"Riches."

"Then you will be disappointed, for we carry no gold or jewels. You would be far better served by preying on a caravan of travelers."

"We'll fight," the leader repeated.

"You have no chance of survival," Alain said, again in that deceptively calm voice. " 'Tis often more valorous to retreat in the face of insurmountable odds. Unless, of course, you are confident of gaining entry at the gates of Heaven.''

"As I reckon, the odds are in our favor.''

Alain shrugged. "Mayhap, but strength is not counted only by numbers. What say you to this? You and I will fight. He who wins takes whatever he wishes.''

There was another low murmur as the brigands considered the challenge. Alain's men remained silent.

The leader hesitated, while his men murmured again. "I'll not battle the Silver Knight,'' he said at last. With a flourish, he led his men away.

When the men had disappeared over the horizon, Alain turned toward Marguerite. For a fleeting instant she did not recognize him. In place of the normally calm, seemingly emotionless visage that he presented to the world, he now wore an expression of almost unnatural excitement. His face was flushed, and his eyes burned with intensity. His grin reflected immense satisfaction and close to physical pleasure.

If she had ever doubted it, she could no more. The man was a warrior to the very marrow of his bones. It was the challenge of battle, the excitement of vanquishing an enemy that kept him alive. Unfortunately, all too often he saw her as an enemy. Marguerite's eyes darkened as she wondered what this would mean for Mirail.

Women. They were totally unpredictable. A normal woman would have been grateful that he had protected her, that he had diffused the danger from the brigands without resorting to force. A normal woman would have recognized that it required far greater courage to face the marauding band without a drawn sword than to have charged into mortal combat. A normal woman would not have retreated into a cold silence. But, Lord help him, Marguerite was not a normal woman.

She had insinuated herself into his life, more like a raging fever than any sort of pleasure. It reminded him of the time when Neptune had been restive, refusing to obey his commands. Only after a careful examination had Alain found the tiny thorn embedded under his destrier's mane. It had begun to fester, causing the animal's distress. Marguerite was like that, a festering wound that refused to heal or to be ignored.

Alain approached Marguerite, slowing Neptune's pace to match that of her mount.

"Jarnac is over the next ridge."

She spoke not, merely nodded her understanding. It had been thus ever since the brigands had departed. She had seemed to disdain his company, leaving him with far too much time for thoughts and worries. A man could spend his days wondering why she found him so repulsive, why even his most ardent caresses failed to arouse her. A man could spend his nights wondering why he heard only the sharp edge of her tongue when even the lowliest of serfs was treated with courtesy.

Today, however, Alain had another worry. He feared the reception that awaited her at Jarnac. The few servants who had remained to care for Philippe would present no problem. It was Philippe himself who worried Alain. For as long as he could remember, Philippe had been open in his hatred of Guillaume and had forbade both Janelle and Alain to speak the man's name. A traitor, Philippe had claimed. Though Alain knew the true reason for Philippe's hatred, that knowledge brought him no comfort, for he feared that his stepfather would transfer his destructive emotions to Guillaume's daughter.

That was not an acceptable thought.

Alain blinked, surprised at the direction his thoughts were taking. He was plotting his defense of Marguerite as he would have a military campaign. It was odd. Never before had he felt the need to protect a woman in this way. Of course he would defend a woman against physical perils. That was his duty as a knight. That was what he had done when the brigands had threatened to attack. Never before had he wanted to keep a woman safe from other harms, from the wounds cruel words could inflict. Alain remembered Marguerite's claim that invisible wounds were the most painful. How well he knew the truth of those words.

It had been a year since he had last seen Jarnac. From a distance, nothing appeared to have changed. The high walls still shone yellow in the sunlight. Today the crenelations that had appeared as fearsome as dragon's teeth to a child seemed no more than ordinary defenses of a castle, and the water in the moat where he and Charles had speared frogs on his rare visits was evaporating in the summer sun.

There was naught to alarm him. Certainly not the man who stood near the portcullis to greet them. The year had not been kind to Philippe. His hair, or what remained of it, was completely gray, and the lines which framed his mouth had deepened. Yet his thin face bore a smile as he helped Marguerite from her mule.

"I welcome you to Jarnac," he said, holding Marguerite's hand far longer than necessary. Alain felt a twinge of fear. Was this a new game Philippe was playing? Lord knew the man was a master at them.

"As Alain has probably told you, I am not as skilled with words as he is, but I wish you to know how happy I am to meet you. 'Tis truly a miracle to see Alain wed."

Alain grimaced. There was no need to tell Marguerite that he had been as reluctant for the wedding as she. All that had changed with Guillaume's death, when he had realized there were no choices. Duty required him to marry Marguerite and protect her lands.

Alain gave Philippe a cautionary look, but the older man would not be silenced. "Indeed, his mother and I worried that he would never wed and that we would not see his children. He was a most reluctant bridegroom."

Enough. Philippe had said enough.

"No one, it would seem, worried that my bride would be reluctant."

Marguerite shot him a quick glance, and Alain wondered if she would continue her silence. "What woman could resist so valiant a knight?" she asked. "Mere hours ago he defeated brigands with nary a thrust of his sword. Truly, my husband is an extraordinary man."

Though her words were sweet, the tone was not. If this was her idea of polite conversation, Alain almost wished she had kept her vow of silence. Almost. For, though she had laced her words with sarcasm, it had been the first time she had referred to him as her husband, and Alain found that the title pleased him. Perhaps his bride was beginning to accept his role in her life.

Philippe, it appeared, found other things to please him. He started to laugh, big guffaws that surprised Alain. "Do I sense vinegar under the honeyed words?" he asked Alain. "Indeed, Janelle's prediction has come true. Marguerite will be the perfect wife for you." He turned to Marguerite, a smile still hovering on his lips. "Tell me, my dear, why did you marry this rogue?"

Alain waited, as anxious for the response as his stepfather.

She smiled and arched one shapely brow. "Ah, m'lord, that should be self-evident."

"You bring an old man much pleasure." Philippe studied the game board then moved his piece.

"You're not an old man," she said as she captured his remaining dame. Each day since she had arrived at Jarnac and had learned of his fondness for the pastime, she had found time to play a game or two of dames with Philippe. In truth, it had been a pleasant respite from the day's work. For, as she had feared, there was much to do to ready the castle for visitors. The servants, grown lax over the years, had required bullying and cajoling to sweep out the soiled rushes and remove the cobwebs that festooned each corner of the many-roomed château.

Philippe shook his head as he conceded the game. "You're a formidable opponent."

"If so, I owe it to my father. He taught me a game was not worth playing unless you played to win."

"Ah, yes. I can recall his saying much the same to me when he took my last silver coin." Philippe's expression bore a hint of sadness. "Your father and I shared many things."

Looking at the man who had been one of her father's two closest friends, Marguerite found it difficult to believe they were of an age. Whereas her father had never seemed old to her, Philippe—despite her protests to the contrary—was aged. He was far different from her expectation, quiet rather than belligerent, sorrowful rather than bitter. What was clear was that the years had not been kind to Alain's stepfather.

"Perhaps I am wrong in asking this, but I have never understood how you could have renounced your allegiance to King Louis after you risked your life to go on a crusade with him."

Philippe's brown eyes held a deep sorrow as he spoke. "It was not a movement against Louis," he explained, "but one in support of Eleanor. She and Janelle were more than queen and lady-in-waiting. They were the closest of friends and confidants. It would have been impossible for Janelle to leave her."

"What was she like?" It was a question that had haunted Marguerite as much as Philippe's change in loyalty. Though she dreaded the answer, she could no longer live in ignorance.

Philippe smiled, remembering. "She was the strongest woman I have ever met. A born queen. But it was more than that. I can't explain how she did it, but she inspired the deepest loyalty in anyone who knew her. Men would risk their lives for nothing more than the promise of her smile."

Though the picture he painted was a vivid one, it was not the one Marguerite sought. "I meant Janelle," she said. "My father would never speak of her."

Philippe's face lit with animation and for a moment he seemed almost boyish. "Ah, Janelle. She was beautiful, more so than the queen, although none would dare admit it. Her hair was the brightest gold, and her eyes . . . You need only look at Alain to see their deep blue." He stood and paced the floor. "She was shrewd, a good judge of people. Eleanor relied on her in that regard. But Janelle lacked Eleanor's strength. Though she was not a tiny woman, there was something about her that made men want to protect her. I think every man in the French army was more than half in love with her."

"Including my father."

Philippe gave Marguerite an appraising look. "Yes."

It was not a surprise, but rather a confirmation of her suspicions. There had been hints over the years. The odd smile Father had worn on the few occasions he had spoken her name.

The animosity he bore toward Philippe, Janelle's second husband. His reaction when Alain and Charles had come to Mirail. Still, suppositions were one thing; knowledge quite another.

Marguerite felt a sharp stab of anger that she had been the pawn in a game of love. Her betrothal was the result not of her father's and Robert's deep friendship, as she had been told over the years, but of her father's unrequited love for Janelle. In a perverse way, it made sense. Father had believed that if he could not marry Janelle himself, he could at least ally his family with hers by betrothing his daughter to Janelle's son. But why, oh why, could she not have married Janelle's other son?

"It was strange." From a distance Marguerite heard Philippe's words. "Though you would have thought otherwise, no one was jealous of Robert. You had only to see him with Janelle to know that they belonged together."

"His death must have been a horrible shock for Janelle." Marguerite had heard the tale of the ambush that had taken so many lives on the way to Jerusalem.

"That whole day was a dreadful, deadly mistake. The rear guard should never have been left alone to face that ambush." Philippe's expression was distant, as though he were reliving the events of that fateful night. "There were some who blamed the queen. They said she sent the wrong messages, that she was trying to show the king she was as skilled a leader as he. Janelle insisted she would never have done that." Philippe shrugged. "So many years have passed that now no one will ever know what really happened. It was simply a day of terrible devastation, and it should never have happened."

"But Janelle turned to you in her distress."

Philippe's face turned white, and he swallowed noisily. "Yes. She did."

"We should plant some medicinal herbs." Marguerite stood at Alain's side, surveying the small garden. Though overrun with weeds, she assured him that some flowers would bloom before fall. "I'll bring shoots from my garden on our next visit."

It should not have mattered. Lord knew that after everything that had happened—and failed to happen—here, he should have regarded Jarnac as nothing more than a piece of land with a pile of stone standing on it. By all rights, he should have given its care to a valued castellan. He most definitely should not have tried to invest it with qualities it had never possessed or to consider it his home. Jarnac was his heritage, not his home. A wise man would remember that the two were not always the same.

But since he and Marguerite had arrived, Jarnac had seemed different. When he had walked to the hollow tree that had been his refuge as a child, he could have sworn that he had felt a woman's hand caressing his hair. Janelle had never done that. Or had she?

Now Marguerite was acting as though she had accepted their marriage, for she was speaking of their next visit. Alain tried not to let his surprise show. Since they had arrived, they had spoken of mundane things, the need for more servants in the castle, the deplorable condition of the rooms. But Marguerite had not volunteered, nor had Alain asked to know her feelings.

Philippe had not waited for an invitation to speak but had been fulsome in his praise of Marguerite, smiling more than Alain could remember as he recounted stories Marguerite had told him. Stories—Alain would never have admitted to his stepfather—that he himself had not heard. Marguerite, it appeared, had charmed the beast in his lair.

"She's the perfect wife for you," Philippe had announced.

Alain's only response had been a raised eyebrow. It was painfully evident that while Marguerite found the other Jarnac males' company pleasant, his own filled her with revulsion. Today, though, was different. Mayhap she was changing.

"Then Philippe is not the ogre you expected?" Alain asked.

"Very little would have been as fearsome as I had imagined," Marguerite admitted with a wry smile. "I had prepared myself for the worst, but I'm glad to say that Jarnac is nothing like my expectations." Absentmindedly, she tugged at a weed.

"I did not expect to, but I like Philippe. Now that I've met him, I understand where Charles got his charm."

Charles. Why did she always have to talk about Charles?

"Actually, Charles spent very little time with Philippe. Like me, he was fostered younger than most boys."

Marguerite rose and brushed off her knees. "Charm like that is inherited, not learned. It's obvious that Charles is Philippe's son in spirit as well as body."

"Is this your much-vaunted woman's intuition?" Alain could not keep the harshness from his voice. If there was one subject he did not want to discuss with Marguerite, it was Charles's parentage. The truth was far too devastating. "Charles is Robert's son. If you think he resembles Philippe, it must be pure coincidence, or perhaps that he learned mannerisms from our stepfather."

But Marguerite was not to be dissuaded. "Alain, it's much more than intuition. Charles looks like Philippe. Surely you've seen that. They have the same brown eyes."

"My mother's eyes were brown. Charles resembles her." It was a lie. Janelle had had deep blue eyes, but fortunately Marguerite had no way of knowing that.

As though she had not heard him, Marguerite continued. "The timing would be right. Charles's birthday is almost exactly nine months after Philippe married Janelle."

"Charles is my father's posthumous son." Why wouldn't the woman accept that? There was nothing good to be gained by continuing this discussion.

She shrugged her shoulders and stared at him for a long moment. "Whatever you say."

By midday, the castle was filled. Knights and their ladies gathered in the Great Hall while squires and pages bustled from room to room, readying armor for the tournament, sneaking sweetmeats from the kitchens and stealing kisses with the maids. Although the cacophony was enough to deafen a dog, Marguerite was relieved by the influx of visitors. It was far better to be surrounded by strangers than to have her husband's constant, undivided attention.

He had been different since they had arrived, and there had been times when she had seen an expression on his face that, had she not known better, she would have called wistful. It was surely her imagination, for it was quickly replaced with his normal sardonic smile.

"Be patient," Philippe had counseled her. "He may appear to be a man, but where love is concerned, he is yet a babe."

A babe who had no desire to learn.

Marguerite sat in the large solar, accompanied by two of the vassals' wives.

"If I were not already married, I would envy you." Heloise, a tall woman with deep auburn hair, sank onto a pile of cushions.

Her companion agreed. "Until you captured him, the Silver Knight was considered the greatest prize in Aquitaine, perhaps in all of France." Emilie, whose lands adjoined Jarnac on the east, was shorter than Heloise, with dark brown hair and a pert nose.

"My husband is indeed a formidable knight." Marguerite kept her voice calm. Though she disliked the gossip on which these two women appeared to thrive, she did not wish to annoy them and provide even greater food for their favorite pastime.

She bent her head to thread a needle. When she raised it, Emilie's smile was guileless. "I vow, you and Alain are well suited. He is the bravest knight in Christendom, and you must surely be the most tolerant wife in the realm. Anyone else would have grown worried when he visited Honore."

The two women were transparent in their desire to arouse her curiosity. Marguerite raised one eyebrow rather than voice her question.

"Oh, Emilie, I can see she doesn't know who Honore is. We must tell her." Heloise's smile left no doubt that she was enjoying the story. "Honore is a close friend of your husband's. Very close." She emphasized the adjective.

Emilie joined the recounting. "Surely you must know he journeyed to Poitiers to visit her before your wedding. 'Twas the talk of the queen's court for many a day, how he barely spoke to anyone and did not even attend to his horse. Once he arrived in Poitiers, it seemed he had only one thought— Honore.''

Heloise smirked. "He fairly flew to her apartments. Of course, we don't know exactly what he was doing with her once they were inside." The woman's intonation supplied the missing pieces.

"Undoubtedly he was bidding her farewell. After all, that is what close friends do when they will be parted." Marguerite watched the women, waiting for their reaction.

" 'Tis likely indeed," Heloise admitted. "That is undoubtedly what they were doing in her bath."

The image was so vivid Marguerite could almost believe she had been there. She saw Alain, that big body of his folded to fit inside the tub, and the woman kneeling by his side, her hands . . .

A shaft of pure emotion stabbed Marguerite, its intensity taking her by surprise, stealing her breath. Jealousy. It could not be. Alain meant nothing to her, and so there was no reason for her to be jealous. 'Twas something she ate that must have disagreed with her. That was all it was.

# Chapter Twelve

For a woman with no great affinity for travel, she was devoting entirely too much of her time to it. Horseback, muleback, on foot. It seemed as though she had spent the majority of her married life journeying either to or from Mirail. No sooner had she and Alain returned from Jarnac than he had announced it was time to leave for Lilis. So here they were, on the road again.

This time, though, was different. This time she need not fear the reception she would receive. For this time Charles was waiting at journey's end.

Marguerite began to hum.

" 'Tis good to see you so happy." Louise rode at Marguerite's side, her lips pursed in an expression Marguerite knew all too well. This was Louise's first long journey, and her bones, ill accustomed to the mule's bouncing, ached.

"It will grow easier," Marguerite assured her maid, remembering how her own body had toughened after the ride to Jarnac. The return trip had been easier—far from pleasant, but infinitely more bearable.

The smile Louise mustered was a feeble one, wordlessly reminding Marguerite that her pain was more than physical.

Though Marguerite had thought Louise's sorrow at being parted from Gerard would lessen with the passage of time, it had not. Instead it had seemed to intensify, leaving Marguerite feeling powerless, for Louise would not accept her offer to negotiate with Henri for Gerard's release.

"Do not worry about me," Louise had told her. "Gerard and I will find a way. I know we will."

Just as Marguerite was convinced that she and Charles would find a way to be together. Soon. Soon she'd see her Lancelot again, and if that was not reason enough for rejoicing, there was one other pleasant possibility. While they were at Lilis, Alain would be so occupied that he would have little time to spend with Marguerite. Perhaps, indeed, there would be so few chambers that they would be unable to share one.

The respite would be welcome. Alain was a man driven by goals, and it appeared that his current goal was to sire an heir. Lord knew, he was persistent enough. Marguerite's humming faded as she thought of what transpired in her chamber each night. Each night he drew her into his arms, and each night it grew more difficult to remain impassive, to steel herself to show no pleasure. She would not grant the man the victory.

'Twas bad enough that during the day he sought to undermine her authority, to usurp her role as chatelaine of Mirail and bind the people to him. She could—and would—fight each of his underhanded tricks. Oh, he was careful never to be overt about it. When he intervened in a minor dispute, he told Marguerite 'twas so insignificant that it did not require her attention. And when he directed Jacques to assist Cook in the kitchens, he said 'twas only because the man had naught else to do. Idle hands, Alain reminded her, were dangerous.

His own were rarely idle, particularly at night. Then he seemed to regard her body as a battlefield where he sought yet another victory. Let him seek. He would not win. Especially now when she was so close to seeing Lancelot, the man of her dreams, again. Though she might not be able to keep her body pure for Charles, she had resolved to keep her spirit untouched, and thus far she had succeeded. Other than their wedding night when her body had betrayed her, she had managed to keep from showing even a hint of pleasure.

Soon they would be together again, she and Lancelot. Marguerite smiled and began to hum again as she thought of Charles. It had been so long since she had seen his face, been warmed by his gentle smile and heard his courtly words. There were times when she could barely conjure his image, when his hair seemed silver, not golden, and his eyes blue rather than warm brown. 'Twas good that they would soon be reunited.

"I see that something pleases you." Louise dropped back as Alain reined his horse in next to Marguerite. "Dare I wager what it is?"

" 'Tis a beautiful day. That would gladden even a curmudgeon's heart."

"Of course." Alain managed to imbue the two simple words with disbelief. "I, for one, will be happy when the wedding celebration is ended and we can return to Mirail."

"I had thought you would return to military life." The man was a warrior. Surely he longed to resume the life for which he had been bred . . . and leave her to that for which she had been raised, running Mirail.

Alain scanned the horizon, gesturing toward gray ramparts in the distance. "Lilis," he said simply. Then he turned to Marguerite. "You surprise me, my dear. I would have expected more subtlety from you."

"And you, my lord, amaze me with that statement. Why should I strive for subtlety when 'tis abundantly clear that you prefer plain, unembellished speech to the polite strains of a courtier? Surely that has not changed."

"You know what Heraclitus said, 'Naught endures but change.' "

"Indeed, and Pindar claims that 'Not every truth is the better for showing its face undisguised.' Still, I see no need to disguise the truth from you or to cloak it in pretty words."

"Then, to respond in kind, let me assure you once again that I have no intention of leaving Mirail unless my lord Richard requires my services. Nay, Marguerite, you'll not be rid of me so easily."

He remained at her side as they approached Lilis, neither breaking the uncomfortable silence that had fallen between them. Marguerite fixed her eyes on the castle walls in an attempt to still the frantic pounding of her heart. Though Alain had sought to intimidate her with his words, 'twas in her power to resist them.

They were perhaps half a mile from Lilis when two riders approached them. One was a woman. The sight of the other made Marguerite smile, and for a moment she was able to ignore the big man next to her. Charles! Her Lancelot had come to greet her. 'Twas apparent he was so eager to see her that he could not wait until she entered the château.

Marguerite glanced at the woman seated next to Charles. She was as beautiful as the troubadours had claimed, with finely chiseled features and dark hair plaited into thick braids. Though she sat confidently in the saddle, an unexpected air of vulnerability clung to her, and she darted uneasy glances at both Marguerite and Alain. But Marguerite had no time to consider Diane de Lilis's weaknesses, for her attention was drawn to Charles.

It was odd how memory distorted reality. In her memory his shoulders were broader and his chin firmer. In her memory he sat taller in the saddle and gripped the reins more forcefully. In her memory his smile was brighter. Memory, it appeared, was decidedly unreliable. Still, memory had not misled her in one respect. In the brief instant that they met hers, she saw his eyes were as warm a shade of brown as she remembered.

When they had crossed the moat and entered the courtyard, Charles and Diane dismounted. Alain and Marguerite followed suit. "Welcome back, Alain." Charles grinned at his brother, but when he turned to greet Marguerite, he kept his eyes on the ground. "Welcome to Lilis." It was surely her imagination that he seemed somehow ill at ease.

Diane flashed him a quick smile then turned to her guests. "I'm so happy you have come." Though she glanced at Alain, she directed her words to Marguerite. "I have always wanted a sister, and now Charles has given me one." She gazed at Charles again, and her smile grew warmer. "But come, Marguerite. 'Twas a long journey, and I am certain you will want to wash off the road dust.''

She seemed guileless, genuine in her wish to provide hospitality. Perhaps it was that sincerity which made Marguerite hesitate. She needed to talk to Charles, to assure herself that nothing had changed between them. Though Alain might claim that change was constant, Marguerite knew some things were unchanging.

She fixed her eyes on Charles, willing him to look at her, but he did not meet her gaze. Instead, he seemed engrossed in a private conversation with his brother.

Alain, it appeared, had seen her hesitation. '' 'Tis so like my bride to worry about me,'' he told the others. "She is concerned that the water will cool before I am able to bathe, and so she is loathe to attend to her own comfort. You need not worry about me,'' he assured Marguerite. "You should know that as a warrior I am accustomed to seeing to my own needs. If naught else, Charles will find me a trough for bathing. I pray you take this opportunity to become acquainted with my brother's bride.''

The man was despicable! There was no doubt that he had emphasized the last two words, reminding Marguerite once again of the impossibility of her love for Lancelot.

"I am certain you have many military matters you wish to discuss,'' she returned.

"Considering the occasion, the delights of the marriage bed would be a more appropriate topic. Don't you agree, my dear?''

Diane blushed and led Marguerite inside.

"Charles is so wonderful.''

They were in the large chamber that Diane had told Marguerite was reserved for the most honored guests and which would be hers and Alain's whenever they visited Lilis. While the servants filled the wooden tub with steaming water, Diane insisted on helping Marguerite and Louise unpack the trunks.

"I'm sure you know how I feel,'' Diane continued. "Truly, I must be the luckiest person on earth.'' She blushed again. "Father Paul would tell me 'tis a sin, but I feel so happy that I sometimes think this must be heaven. Even though I've dreamed about marrying all my life, never did I dare hope it would be to someone so wonderful.'' She tested the bath water with her hand, then nodded to Marguerite, urging her to disrobe. ''Charles is perfect,'' she said.

Sweet Mary above, Marguerite prayed, give me strength to endure this. The woman's simpering was enough to make a saint curse, and Marguerite was far from a saint. Charles might be wonderful. She would not deny that. But perfect? Hardly. Couldn't the woman see what was before her very eyes, that Charles was handsome and charming but naught else? Marguerite blanched. Where had that thought come from? 'Twas nonsense. The journey must have been more arduous than she'd realized if it was causing such foolish thoughts to pop into her head.

''Tell me, Marguerite. Is it as wonderful as the troubadours claim?''

''It?''

Diane's blush deepened. ''You know. It. The . . . er . . . bed. Um . . . that is . . . the act.''

So Alain had been wrong. Marguerite felt a shaft of satisfaction that Charles and Diane had not anticipated their wedding vows. What would happen, she wondered, if Diane feared the consummation of her marriage? Would she seek to break the betrothal? Marguerite gave Diane an appraising look. The woman's eyes radiated trust, reminding her of a forest animal, beautiful and guileless. No, she could not mislead her.

''With the right man,'' Marguerite said finally, ''it can be very pleasurable.''

Diane's relief was palpable. ''I had hoped so. My mother told me it was pleasant, but I feared she exaggerated, for I know how dearly she wishes me to wed Charles. Somehow I knew you would tell me the truth.'' Diane handed Marguerite a piece of soap. ''I'm happy that you've found marriage so enjoyable.''

Had she said that? Marguerite started to correct Diane, but the other woman continued, giving her no chance to speak. ''In truth, 'tis easy to see you and Alain are made for each other, just as Charles and I are. I sometimes think we are two halves of a single whole.''

What an unpleasant thought. Charles was hers, her Lancelot. When Diane left the room, Marguerite called to Louise. ''You must get a message to him.''


Diane had ordered the noon meal served on the wide grassy expanse along one side of the castle walls. Though Marguerite normally enjoyed eating outdoors, today she was preoccupied. Would Charles respond to her message? Although he was seated next to her, he rarely spoke to her, turning instead to Diane on his left.

''I heard that Pierre the Strong uncovered a plot to kill Louis.'' Charles addressed his words to Alain.

Without giving her husband a chance to reply, Marguerite responded, ''Do you know who was behind the plot?'' 'Twas serious news. Though the king had his share of enemies, until now few had gotten close enough to threaten him.

''As I heard the tale, no one is certain.'' Diane joined the conversation. ''But had it not been uncovered, we would have had a new king. The plan was to separate him from his guards, then attack.''

''It appears someone studied the Second Crusade. The Saracens used that tactic all too well then.'' Alain offered Marguerite a morsel of stewed fish.

She chewed slowly, remembering Philippe's description of the day Alain's father had been killed, the day her own father had lost his arm. ''Mayhap the traitor was someone who was on the crusade and remembered the ambush. There must be men close to the king who were in Outremer then.''

Diane nodded. ''I suppose we'll never know, but at least the king is safe. Now that he's been warned, he's doubled the number of his guards.''

''I don't understand Pierre.'' There was a note of disdain in Charles's voice. ''The king gave him the choice of any reward for uncovering the plot, and he chose only Arnot. 'Tis a small castle. Why wouldn't he have asked for more?''

"Perhaps he preferred not to be greedy," Marguerite suggested.

"Or maybe he liked Arnot." Diane laid her hand on Charles's.

Alain speared another piece of fish. "Mayhap you're both right. He may have wanted more but didn't want to appear greedy. 'Tis unfortunate he did not have a bull's hide with him."

Marguerite chuckled. Alain was right. 'Twould have been an ideal way for Pierre the Strong to extend his reward without the stigma of greed being attached to his request.

At her side, Charles stiffened then shot a puzzled glance at his brother. "A bull's hide? Why would he want that?"

It appeared that Charles did not recognize the reference to one of the most famous classical tales. "Legend has it that that was how Dido founded Carthage," Marguerite told him.

When Charles continued to look puzzled, Diane explained the story of how Dido, exiled from her home, had arrived on the coast of Africa. Seeking refuge, she had asked for only as much land as she could contain within a bull's hide. When the king had agreed, crafty Dido had cut the bull's hide into thin strips and had measured out an area far greater than the king had expected.

"Legends!" Charles scoffed. "That never happened."

'Twas odd, Marguerite reflected, that Charles cared so little for learning. He had thought Sophocles was a Roman, and it appeared he had paid little heed to the myths. Yet surely that mattered not. What was important was his sense of chivalry.


The afternoon sun streamed through the stained glass window, sending shafts of blue light onto the floor. At this hour of the day, the chapel was empty, with only a few votive candles still burning. She waited, wondering whether he would come. Moments later the sound of footsteps rang on the stone floor.

"You came!" She gave Charles a smile of pure delight. At last they would have a chance to talk, to explain all that had occurred, to renew their pledges.

"How could I stay away? When my lady calls, I must come, for there is much I must tell you." He knelt before her and pressed a kiss on her hand.

The door swung open.

"What have we here? A recreation of Camelot? I fear the stake has not yet been prepared, but surely 'tis appropriate for the sinners to meet in the very spot where Charles will soon wed another."

Had she ever thought that anger was hot? Alain's fury was colder than the winter wind, his voice flaying her senses as surely as a lash.

"Charles, I must give you credit," he continued. "You are truly the master of the dramatic scene. Or is it the absurd?" As Charles scrambled to his feet, Alain extended one hand and pushed him toward the door. "Get out of here before I forget that this is a place of peace and bloody your nose again."

Charles scurried away with nary a backward glance.

"How could you treat him like that?" If Alain was angry, so was she. The man had no right to humiliate Charles.

"Like what?"

"As though he were a child." Alain would have challenged a man to a joust; it was only a child that he would threaten with a bloody nose.

Alain gripped her forearm, forcing her to meet his gaze. "Mayhap I treat him like a child because he acts like one. How else would you describe his behavior and yours?" Alain shook his head in disgust. "I can almost excuse Charles. He never could resist a pretty face, and Lord knows yours is pretty enough to distract him. But you should know better. How could you destroy his chance at happiness?"

Though she would not have thought it possible, Alain's anger had intensified.

"I am not destroying Charles's happiness," she asserted.

"Oh, yes, my dear, you are." Alain increased his hold on her arm and led her out of the chapel. "Are you so blinded with emotion that you cannot see that Diane is the perfect wife for him? When you're not here, even Charles realizes that. But when you're near him, he wavers. All he can see is that you're more beautiful than his bride-to-be.'' Alain turned Marguerite to face him. ''Don't do it. Don't ruin both of their lives. They deserve happiness.''

''What about me?'' she asked softly. ''Don't I deserve my share of happiness? You're so eloquent on the subject, but Lord knows you have brought precious little of it to Mirail.''

''' 'Tis most unfair. Once again you have seated me so far from you that I cannot enjoy the pleasure of your company.'' Were those courtly words and the gentle teasing coming from Alain? Marguerite turned in surprise as they approached the high table and Diane ushered them to their seats.

Diane blushed. It appeared the woman could do naught but color when a man spoke to her.

''I assure you, 'twas not intentional. I simply thought you would find Marguerite and Charles's conversation more stimulating than mine.''

''Ah, you do yourself a disservice. What man would find mere conversation more stimulating than your company? Certainly not I.'' As he spoke, Alain guided Diane into the seat on his right, then placed Marguerite on his left, leaving the position on Diane's right for Charles.

It was, Marguerite reflected, another of his masterful strokes. For, while appearing solely to crave Diane's company, he had managed to separate Marguerite and Charles. At the noon meal, they had been seated next to each other, with Diane and Alain on the ends. Now it was Marguerite and Charles who occupied the distant seats, making private conversation impossible. She had had no opportunity to talk to Charles since the debacle in the chapel. Though he had said little, Alain had remained at her side throughout the afternoon, forestalling any attempt she might have made to see Charles alone.

''Yes, please,'' Marguerite said as the page offered to refill her goblet. The cool liquid slid down her throat, helping to wash away the bitter taste of the stewed eels. 'Twas obvious the Lilis cook had not learned that a clove of garlic would

enhance the flavor of even an aging fish. Perhaps the wine
would cleanse her palate.

"My brother is a most fortunate man to have so beautiful
and gracious a bride." Though Alain directed his words at
Diane, Marguerite knew that he meant her to overhear, that
he was making a deliberate—and unfavorable—comparison
between Charles's wife and his own. Damn the man! It was
his own fault that she was not gracious to him. If he had treated
her with half the courtesy he displayed to his future sister-in-
law, he might have found her a more willing bride. But, no,
he had waged a battle for her rather than woo her.

"Yes, please," she said as the page returned with another
pitcher of wine.

"I count the minutes until you will be mine." Charles
entwined his fingers with Diane's as he spoke. " 'Twill be the
most joyous day of my life."

There had been a time, not so very long ago, when he had
murmured the same words to her. This time 'twas all for show,
of course, a noble pretense to keep his wealthy bride happy.
But it hurt. Ah, yes, it hurt.

She accepted another glass of wine then, on legs that were
barely steady, she climbed the stairs to her chamber. Her eyelids
felt oddly heavy as she brushed her hair, but her thoughts were
clear. He was coming soon, the man who would make her body
sing with pleasure. The August breeze that stirred the rushes
on the floor was sweet, redolent with the scent of flowers.
'Twas a most beautiful night.

Marguerite slipped into the bed, drawing a light sheet over
her but leaving the bed curtains open. The air was far too
fragrant to block with heavy cloth.

Soon. He would be here soon. She felt the mattress dip, then
the scent of flowers was replaced with a more powerful aroma,
spicy yet tart, like the most delicious of pastries. She shifted,
moving closer to the intoxicating fragrance, and as she did a
warmth began to steal over her body. She moved ever closer
until she reached the source of the warmth.

"Ah, Marguerite, you must be a witch."

Her eyes opened at the sound of Alain's voice. It was he

who was the source of the wonderful fragrance, the enticing warmth. It was he she had been seeking. She snuggled closer, unwilling to lose the comfort his nearness brought.

"Indeed, you must be a witch, for what other than sorcery could make me want you so?" He turned on his side so that he was facing her, and she could feel the warmth of his breath on her lips. With one hand, he reached out to touch her cheek, drawing his fingers slowly along the line of her chin and down her throat, lingering on the sensitive spots at the base of her neck.

'Twas wondrous what a mere touch could do, what magic it would work. "I'm no witch," she whispered. "Just an ordinary woman." As his hand continued its downward motion, a soft moan escaped her lips. By all the saints above, 'twas he who was using witchcraft. For what else could set her body afire? What else could make her feel that this was what she had sought all her life?

His lips nuzzled her neck, following the trail his fingers had blazed. " 'Tis there you're wrong." He shook his head slightly, and the faint stubble of his beard scraped her cheek. It was an unexpectedly pleasant sensation. "No ordinary woman's lips would make my blood boil like this."

Suiting his action to his words, he captured her lips with his. As she parted hers willingly, he thrust his tongue inside her mouth, continuing the exploration he had begun.

When at length he drew his lips away, Marguerite's pulse was pounding. " 'Tis not only *your* blood that boils," she whispered. She raised her hand to touch his shoulders, glorying in the feel of his firm muscles and the springy hair which covered his chest. She had touched men's bodies hundreds of times, dressing their wounds, caring for their illnesses. Never had she thought of touching a man's body for pleasure. Yet pleasure her, it did. Who would have dreamt that such a simple thing as pressing her fingertips to his warm, fragrant skin would be the source of such delight?

"You are indeed a witch." Alain groaned as her fingers continued their exploration. "But you're mine, my witch."

He renewed his caresses, and she followed his lead, matching touch for touch, exulting in the pounding of his pulse under her fingertips and the knowledge that it was she who had caused his breath to grow ragged, his blood to race. Together they climbed to the heights of passion, and when the world dissolved into shooting stars, they drifted back to earth together, their bodies entwined.

*She was cold, oh, so cold. Though she could see the sun through the tiny slit that was her sole contact with the outside world, no warmth permeated the thick walls. Inside the small room there was no source of heat, no fire, no tapestry to block the chill that radiated from the walls, not even a layer of rushes to insulate the floor.*

*She shivered, wrapping her arms around her body in a futile attempt to warm her trembling limbs. But it was for naught. If the cold was pervasive, the fear was worse. It was faceless and nameless, gaining power from its very ambiguity.*

*She had to get out! The words drummed in her head. Her eyes moved frantically, but there was no door in the small room, only the slit of a window in the curved wall.*

*He needed her. She knew it.*

*She moved to stare out the window. The ground was far below, and the sight of a moat told her she was in a high tower. One with no entrance, no means of escape.*

*She had to reach him.*

*She tried to lean through the slit, but it was too narrow for even her slender form. There had to be a way!*

*She looked down. The great gray destrier stood grazing placidly. Where was his rider? Where was her knight?*

*Her eyes moved frantically, searching.*

*She gasped. He was there, sprawled on the ground, and even from a distance she could see his lifeblood seeping away.*

*There was another. She could not see* him, *could only feel* his *presence—the danger, the evil. He lurked in the shadows, waiting to strike, waiting to end her knight's life.*

*She had to stop* him. *She had to save her knight. There had to be a way.*

*As her blood pounded, she heard another sound. Hoofbeats. She leaned further out the window. Someone was coming. A knight.*

*"Help!" She screamed her plea. The knight drew closer.*

*"Help!"*

*He spurred his destrier. As she shouted, he looked up at the tower and raised his visor.*

*It was Charles.*

*"Help!" she screamed. "Help him!"*

*The cold had grown more intense, setting her limbs to trembling. She knew that without help the end was imminent. The other would have his way.*

*Soon. He must have help soon.*

*Charles raised his lance in salute, then turned his back and slowly began to ride away from the tower, away from his brother.*

*"Charles!"*

When she woke, there were tears streaming down her cheeks.

# Chapter Thirteen

This was worse, far worse, than the Saracen's blade. Though that pain had been intense, the wound had been clean and healed easily. This was different. It was a jagged, festering cut, one which brought fresh pain each time he moved.

He should have anticipated it. After all, there was no reason to believe she was any different from any other woman and far too much evidence to the contrary. He should have been prepared. The saints above knew he had not gained his reputation as a fearless warrior by going into battle without his armor. Unfortunately, this time he had. He had been utterly defenseless, and so the attack had caught him unaware.

Who would have thought a lie would be so painful? 'Twas what she herself had said: the invisible wounds were oft the worst.

The strategy was brilliant, worthy of a veteran tactician. She had found his point of vulnerability and exploited it, causing him to lower his defenses. For a few moments, yes, even a few hours, he had thought she was happy, and, oh, what that had done to him. She had responded to his caresses so passionately that he had—fool that he was—deluded himself. For the space of one night, he had thought that the passion was for him, that there was, despite all the odds, a chance that this time it might be different. And then, when he had least expected it, she had delivered the *coup de grâce*.

It had all been a sham, the ultimate pretense. The passion was never in question, but the simple, painful fact was that that emotion had been for his brother. He had been no more than a convenient substitute.

Though she had plied him with kisses and touches that inflamed every inch of his body, her untutored caresses arousing him more thoroughly than Honore's most practiced seduction, the truth was easily revealed. When terror had overtaken her in the night, it was not his name she had called. No, in the moment of truth, she had confirmed Alain's deepest fears. What Marguerite felt for Charles was far more than infatuation. She loved him.

She had claimed otherwise, saying that she had seen him— Alain—wounded and that she had cried to Charles to assist him. She had said the words, but the trembling in her voice had told Alain the truth. She herself had been threatened, and 'twas Charles she had turned to, Charles whom she believed could save her, Charles whom she loved.

He had been a fool to think otherwise, and now he would pay the price for his foolishness. So be it. That was one mistake he would never again make.

It would be a close to perfect wedding, one that needed none of the embellishment it would receive in the retelling. The bride, Marguerite had to admit as she helped Diane dress, was radiant with happiness. The kitchens were overflowing with sumptuous dishes, and the kegs of wine and ale which had been brought to the Great Hall promised the guests a merry evening.

Wine! Marguerite grimaced. Just the thought was enough to set her head to pounding again. She should never have accepted that last glass, and yet . . . She blushed at the memory of what had transpired in her chamber, what might never have happened had the wine not lowered her defenses.

It had felt so good, so very, very good. Nothing in her experience had prepared her for the sheer physical pleasure of the hours she had spent in Alain's arms, the hours when they had been as one.

And then the nightmare had come, destroying the fragile truce she and Alain had forged, reminding her that Alain was not the man of her dreams. For when she had clung to him, seeking comfort from the hideous nightmare that even now had the power to send a frisson of fear down her spine, he had turned away, leaving her feeling more alone than ever before.

She had been a fool to think he cared for more than her body. Now she knew the truth, and that was one mistake she would never again make.

He was waiting when she entered the small chapel with Diane. When she had escorted the bride to the altar and given her to Charles, Marguerite took her place next to Alain. For the sake of everyone who was watching them, she fixed a smile on her face, though her heart ached even more than her head.

As the priest began to intone the words of the marriage service, Marguerite's eyes strayed to the bridal couple. Yes, Diane was lovely with her coronet of pearls setting off her dark hair, while the dark green of her bliaut turned her eyes from hazel to pure green. And Charles looked so proud, standing at her side.

Marguerite's eyes narrowed. How had she thought him more handsome than his brother? Oh, Charles was an attractive man, but he lacked Alain's strength. Compared to Alain, Charles appeared a mere boy. Her husband was a man. A most despicable, cruel man, but a man nonetheless.

Marguerite turned slightly to look at Alain. His eyes were fixed on her with an expression she had never before seen. It was almost as though he were hurt, or perhaps angry. Yet when his gaze met Marguerite's, he smiled, and his eyes were once again clear blue. It must have been the lighting in the chapel that made her imagine something more.

It seemed an endless day. First the interminable nuptial mass, then the banquet with its dozens of courses of food. And now there were scores of toasts and speeches to endure. Under the best of circumstances, the speeches were tedious. Tonight they seemed deadly. Not only were they delaying her departure from the feasting table where the very smell of food made her head ache, but their ribald content reminded her all too painfully of last night. Why couldn't the courtiers be done with it all?

At last Diane rose. Though there was still the disrobing and the ceremony in the bridal chamber, the evening was approaching its end. Marguerite escorted Diane up the staircase. An hour later she returned to the chamber she and Alain were sharing. It was time to confront Alain, to tell him that henceforth he would have to slake his lust with someone else.

At the sound of men ascending the stairs, she slid into bed, but the raucous voices passed her door, and Alain did not appear. She turned onto one side and stared out the window. The stars were bright, and a sliver of a moon illuminated the sky. It was beautiful, but tonight it mattered not. All that mattered was that Alain understand that she would no longer allow herself to be used.

Where was he?

She could tell by the position of the moon that several hours had passed before she heard the rattle of the door latch. Alain was here.

"We need to speak about last night," she said as he slipped into the other side of the bed.

"*Au contraire,* my sweet wife. *You* may have a need to speak, but I have no desire to listen. Indeed, I heard far too much last night." Alain rolled onto his side, leaving the width of the bed between them. "I bid you sleep. 'Tis a long ride we have tomorrow." Moments later he was asleep.

Their days formed a pattern. When others were close enough to observe or overhear them, Alain was unfailingly polite to Marguerite. Indeed, he seemed the model of a chivalric knight paying homage to his lady. But when they were alone, he was as silent as the stone floor. Though he would answer when Marguerite addressed him, his responses were monosyllabic and so unsatisfying that she quickly learned the futility of questioning him.

The nights, too, formed a pattern. Alain would wait for

several hours after Marguerite retired to their chamber before he joined her. And when he did enter the room, it was only to sleep.

It appeared she had been wrong. She had thought his goal was to sire an heir and that that was the reason he had bedded her each night. But she had been mistaken, for although she was not breeding, they had not made love since the night before Charles and Diane's wedding. The night when she had given herself to Alain, finally admitting how much pleasure his kisses and caresses could arouse. The night that, despite everything, she could not forget. The night that obviously had meant nothing to Alain.

His goal, it appeared, had been to force her to respond. Now that he had achieved that victory and had proven that she was like every other woman, that she craved his touch, the challenge was ended.

She should have been happy. It was what she had wanted: a marriage that would protect her lands and her people but which required no intimacies of her. Why, then, did it seem so empty? Why, now that Alain was unfailingly polite, did she miss the arguments that had sparked their conversations? And why, oh, why, did she miss his arms, his lips and his love?

It was not fair. Henri unlatched the small oak chest and pulled out a handful of gold coins. He clenched them in his fist, then let them trickle back into the chest in an action that never failed to soothe him. Today for the first time the sight and sound of his fortune had little effect.

The man had everything. The adulation of the masses, the beautiful Marguerite in his bed each night, the riches of Mirail. And now he wanted Henri's homage. Henri grinned. He knew the form of homage he'd like to give Alain de Jarnac. A swift thrust of the sword between his shoulder blades. That would be a fitting payment for the humiliation he had dealt Henri.

Henri's grin became a low chuckle. It would happen. Indeed it would. The only question was when. The time had to be right. Though the thought of watching the man die a slow and painful death was most appealing, he must be careful that no one could connect him to the deed. Alain's death would have to appear an accident. A most unfortunate accident that left Marguerite a widow needing comfort, protection and a husband.

Soon. But not quite yet. For the present, he would journey to Mirail as bidden and would go through the pretense of paying homage. Galling though the homage would be, there was much to be gained by the trip. Only a fool would not turn the visit to his advantage, and Henri de Bleufontaine was no fool.

"Where is Sir Alain?"

Marguerite looked up in surprise at the sound of Clothilde's voice. 'Twas rare for Clothilde to climb to the solar. Indeed, the last time Marguerite could recall it happening was the day Jean had gouged his arm with an ax.

"I believe he's in the stables," Marguerite said.

"No." Clothilde shook her head, her three chins wagging. "We looked there."

"Then I don't know where he is." The man saw no reason to tell her where he was going or what he was doing. Most days he acted as though Mirail were his home and Marguerite the visitor. "What is the problem?" she asked, for it had to be a problem which induced Clothilde to mount the stairs.

"We're missing three sacks of flour and a side of pork." Clothilde was clearly outraged by the pilfering. "Someone must stop the stealing."

Anger sprouted as quickly as weeds after a spring rain. "And why, pray tell, do you believe you need Sir Alain for this matter?" Marguerite demanded. "Have I not always handled all the kitchen affairs myself?"

Clothilde nodded, her face whitening under the onslaught of Marguerite's anger.

"Then be gone. I'll attend to this later. And if I hear that any one of you has gone to Sir Alain in my stead, I shall see you whipped."

* * *

His kisses were even sweeter than she had remembered. Louise entwined her arms around Gerard's neck and pressed her body close to his.

"I've missed you so!" she whispered when he trailed his lips along her neck, sending shivers of delight down her spine. 'Twas wondrous having him once again at Mirail, truly the answer to her prayers. Each day she had knelt on the cold stone floor until her bones had ached, imploring her patron saints to allow Gerard to return. And here he was, holding her again.

"I feared he would not let me return," Gerard said in the strangely coarse voice that was his alone. "I had to pretend that I had no wish to come to Mirail, or he would have forced me to remain behind."

Louise shuddered. "I would have died had you not come. When we're apart, I feel only half alive, but now . . ." She opened her mouth to his questing tongue. "Nay, do not stop."

"I must," he said.

"But why?" She felt bereft now that his hand no longer traced the softness of her curves. " 'Twould not be a venial sin for us to lie together."

"The risk is too great. You might conceive a child."

Slowly she moved her fingers along the hard planes of his face. "And if I did, I would count it a blessing to have a part of you to love."

For a moment the only sound was Gerard's quick breathing. When she spoke, his voice was low. " 'Tis I who am blessed to have your love," he told her. "At Bleufontaine the women run from me. They hear my voice and tell their children I was sent by the Devil. But you have never done that. From the beginning . . ."

She laid her fingers across his lips, silencing him. "From the beginning I loved you."

"As I love you."

"Then why would a child be so wrong?"

"It would. You must trust me in this. It would. But a kiss . . ."

Long minutes later Louise murmured, "Tonight. When the banquet is over and Sir Henri does not need you any longer, come to my parents' house. They wish to meet you."

Her eyes had grown accustomed to the semidarkness of the storage room, and she saw Gerard's smile while she felt the warmth of his breath on her cheek. "I would be honored," he told her.

"Your visit is all my brother Jean can talk about. But you know how younger brothers are. Jean is very protective of me, for all that he's only ten."

It must have been her imagination that Gerard seemed to hesitate. "I would not know," he said. "I have no brothers."

"Have you any sisters?"

Again there was the shortest of pauses. "I have no family at Bleufontaine. But come, my sweet, let us not waste time talking."


"We caught him in the forest." Though the guard kept his voice low and respectful as he addressed Marguerite, his grip on the felon's arm was harsh, as if he feared his prisoner would attempt to escape.

When she had heard the guard's shout and the summons to sentence a criminal, Marguerite was not certain what she had expected. She had felt a moment's relief that the guard had asked for her rather than Alain, but it was quickly overshadowed by concern. Serious crimes were so infrequent at Mirail that the sound of an urgent summons had startled her. She had descended the stairs, trying to imagine what misdemeanor had occurred. Mayhap one of the visiting vassals, having imbibed too much ale, had stolen another's armor.

Whatever she had expected, it had not been this.

"What happened?" she asked the child.

Though he met her gaze, Jean's entire body was trembling with fear. He opened his mouth, but no words came out.

Marguerite waited.

"He killed one of the barony's deer." It was the guard who answered.

A silence descended on the room as serfs who a moment before had been raking soiled rushes and gathering bones for the hounds stopped their work.

"Is that true?" Marguerite felt her heart sink. 'Twas no wonder the guard had summoned her, if this was the felony.

Jean managed a small nod. "Louise invited her man to join us for dinner tonight, and I knew Mère wanted to serve something other than pork." Jean spoke quickly, almost babbling now that he had found his voice. " 'Tis a big celebration, you know, and venison is more tasty than pork."

Unfortunately, the flavor of the meat mattered little.

"But you knew it was forbidden." Marguerite forced her voice to remain impassive. She could show no favoritism, no matter how fond she was of Louise's younger brother.

"Yes." His voice cracked.

"And you knew the penalty for killing a deer?"

"Yes."

There was a low murmur as the servants waited for Marguerite's reaction.

"Do you want me to hang him now?" When the guard yanked on Jean's arm, the boy whimpered, as much from fear as pain.

Marguerite shook her head. She needed time to think. "Put him in the dungeons. You need not chain him, but ensure that the door is locked."

As the guard led him away, Jean gave Marguerite one last imploring look, the terror in his eyes reminding her of a wounded animal. If only he had chosen a peacock, a sheep, anything but a deer.

"Please, my lady. I beg you." Tears streamed down her face as Louise knelt before Marguerite. "Don't hang my brother. He's merely a boy."

But a boy who had violated one of the primary laws of the realm. Deer could trample fields or consume the serfs' crops, and the farmers had no recourse, for only a noble could hunt them.

Though it wrenched her heart, Marguerite's voice was stern. "You know the penalty is death." While it was not a rule that she and her father had liked, they had enforced it on the few occasions when one of the serfs had poached the barony's deer. Guillaume had insisted that order would be maintained only if there were a healthy respect for laws.

"But he's the only son, and Mère can have no more children." Louise continued to plead.

Marguerite drew Louise to her feet. "Even if I could mitigate the sentence, this would not be the time. The vassals are here, and what has happened is no secret. If I relent, they will think I am weak, that I am swayed by sentiment. I cannot let that happen. Surely you see that, Louise. Mirail's safety is at stake."

Louise raised a tear stained face. "But this is Jean," she said simply.

"I know."

The banquet that night was the most festive since Marguerite's marriage. Cook had prepared a series of tempting dishes, and the minstrels who sang while the guests gorged themselves on the rich food were among the best Marguerite had ever heard. Though the visiting vassals appeared to revel in the entertainment, it was wasted on Marguerite. She was able to enjoy neither the cuisine nor the music. Instead, although she forced her mouth to form a smile, she felt no gladness.

How could Jean have been so foolish? If he had asked, she would have told Cook to give him some of the venison that was being prepared for tonight's meal. Marguerite would gladly have helped Jean make Gerard's visit special. There was no need to kill a deer. Now it was too late. The deed was done.

Marguerite's stomach churned as she thought of the fate awaiting Jean. Though swift, hanging was not a pleasant way to die, or so she had been told. It would have been easier, had he been a hardened criminal. But Jean was, as Louise had reminded her several times, only a child. A foolish, foolish child who loved his sister dearly. A boy who thought he was a man.

If only the vassals weren't here, perhaps she could have shown clemency. But the risks were too high. Alain had sum-

moned them because he shared her father's concern that their
loyalty might waver. If she displayed weakness now, their faith
in her would be diminished, for she would give truth to their
fear that she was a powerless woman.

If only there were some other way. For the first time the
responsibility of Mirail weighed heavily, and she found herself
wishing her father were still alive, that she could seek his
advice. Marguerite's eyes strayed to the big man who sat next
to her. Though he had undoubtedly heard about Jean's crime,
he had said nothing. Perhaps he thought the guard should have
brought Jean to him for sentencing. The man had done much
to insinuate himself into the very fabric of Mirail.

It was likely that he would have wise counsel. Marguerite
could not fault the judgments he had handed down, merely the
fact that he had usurped her authority by making them.

She would not; indeed, she could not ask him for advice.
That would be proof that she was vulnerable, that she needed
him. She'd not give the man the satisfaction of another victory,
not after the way he'd scorned her, showing her how little her
happiness meant to him. No, there had to be another way.

"Please, Marguerite." Louise dropped the hairbrush for the
third time in as many minutes. "You must save him."

With a weary sigh, Marguerite dismissed her servant. As
galling as it was, she had to concede that there was no alternative.

"I must talk to you." She was seated by the window when
Alain entered the chamber.

"Indeed?" He began to undress, folding his clothing and
arranging it on the trunk as he did each night. When he spoke,
his voice bore as little expression as a child reciting a rhyme.
"I thought the jongleurs were exceptionally skilled tonight."
It was the polite conversation he had employed for the past
month. She had endured it and had even managed to smile,
because she had known how important it was to maintain a
façade in front of her people. But not tonight.

"We need *real* talk," she said, her voice harsh with anger
and pain, "not the meaningless drivel we've exchanged since

we returned from Lilis. Now, listen to me.'' Quickly she outlined the problem.

''You want my advice?'' At another time Marguerite would have responded in kind to Alain's sarcastic tone, but tonight there was too much at stake to be bothered by pettiness.

''I asked for it, didn't I?''

Alain was silent for so long that she feared he would not answer her. Then he spoke. ''You need to administer a harsh punishment, because the crime is a severe one. But you also need a reason for leniency, something that everyone will believe.''

Marguerite nodded. He had understood and summarized her dilemma.

''Let's start with finding a reason for clemency,'' he suggested. ''What about Jean's age?''

''I considered that,'' Marguerite admitted. ''Unfortunately, there is a precedent. Younger boys have been hanged on other baronies.'' Her voice cracked as she spoke the words, knowing they might soon apply not to a faceless, nameless child on another barony but to Jean.

As if he understood her distress and wanted to comfort her, Alain took her hand between both of his. ''Can we claim today is a special occasion? Perhaps having assembled the vassals?''

The warmth of his hand spread up her arm, and Marguerite felt herself begin to relax. For the first time since the guard had dragged Jean before her, she believed there might be a solution. ''Mayhap it would work, but we need something more important than the vassals' visit. They'd see that for the pretext it is.'' She thought for a moment. ''A saint's day. We can exonerate Jean on religious grounds.''

''I hesitate to tell you this, but today is not . . .''

''. . . St. Jean's day.'' Marguerite completed the sentence. ''No, it is not. Today is something much better. 'Tis *your* saint's day.''

''Mine? Mine is in January, not September.''

''Not any longer.''

Marguerite laughed for the first time since the guard's summons. ''Oh, Alain, don't you see? 'Tis the perfect solution. No one at Mirail knows when your saint's day really is, so we can claim it is today. 'Tis perfect.''

" 'Tis a plausible story,'' he admitted, ''but have you considered what this will mean? The people will give me the credit for saving Jean, not you.''

Marguerite nodded. " 'Tis better this way. Had I mitigated the sentence, the vassals would have called me weak, but that's one word no one will ever use toward you.''

The warmth that spread throughout her body owed little to the late summer night. It felt so good to be talking, really talking, to Alain again.

"What punishment would you suggest?'' she asked.

This time he did not hesitate, and Marguerite knew he had been considering an appropriate penalty, one that met the criteria they had outlined. "Eleven lashes. One for each of his years, the last for the deer he slaughtered.''

Marguerite shuddered, thinking of Jean's tender back. " 'Tis a harsh sentence.''

"Far more lenient than death.'' Alain tightened his grip on her hand. "You are a healer,'' he reminded her. "Surely you can heal Jean's flesh, but even you have not the power to undo a hangman's noose.''

Slowly Marguerite nodded. "You are right.'' Though it was not a punishment she liked, she knew Alain had chosen it carefully. The vassals' sense of justice would be served without Jean's forfeiting his life. The solution seemed so simple that Marguerite wondered why she had not conceived it herself, and yet she had not. Nor had Alain. It had taken the two of them working together to accomplish what one alone had been unable to do.

"Thank you,'' she said softly. Maybe this would be the beginning. Maybe they could put their differences aside. But the spell was broken.

Alain released her hand and rose. " 'Twas my pleasure, my lady.''

The moment of closeness had ended, and the cold stranger who shared her chamber ever since Lilis had returned.

# Chapter Fourteen

For the first time that day, the tears which filled Louise's eyes were tears of joy. Jean would live! When she had heard Sir Alain's pronouncement, she had knelt at his feet and kissed his boots. Surely Mirail was fortunate to have such a wise and compassionate lord.

Now she had a double cause for celebration. Her brother was safe, and the man she loved had come to meet her family.

"Welcome to our home." Her parents stood on either side of the doorway, greeting Gerard. Louise felt the tension that had been building all day begin to release as she heard the warmth in her father's voice. She had not been certain of the welcome Gerard would receive. Both Mère and Père had been as overwrought as she at the thought of losing Jean, and she had feared that they might have blamed Gerard for Jean's foolishness, thinking that the man had in some way encouraged Jean to hunt the deer. But the smiles they gave Gerard, tempered as they were with the knowledge that their son had yet to suffer his full punishment, told Louise her concerns were unfounded. Though Jean remained in the dungeon, the family would continue its celebration.

"We are pleased to have you join us." While her father

spoke, Louise's mother nodded her agreement, then gestured to the table. Tonight it held only four trenchers of bread rather than the five Louise had prepared, and the small room was redolent with the aroma of roast pork rather than venison. Mère obviously wanted no visible reminders of Jean to spoil the festive occasion. It would be, Louise suspected, a long time before anyone in her family ate venison, no matter who had killed the animal.

Despite its almost tragic beginning, the evening proved to be an enjoyable one. To Louise's delight, Gerard and her father found many areas where they held similar opinions, and her mother smiled with pleasure when he complimented her on the succulent pork. Within a few hours, it seemed that Gerard had become part of the family. Still, it was a surprise when her father brought out a bowl of sultanas at the end of the meal.

A quick blush heated Louise's cheeks, and for a moment she dared not look at Gerard. It was too much to hope that he was unaware of the fruits' significance, for who did not know that when a parent offered sultanas, he was approving a man's request to marry his daughter? The problem was, Gerard had not asked for her hand in marriage. 'Twas simply that Père knew how Louise loved Gerard and that she longed to be with him, and so he was attempting to encourage the man's suit.

Before her father could verbalize his thoughts and destroy the gentle camaraderie that had grown throughout the evening, Louise rose and took Gerard's hand. "We must return to the castle," she told her parents. "Lady Marguerite has asked me to attend her tonight." It was a lie, and Father René would demand a penance for it, but Louise could not allow her parents, no matter how well-intentioned they were, to embarrass Gerard. He had said he could not leave Bleufontaine to marry her, and no amount of sultanas would change that. 'Twas a matter for the two of them to resolve, no one else.

The sky was dark and moonless, lit only by the distant stars, and the air held a hint of the coming winter's chill. Though it was not a night for lingering out of doors, Louise led Gerard into the apple orchard. Before they parted, she wanted to ensure that nothing had changed between them, despite her father's clumsy attempts at matchmaking. They wandered slowly, hand in hand, listening to the soft soughing of the wind and the occasional plunk of ripe fruit on the ground.

"You are so very fortunate," Gerard told her. "You have a wonderful family, and Lady Marguerite and Sir Alain are as different from my master as this night is from a summer day." A shudder wracked his frame.

"You could be part of our family." She spoke slowly, hesitant to voice her deepest wish for fear that once again he would tell her it was impossible. "You know I love you, and you've seen how my parents accept you. 'Twould be wondrous to have you here at Mirail."

Gerard shook his head, and his voice was harsher than usual when he spoke. " 'Tis not possible."

The bleakness in Gerard's words chilled her as much as the night breeze.

"Please let me try. Let me ask my mistress to intercede for you." If Sir Alain could mitigate Jean's sentence, anything was possible, even Gerard's coming to Mirail. "I am certain she will be able to convince Sir Henri to release you."

A soft cry escaped from Gerard's lips. "I wish it were that simple." He stared at Louise for a moment, then sank to the ground and drew her down next to him. "Do you remember this afternoon when I told you I had no relatives at Bleufontaine?"

Louise nodded. Gerard sounded so solemn that her heart began to pound. Something was wrong, very wrong, but she knew not what it was. Unless . . . could Gerard be married? 'Twas something she had once feared. Mayhap 'twas true.

"What I told you was the truth, but not the whole truth," Gerard said. "I wanted you to think I had no sisters or brothers, but I do."

Whatever it was that was causing his anguish, it was not that he was already married. Louise took a deep breath. She could deal with most anything else.

"I don't understand." Louise gripped his hand, hoping that somehow her touch would relieve his pain.

" 'Tis not a pleasant story," he told her. "Are you sure you wish to hear it?" When she nodded, Gerard continued. "I have a sister. A younger sister. When they first meet her, Marie-Claire reminds everyone of an angel. She's so pretty that men were attracted to her from the time she became a young woman, but it didn't matter who they were. She never cared for their attentions. Ever since she was a small child, old enough to say the rosary, we've known that Marie-Claire was different from other children. The only thing she ever wanted was to become a nun.''

Louise smiled. Was it not every family's dream to have either a son or a daughter who would dedicate his or her life to the Church? '' 'Tis wonderful.''

"It would have been, had it not been for Sir Henri." Gerard could not contain his bitterness. "My master is zealous in exercising the *droit du seigneur*. There's not a single young woman on Bleufontaine who has not given her maidenhead to him. I've heard tales that he's no more than a rutting beast and that he likes to cause pain. He even encourages early marriages, because he enjoys deflowering young virgins.''

"But Marie-Claire is safe. Surely he would not violate a nun." It was Louise's turn to shudder. Only a monster would flout the Church's authority in such a heinous way.

Gerard tightened his grip on Louise's hand. "Even Sir Henri is careful not to antagonize the Church. No, he sought another way to gain my sister. He refused to let her enter the convent. Instead he insisted she marry one of the other serfs. She had no choice but to flee Bleufontaine and take sanctuary at the convent.''

Louise's heart went out to the young woman whose deepest beliefs had been threatened. "Did she reach it?''

Gerard nodded. "She is now Sister Marie-Claire at Saint Lazaire. As long as she remains within the convent walls, there is little Sir Henri can do to harm her, but there's still danger. When he's angered, he threatens to storm the convent. I doubt he would do it, but I cannot take the chance. I swear if he tries to hurt my sister, somehow I'll stop him.''

Gerard touched Louise's face, his fingers tracing the outline of her lips. "I cannot leave Bleufontaine, nor can I ask you to come there. You're so beautiful you would not be safe from

Sir Henri. He'd find a way to take you." Gerard groaned. "Louise, I could not bear it if he hurt you the way he has all those other women."

"Oh, my darling, how terrible this all is for you!" Tears streamed down Louise's cheeks. A day ago she would have heard Gerard's tale and felt great compassion, but today, after living through the heart wrenching experience of believing Jean would be hanged, of facing life without her beloved younger brother, Louise felt more than compassion. She knew Gerard's fears and the pain they brought, for she had shared them.

"I knew Sir Henri was not a good master, but never did I dream he was evil. We must stop him. There must be a way we can save your sister and get you released from him."

"You don't know my master. The man is ruthless when he wants something, and he wants my sister. No, my sweet, I fear our love is hopeless."

Gerard's voice was flat with despair. Aching to ease his pain, Louise wrapped her arms around him and drew him close to her.

"We'll find a way," she whispered as she pressed her lips to his.

It was meant to be a comforting gesture, nothing more, but the touch of their lips ignited a spark of passion. All the fear Louise had felt for her brother, all the anguish Gerard's tale had aroused were subsumed by the pure pleasure of their kiss. She tightened her arms around him, then slid one hand underneath his tunic.

His skin was warm against her palm, sinewy rather than smooth. She stroked his back in ever-widening circles.

Gerard groaned. "Oh, my love, that feels so good."

In a day that had been filled with fear and pain, suddenly nothing mattered but to celebrate life in the most time-honored way. This time there would be no stopping. This time they would prove their love in deed as well as word.

With hands made bold by desire, Louise tugged Gerard's tunic over his head and began to loosen the laces of her bliaut. Though his breathing was as ragged as her own, his heart pounding underneath her hand, Gerard took both her hands between his.

"We must stop," he said.

Louise slid her hands from his grip. "No." With a deft movement, she slipped out of her bliaut. "I love you, Gerard, and I want to show you that love in every way I know how."

"But we have no future." It was an argument he had used before. Tonight it held no power over her.

"Only God knows what the future will bring. For myself, I cannot continue to live in the future. What matters is right now."

She punctuated her words with a long, lingering kiss, then removed her tunic. The night air felt cool against her fevered body, and she pressed close to Gerard, seeking warmth and comfort.

Tenderly Gerard placed a hand on either side of Louise's head. "Are you sure?" he asked.

She nodded. "My love, I have never been more sure of anything."

The woman was an enigma.

Alain urged his horse forward, and for a few moments he found comfort in the familiar motion. The steady, predictable sound of Neptune's hoofbeats provided a counterpoint to his turbulent thoughts, reminding him that there were some constants in his life. His wife was not one of them.

It was not that she was mercurial, shifting from one mood to another, for she was not. It was quite simply that he did not understand her. How could the same woman whose head was filled with foolish dreams of chivalry and his brother be such a wise, capable chatelaine? In truth, she was more than a chatelaine. After observing the way she ran the barony, Alain suspected that she had done it for years, that Guillaume had long ago abdicated his responsibilities to her, remaining only as a titular head of the estate.

It was logical. Guillaume had been a dreamer, more suited to scholarly pursuits than the daily running of a large barony.

He must have been relieved when his daughter had proven so capable of assuming the tasks he disliked.

As for Marguerite, it was most unfortunate that she appeared to have inherited not only her father's barony but also his luck in love. First Guillaume and Janelle, now Guillaume's daughter and Janelle's son. Was there some cloud over Mirail that two generations had the poor sense to fall in love with the wrong person?

Alain scanned the horizon, studying the wheat fields. In a fortnight, the fields would be filled with serfs wielding their scythes, preparing another year's harvest. Autumn was the season Alain loved best, a time of maturity, when spring's promise was finally realized and the earth could prepare for its winter rest.

In other years he had found that his own life mirrored the seasons, and that each autumn he would seek to complete tasks to clear the slate for the new year. But this year autumn with Marguerite had brought nothing to fruition. Instead, though he was as ripe as the sheaves of grain, ready for harvest, there was no release for him.

If a man gained sainthood for abstinence, Alain was certain he would soon be canonized. Each night he steeled himself not to touch her, and each night it grew more difficult. She was the most alluring woman he had ever had the misfortune to meet. Just being in the same room with her was enough to make his loins ache, and sharing the same bed! If there were a hell on earth, it could scarcely be more painful than lying only an arm's length from her and being unable to touch her.

He could not. He would not. Though it might bring his body temporary relief, it would surely damn his soul to hell to make love to his wife when it was his brother she desired.

A distant swirl of dust alerted Alain to the emissary's approach. When he recognized the livery, Alain grinned. Perhaps prayers truly were answered. At a minimum, Richard's summons would provide much-needed action. And who knew? Perhaps the time away from Mirail would help him understand the woman he had married.

* * *

"Do you hear me?" Marguerite knelt next to her father's grave. "I need your advice so desperately. I know not what to do."

She laid the sheaf of brightly colored flowers on the ground. The grass had not yet covered the spot where her father had been buried, and she sought to camouflage the raw dirt.

"There are times when I think I imagined that night at Lilis. Oh, Father, Alain was wonderful that night. He was the most tender lover I can imagine. I blush to tell you this, but it was more than a physical act. I truly felt we were part of each other, and that you were right. He was the man for me."

She rocked back on her heels, studying the arrangement of flowers. "That man disappeared as soon as he fell asleep. Now I live with someone who looks like Alain. He wears Alain's clothes and rides his horse, but he acts so differently. 'Tis as though that night never happened." Marguerite fanned the blooms slightly. "The night that Jean killed the deer, I caught a glimpse of the other man. We shared a problem and we worked together to resolve it. But that moment of closeness ended almost before it began. Now we're strangers who share no more than a room."

The autumn breeze ruffled the ends of her hair, setting her braids to swinging. " 'Tis most strange. A year ago, I would have told you I was happy. My life seemed complete, and I could imagine wanting nothing more, save marriage to the courtier of my dreams. Then Alain came. He was not the man of my dreams, but he showed me a side of life I hadn't even dreamt of. At first I thought 'twas only lust, but now I no longer believe that. What we shared was more than that." She tossed her braids over her shoulders as she rose to her feet. "I don't want to continue living the way we do, but I don't know how to change it. None of the books I've read has any advice. Oh, Father, you taught me to rely on myself, and I do. But what if I don't want to? How do I tell Alain that I want to share my life with him?"

Marguerite walked a short distance from the grave, then

turned and regarded the dark mound as though seeking an answer from it. A shudder shook her delicate frame. "Even if I could find the words to tell him, what will I do if he says he doesn't care? Perhaps he sees our marriage as a burden and seeks to escape it. After all, Philippe admitted that he and Janelle feared Alain would not honor the agreement you made and that our marriage would never take place."

As she remembered the gossip the vassals' wives had been so eager to share with her, Marguerite's eyes darkened. What if their stories had been founded on truth? In Marguerite's experience, there was always at least a grain of truth in the tales the troubadours brought. What if Alain loved Honore and that was the reason he had been so hesitant to marry?

She straightened her shoulders and held her head high. Worrying would accomplish nothing. Only Alain could resolve the problem.

Tonight. Tonight they would talk.

"You cannot go!" Marguerite faced Alain, a look of horror on her face. In the distance, a crack of lightning split the sky. Several seconds later the low rumble of thunder reached them, announcing the approach of the storm that had been hovering on the horizon all day.

"What do you mean 'cannot'?" Alain raised one eyebrow in the maddening way he had of telling Marguerite he was displeased. "Serving Richard is my duty."

Her heart plummeted. She had wanted to talk to Alain tonight, but not about this.

"You claimed you wanted to ensure my vassals' loyalty," she told him. "How can you accomplish that if you are traveling with Richard rather than King Louis?"

Alain lowered his eyebrow and regarded her steadily. "This is no surprise to you or to them. From the beginning you have known that my fealty is to Richard. He is my sworn lord, and I owe him my service. Besides," Alain spoke slowly, as though explaining a difficult concept to a child, "it is not as though I were waging war against Louis. I am simply accompanying my liege lord on a journey.''

A glint of excitement lit Alain's eyes, telling Marguerite more clearly than words that he was anxious to join Richard's forces. Or was it simply that he sought a way to leave Mirail?

"All you care about is fighting."

Fat drops of rain began to fall. When one landed on her eyelashes, Marguerite brushed it away.

"As you have pointed out on numerous occasions, my dear Marguerite, I am a warrior. Warriors fight. It is what we are bred to do. Surely that comes as no surprise to you."

"Is it that?" she demanded. "Or are you so bored here at Mirail that you seek any excuse to leave?"

The heavens opened, releasing sheets of rain.

"What I seek is an excuse to get out of the rain." Alain took Marguerite's hand in his and began to run toward the castle. When they reached the Great Hall, he shook the water from his hair. "What is the real issue, Marguerite? Why are you concerned that I am leaving? It is not as though you needed me. You are eminently capable of running the barony alone, a fact you've sought to impress on me on numerous occasions. Every time I've tried to contribute even the slightest assistance to the running of the barony, you've acted as though I were stealing your first born child."

Alain paused for a moment and stripped off his sodden cloak. "Don't think I'm unaware that you threatened to whip anyone who sought my advice and that you've done everything in your power to keep the people of Mirail from me. So tell me, Marguerite, why do you care that I am leaving?"

Though his words were matter-of-fact, there was an underlying tone that startled Marguerite by its intensity.

"What if I did need you?" she asked. "Would you stay?"

Alain shrugged. "The question is rhetorical, since you don't need me."

"Answer me. Would you stay?" Silence was his only response. Goaded by Alain's continuing refusal to answer, Marguerite said, "A true chevalier would stay with his lady." She paused a moment, then added, "Charles would not leave."

Alain narrowed his eyes, and the foreboding expression on his face made Marguerite flinch. When he spoke, his voice was calm, almost amused. "To your everlasting regret, my dear, it should be apparent that I am not Charles."

# Chapter Fifteen

"I knew you would welcome her as a sister."

They had arrived without warning, Charles and his bride. For a few hours there had been a flurry of activity as Diane supervised the unloading of the household goods she had brought with her, their completeness telling Marguerite more clearly than words that Diane expected her stay at Mirail to be a lengthy one. Servants had scurried in all directions under Diane's quiet but firm commands. Then silence had descended once again on the Great Hall. Now it was deserted save for Marguerite and Charles, who had remained behind when his bride made one last trip to the chamber they would share that evening.

Marguerite looked at Charles, remembering the first time she had seen him. So much was the same. She had first met Charles here, before the still glowing embers of the fireplace. Then, as now, his clothes had been stained with travel. Then, as now, they had been alone in the room. And yet so much was different. 'Twas more than the fact that they were both married, much more. Today it was difficult to imagine how she had ever mistaken Charles for Lancelot. Oh, he was pleasant enough to look at, but he was certainly not heroic. And the words which came from his lips were mundane rather than poetic.

"Diane is precious to me," Charles continued. "I beg you keep her safe for me."

Though her smile never faltered, Marguerite felt a twinge of annoyance. The last thing she needed now that Alain was leaving was the burden of Charles's simpering bride. Was it not enough that she would have to deal with the harvest and the winter preparations alone? Now she was expected to entertain a woman who appeared to need constant attendance.

"Was there a reason Diane could not remain at Lilis?" She understood why Charles had stopped at Mirail on his way to answer Richard's summons. Not only would it be preferable to travel with his brother rather than alone, but Mirail was directly between Lilis and Poitiers, where the men were to meet their liege lord. Diane's arrival was not so easily explained.

"Hugh and Gisaine have journeyed to Lancy," Charles explained, referring to Diane's parents. "They left almost immediately after our wedding, saying they needed to meet with the bailiff there. Diane suspects 'twas only an excuse and that they wanted to give us time alone." His eyes sparkled as he added, "I don't have to tell you what it's like for newly married couples, do I? You know how important it is to have time together. When Richard's summons came, Diane decided she would prefer to come here rather than stay alone at Lilis."

Marguerite suppressed a smile. "Alone" at Lilis meant having the company of a hundred serfs as well as a well-provisioned troop of guards. She could not imagine how Diane would have been lonely there or how she could have lacked activities to occupy every waking moment. Any barony, even the best managed, needed constant attention. How could Diane have left her home without proper supervision?

There was no point in raising questions that had no answers, and so Marguerite said simply, "Of course Diane is welcome at Mirail, but 'tis a busy season. I fear I will have little time to visit with your bride."

Charles shook his blond head. "She came here for safety as much as companionship."

"Safety?" This time Marguerite was unable to disguise her surprise. Lilis's guard was larger than Mirail's, and the château was so well fortified that it had never been attacked. If it was her personal safety that worried Diane, she could always do as Marguerite had been taught and sleep with a knife under her pillow.

"You may not understand, for you are much stronger than Diane, but she was afraid to remain alone. I know you'll keep her safe."

Indeed much had changed from that first day she had met Charles. Then he had sung her praises, vowing to protect her from all dangers as though she were weak. Now he recognized her strength and was begging her to protect his wife.

Charles gave a furtive glance around the room, as though assuring himself they were alone. Then he reached a hand into his tunic and withdrew a piece of parchment. "I beg you to accept this humble offering." He unrolled the parchment and presented it to her.

It was a poem, one which even the most skilled of troubadours would have been proud to call his own. As she read the neatly inscribed words, tears stung Marguerite's eyes. 'Twas a beautiful piece of poetry, a work of art. In another time and place it would have stirred her senses. Today it merely aroused a faint nostalgia, and when she reached the final stanza, Marguerite felt naught but a sense of relief.

In beautifully rhyming verses, Charles had declared his love for her, tempering the words with the explanation that the love was that of a brother for a sister. Though they had shared a few magical moments, he now knew that his feelings for Marguerite were a pale shadow compared to his love for Diane. While he vowed that he would never forget Marguerite, it was Diane who had captured his heart and whom he would love for eternity.

Much, indeed, had changed, and for her part Marguerite had no regrets.

" 'Tis beautiful," she told Charles as she tucked the poem into her bliaut. "I shall cherish it as a memory of the dreams we once shared."

Charles smiled. "You have found your Lancelot, and I have my Guinevere."

Later that day as Marguerite slipped the poem into the wooden trunk at the foot of her bed, she sighed. If only Charles's words had been true! If only Alain were Lancelot.

Sheets of rain obliterated the horizon, and puddles had begun to form on the floor. When it rained, Bleufontaine was not a pleasant place to live, for water trickled through gaps in the walls, and the cold breeze brought a pervasive dampness to even those rooms where fires were permitted. On days like these, Henri cursed his ancestors for failing to hire skilled artisans and himself for having to live in such squalor.

Today was different. Though the rain pelted down and his shoes squished as he stepped in a puddle, Henri could not repress a grin. Truly, the fates were with him. Though the sun might not be shining, his lucky star was.

The traveling peddlers had brought the story, and if they were surprised by the extra coin Henri had thrown their way, they had said naught, merely repeated the tale that Richard the Lionheart had summoned his vassals to Poitiers. There was no doubt about it. The despicable cur would soon be gone, following his liege lord's command. That would leave the beautiful Marguerite alone. Lonely, unprotected, more vulnerable than ever. Yes, indeed, fate was with him.

He had been right to bide his time, to plot his course. Now the planning was complete. It was time for the execution.

"Oh, Marguerite, I don't know how you can bear to have him leave."

Louise drew a strand of crimson wool through the altar cloth she and Marguerite were embroidering. They sat in the solar, alone for the first time since Diane and Charles had arrived the day before. Though a damp chill kept Marguerite indoors, Diane and Charles had announced their intention to stroll in the garden.

As for Alain, he was outdoors somewhere, perhaps with his destrier whose company he appeared to prefer over his wife's.

Louise's dark head was bent, but as she raised it to face Marguerite, her eyes glistened with tears.

"There is no choice." Marguerite's reply was pragmatic. "Alain has made it quite clear that his duty to Richard is greater than his duty to me and to Mirail." She would not tell Louise that Alain had appeared anxious to leave, for the woman—like everyone else on the barony—would hear no ill of her new master. He had saved Jean's life, and that alone made him a hero to Louise.

" 'Twill be lonely with him gone."

The unmistakable pain in Louise's voice made Marguerite pause. Such anguish was not caused by Alain's imminent departure. Though the man appeared to inspire loyalty, Marguerite knew he was not the reason for Louise's sorrow.

"You miss Gerard." It was a statement, not a question.

Louise nodded, and the tears which had been threatening spilled from her eyes. "I never dreamt it could grow worse, but 'tis far worse now."

For a moment Marguerite looked at her, uncomprehending. Then she asked softly, "Now? What is different now?" Louise's blush answered her question. "When did it happen?"

Brushing the tears from her cheeks, Louise smiled. "The night Sir Alain pardoned Jean." Louise clasped her hands together. "Oh, Marguerite, it was more beautiful than anything I ever dreamed. I never knew there could be pleasure like that." She began to sob again. "Now it is worse. I cannot bear the thought that we may not see each other again. How can I live without him? Gerard and I belong together."

Marguerite placed a comforting arm around Louise's shoulders. "You will see him. I promise. When Alain returns, he and I will visit my vassals. You may go with us on the journey to Bleufontaine."

A glimmer of hope lit Louise's face and Marguerite smiled. At least one person at Mirail ought to be happy.

* * *

She tugged on the weed for the third time, then when it refused to leave the ground, dug her knife into the earth around it. It had only been two days since the rain. The ground ought not to have dried so thoroughly. But nothing at Mirail appeared easy these days. Even so simple a task as weeding her herb garden proved exasperatingly difficult.

"Did you hear the news?"

Marguerite looked up at the sound of Jean's voice. The boy was skipping as though he had not a care in the world, and his voice bubbled with glee.

"No," she said with a quick smile. His exuberance was contagious, reminding her of the time when life had seemed simple.

"He told me when he returned he'd teach me how to care for his armor." Jean thrust his shoulders back, strutting with pride.

There was no need to ask who "he" was. Only one man on the barony would have had that effect on Jean. "Our lord is very wise," she said calmly. "He knows that of all the young men on Mirail, you will surely be the most careful with his armor. Good armor, you know, is valuable."

Jean nodded solemnly. "He told me that. He said a knight owned nothing of more value than his armor. Not even his horse."

And most assuredly not his wife.

"Mère says he's the best lord Mirail has ever had. We're very lucky to have him."

Indeed! It appeared everyone on the barony shared the same opinion of their new lord. It was what she wanted, of course. Her people were contented, and that was important, for happy serfs were more productive. There was no need for them to know the truth, that the man who showed such warmth and such wisdom in dealing with them was a cold, heartless stranger to his wife.

"Mère says we will celebrate his saint's day every year."

Undoubtedly so would everyone on the barony. They would

never know that Alain's saint day was no more real than the courtesy he accorded his wife in public.

"Let me look at your back." Under different circumstances Marguerite would have cared for Jean's lacerated back herself, but this time she had recognized that her authority as chatelaine of Mirail was at risk, and so she had given Jean's mother a special unguent to apply to his wounds rather than care for him herself and lessen the impact of the punishment.

The flesh was still red and puckered, but it was no longer raw. "You are nearly healed," she told Jean.

He grinned. "All the other boys want to see my back," he confessed. "They think I was brave."

Marguerite rolled her eyes. There was no accounting for popular opinion. Though it should have been otherwise, it appeared that rather than being a stigma, Jean's scars had become a badge of courage. If this was the barony's idea of logic, 'twas no wonder those same people thought Alain was the perfect lord.

"Where is my gray tunic?"

Marguerite looked up in surprise. Alain did not normally enter her chamber until far later in the evening when she had retired to bed.

"I believe 'tis in the chest." She rose from her seat by the fire and took a step toward Alain, meaning to help him find the tunic. It was too late. He had already thrust back the lid and was rummaging through the contents. Marguerite sighed. The care she and Louise had taken to fold each garment was lost as Alain pushed fine silk and woolens aside in his search.

"M'lord, let me help."

More clothing tumbled onto the floor.

"Are you sure . . . ?" Alain stopped in midsentence. "What is this?" He held up a piece of rolled parchment.

Marguerite felt the blood drain from her face. Sweet Mary above, how was she going to explain this? She had given no thought to Charles's poem since she had tucked it into the chest. Indeed, it had been nostalgia, pure and simple, which had led her to keep the verses, nothing more damning. 'Twas nothing more than an innocent poem from a friend, as Alain would discover if he read the words, and she had kept it as a memento of that friendship. Unfortunately, Marguerite held little hope that her husband would believe that. If there was one thing she knew, it was that Alain was not reasonable where she and his brother were concerned.

" 'Tis naught." She reached for the scroll. "A receipt for special unguents."

The firelight flickered, casting shadows on Alain's face. "A most unusual place to store receipts, is it not? Surely the book of records where the other *receipts* are kept would be more appropriate." He straightened the parchment. "Still, I confess I'm curious about the ingredients in this special unguent." He looked down at the carefully penned letters, obviously recognizing the handwriting. For an instant, an emotion Marguerite could not identify crossed his face only to be replaced with one she knew well.

"I had hoped you would outgrow this foolishness."

His words were cold, clipped and so filled with anger that Marguerite took an involuntary step backwards. When she realized what she had done, she took two steps forward. The man was not going to intimidate her. After all, there was no crime in saving a poem.

"It is not what you think it is."

He raised one eyebrow. "Spare me the lies. I can see quite clearly that this is no receipt for an unguent, special or otherwise. Now, tell me the truth . . . if you can, that is. Is it or is it not a poem from my brother?"

"It is, but . . ."

Alain crumpled the parchment, his knuckles turning white from the tight grip he kept on it. "At least you don't deny it."

" 'Twould indeed be foolish to deny something so obvious." Marguerite felt the anger which had been simmering deep inside her begin to bubble to the surface. She was not a recalcitrant child who needed discipline, and she would not be treated as one. " 'Tis obvious that it *was* a poem before you decided to destroy it. I kept it as I would other possessions, a ribbon . . ."

Alain shook his head. "Do not try to convince me that this meant nothing special to you. You would not have saved it if it had not."

Marguerite met his gaze, her eyes as angry as his as she bit her tongue to keep from speaking. 'Twas apparent Alain had not read Charles's words, for if he had he would have realized the poem was not a lover's. 'Twould be so simple to tell him to unfold the parchment and read the words inscribed on it. But that would prove naught. The man should believe her and not require further proof. Her word alone should be enough. If he did not trust her on something so basic, there was no hope for them.

Alain brandished the parchment as though it were a sword. "Marguerite, I vow I do not understand why you persist in these foolish dreams. All I know is that I must put an end to them."

With three long strides, he reached the fire and tossed the parchment onto the flames. As Charles's words turned to ashes, Alain turned to his wife, and this time his mien was devoid of anger.

" 'Tis apparent you crave things I have not given you. Mayhap I'm at fault for that." He glanced at the fire, as though assuring himself that no trace of Charles's poem remained. "You have oft accused me of lacking chivalry, though even you must admit that I have provided you with the protection a knight owes his lady. Still, you are right when you say that I have failed to give you poetry." Alain stared at her for a long moment, as though daring her to dispute him. At length he said, "If it is poetry you want, then poetry you'll have. But make no mistake, Marguerite. 'Tis I and only I who shall give it to you."

Slowly and deliberately, he walked to the door and latched it.

"What are you doing?" Marguerite demanded. Never before had she or Alain latched the door, for no one at Mirail would dare disturb them. The closed door was as effective a barrier as a lowered portcullis.

"I am preparing to be a poet," he said simply. "Now come

here, my sweet bride.'' Alain gestured to the carved chair where
Marguerite had sat earlier that evening. Though his voice was
once more calm, there was no mistaking his intent. It was a
command, not an invitation.

Marguerite hesitated. This was a side of her husband she
had not seen, and she mistrusted it. Though Alain might claim
he was going to give her poetry, 'twas so foreign to his nature
that she could not believe it. Nay, the man had something else
in mind. This was another tactic in his battle plan.

''Charles's poem was harmless.''

''As indeed this will be,'' Alain replied smoothly. ''I assure
you, I mean you no harm. All I ask is your time. Surely that
is not too much to request. After all, I *am* your husband, the
man to whom you pledged your vows. If you can spend hours
reading Charles's poetry—or shall we continue to call it a
receipt for your special unguent?—surely you can spare a few
moments for my poem. Now, come.''

He took her hand and led her to the chair, waiting until she
sat. For a long moment, he did naught but stand staring at her.
It was unnerving, having him tower over her. Undoubtedly
Alain had planned this carefully, recognizing that being seated
would place her at an even greater disadvantage. However, if
he thought she'd capitulate so easily, he had sorely misjudged
his opponent.

Marguerite met Alain's gaze, determined that he would be
the first to break it. Though there was no way she could best
him in a physical challenge, she would not let him win in a
contest of wills. This was one time when Alain would have to
accept defeat. His eyes were dark, and she had no need to see
his clenched jaw to know that he held his anger under a tight
rein. Indeed, the anger emanating from him heated her more
than the fire at her back, fueling her own fury. She had done
naught to deserve the suspicion with which he regarded her
every act.

''Poetry, that's what the lady wanted.'' Alain spoke as though
to himself. ''I believe a *preux chevalier* would kneel.'' He sank
to his knees in front of Marguerite. Oddly, though it was the

position of a suppliant, Alain seemed no less a warrior when
he knelt. Was this yet another weapon in his arsenal?

"Flowers and poetry, they tell me, are what my lady desires.
Alas, I have no flowers, and so my rhymes will have to suffice."
His tone, laden with sarcasm, gave lie to the gentle words.

"What are you trying to do?" Marguerite demanded.

"I thought 'twas obvious. I seek to give you what you desire:
courtly words and empty promises. Correct me if I am mistaken,
but I distinctly remember your saying those were important to
you. If that were not enough, you further underscored your
preferences by the fact that you cherished my brother's poem.
As I told you before, since you crave poetry, I shall give it to
you. Now, do not interrupt me, I beg you."

Alain reached for her hand, capturing it between both of his.
When she tried to withdraw it, he shook his head in a silent
command. He stared at her hand for a moment, his expression
pensive; then he spoke.

> The scent of flowers fills the land,
> But none compares to Marguerite's hand.

His voice was soft, his words as pretty as any courtier's.
Only the inflection told Marguerite that this was a charade, that
he sought to mock her dreams. Because there was no feeling
behind them, his words were as empty as he had promised they
would be, a shell with no substance.

This was not the poetry she craved, and well he knew it.
But, oh, how easily it could be! If only Alain trusted her. If
only he loved her.

Unfortunately, he did not.

Marguerite felt the anger begin to drain from her, replaced
by a deep sadness. She waited for his next mocking words, but
instead Alain raised her hand to his mouth and pressed a kiss
on her smallest fingertip.

"Stop!" She had not bargained for this.

"I thought I told you that I did not wish to be interrupted."
His lips were so close to her fingers that she could feel them

move as he spoke. Then he lowered them a fraction of an inch and kissed her ring finger.

Marguerite shuddered. Alain's lips were warm and moist. She closed her eyes, and for an instant she was back on the riverbank, reliving the night Alain had first kissed her hand. He had been playing a game then, as he was now. Unfortunately, though his words and his kisses were a mockery, the pounding of her blood was all too real. He had done naught but kiss two fingers, and her memory, her traitorous, traitorous memory, reminded her of the magic his lips could conjure, of the exquisite joy he had wrought that night at Lilis.

As he drew her small finger into his mouth and began to suckle it, reason returned. Marguerite jerked her hand away from him.

"No."

Alain's only response was a soft laugh as he recaptured her hand and began to kiss her palm. When he withdrew his lips, he kept a tight grip on her hand and once again raised his eyes to meet hers.

> Magicians seek the hidden charm
> That will keep the land from harm.
> No sorcery found on field or farm
> Can match the sight of my lady's arm.

He pushed back the sleeve of her nightrail. Though his words spoke of sight, Alain was not satisfied with looking at Marguerite's arm. Instead, he trailed kisses up her forearm, then stopped when he reached her elbow. As he recited another rhyme, Marguerite giggled.

"Is aught wrong?" he asked.

" 'Tis only that no one has written a poem to my elbow."

"Perhaps you've not had the right lover." Alain kissed the body part in question, tracing circles with his tongue. When he spoke again, there was a catch in his voice, and Marguerite was not certain whether it was caused by laughter or something else.

"Your elbow is so fair it, and not Helen's face, could have

launched the Trojan ships. As it is, you have launched my desire.''

This time it was Marguerite's breath that caught as his lips moved up her arm. 'Twas not only Alain's desire that had been unleashed. Her blood was pounding, and every nerve ending tingled. When he reached her shoulder, she shivered in anticipation, remembering the nights they had shared and how his lips and fingers had caressed the sensitive hollow of her throat.

She ought to resist him. Dear Lord, she ought to. The man had accused her of being a witch, when in truth, 'twas he who had bewitched her. Though her mind urged her to resist, her body ignored the commands, remembering instead the sweet magic he had made. Soon he would reach her throat, and then her lips. And then . . .

But instead of continuing upward, Alain lowered his head. He reached for her foot and carefully removed the soft velvet slipper. For a moment he did nothing more than hold her foot in his hand, his palm clasped around her instep. Then his fingers began to move, gently stroking the sensitive skin.

She had never thought of her foot as a sensuous object, and had never dreamt that a man's touch—Alain's touch—could ignite such feelings of delight. Something so wondrous must be sinful; 'twas the only explanation.

> Like petals on a fresh pink rose
> So I find my lady's toes.

The mocking tone he had employed when he composed the verse in honor of his fingers was gone, replaced by the huskiness she had heard once before, on that night in Lilis.

As he had with her fingers, Alain kissed each of her toes, then transferred his attention to her instep. His hands moved upward, caressing her leg, sending an almost unbearable warmth spreading throughout her as his lips followed the trail his fingers had blazed.

Marguerite gasped with pleasure. This was magic, pure magic.

"Does my poetry please you?" His voice was low and intimate.

She chuckled, a soft, joyous sound like the babbling of a brook. "In truth, Alain, 'tis your actions I prefer."

His laughter joined hers, resonating from the walls. "Then we are most fortunate that I am a man of action, are we not?"

Alain rose to his feet and in one fluid motion drew Marguerite from the chair into his arms. A moment later all words were forgotten.

# Chapter Sixteen

The morning air was cold, the sky filled with flocks of birds obeying their centuries-old instinct to fly to warmer lands. It was a time when most men would have preferred to remain at home, enjoying the warmth of their hearths and the even warmer embraces of their wives or, should they not have been so blessed, a willing wench. As he spurred his destrier, Alain thanked the Lord and all His saints that he was not most men. This was what he loved above all—being back in armor, ready to serve his liege lord. This was where he belonged—with men who knew the meaning of loyalty. And if this time the satisfaction he had always derived from commanding a group of highly skilled warriors seemed somehow lacking, 'twas surely only that his memories had glossed over the petty aggravations that seemed to weigh so heavily on this journey.

"Mornings! How I hate them!" Charles grumbled as he reined his horse in next to Alain. "The only good thing about mornings was waking up with Diane in my bed."

Alain grinned. His brother made no pretense of enjoying the journey, but took every opportunity to remind Alain of all that he had left behind, bemoaning the fate that had taken him from his bride and the pleasures of the marriage bed.

"A year ago, even six months ago, 'twould not have been so bad. But now that we're both married, we have other responsibilities." Charles's complaints formed a familiar refrain, punctuating the days they spent on the road.

"Indeed, it is different," Alain admitted. Marriage to Marguerite had proven far different from his expectations, although that was one confidence he would never share with his brother. He had expected an empty-headed bride, concerned with little more than matching ribbons to her gowns. Instead, Marguerite had proven both sharp witted, and—as he had learned from bitter experience—sharp tongued.

There were times when Alain thought that an empty head might have been preferable. Then at least he could have excused her silly infatuation with Charles as the product of a mind incapable of deeper reasoning. But Marguerite was no addle-brained chit. She was a highly intelligent, eminently capable woman who made no secret of the role she expected him to play in her life. He was to be the figurehead baron and, it appeared, he would be welcomed into her bed only if he plied her with poetry and all the other senseless trappings of what she called chivalry.

'Twas galling to realize that his bride had responded to his lovemaking only twice, and in both cases he had been no more than a proxy for his brother. For the first time, that night in Lilis that even now haunted his memory, she had dreamed of Charles, turning to him in her distress. And the night he had found Charles's poem, he had behaved as she would have expected Charles to. Not once had she wanted him—Alain de Jarnac—as he was.

What a fool he had been to believe it could have been different.

"I never thought marriage would be so satisfying."

Alain gave Charles a sharp look. "Then you are happy?"

"By all the saints above, I am." Charles shifted his shield, then admitted, " 'Tis not what I had expected, although I wonder how either of us could have formed any valid opinion of the state of matrimony. 'Twas not as though we had a shining example to study."

Alain looked at Charles, surprised by both his comment and the introspection it revealed. Though he and Charles were brothers, they had spent most of their lives apart, first being fostered at different baronies, then being separated while Alain was in Outremer. During the few hours they had been in each other's company over the past decade, Charles's conversation had centered on his latest dalliance with one or more ladies of the court. Never had he expressed a thought more serious than speculation over which of the Queen's attendants was still a virgin.

"What do you mean?" Alain asked.

"I would not call our mother and Philippe's marriage one of the world's best. Would you?" As a rabbit scurried in front of them, Charles gave the reins a light tug, keeping the horse's hooves from striking the small body. "Did you ever wonder if Mère was happy?"

The image of Janelle's tear-stained face and his own confrontation with Philippe flashed through Alain's memory. That was one particular conversation he had no intention of sharing with Charles. Instead he said mildly, "Happiness is a much overrated commodity, as Janelle herself would have told you. I doubt she expected it. After all, we know that she married Philippe to protect herself and her unborn child, not because she had suddenly developed a passion for the man. He was her friend." That much was true. There was no need for Charles to learn the other reason Janelle had married when she did or the relationship she had had with her other "friend."

Alain shifted in the saddle, moving deliberately so that his brother could not see his face as he spoke. "Janelle was probably as happy as she could be under the circumstances. I suspect she never fully recovered from Robert's death." Knowing what he did, Alain could not force himself to refer to the man as Charles's father.

"Then you agree with me that there was no outward sign of affection between Janelle and Philippe."

Alain's laugh was rueful. "Charles, I must defer to your judgment on this topic. After all, you spent far more time in their company than I did. I rarely saw the two of them together."

"Diane is so different from our mother." Charles's voice warmed as he spoke of his bride. "She does not hesitate to show me how much she loves me. Sometimes it's just a smile; other times a touch."

The sharp pain Alain felt in his stomach must have been the result of an overripe apple. It could not possibly be caused by the realization that not once had his bride given him a special smile or a touch.

Charles continued speaking. "Diane was fortunate. She had Hugh and Gisaine as an example. You'd be amazed, Alain. Though they've been married almost two score years, they still act like newlyweds. Diane tells me that the serfs take great pride in the fact that not once has Hugh exercised the *droit du seigneur.*"

"And you?" Alain could not resist teasing his brother. "In your lengthy marriage, have you felt the need to deflower a virgin?"

"Of course not! Diane is the only woman I need."

Marriage had indeed changed his brother. As they rode toward Poitiers, Alain reflected on Charles's comments. Perhaps there was some truth to the theory that a man and woman needed to learn about marriage by observing others. That was how a boy learned to fight, first by watching knights, then by emulating them. 'Twas true that Marguerite had been raised without a mother and, therefore, without an example of marriage. It was possible that that lack was one reason she had such unrealistic expectations of her own marriage. The question was, how did one overcome such a handicap?

"I am most grateful to be here. Lilis would have been lonely with Charles gone."

Diane had joined Marguerite and Louise as they sat in the solar, embroidering the border on another altar cloth. Though her fingers moved swiftly when she worked, Marguerite noticed that Diane spent as many minutes apparently contemplating the design as she did plying needle and thread.

"Surely you found much to occupy you at home. Lilis is as large as Mirail, and the chatelaine's role is a full one."

Diane rested the fine linen on her lap before she looked at Marguerite. "Like any barony Lilis needs but one chatelaine, and that's my mother. Although she'd deny it if you asked her, I know she would be hurt if I tried to assume more responsibilities." Diane lowered her voice, as though to keep her words from becoming the subject of castle gossip. "I believe she fears growing old, and if she were to relinquish those tasks that have made her life complete, she would be admitting that she is no longer in her prime."

Parents, Marguerite reflected, were as different as the blossoms in her garden. Her father had been more than pleased when she had been able to assume much of the daily running of Mirail, for that had freed him to hunt and devote himself to his books. But Diane, it appeared, had been frozen in perpetual childhood, unable to assume the responsibilities of a normal adult. 'Twas no wonder she often seemed childlike.

"Surely you know how to spin and weave." Louise exchanged a glance with Marguerite, expressing her surprise at Diane's revelations.

Diane picked up her needlework and took another stitch. " 'Tis not knowledge I lack. In truth, I can both spin and weave well. What I lack is practice in directing others."

"Marguerite has been doing that—and much more—all her life." There was pride in Louise's voice. Because of Marguerite, Mirail was an unusual barony, a fact that had become a source of pride for its inhabitants.

"The peddlers and troubadours brought that tale to Lilis. 'Twas one of the reasons I sought to come here." Her eyes met Marguerite's, and there was a gentle pleading in them. "I need to prepare myself to be a proper wife for Charles, and so I would like to learn how you run the barony."

Marguerite raised one brow. This was not the story Charles had given her when he had explained why Diane wished to live at Mirail. "I thought you were . . ." Marguerite searched for a polite term. She would not embarrass Diane by admitting that Charles had told her his bride was afraid to remain alone.

". . . reluctant . . ." There were no especially pejorative connotations to that word. ". . . to stay at Lilis."

The peal of laughter which escaped from Diane's lips startled Marguerite. "Let us not mince words. You heard that I was afraid." Diane laughed again. "That was the story I told Charles, because I knew it was one he would understand and which would provoke no argument. How could he refuse to bring me here when I had such a compelling reason for leaving my home? Besides, my confession made him feel needed. Like any man, he excels when you arouse his protective instincts." Diane looked from Marguerite to Louise and back. "The ploy worked; did it not?"

Marguerite lowered her eyes, lest Louise read her speculation. It appeared there was more to Diane than the brainless female she had first seemed to be. In her own quiet way, she could be a formidable opponent.

"He's nigh!" The glow in Louise's cheeks owed naught to artifice. Indeed, her face had been radiant from the moment the guards had announced the identity of the approaching visitors. "He says he brings you a message from the king."

Marguerite suppressed a smile but could not prevent a hint of humor from making its way into her words. "I would venture that your enthusiasm is for the possible presence of a certain member of Henri de Bleufontaine's entourage rather than for the message he brings me."

"Mayhap." Louise blushed as she met Marguerite's steady gaze.

Marguerite rolled up her needlework and walked toward the stairway. With Alain gone, she would greet Henri in the Great Hall rather than the courtyard. Still, she wished to be there when he entered the room. "If Gerard is here, spend every minute you can with him."

Louise's grin widened. " 'Tis generous of you to offer, but who will assist you dressing tonight?"

"Béatrice can help me," she said, referring to Clothilde's

youngest daughter. "Clothilde mentioned that she wanted to learn how to handle my clothing."

As they descended the steep staircase, Louise said, "It seems you're running a school for females in training. First Diane and now Béatrice. But," she added quickly, "I'm not complaining. Not if I can be with Gerard."

Henri was garbed in his finest blue robes, and Marguerite noted that he was freshly shaven. Even his hair seemed to have been recently groomed. Although he was normally well dressed, never had Marguerite seen him take such pains with his appearance. Perhaps this was the result of his meeting with the king. If a man viewed himself as a royal messenger, there was no telling how he might react, what airs he might assume.

"What is the message you have brought?" she asked. They were standing in a window embrasure of the Great Hall, Henri with his back to the light.

He lowered his voice. "Later, when we are alone. I promised the king I would deliver it in private."

The sun in her eyes kept Marguerite from seeing the nuances of Henri's expression. "When were you in Paris?" Never before had King Louis sent messages other than through his royal emissaries, but if Henri had been at the court, perhaps Louis had felt no need for a member of his entourage to make the journey.

Henri shook his head. "I have not been to Paris," he admitted. "I met the king by chance when we were both hunting near Angers."

Though his voice was steady, it had an undertone, a note which disturbed Marguerite. There was something false about Henri's story. Perhaps he had not met the king by chance. Perhaps he had deliberately approached their monarch. But if he had, what had been his motive? Could it be, as Alain and her father had feared, that the vassals were truly dissatisfied? Marguerite felt her stomach knot as she considered the possibility that Henri had asked the king to relieve him of his fealty to Mirail.

"We most certainly will discuss this later," she told Henri.


The room was dark, lit only by a single torch. With no windows, it should have been musty, yet it smelled of springtime, for Louise had swept out the old rushes, replacing them with freshly gathered ones, and she had sprinkled some of Marguerite's herbs in the corners.

"Oh, Gerard." Her heart caught in her throat as his familiar form appeared in the doorway. When Henri's entourage had filed into the Great Hall, she had managed to whisper a message, telling Gerard she would be waiting in the storeroom that she had come to think of as their chamber, but until he had arrived, she had feared that Henri would demand Gerard's presence.

"I was so afraid we would not be together again." She breathed the words against his mouth, savoring the sweetness of his breath, trying to erase the memory of the nights she had spent alone, dreaming of his embrace.

" 'Tis most unusual. Henri seems almost carefree these past few days, and he has not threatened my sister at all. I've never seen him like this."

"I shan't question the reason, not when it's brought you to me. Oh, Gerard!"

Louise drew him down to the pallet she had placed in one corner of the room. As her arms encircled his body and her hands moved greedily along his back, relearning the patterns of his muscles, she spoke softly. "I feel almost guilty being here with you when Marguerite sleeps alone."

Gerard, who had been nuzzling the side of her neck, stopped. "Did your mistress ask you to stay with her?"

"I beg you, don't stop. Um . . . that feels so good." Louise swallowed deeply. "In truth, Marguerite sent me to you."

With a low chuckle, Gerard resumed his exploration of her body. "In that case, I can think of far better uses for your lips than talking."

* * *

She was almost asleep, in that hazy state where reality blends with dreams and where reactions are dulled by the approach of sleep. When she heard the sound of the door opening and footsteps crossing the room, she snuggled deeper into the mattress. It must be late, or Alain would not have come to their chamber.

Seconds later, the bed curtains were jerked aside, and a heavy body landed on the bed. The last vestiges of sleep vanished, swept away by the unfamiliar scent and sounds that invaded her senses.

The man in her bed was not Alain.

Blood began to pound in her temples as fear replaced surprise.

"Henri! What are you doing here?" Even in the dim light, Marguerite recognized her vassal and the fact that he was stark naked.

His laugh sent a chill through her bones. "I have come for what should by rights have been mine. You, my sweet Marguerite."

With one of the deft movements that made him so successful as a warrior, Henri grasped Marguerite's face in both hands and pulled her toward him. He ground his lips against hers, forcing hers to part, and thrust his tongue inside her mouth.

"No!" Marguerite's scream was lost, muffled by his wet embrace. She pushed with all her might, trying to break away from him, but 'twas for naught.

He chuckled, as though her struggles amused him.

Henri gripped her wrists in one big hand, then used the other to push her back onto the mattress. When she started to move, he covered her body with his.

"Better. Much better." He began to move rhythmically against her, matching his movements to the thrusts of his tongue.

Marguerite started to gag. His breath was fetid, his tongue a disgusting instrument of humiliation that threatened to choke the very life from her. She struggled to loosen the grip of his hands, but to no avail. The man was bigger and stronger than she. Her only hope was to use surprise as a weapon.

She opened her jaw as wide as she could, then clamped it closed, biting his tongue.

"Ow!"

Henri jerked his face away from her. For a long moment he stared at her, his expression malevolent. Then he laughed. "So you like it rough, do you? How fortunate that I do, too." He grasped a lock of her hair and gave it a sharp tug that brought tears to her eyes.

"You will never get away with this."

Henri twisted the hair between his fingers, drawing another gasp of pain from Marguerite before he gripped her chin with one hand. "That is where you are wrong, my sweet. I shall indeed escape scot free. You will have no proof, for tonight there are no witnesses. There never are."

He chuckled as his hand tightened the pressure on her chin, bruising the smooth skin. "Besides, no one would believe I forced you. They all know you want me. They've seen the way you look at me. Who will say nay when I tell them how you begged me to come to your bed?"

The man was deranged. 'Twas the only explanation. But Marguerite knew that a disturbed mind did not diminish a man's power. To the contrary, it could increase it, if he was reckless or was so convinced of his omnipotence that he took fewer precautions than a sane man would have.

Marguerite's mind raced, seeking an answer. The odds of success were slim, but they were better than the alternative. She had only one chance of escaping him, and even that was lost if she could not free her hands.

"M'lord," she said, trying to keep the pain and fear from her voice, "surely you know a maiden wishes to be wooed with words first."

Henri's lip curled. "I have no need for words. What I need is to feel you." He squeezed her breast, bringing tears to her eyes. "Every bit of you." His hand moved to her other breast, bruising it with the force of his grip.

"I want to plant my seed inside you . . . see my child swelling your womb." His laugh held more than a hint of madness. "What sweet justice it will be, knowing that the mighty Alain de Jarnac is raising a bastard as his son. My bastard. Oh, Marguerite, you should have been mine." His hand roved down her body. "And now you will be."

As his lips captured hers, his hand reached for the hem of her nightrail. With one swift movement, he ripped it, exposing her body to the night air and his gaze.

"Ah, sweet!" His eyes glazed with lust as he stared at her flesh.

Marguerite tried not to cringe. Though the man's gaze was as great a violation as his hands had been, she could not . . . would not . . . admit her fear. That would give Henri yet another weapon in this unbalanced contest.

She would escape. She had to. Marguerite tugged again, trying to loosen her hands from his grip.

"Please, m'lord. Would you not grant me the pleasure of touching you?" It was a lie, a monstrous lie, but mayhap the man was deluded enough to believe it. Dear Lord, please make him believe it.

Henri looked at her for a moment, then released one of her hands. He believed her! For the first time hope began to well up within her, displacing the fear. She placed her palm flat against his chest and began to stroke him. "So good," she murmured. The lie would cost her another penance, but it was a small price to pay for her freedom. She moved her hand lower, circling the muscles of his abdomen, trying to fight back the revulsion that touching him created. He must not see how disgusting she found every part of him.

"More." This time it was Henri who spoke, and as he did he released his grip on her other hand.

It was all Marguerite needed. She had one chance, and only one.

She slid her hand under the pillow and felt the cold metal. It was there. With a motion so quick that Henri had no way of anticipating it, she pulled out the knife and pressed it firmly to his throat.

"Let me go, or I'll use it." Her voice was as firm as the point of the knife.

Henri moved, as though to wrest the weapon from her grip.

Marguerite pressed harder, and this time a drop of blood welled from Henri's throat.

"Get out of here before my hand slips." Marguerite punctuated her words by increasing the pressure on the knife.

Henri's eyes widened in amazement, and Marguerite watched as his gaze darted from side to side, as though assessing his chances of overpowering her.

"I would not risk it, if I were you." Miraculously her voice betrayed none of the fear she felt, only cold, harsh anger.

Henri gave her one final malevolent stare, then rolled off her. Grabbing his robe, he stalked to the door, then turned.

"You'll regret this. I promise you that. If it's the last thing I do, I'll make you sorry you drew a drop of my blood. No one—man or woman—does that and lives."

# Chapter Seventeen

It was the third day of rain, a cold, pelting downpour that made even the hardiest warrior long for shelter. Only the leader of the small entourage retained his native optimism.

"At least 'tis rain and not ice." Though the tall man's distinctive red hair was hidden under his helmet, nothing could disguise his bearing. Some might call it arrogance, but Alain knew it for what it was: the inborn pride of a natural leader. Even from a distance and mounted on horseback as he was, no one would mistake Richard for an ordinary knight. The set of his shoulders and the way he held his head proclaimed his rank more clearly than his finely woven clothes and jeweled sword.

"What do the men say? Have they accepted me?" Richard, it appeared, was beset by the same insecurities that plagued men of less exalted birth.

"It will take some time for the vassals' allegiance to be complete." Alain pulled in Neptune's reins and faced his sovereign. He did not want to prevaricate, but neither did he want to exaggerate the level of acceptance. No good would be served by that, and indeed much harm could result if a man relied too heavily on vassals whose allegiance was less than complete.

" 'Tis a good beginning," Alain told the Duke of Aquitaine.

The men had sworn fealty, and if they did not yet offer their new lord their full devotion, at least there had been no refusal to give yet another oath of loyalty. "I believe that is all we can expect for the present."

Richard met Alain's gaze, and his eyes were the first to fall. "I want them to accept me for myself, not because of my mother."

Once again Alain chose his words carefully. Though Richard's desire was understandable and in fact perfectly natural, it would not be satisfied in the near future.

"That will happen," he told Richard, "but 'tis unrealistic to expect your people to forget the queen. She is a strong woman, and for years the people of Aquitaine have known her as their sovereign. Remember, my lord, that their allegiance was always to her, not to her husbands. 'Twill be difficult to change that overnight."

Richard nodded, and a rivulet of rain ran down his nose. "But now I am the duke."

"Indeed. And your courage is legendary. That will serve you well with your people, for they seek a strong ruler who can keep them safe. 'Tis one way whereby you can quickly establish yourself as their sovereign."

Alain and Richard rode at the head of the small group, trailed by a dozen of Richard's vassals and their men. At Alain's request, Charles remained at the rear of the entourage. Though Alain had no real concerns over the other knights' loyalty, their battle skills were unknown. If there were a need, Charles could lead them.

The rain continued, penetrating their clothing and covering their horses' flanks with mud. Alain cursed the fact that he was forced to wear a helmet. Normally he preferred to ride bareheaded, for a helmet sorely limited his vision, but in a steady rain, the helmet served a useful function, keeping the water from streaming into his eyes.

They had ridden across open fields throughout the day. Now a dense forest loomed before them. Instinctively Alain looked around, his eyes surveying the approach to the forest. Nothing appeared amiss. But as they were engulfed in the darkness of the trees, Alain felt the hair on his arms prickle. The silence was complete, broken only by the sound of their horses' hooves and the steady drip of rain. No small animals scurried for cover, no birds warbled, no deer loped between the trees. The silence was unnatural.

Alain drew his sword. "Richard!"

But the alarm was too late, for as Alain moved to protect his liege lord, a shout echoed through the forest. Within seconds, Alain and Richard had been separated from the rest of their entourage, surrounded by a band of men brandishing swords and spears.

"We've got him! We have the duke!" The man's voice was hoarse with triumph.

It was an unfair contest, two men against twenty. Quickly Alain looked behind him, trying to assess the situation. It was at best close to impossible. Charles and the rest of Richard's men were out of sight. Whatever ruse the enemy had used to separate them had been effective, dangerously so.

Their only hope now was brute strength, for one look at the men had told Alain there was no chance of intimidating or outwitting this group. These were not knights, men trained in the rules of fair play. No, this was a motley assortment of men, their poorly fitting armor clearly the spoils of war. They were likely outlaws, men whose loyalty was to themselves, whose code of honor was nonexistent. What they shared was a fierce desire for victory and the riches it brought.

Alain darted a glance at Richard, and in that moment his regard for his lord grew tenfold. The troubadours' tales of the man's courage had not exaggerated, for he bore no sign of fear. Instead, his face remained as calm as if he were entering a parade. A faint smile crossed his lips; only his eyes were serious, telling Alain he was fully cognizant of the danger they faced.

Richard smiled again and reached for his sword.

Alain aimed his lance.

The melee had begun.

Though the attackers had the advantage of numbers, both Alain and Richard were mounted on destriers, battle-trained horses whose hooves were more dangerous than many spears.

Schooled to move quickly, deflecting sword thrusts and trampling men who had the misfortune to be unhorsed, the destrier was one of a knight's most valued weapons. God willing, it would be enough to save their lives today.

They fought as one fierce battle machine, the two knights and their horses, united by unspoken communication and an unquenchable desire to live. Recognizing the danger of being separated, Alain remained at Richard's side. While Richard used his sword to dispatch those who came too close, Alain's spear unhorsed more distant opponents. And through it all, the destriers whirled, changing direction so quickly that men who were attackers one moment found themselves on the defensive the next.

The outlaws screamed, cursed and shouted commands. Alain and Richard remained silent, their only noise the clash of a sword, the thud of a lance.

When the skirmish was over, ten men lay in the mud. The others had scattered. Alain raised his lance in a gesture of victory and, yes, relief. He and Richard were alive! There was no need for words as he and his lord stared at each other, for their grins were more eloquent than the troubadours' most polished verses.

For an instant the forest was silent. Then Alain heard the pounding of hoofbeats and the sound of Charles's cry. The rear guard had found them.

When the tale had been told and retold, Richard turned to Alain. "The minstrels did not exaggerate." Richard's face was still flushed with exertion and excitement. "You are truly a valiant warrior."

"I had the best of leaders." It was more truth than flattery. In all his years of battle, this was the first time Alain had fought with a man whose skill matched his own, a man who had known instinctively what moves Alain would make and how to best complement them.

If he had been asked who had been the leader, Alain would have had difficulty replying, for at times he had felt he was following Richard, while at others he had clearly been the one setting the plan of attack. It had been a unique and yet oddly exhilarating experience, for this time the excitement had come not only from the victory but also from sharing it with Richard.

The man had to be punished; of that there was no doubt. The only question was the nature of the penalty she should exact.

Marguerite poured water into the basin, dipped a cloth into it, then began to scrub her body. Though the bruises would remain, somehow, some way she had to eradicate every other reminder of Henri's touch.

The crime was heinous. It was not only the attack on her person; that was serious enough. But the fact that she was his sworn liege lord and that Henri owed her loyalty rather than treachery compounded the wrong. The very fabric of society, her father had taught her, was dependent on men's adhering to basic laws, and among those laws there was none more fundamental than the vow of fealty a vassal took. Henri had broken that vow of fealty, not in a moment of passion or foolishness, but deliberately after days—perhaps even weeks— of planning.

It was a transgression of enormous magnitude, and the punishment must be commensurate. She could disenfranchise him. Short of death, it was the ultimate penalty and the punishment which best suited his crime.

Marguerite shuddered. Like excommunication, disenfranchisement was not an act to be taken lightly. Not once in the past three generations had one of Mirail's knights been disenfranchised. But not once had a knight been so perfidious.

Marguerite emptied the basin, then refilled it with fresh water. As she scrubbed her skin fiercely, trying to remove the memory of Henri's loathsome touch, she bit her lip. Henri deserved to lose his lands, to be publicly disgraced. And yet the decision was not so simple. Though she longed to bring Henri to justice, to exact vengeance for his attack on her, Marguerite knew there was more at stake here than her own honor. The safety of her people could depend on the decision she made tonight.

Her torn nightrail gleamed white in the near darkness. Touching it as gingerly as if it were on fire, Marguerite crumpled the fine linen into a ball, then tossed it into the garderobe. Though Louise's skillful fingers could mend the rents, Marguerite knew she would never again wear the garment, and she could not bear to think of someone else's body being clad in the defiled linen.

Henri's brutal act had done more than violate her body. He had created a dilemma. If she disenfranchised him, not a soul would dispute her, for in the moment that he had sworn fealty to her, Henri had conferred that right on her. And yet . . . Marguerite sighed. Although they had renewed their vows, the vassals were still restive, and many viewed Henri as a natural leader. Who knew how they would react if his humiliation were made public?

Marguerite remembered Henri's boast that people would believe his tale that she had encouraged him. Perhaps they would. Though the mere thought of the man made her want to gag, Marguerite knew that Henri presented a far different image to the world. He was a polished speaker who could make lies sound convincing. If he told his tale, she would be painted as petty, vengeful and weak. It was possible, indeed likely, that at least some of her vassals would side with Henri, and though there would be no outcry, the private discussions would be all the more dangerous for being conducted in secret.

There was no choice. While Henri must be punished, Marguerite could not jeopardize her people by making the sentence known. She could not disenfranchise him.

Marguerite moved to the window and stared into the darkness, as though seeking an answer from the evening air. She managed a small smile, remembering the last time she had faced a similar decision. Then she had had Alain, and together they had been able to find a fitting punishment for Jean. Tonight, though, she was alone. There was no one to help her, no one to share the burden of responsibility.

If only Alain were here!

The longing was so deep it was almost painful. She wrapped her arms around her waist, trying to quell the need. It was simply a reaction to Henri's attack, the natural aftermath of fear. It signified nothing.

Not wanting to pursue that thought, Marguerite turned abruptly and walked toward the carved chair. She needed to make a decision quickly, for she would insist that Henri and his men leave at dawn. He could not be permitted to stay a moment longer. Indeed, were it not for her desire to avoid public speculation, Marguerite would have summoned her guards and ordered them to evict Henri bodily. But that was not the answer.

If only she had the right answer.

"What has happened?" Louise threw open the door to Marguerite's chamber. She was breathless, as though she had run up the stairs, and her eyes were wide with alarm.

It was safest that no one—not even Louise—know of Henri's perfidy, and so Marguerite forced a slightly humorous tone to her voice. "Is aught amiss? Did you and Gerard exhaust each other? In truth, I did not expect to see you until morning."

There was no humor in Louise's words. "Gerard could not leave his master alone for the entire night, and so he left me after a few hours. I told him I would wait for him to return, but he never came back." The pain in Louise's voice was palpable. "I'm afraid I fell asleep. When I woke up, the candle had burned out and Gerard had not come back. I was so worried about him that I went to the Great Hall." Louise gripped the back of a chair for support. "Marguerite, they're all gone."

"What?" Once again Henri had taken her by surprise. She had thought he would remain until morning, then leave as though nothing unusual had occurred. Fleetingly Marguerite wondered what excuse Henri had given his men for their surreptitious departure.

"Why did they leave? Did the king summon them?"

Marguerite was silent for a moment. Then she smiled, for unknowingly Louise had provided her with Henri's punishment. "I fear it is much simpler than that." Slowly she recounted the tale of Henri's attack. "You must never tell anyone—not even Gerard—about this. The well-being of Mirail depends on your silence." She had told Louise only because the woman would be part of Marguerite's retribution.

"Oh, my lady, it was my fault," Louise wailed when Marguerite had finished her story. "Henri would not have come to your chamber if I had remained with you."

Marguerite knew it was unlikely that anyone or anything short of a sword could have prevented Henri's attack. "Nonsense. You were not to blame. After all, 'twas I who insisted you spend time with Gerard. No, Louise, if there is any fault, it is my own. I knew there was something odd about Henri's visit, and I should have taken extra precautions. Now, summon the men. Henri will not escape so easily."

"Father, I have sinned most grievously." Louise knelt on the stone floor of the confessional. Her wrongdoing had weighed so heavily that she had not attended Mass that morning, and now she sought the comfort of confession.

"Have you had more lustful thoughts, my child?" Father René's voice was soothing.

"Oh, Father, it was far worse. I have sinned in deed as well as thought, and my mistress has suffered for it."

At the priest's urging, Louise outlined her sins. When she finished, there was silence on the other side of the curtain.

"This is serious, indeed, but our Lord forgives all who are truly repentant." He enunciated each word clearly as he gave Louise her penance, ending with the admonition, "Go forth and sin no more."

Tears streaming down her face, Louise left the confessional box.

"I wish there were a way to get a message to Charles."

Diane walked at Marguerite's side as they approached the weaving shed. For the past two weeks, Marguerite had turned the supervision of the weavers over to Diane. She had accompanied the other woman each morning, greeting the weavers and praising their work, but then she had left Diane to ensure that the cloth they produced met Mirail's standards.

"If it is important, I can send messengers. They should be able to learn where Richard and his men are camped."

"Would you?" A smile lit Diane's face. "The message is indeed important. At least," she added slowly, "to Charles."

Though there was frost in the air and they had been walking briskly, Marguerite paused and raised one brow. It was a gesture she had found rarely failed to elicit the information she wanted.

Diane drew her cloak closer, then responded to the silent question. "I wanted Charles to be the first to know, but I am so excited that I cannot wait. I must tell someone or burst." She placed a hand on Marguerite's arm. "If Charles can't be the first, then it's right that I tell you, for you are the sister I have always wanted. I know you'll share my happiness." Though there was no one near, Diane lowered her voice. "I think I am with child."

It should not have been a surprise. After all, Charles and Diane had been married for over a month before they came to Mirail. That was more than enough time for Charles to plant his seed. Still, Marguerite felt a pang of longing. Not for a child, of course. That was Alain's desire, not hers. But a marriage as simple as the one Charles and Diane shared suddenly seemed attractive.

" 'Tis wonderful news." Marguerite gave Diane a congratulatory kiss.

"I knew you'd be glad. Oh, Marguerite, this will make my life complete."

When she left Diane in the weavers' shed, instead of returning to the castle as she normally did, Marguerite walked slowly toward the river. A child. What would it be like if she were pregnant? A vision of a small boy with silver blond hair and deep blue eyes filled her thoughts.

Diane had no doubt that Charles would be thrilled by the news of her pregnancy. But that was Charles, not Alain. The two brothers were so different that it was impossible to predict how Alain would react under the same circumstances. Would he be happy, or would he view a child as yet another burden? It had been a long time since he had spoken of an heir for

Mirail. Perhaps he no longer wanted one. Strangely, the thought brought sadness, not the relief it should have.

In all his years as a warrior, he had never had difficulty sleeping. Yet the past few weeks had made mockery of all that had come before, and Alain had found himself spending nights outdoors, staring at the stars or walking through muddy fields, trying to ignore the image that seemed indelibly etched on his memory.

Damn her! She was just a woman. There was no reason the mere thought of her should disrupt his sleep, indeed his whole life, so completely. It had nothing to do with Marguerite; it was undoubtedly the result of the rabbit stew he had eaten.

Alain paced a triangle between three pine trees in the vain hope that the rhythm of his steps would somehow ease his turmoil.

"Has Richard said how long we will be on tour?" Charles interrupted Alain's thoughts, matching his stride. As the weeks had passed, his brother had spent most evenings with him. It was almost as though he guessed how difficult Alain found those nights, or perhaps Charles suffered from the same malady.

Alain shook his head. It was a question he had asked their ruler on numerous occasions, and on each he had received the same answer, which was no answer at all.

"All I can surmise is that since we are heading for Poitiers, he may disband us once we arrive there." When he realized that he had been pacing and what that revealed about his mental state, Alain sank to the ground, leaning back against a tree.

"But that could be months."

Alain could not dispute his brother's complaint. They had been traveling slowly, spending time at each of the castles in Richard's duchy, establishing their lord's dominion. If the duke had been alarmed by the ambush in the forest, he had not allowed the attack to disrupt his plans, and he had continued at the same deliberate pace, as though he had all the time in the world.

By law they were bound to give Richard forty days of service each year, and those forty days would soon be over. Still Alain doubted any of the vassals would leave Richard even when the time had expired. He knew he would not, for his lord needed him.

"I know you enjoy this." Charles gestured to the hard ground which served as their bed each night they were not at a castle. "I do not. I want to be home in a soft bed with my wife."

It was not an unreasonable wish, and Alain could not fault him for it, particularly when the same thought had haunted him for more nights than he cared to remember.

"This is our duty," he said simply as Charles took a seat next to him.

"I don't dispute that, and I'm here, fulfilling my duty just as you are. The difference is that you're the true chevalier. You seem to thrive on this. I do not."

Idly Charles picked up a pinecone and tossed it from one hand to another. "Do you ever wonder why we are so different? It is almost as though we were not related."

That was a topic Alain had no wish to pursue. "But we *are* brothers," he said shortly. Then, sensing that Charles would not dismiss the subject so easily, he continued. "If we are different, it is because of our ages and the way we were raised. I spent my early childhood at the queen's court. The first memories I have are of people talking about war. Stories of the crusade filled every day."

Charles bounced the pinecone off the ground. "Mayhap you're right. What I remember most is our mother reciting poetry. She used to love it when the troubadours would visit and bring new rhymes."

The explanation of their differences was plausible, and it appeared Charles was accepting it. "Is it any wonder we're not alike?"

"None of that changes the simple fact that I want to be home. It doesn't matter whether it's Lilis or Jarnac, so long as Diane is there."

Alain turned his head aside, unwilling to let Charles see what a sympathetic chord he had struck. It was nonsense, pure and simple. He was a warrior, doing what he loved most. There was absolutely no reason for him to feel this longing, this almost magnetic force drawing him back to Mirail.

He would never again eat rabbit stew if this was the result.

"Did you ever think that Diane and Marguerite could be pregnant?"

A babe. Alain had spent more time than he'd admit thinking of a tiny girl with golden blond hair and blue eyes, wondering how Marguerite would react if she were indeed with child. Would she love their daughter, or would she wish Charles had been the father?

Apparently not noticing that his brother had not spoken, Charles continued, "Alain, I don't want to be like our father and miss seeing his sons growing up. I want to be there!"

And I, my dear brother, have a different need. When my wife bears a child, I want there to be no doubt whatsoever of the babe's parentage.

# Chapter Eighteen

"It is all your fault, you worthless cur! You should have warned me that she was armed." Henri raised his arm again, punctuating his words with blows to Gerard's stomach. "I told you to learn everything about the bitch."

Though there was no way he could control the whoosh of his breath as Henri's fist pummeled him, Gerard steeled his face to show no fear. Years of experience had taught him that his master thrived on others' fear and that his punishment would be more severe if fueled by cringing and pleading.

Tonight was no different than a hundred other times when Henri had vented his frustration on the closest serf, blaming the hapless man for whatever had gone wrong. Though painful, Henri's blows did not engender any real fear, for Gerard knew that Henri would content himself with a mild beating. After all, if he were to seriously maim a serf, he would lose the man's service, and Henri was nothing if not practical. Serfs were more valuable than gold, and everyone knew how Henri prized gold.

"Your imbecility has made it far more difficult. Fear not; you will pay for your disobedience." Henri aimed another punch at Gerard. Then, apparently satisfied when his servant doubled over in pain, he turned and picked up the scrap of parchment. "She ordered me to come back." His voice, which seconds before had been filled with hostility, turned to gloating as he stared at the parchment. Though Henri was unable to read, he had insisted the priest leave the missive with him. "I was right. She is like every other female. She wants me back . . . in her castle and in her bed. She's a bitch in heat, and I'm the one she's panting for."

Henri tossed the parchment onto the chest that stood in one corner of the chamber. "I was right. I knew she'd regret her hasty action." He grinned. "Now she can wait. I'll go to Mirail when I choose, not when some haughty female thinks I ought to go. Imagine! Summoning me, Henri de Bleufontaine. The fool! Little does she know how much she will regret that folly."

Henri's chuckle sent a shiver down Gerard's spine. Marguerite de Mirail might be a strong woman, but she was no match for Henri, for the man had no peers when it came to cruelty and brute strength.

"As for you, you flea on a dog's hide." Henri turned toward Gerard. "I'll teach you to defy me."

The last sound Gerard heard was Henri's fist connecting with his head.

It was one of her favorite tales, Virgil's story of the wanderings of Aeneas. Today when a pounding rain made all except the most essential outdoor tasks unthinkable, Marguerite sought refuge in her solar. Never before had Virgil's iambic pentameter lines failed to transport her back to a simpler, more heroic era. Today, though, the words wrought no magic. Instead, as she read of Aeneas's adventures, Marguerite's mind conjured pictures of another man, a tall man with pale blond hair. Where was he? Was he facing enemies as the Roman hero had? Or was he perhaps dallying with another woman, his own Dido? If Richard had taken his men back to Poitiers, Alain could be reunited with Honore.

The thought caused Marguerite's stomach to ache more than the meal she had once made of green apples.

"I envy you."

Marguerite raised her head. Normally she preferred not to be interrupted when she was reading, but today she welcomed the distraction of Diane's company. She motioned the other woman into the chair next to her.

"Why would you envy me?"

"You can read."

Marguerite was silent for a moment, nonplused. "You know so many stories that I thought you had read them."

Diane shook her head. "Neither of my parents can read or write, so they saw no reason for me to learn. Pleading with them was for naught, and our priest refused to teach me."

"Did he tell you it was against God's will for a woman to read?"

"How did you know?"

Marguerite laughed. "Father René tried that argument with me."

"But you read. He must have taught you."

"No, he refused. I was more fortunate than you, though, for my father could read. When he realized that I was determined and that no amount of arguing was going to convince me otherwise, he agreed to teach me." Marguerite's smile was wistful as she thought of the long hours she had spent with her father, devouring the books in his library, pleading with him to commission the monks to copy new ones.

"How did you learn so many stories?" she asked Diane.

"I guess I am a good listener. Mayhap I should have been a troubadour." Diane giggled. "Can you imagine what Father Albert would have said to that? Still, I confess I have always been fascinated with heroic tales."

Marguerite gestured toward the book in her lap. "The *Aeneid* is one of my favorites. I know you've heard it, because we talked about Dido and the bull's hide. But did you like the tale?" Diane nodded her agreement. "Do you also like the story of Camelot?"

"No." There was such venom in Diane's voice that Marguerite looked up, once again surprised. "In truth, I cannot understand how Guinevere could have left Arthur, even for

Lancelot.'' Diane's eyes darkened, and she leaned forward to emphasize her point. "Guinevere plighted her troth, and then she broke those vows. No, Marguerite, I cannot believe that is a heroic act no matter how often it happens. Oh, I know about the ladies at the court and how little they prize their marriage vows, but I cannot countenance their infidelity." Diane laid a hand on Marguerite's arm. "How could Guinevere have done that? I love Charles so much that I would not willingly hurt him."

The wind lashed another sheet of rain at the narrow window. Diane shivered, then renewed her grip on Marguerite's arm. "I know you well enough to say that you would never betray Alain."

It was true. Though Marguerite had not thought of it in those terms, she could not imagine lying with a man other than Alain. In fact, just the thought of another man touching her was distasteful. Reality had been even worse. Henri's touch had been physically repulsive. At the time she had thought her reaction was so strong because he had tried to force himself on her, but now she knew the cause was far deeper than that. Quite simply, Henri was not Alain. It mattered not that many women found Henri handsome and charming. He was not the man she had married. He was not the man she wanted in her bed.

It was oddly disconcerting to realize how quickly she had developed a deep and abiding loyalty to a man she had married so reluctantly, a man who had done nothing to inspire that loyalty.

"I wish there were some word about our men." Diane's voice was soft but plaintive.

"'Tis natural you would want to tell Charles about the babe." Though Diane did not speak often of the child, she was given to frequent bouts of introspection, when a faint smile would cross her face as though she were envisioning her child at play.

"There is no babe. My courses came this morning."

Diane's voice was flat, almost emotionless, belying the sorrow Marguerite knew she must be feeling. Impulsively, Marguerite reached over to hug the other woman. "I know not what to say to comfort you."

For a long moment Diane was silent, her uneven breathing the only sign of her emotion. "Do not worry," she said at length. " 'Twould be a lie if I were to say that I was not disappointed, for I am. Sorely so. It would have been wonderful to bear Charles's son so early in our marriage. But naught is to be gained by railing at the Fates. I cannot bring the baby back. All I can do is wait until Charles returns. Then, if God is willing, we will make another one."

The look Marguerite gave Diane was long and appraising. Though the other woman might envy her because she had learned to read, at this moment it was Diane who seemed the more fortunate, for she possessed an evenness of temper, a pragmatic disposition that Marguerite wished she could emulate. Her new sister was a far more intriguing person than Marguerite had guessed.

The small hut was dark and silent, save for the bitter sobbing. Louise huddled in the furthest corner, her shoulders shaking as she released all the sorrow, all the despair that had filled her soul.

"My child, what ails you?" Adele knelt next to her daughter and put her arms around her, trying to comfort her. She had not seen Louise give way to tears since she, a child of six, had lost the Christmas orange that the master had given her. Then she had cried as if her heart would break, all for the loss of a piece of exotic fruit. Whatever had caused her daughter's despair today, Adele knew it was far more important than fruit.

Louise turned, and the sight of her tear-stained face wrenched Adele's heart. "What is it?" she asked again.

" 'Tis too cruel." Louise grasped her mother's hand. "I know it is a sin to question Father René's word, but surely he is wrong. The good Lord would not ask me to bear such a heavy burden. Mère, I cannot do what Father commands."

Adele's eyes widened with shock as she realized that her daughter was planning to disobey the priest. Louise, quiet, biddable Louise, had suddenly become defiant. What she was suggesting was blasphemy, punishable by excommunication, for everyone knew the Church was God's instrument, and her priests His spokesmen. Their word was God's word, sacred and not to be questioned.

"What is wrong? What has Father René commanded you to do?"

Her words broken by sobs, Louise told her mother of the night she had left Marguerite's chamber to be with Gerard, the night Sir Henri had found her mistress unprotected and had attacked her.

" 'Twas my fault, Mère, and I confessed my sin to Father. I knew he would give me a severe penance, but never this." She began to cry again, her shoulders shaking with the force of her sobs. "He forbade me to ever see Gerard again." Louise brushed the back of her hand across her cheeks, scattering teardrops. "I know I should be strong, but I cannot bear it. I cannot live without Gerard."

Neither of the women heard the small figure pause in the doorway, then scurry away.

There were no complaints from the men as they filed across the drawbridge. Indeed, a festive air surrounded the small entourage. Voices were cheerful, punctuated with laughter, and one man could be heard whistling. Oh, his whistle was tuneless, closer to the shriek of a mouse caught in an owl's talons than a songbird's warbling, but his companions did naught to discourage him.

It was a masterful ploy. The knights who accompanied her were pleased by the diversion. Any excuse to leave the barony after weeks of inactivity was welcome. They would not have dissented if she had bade them pick herbs along the riverbank. But a hunting party. That was a diversion of the highest kind. Far from raising complaints, the news that they were to hunt had roused cheers.

Yes, Marguerite reflected, it was one of her better ideas. The men were happy, the barony would have its store of meat replenished in time for the Yuletide festivities, and she would resolve the issue of her recalcitrant vassal. An excellent plan, for it was a hunting party where only she knew the real quarry.

It was their second day of riding. They had flushed a few hares the previous day, and they had killed a large boar, but thus far the men's primary goal—a buck—had eluded them.

As they emerged from the forest onto a small rise, Marguerite reined in her horse. Shading her eyes with one hand, she surveyed the horizon.

"I believe we are near Bleufontaine." She spoke with a measure of uncertainty, as though she had not carefully guided them in this direction. Oh, she had appeared to be wandering almost aimlessly through the forest, and when she had followed the river, she had announced it was to hunt for fish. Similarly, the detour across the wheatfield was merely a short cut to the forest where she had heard there was an unusually large herd of deer. It had all been done so artlessly that no one would guess their route had been planned long before they left Mirail.

Marguerite motioned to two of her most trusted men. "I bid you deliver a message to Sir Henri. Tell him I am weary from the hunt and request that he prepare refreshments for me and my party. If you hurry, he should be ready for us when we arrive."

And I will be more than ready for him. If the man refused to answer her summons—and it appeared that he was feigning ignorance of her demands, for weeks had passed since Marguerite had sent two men to Bleufontaine with a strongly worded message for Henri—she would deliver her command directly.

" 'Tis an honor to have you here." Henri's hair was still damp, as though he had been in the midst of his ablutions when Marguerite's messengers had arrived.

Marguerite smiled sweetly, trying to conceal the revulsion that the mere sight of Henri raised. The man was a liar, but prevarication was a game two could play. "I grew thirsty from the hunt."

As Henri guided her into the Great Hall, Marguerite darted shrewd glances at the castle. The years since she and her father had been in Bleufontaine had taken their toll on the building.

Mold grew in the corners, and the tapestries appeared so faded that she knew they had not been beaten in many years. Though there was no dearth of servants, the Great Hall suffered from both a lack of cleaning and repair.

It appeared her father had been correct, and Bleufontaine needed a woman to oversee it. Marguerite thanked the Lord and all His saints that she was not and never would be that woman.

Henri gestured to a tall-backed chair. When Marguerite raised one brow and looked pointedly at the thick coating of dust which turned the seat cushion to gray, Henri had the grace to flush. He brushed his hand across the seat, scattering dust motes into the air. Then he shouted for a servant to bring them flagons of ale.

While she sipped politely, Marguerite studied her vassal. It was apparent that he was uneasy having her in his castle, as well he should be. Though he managed to converse with her, discussing topics that ranged from the unseasonably warm December weather to the King's plans for his son, Henri was visibly nervous. A truly good woman would have put an end to his apprehension, but Marguerite had no illusions about her goodness. Henri had defied her not once, but for weeks. It would do his soul good to worry a bit longer.

As Henri fidgeted, trying to turn the conversation to the reason for Marguerite's visit, she watched the servants who moved through the Great Hall, her eyes searching for Gerard. But, though there were many brown-haired men, none was Gerard.

"I would like to see your solar," she said when she had drained the flagon. "I have heard that the new stained glass is most beautiful." In reality, all she sought was a measure of privacy that the Great Hall did not afford.

She gestured to two of her men to follow them as they ascended the stairs. When they reached the solar, Marguerite bade her men to remain outside. Though she wished no one to overhear her conversation with Henri, she was not fool enough to face him with no protection.

When the door had closed behind them, she turned to Henri.

"I would not shame you in front of your people, but you leave me little choice. I suggest you explain now why you disregarded my summons."

"What summons was that?" Though his words were smooth, Henri's eyes betrayed the lie.

"I am not such a fool as you think." As her anger grew, Marguerite's voice grew lower. She enunciated each word carefully, lest the man claim he had not understood her. "The message was delivered to you personally by two of my most valued men. 'Twas not a failure in the delivery but rather in your response to it."

Louise need never know that this sham of a hunting party had been arranged for her benefit. When Jean had come running to Marguerite, bearing the tale of his sister's tears because she could not live without Gerard, he had insisted that neither Louise nor their mother learn he had overheard the conversation. "I fear they would be angry that I told you," he said, his face pale with worry.

Marguerite had reassured the boy, then begun to plan a way to resolve the problem. The action, she found, was therapeutic, helping to channel some of her anger at Henri constructively. It was also far easier to address Louise's dilemma than to solve the riddle of her own marriage.

When Henri did not speak, Marguerite continued. "Since you appear to have forgotten the content of my summons, let me reiterate it for you. You have a choice. As payment for your unlawful attack on my person, you may either forfeit one of your serfs, Gerard the son of Albert the cobbler, or I shall disenfranchise you. The choice is yours. Tell me now which you prefer."

Henri looked at her, then quickly dropped his gaze. "I meant you no disrespect," he said.

Marguerite raised an eyebrow. Surely the man did not expect her to believe such a bold-faced lie.

"I have prayed daily that I could give you the answer you seek, but God has not answered my prayers." The anger in Henri's voice gave his words the ring of truth, and for the first time since she had set foot in Bleufontaine, Marguerite knew that Henri was not lying. He had indeed prayed and was incensed because the deity had not seen fit to respond to his pleas. She almost smiled at the audacity of Henri's attitude, at his expecting God to bend to his wishes, whatever they were.

His next words caught her unprepared.

"My prayers were for naught. The serf Gerard has been gravely ill, and he died just last night."

# Chapter Nineteen

"Tell me, Alain, what is it like to be on crusade?"

Mercifully, the sun had decided to shine, and though it was a pale winter sun that barely melted the frost from the fields, its very presence raised the men's spirits. The bickering and petty arguments that the days of rain had seemed to engender had disappeared more quickly than the frost.

A crusade. Alain was silent for a moment, considering the import of Richard's question. There had been hints that he was considering taking the Cross, but Alain had dismissed them as mere rumors. Now he wondered.

"I wish to fight the infidel." Richard's words confirmed the whispered tales.

And I have no wish to fight anyone. The thought came unbidden, surprising Alain with its intensity. What had precipitated that? Fighting had been his whole life, and while he hadn't sought battles, there was no denying the fact that a decisive victory brought exhilaration and great satisfaction.

"In truth, my lord, a holy war differs very little from any other kind. There is the same bloodshed, fear and tedium. The primary differences I found were that the sun burns hotter in

Outremer, and the men spoke a language I could not understand."

It was, Alain reflected, no less than the truth. In the past he had shared Richard's craving for the excitement and, yes, the danger of battle. Today, though, the prospect of months, even years, of skirmishes held no appeal. Instead his mind conjured the fleeting image of a small child with golden hair.

"Of course, my mother would insist on accompanying us. She believes no crusade has a chance of success without her."

It was an odd opinion, given the problems that had beset the one crusade Eleanor had made. Though none would dare voice the fact that Louis's and Eleanor's crusade had been a failure, few would tout its accomplishments.

" 'Tis natural she would want to be part of such a noble expedition," Alain said. "Who has not heard of your mother's valor on the Second Crusade? My own mother spoke glowingly of how the queen led her women through treacherous passes, showing less fear than many of the knights."

Richard grimaced. "That is my mother, a fearless woman. But, Alain, I have no desire to take women on my crusade. They are naught but impediments."

If the stories Alain had heard were true, the newly crowned duke of Aquitaine had no desire to take women anywhere. That, however, was a subject Alain had no intention of raising. Instead he said mildly, "I can understand why you would feel that way about most women, but surely not the queen."

With an angry snort, Richard spurred his destrier, leaving Alain behind. When Alain was once more at his lord's side, Richard announced, "Your ploy is transparent, my good man. I can see that you plead my mother's cause in the hope that you might bring your bride with you."

Alain masked his surprise. Surely he had not thought of her accompanying him on a holy war. Not Marguerite of the sharp tongue, Marguerite of the foolish fancies. And yet a part of him wondered how it would be to have her with him. Would she be the delicate rose he had seen the last night they were together, or would her thorns be all too apparent?

"The simple fact," Richard continued, "is that I cannot

mount a crusade yet. I must secure the duchy first before I ask my vassals to take the Cross with me.''

'' 'Tis a wise move,'' Alain agreed. ''Have you decided where we will journey next?'' Although Richard had confided little of his itinerary to Alain, he was more expansive than normal today. Perhaps he would reveal their destination.

When Richard named the next two fiefdoms they would visit, Alain's mind began to whirl. The thought was tempting. So very tempting.


'' 'Tis a monstrous lie!'' Louise's face, which had grown so pale that Marguerite had feared she would faint, flushed with anger.

Marguerite sank into a chair and tugged on Louise's hand to urge her into the seat next to her. Only minutes had passed since Marguerite and her men had returned from their hunting trip to Bleufontaine. Though she was weary and longed to wash away the travel dust, this could not wait, and so she had asked Louise to join her in her chamber.

''Sweet Mary above knows that I would have done anything to spare you this pain.'' Marguerite grasped Louise's hand, praying that the simple physical contact would grant her some measure of comfort. ''I wish it were not true, but I could not let you continue to dream when I knew there was no hope those dreams could ever come true.''

The trip back from Bleufontaine had been much shorter than the journey there, for there had been no need for a circuitous route. Marguerite had gotten the answer to her question, and though it was far from the one she had desired, it had left her with only one responsibility remaining.

Her stomach had tightened with dread, keeping her from eating even the light repast Henri's cook had sent with them. She had ached, knowing the pain she was about to inflict, wishing there were a way she could keep the horrible truth to herself, knowing she could not.

She had expected tears and raging anger. She had not expected denial.

"Gerard is not dead." Though low, Louise's voice was fierce. "That wicked, wicked man lied to you. Gerard is alive. I know it, just as I would have known if he had died. Part of me would have died with him."

Remembering the sense of dread and the sharp pain she had felt at the moment her father had died, Marguerite conceded the possibility that Louise might have been able to sense her lover's death. And yet there was no denying Henri's tale.

"Henri lied."

Sadly Marguerite shook her head. "Believe me, Louise. I thought of that. I know the man is a liar. That's why I questioned two of the squires, and my men spoke to the other servants. Everyone gave the same response. No one has seen Gerard in weeks, ever since he contracted the pox. Nay, my friend, this is one time when Henri did not lie."

"He is alive," Louise insisted. "I know it."

It was insanity, pure insanity. Alain drew the brush through his horse's mane with more force than normal. How could he even consider it? It would be violating everything he held most dear, his vows, his honor.

The rain had resumed that morning, dampening the men's spirits, coating their horses with mud, subsiding only at dusk when Richard had declared they could camp for the night. Though the other men had quickly finished rubbing down their horses, eager to escape to the relative dryness of the campfires, Alain had remained with Neptune. Tonight, he longed for companionship, but it was not that of his brother or the other men in Richard's entourage.

Neptune whinnied. Alain placed a soothing hand on his neck.

"You are right," he told the horse. "I cannot leave my liege lord, not even for one night."

A loud snort greeted his words, and Neptune pawed the ground. Alain stared at his destrier for a moment, then laughed. Whoever had said that horses were stupid animals had not met this one.

It was only one night, and Richard was well-guarded.

No one need know.

Alain drew the brush through Neptune's mane one last time, then patted him on the nose. Whistling softly, he turned toward the campfire. Three paces later, he stopped.

The rain must have addled his brain to make him even consider it. Sacrifice his honor for a mere woman? Never!

The troop of peddlers crossed the drawbridge, their noisy greetings and careless jostling reminding Marguerite of a flock of sheep searching for fresh grass to devour. This was a band she had not seen before, and she welcomed them with more than normal enthusiasm. The diversion they would bring Mirail was sorely needed, for in the days since she had returned from Bleufontaine, a pall had settled over the barony. The tale of Gerard's death had spread quickly, causing the people to rally around Louise. Yet their sympathy, well-meaning though it was, had brought Louise no solace. She had stubbornly refused to acknowledge Gerard's death, retreating into an uncustomary silence.

Marguerite knew it was vain to hope that the peddlers would cheer Louise, but the sight of their wares and the colorfully embroidered tales that accompanied them would be a welcome relief for the barony's other inhabitants.

"Do you bring any word of the duke of Aquitaine's men?" Diane, who had accompanied Marguerite as she greeted the band of peddlers, spoke to their leader.

The man tipped his head to one side, as though considering her question. "Nothing recent," he said at last. "We have not encountered them on our travels. When last I heard, the duke had assembled a group of his most loyal vassals and was journeying to the other parts of his lands." He counted on his fingers. "That was nigh onto five weeks ago."

A dark-haired man standing at his left side pulled out a length of silk ribbon for Diane's approval. "There is a tale that the duke wishes to mount a crusade."

Fingering the deep blue ribbon, Diane turned to Marguerite. "If it is true, mayhap we could accompany them. 'Twould not be the first time women went on crusade.'' The enthusiasm in her voice told Marguerite more clearly than her words how deeply she missed Charles. Though Diane had remained outwardly cheerful, each day her smile seemed a little less bright.

''What we should hope is that there is no truth to the tale,'' Marguerite said more sharply than she had intended. ''A crusade is far from glamorous. 'Tis more a pestilence than something to be desired. I have heard far too many stories of the Second Crusade to think otherwise.'' She gestured toward a dark red ribbon. It would make a fine gift for Louise. ''Indeed, we should say special prayers that it does not come to pass.''

''Mayhap you are right, but we would be with our husbands. Surely that is worth any amount of danger.''

It was fine for Diane to say that, for she had no doubts that Charles would welcome her company. But Alain? Who knew what sort of reception he'd give his wife?

Jean hefted another sack over his shoulder. The metal pans inside clattered, and a handle dug into his back, grazing the tender skin where the lash had flayed his flesh. It mattered naught. He would endure far greater pain for his sister.

Until today his plan had been vague. All he knew was that there had to be a way to help Louise. Ever since Lady Marguerite had returned from Bleufontaine with the story that Gerard had died, Louise had been different. She no longer laughed or sang when she visited with the family. Oh, she still spent time with their parents. Louise knew her duty, as did Jean. But it was not the same. *She* was not the same.

Louise was convinced that Sir Henri had lied, that Gerard was still alive, and naught but seeing his body would convince her otherwise. Jean had heard Mère tell her she was foolish, that she must accept God's will. But his sister was as stubborn as a mule. She needed proof, she said. If it was the last thing he did, Jean would find it for her. The question was, how.

He had had no idea until he had heard the peddlers talking. After they left Mirail, they were going to Bleufontaine. It was a sign from Heaven, Jean was certain. Why else had these peddlers come to Mirail at this time if not to help him? It was so simple. When the peddlers left, he would go with them. He would be safe traveling with them, and—more importantly—as part of their band he would be able to gain entry to Bleufontaine. Once there, he would learn the truth. Then Louise would smile again.

The drawbridge was down; only the portcullis defended the castle from attack. On another day, Alain would have chastised the watchman for the breach of security, but tonight Alain praised the man's foresight. The open drawbridge meant there was one less obstacle between him and Marguerite.

"M'lord!" The sight of his master chased the last remnants of sleep from the man's voice. "I did not know you were coming." He opened the portcullis and ushered Alain into the bailey. "I'll send a message to Lady Marguerite."

"There is no need to announce me." Alain slid off his horse and handed the man the reins. "See to Neptune, but say naught to anyone."

As he raced up the stairs, taking them two at a time, Alain wondered for the hundredth time at the wisdom of his action. Not only had he broken one of his vows of fealty, leaving his liege lord unprotected, but this foolhardy trip might be in vain. For there was no guarantee of the reception that waited for him. Despite the passion and the tenderness of their last night together, Alain had no assurance that his bride would welcome him. She might have sharpened her thorns during his absence and might order him from the room. She might—Alain's face darkened at the thought—have a man with her. With Marguerite, anything was possible. But he needed, Sweet Mary above, how he needed to be with her if only for one night.

Alain flung open the door. The chamber was dark, the only sound soft breathing and a light snoring. Two people! Alain gripped his sword. He'd kill the man. As for her . . . He crossed the room in three swift strides, then jerked the bed curtains apart.

She was waiting. His wife knelt on the mattress, a wary

expression on her face, and in her hand . . . Alain blinked. Yes, her long slender fingers were curved around an even longer curved knife.

"This was not quite the welcome I expected." Somehow his voice did not betray the pounding of his heart or the exultation he felt at the sight of her in bed alone, the knife telling him more clearly than words that no man had taken his place in her life or her bed, that she relied only on herself for protection.

"Are you all right, Marguerite?" Louise spoke. She was the one who had snored. If she was such a sound sleeper, 'twas no wonder Marguerite kept a weapon close.

" 'Tis all right, Louise. You may leave us." Marguerite marveled that somehow her voice sounded calm, despite the fierce pounding of her heart. The fear she had felt when her door had been flung open had subsided, and yet her heart continued to thud, fueled by questions she could not answer. Why had Alain come like this, with no warning? Had he somehow known how much she longed for him? Or was the reason for his visit more sinister?

Alain stood at the edge of the bed, his eyes moving from her face to the knife that she still held.

"I wasn't expecting you," she said as she slipped the knife back under her pillow. "A woman alone cannot be too careful."

He laughed. " 'Twould be quite a tale, were I to return to the camp with wounds I could not explain."

"Then Richard's tour is not over?"

The moonlight streaming into the room was bright enough that Marguerite could watch the play of emotions on Alain's face. His initial shock had faded, replaced by a slightly embarrassed grin.

"No," he admitted. "We're camped but a few hours' ride from here, and I could not pass so close to Mirail without coming back."

The words were simple, and he did not imbue them with drama, yet he could not hide the significance of his action from her. For some reason, Alain de Jarnac, the perfect knight, had left his liege lord without his permission. For some reason.

Marguerite's heart stopped for an instant. If she were to judge from the way he looked at her, she was that reason.

A flush stained her cheeks, and her pulse accelerated. "How long do we have?" she asked.

"Not nearly long enough."

How had she ever thought the man disdained chivalry? Marguerite had once told him that he was not a true chevalier, that he did not put his lady's needs above his own. How wrong she had been! Though Alain might not know the language of flowers, he most assuredly knew the acts of courtly love. For what else could have led him away from his lord?

"If we have but a few hours, let's not waste them." Marguerite rose from the bed and started to remove Alain's mail.

He was here! Alain had come to her, though duty had dictated that he not. He had put aside years of training, disregarding a tenet of his code of honor—all to be with her. What woman would not have been thrilled?

As she tugged the shirt over his head, Marguerite murmured, "Had I known you were coming, I would have written a poem for you."

Alain laughed and placed an admonishing finger on her lips. "In truth, I would rather have your smiles than your poetry." She couldn't help it. She smiled. But Alain continued. "Your kisses are far more precious than even your smiles."

Had she once thought he lacked a courtier's way with words? Marguerite laughed softly. This was the man of her dreams, the perfect knight, the perfect chevalier.

"If 'tis kisses you desire, then let me try to oblige you."

Capturing the hand that had touched her lips between both of hers, she pressed a kiss on each of his fingertips, then began to trace circles on his palm with the tip of her tongue.

Alain groaned. "Later, my darling. There'll be time for this later. Right now I cannot wait." He threw off his remaining clothing, then swept Marguerite into his arms. When he laid her on the bed and stretched out next to her, he cupped her chin in one hand. "Have you any idea how many sleepless nights you have caused?"

His voice was husky with passion, and there was no ignoring

the desire that shone from his eyes, desire that matched her own.

"I, m'lord? You accuse me of causing sleepless nights? Mayhap you should answer for those you have wrought. I cannot count the number of times I have wakened in the middle of the night, wanting you next to me."

"Then you missed me?" There was an undertone of surprise in Alain's voice, as though he doubted her answer.

"More than I ever dreamt possible."

"Oh, Marguerite."

And then there was no need for words, for in the darkness of the room she gave herself heart and soul to the man she had married.

Later when she wakened, feeling replete and happy, glorying in the weight of Alain's leg draped possessively over hers, Marguerite touched her fingers to his chin. It had not been a dream. Alain was indeed lying next to her.

His eyes opened slowly, and he grinned at her. "Why did no one warn me that I was marrying a lusty wench?" he demanded. "I'll have to concoct a tale to explain away these scratches."

"A blackberry bush?" Marguerite suggested.

"Richard's men have no time for berry picking. Besides, 'tis not the season."

"A pity." Marguerite managed a long sigh. "I suppose 'tis fortunate it is winter and few will see your back. Now, tell me, m'lord, how has the tour been?"

Alain laid his head back on the pillow and stared at the ceiling. "Richard is an extraordinary warrior and a born leader. He is so good with his men that I often forget how young he is." Alain turned to Marguerite, his fingers grazing her cheek in the lightest of caresses. "When you think about it, Richard could almost be my son."

"Don't tell me you were seducing maids when you were eleven. I shan't believe it."

"How do you think I got to be so good?" he demanded. "Performance like this takes years of practice."

'' 'Tis a shame, is it not? Since you've reached perfection, there is no need to practice any longer, is there?''

Alain laughed. '' 'Tis not only your nails that are sharp. Ah, Marguerite, how I've missed you.''

Tracing her fingers down his arm, Marguerite smiled. 'Twas wondrous to have Alain back, if only for one night.

"Is there any truth to the story that Richard is planning to go on crusade?" she asked when Alain's lips had ceased their forays along her body and she could once more breathe normally.

"Rumors spread so quickly!" Alain propped himself on one elbow. "The truth is that Richard mentioned the idea to me. We were riding at the time, and there was no one near us, so I've no idea how anyone could have overheard us. How could the story have spread to Mirail?"

"Peddlers." Marguerite's reply was succinct. "Somehow they hear everything. But of course they never reveal their sources. So," she asked, returning to her original question, "is it likely Richard will take the cross?"

Alain shrugged. "Eventually. I doubt it will be too soon, because he has much to resolve here in France." Alain's hand roamed freely down her body, stirring her blood once more. "Why did you ask? Were you hoping for the adventure of a crusade?"

"Diane . . ." Marguerite stopped, one train of thought interrupted by another. "Is Charles with you? Diane will be so happy."

Alain's hand stilled. "Charles does not know I left the camp, and if the saints are willing, he never shall. No one must know I left Richard."

The tone of Alain's voice told Marguerite he was concerned about more than his own reputation. He did not want others, innocent people, hurt by his actions. Marguerite concurred. "Especially not Diane. I don't want her hurt, and she would be deeply wounded if she thought that Charles could have come with you but did not."

Alain stared at her for a moment, his eyes warm with approval. "Then it's true, you care for Diane?"

"Oddly enough, yes. She's very different than she appears at first. Not witless at all. I couldn't tell you how, or even when it happened, but she has become a good friend to me."

The moon was beginning to set as Alain pulled on his clothing. "Tell me about Mirail. What has happened here?"

Marguerite busied herself tying his chausses. It was an intimate task she enjoyed performing, and it had the advantage of hiding her face from his scrutiny. As she knotted the laces, Marguerite considered Alain's question. Had he somehow learned about Henri's perfidy? But if he had, surely he would have raised the question earlier. No, it was likely an innocent inquiry. What was certain was that she had to give him an equally innocent answer.

If she told him about Henri, Alain would demand vengeance, and they could not afford that. Not now. Alain's responsibility to his lord must be satisfied before he could deal with a disobedient vassal. Moreover, were Alain to seek out Henri now, the fact that he had come to Mirail would inevitably be revealed. Marguerite would not let that happen, for it would jeopardize Alain's position with Richard.

"We have had an excellent harvest," she said. Though Alain might not be passionately interested in Mirail's production, it was both the truth and a noncontroversial subject. "Diane helped me dry many herbs this autumn."

Alain raised her to her feet and kissed her soundly. "Mayhap you should send some with me. Have you any herbs that will make me want you less?"

Marguerite chuckled as she shook her head. "Even if I did, I would not give you one. On the other hand, perhaps the antidote would be useful for your next visit."

"Are you intimating that I failed to satisfy you?" Alain pretended to be outraged.

"Quite the contrary. 'Twas merely that I was concerned about your strength for a repeat performance."

Alain rolled his eyes to the ceiling. "Didn't I tell you that I married a lusty wench?"

"You may have said that, but 'tis far from the truth. I was not a lusty anything when you married me, and if you find me that way now, 'tis solely your responsibility. Until I married you, I had no idea of love other than the troubadours' songs. Now . . .''

''Be not so disdainful of the troubadours. After all, I too gave you poetry,'' Alain reminded her.

She touched her lips to his. '' 'Tis not your poetry I crave now.''

''And what is it my lady desires?''

''This.'' She wrapped her arms around him.

The sun was rising before Alain left Mirail.

# Chapter Twenty

"He's gone."

Marguerite looked up from the column of accounts she had been trying unsuccessfully to reconcile. No matter what she did this morning, her thoughts seemed to stray to a certain tall man with silvery blond hair. Where was he today? Was the rain which had curtailed Marguerite's outdoor activities making travel difficult for him? While horses were not so easily bogged down in mud as heavily laden wagons, it was nonetheless unpleasant to spend weeks wearing sodden, mud-covered clothing and to be unable to find dry wood for the evening fires. Tempers grew short, and skirmishes were far more dangerous than in sunny weather, simply because the men used the excuse of battle to unleash their frustration. When they swung an ax at an opposing warrior, they were striking a blow against the fates that had sentenced them to travel in a climate which grew less hospitable as winter deepened.

Each morning Marguerite knelt in the chapel and prayed that Richard's tour would soon end and that Alain would return home. Then she tried to resume her normal activities, only to discover that the sight of her accounts triggered memories of his kissing each of her fingers and toes, counting aloud as he did. As she drew strands of finely spun wool into the loom, she remembered the texture of Alain's hair and the joy that running her fingers through it brought. The scent of drying herbs reminded her of the tangy scent that was Alain's alone. Who would have imagined that she, sensible Marguerite de Mirail, would be so ensorceled by a man that he dominated her every waking moment?

"Marguerite, he's gone." Louise repeated her statement, more sharply this time.

"He'll be back." The only question was when.

Louise stood directly in front of Marguerite and placed one hand over the page of accounts, silently demanding Marguerite's attention. "We've searched everywhere, but no one can find him. Mère is beside herself with worry, and even though I've told her that a ten-year-old could not have gone far, I share her fears. What if he fell into the river and drowned? We might never find his body."

A ten-year-old? Marguerite's eyes widened as she realized that Louise was speaking of Jean, not Alain.

"How long has Jean been missing?"

Louise shrugged, her frustration apparent in the tensing of her muscles. "At least several days. In truth, no one can remember when they saw him last. Mère thought he was with me, that you had summoned him for some task in the castle. I had no reason to think he was anywhere but at home."

It was puzzling, for Jean was unusually responsible for a young boy. He knew how dearly his mother loved him, how he was the son she had prayed for. It was not like him to disappear. Of course, he was but a boy, and who knew what mischief a boy could invent? Mayhap he had been punished and had felt the judgment unfair. Causing his mother to worry might be a ten-year-old's idea of justice.

"We'll find him." Marguerite used her most reassuring tone, and for a few days she believed her own words. But as the days passed and the men she had sent to scout the neighboring forests returned with no word of Jean, her concerns grew. Where could the boy be?

Adding to her fears for Jean were her worries over Alain,

for the same men who had searched for Louise's brother had been instructed to seek word of Richard's men. It was as though the troop had vanished, perhaps been swallowed by one of the deep forests, for no one seemed to know where they were.

The days became a week, then two, and with each day the lines around Louise's mouth deepened. With each day, Marguerite's smile faded. The night she and Alain had shared had been perfect, the most glorious time of her life. For a few hours, they had been truly man and wife, sharing far more than physical pleasure. It had been wondrous, but it was only one night, and as the days and the nights passed with no word from Alain, Marguerite began to wonder whether she had only imagined it. Had it all been a dream?

Oh, how his legs ached. The calves burned, their muscles so tightly knotted that he had to stop to rub them every few steps. His toes had blistered on the first day, and now the bottoms of his feet were a mass of broken blisters that ached with each step. Why had no one told him how far away Bleufontaine was?

It was to have been easy. He would ride hidden in one of the peddlers' wagons, coming out only when they reached Bleufontaine. It was a wonderful plan, and it had worked for almost a whole day. Then, when the men unloaded the wagon they had discovered him, curled into a small ball in one corner, trying to remain motionless. The leader had been angry and had insisted that he return to Mirail, but Jean had pleaded, telling the story of how he had to prove Gerard's death. In the end, the leader had relented, although he had stipulated that there would be no free rides. In truth, there were no rides at all. From that day onward, Jean had walked.

The leader's mouth had twitched ever so slightly as he told Jean his responsibility was to lead Sheba, one of the mules. It took only a few minutes for Jean to discover that Sheba was no ordinary mule. Ordinary? Not she, queen of the mules. She was the most ornery, balky animal Jean had ever seen. When she was supposed to walk, she would plant her hind legs firmly on the ground and refuse to move. When the band stopped for the midday break, Sheba would decide it was time to trot . . back along the road they had just traveled.

One of the peddlers had taken pity on Jean and had given him a carrot to hold in front of Sheba's nose. It was, the peddler had assured Jean, a sure way to induce the mule to move. And it had worked. With one swift movement, Sheba had snatched the carrot from Jean's hand and devoured it. Then she had returned to her motionless stance.

Another peddler had handed Jean a stout stick, admonishing him to use it firmly on Sheba's hind quarters. Though Jean had wielded the stick manfully, Sheba had paid no more attention to his blows than to the flies which buzzed near her ears. She moved when she saw fit and at no other time.

Sore feet and legs, the most infuriating mule ever to grace God's earth and food that turned his insides to jelly. Louise had best appreciate the sacrifices he was making for her.

He was becoming an accomplished liar. Indeed, he had shown a remarkable aptitude, mastering the art with no instruction. Of course, it was hardly a skill of which he would boast. He could hear it, the troubadours chanting tales of his prowess in battle, his amatory exploits and his lying tongue. The Silver Knight's reputation would be permanently tarnished.

He had planned to be back at the camp before anyone woke. Instead, because he had been unable to resist the lure of Marguerite's sweet kisses, it had been late morning when he had rejoined Richard's men. Fortunately the fates had been on his side. Not only had Richard followed the route he had outlined, taking none of the detours for which he was becoming noted, but that route had brought them near a dark forest at the same time that Alain saw them. He had guided Neptune into the trees. A few minutes later Alain had emerged from the forest, signaling that there was no danger. If he were lucky, the men would believe he had spent the early morning hours searching the forest, ensuring there would be no further ambushes.

Whether it was luck or the fact that his lies were convincing, no one had questioned him further.

And when Charles had commented on the flowery scent that clung to him, he had said mildly that he must have ridden through more bushes than he remembered. It was only later that Alain remembered that flowers were no longer blooming. Fortunately, Charles had seemed oblivious to that as well as the fact that his brother had not spent the night at the camp site.

It had been a wondrous night. For the first time in his life Alain wished he were a poet rather than a warrior, for the night he had spent with Marguerite deserved to be immortalized in poetry. Good poetry, not the poor imitation he had once concocted for her.

Just the thought of the pleasure they had shared sent the blood rushing to Alain's loins. She had been so responsive, so passionate . . . so loving. The thought made him pause. He had little experience with love, but her tenderness, the way she had spoken his name, and caressed his face was so different from every other night that he could attribute it to nothing else. She had responded to him with passion the night his mockery of Charles's poetry had turned into true love making. At the time, he had reveled in her newfound lust, but that night paled when compared to their stolen hours together.

Last night had been different. There was no denying they had lusted, craving each other's bodies. But it had been far more than that, transcending mere physical union. This time Alain felt they had merged their spirits as well as their bodies.

He grinned, thinking of the myriad ways they had found to pleasure each other. And yet nothing Marguerite had done, not even her most inventive caresses, had stirred him the way her simple words had. She had missed him.

The sun broke through the dense clouds, sending a ray of light onto the muddy road. Alain's grin widened. 'Twas an omen, a sign that Marguerite was over her foolishness and ready to be the wife he wanted. Alain chuckled, thinking how appropriate his choice of words was. The good Lord knew he was ready. As for wanting, he most definitely wanted his wife.

If Richard would only end this foolishness he called a tour, Alain could have what he wanted. It could not happen soon enough.


Her fingers, normally deft as they plied wool through the loom, fumbled and she muttered soft imprecations. At this rate, she would never have Alain's cloak finished. 'Twas foolish to think he would be home by Epiphany, but that thought had so brightened her days that she had begun weaving in anticipation of the holiday.

She had chosen an intricate pattern, one which would make him a rich, warm cloak. For the first few days, her fingers had flown, transforming fine strands of wool into a soft fabric. Today was different. No matter how she tried, she could not force her fingers into the soothing repetitive motion that was needed for a smooth even weave.

Today, though the sun shone for the first time in over a week, she was filled with an inexplicable sense of doom. Louise was humming softly, as though she had managed to put her fears for her brother aside for a few moments. Diane's step was lighter than it had been in weeks. Only Marguerite was unable to share her friends' delight in the beautiful day. Instead, she felt as though a heavy weight had been thrust upon her shoulders, dragging her slowly, inexorably toward the ground. She shuddered, for she had known this feeling once before, the day her father had died.

Marguerite shut her eyes, trying to block out the image of her father's body slumped over the table. That was a mistake. She should not have closed her eyes, for the image she saw then was not Guillaume but Alain, his body bloodied and lifeless in the middle of an empty field.

Nerves. That's all it was. There was no reason to believe he was in danger, for had he not said that Richard was a cautious leader, seeking peace rather than battle? It was merely the fact that her days seemed empty that made her react so foolishly.

She missed him. She had not lied that night when she had told Alain how she had longed for him, and yet what she had felt before was nothing compared to what she felt now. It was natural that she missed Alain's lovemaking. It was natural that her nights felt empty without him. This was more—far more—than that. At odd moments during the day she would find herself turning to talk to him, to ask his advice, but he was not there, and the realization left her feeling even more bereft.

She wanted Alain home again. He might not know how to console Louise or where to find Jean, but together they would be able to devise solutions to her problems. Alone she was but one person. Together they would be invincible.

But Alain did not return. And so she took long walks to soothe her spirit, she drank herbs to make her sleep and she prayed to every saint she knew. Nothing worked.

*She would never be warm again. The cold permeated the small chamber, seeping through the thick walls, chilling her to her very marrow. She sat huddled in one corner, her knees drawn up, her arms clasped around them as she tried to conserve what little warmth remained in her body.*

*Soon. It would be over soon. He had told her that the end would come on the third day after the full moon. 'Twas now two nights since the moon had cast its light through the tiny slit. Today, or mayhap tonight, would be the end.*

*He would come for her. Those heavy footsteps would ring on the stairs. The coarse laugh would reverberate, echoing off the walls. Those hands would reach out . . .*

*With a cry she rose and crossed the chamber, seeking the sun's warmth, a gentle breeze, the fragrance of a flower, anything to blot out the images of what was to come. She stared at the fields of golden wheat rippling in the breeze, a breeze that could not penetrate the tower walls, but she found no solace in the pastoral beauty.*

*And then she heard it, the sound of boots climbing the stairs, slowly, inexorably drawing nearer.*

*No! She could not let him do it!*

*Her breathing grew ragged as she leaned into the narrow slit. Where was he? Where was her knight? He had vowed to*

*help her if she ever needed him. Nothing on God's earth, no
creature that could live or die, would keep him from her. He
had sealed his pledge with the most tender of kisses and had
given her a rose as a sign of his love.*

*The rose was long since gone, its petals scattered to the
wind. Now all that remained was the memory of his promise.
That had been her sole shield against the nightmare she had
endured, the cold, the hunger, the waiting. He had promised,
and his promise was sacred. He would come.*

*Her eyes scanned the horizon, searching for him.*

*There was no one.*

*The footsteps grew closer. They were faster now, as though
he were anxious.*

*Where was he?*

*"It is time, my sweet." His voice echoed in the stairway,
and the laugh that accompanied his words sent a tremor down
her spine.*

*She leaned further into the slit, pressing her body into the
tiny opening.*

*And then she saw him. The great destrier stood a few yards
away, placidly grazing while his master lay on the ground,
not moving, his heartbeat growing weaker with each passing
moment.*

*"Help him!" she cried.*

*But there was no one to hear her plea, no one save the
creature whose laugh even now filled the room with evil.*

*"Only God can help him now."*

*He laughed again.*

*She screamed.*

Marguerite awoke, tears streaming down her cheeks. For a
moment she stared at the room, her eyes moving from the
tapestried walls to the deep window embrasure, drawing comfort from the familiar surroundings. It was naught but a nightmare. She had had it once before, that night at Lilis, but this
time it had been far worse. Marguerite dismissed the fact that
this time she had been in danger. From the moment that she
had seen Alain lying in the field wounded, perhaps dying, her

own peril had seemed insignificant. What had mattered was that Alain was in danger.

A shudder wracked her slender frame, and she felt the sharp metallic taste of fear. Unless she could learn who threatened Alain, she was powerless to help him, and that was a situation she could not tolerate.

Bleufontaine was not like Mirail. At home if people grumbled, it was good-natured grousing. In truth, most of the time there was little enough complaining. People were fed and clothed; their houses rarely leaked. Why would they complain? Instead they joked and helped each other.

Here the serfs and even squires cowered, slinking through the shadows in the vain hope they would not be noticed. Meals were silent affairs, with no one speaking unless Sir Henri addressed them. Even the dogs did not bark. It was as though they knew they would get fewer bones if they made a noise.

Jean did not like Bleufontaine.

It had been easy enough getting into the castle. He had marched in with the other peddlers, carrying a sack of pans over one shoulder, leading Sheba with the other arm. For once she had seen fit to walk with the other mules. Jean would never again doubt the power of prayer. He knew those hours he had prayed to every saint whose name he could remember had resulted in Sheba's unusual docility. Jean raised his eyes to the heavens in a silent prayer of thanks. He was inside and unnoticed. Now all he had to do was find Gerard.

With the unerring instincts of a hungry ten-year-old, Jean made his way to the kitchen. Cooks knew everything. They would know if Gerard were still alive and, if he were not, where he was buried. Besides, they usually had an extra pastry for a boy who was willing to do errands. Jean never minded errands, for if there was one thing he could always use, it was more food.

"That smells good." Jean pointed at the row of meat pies the cook had taken from the oven.

"There'll be none for you, my lad," the cook said. There

was no malice in the man's voice, only the statement of a fact. "My master ordered twenty, and twenty he will have."

"But he won't miss one."

Cook shook his head. "You peddlers will leave tomorrow. I stay, and I won't risk my skin for you."

Jean rubbed his stomach and wondered if Lady Marguerite counted meat pies. Somehow he doubted it.

"I'm mighty hungry," he said, moving his gaze from the meat pies to the bubbling kettle of soup. Surely Sir Henri hadn't measured every ounce. "I'm stronger than I look, and I can be real helpful if there's some extra food."

The cook shook his head. "There are others in this castle who are a lot hungrier than you." He looked at the beef bones piled on one corner of the table. Though nearly clean, there were still some shreds of brown meat clinging to them. "If you want to be useful, drop these into the dungeon. The poor chap there needs them more than the dogs. Then come back. I'll find something else for you to do. And maybe . . ." There was a hint of amusement in the man's voice, ". . . maybe I'll let you taste the soup."

With the prospect of food as a lure, Jean gathered the bones into his arms. When he returned from this errand, he would ask the cook about Gerard.


The saints were smiling on Giles, the baron of Valraux. Not only was he blessed with a visit from his liege lord, the duke of Aquitaine, but by the happiest of chances a troupe of troubadours had come to the castle. Now Giles could provide his lord with entertainment as well as finely cooked victuals. Perhaps Richard would recall his visit to Valraux with favor, enough favor to increase the rents Giles received. Indeed, it was a most fortunate day.

Giles had spoken with the leader of the troubadours, telling him of the honor that had been paid him, begging him to earn his keep tonight. Now, as the squires cleared the table, the troubadours filed into the Great Hall, their brightly colored raiment setting them apart from even the duke. Though Giles had been distressed that his lord had chosen to dine dressed as a common soldier rather than wearing royal robes, he had managed to hide his disappointment. The duke was, after all, a warrior. Maybe he felt it appropriate to dress as one.

The troubadours' first tale was one calculated to please the duke, for it told of a young warrior, recently installed as duke of the most powerful lands in all of France, a warrior who inspired such loyalty among his men that they would willingly die for him. Though no names were mentioned, as the lay continued, detailing the man's valor, there was no doubt of the proud and powerful duke's identity.

Alain listened in amazement to the second tale which recounted the same duke's pilgrimage to Jerusalem. Not a crusade, but a pilgrimage. It was only in the last week that Richard had changed his goal, admitting that he would make a pilgrimage. How had the rumor spread? He had asked Marguerite the same question. Peddlers, she had said. By now he should have been used to it, for each time they stopped at a castle, people had heard of Richard's yearning to take the Cross. Now it appeared they had learned of his new intentions.

In the past Alain had paid scant heed to troubadours' tales, believing them to have little basis in fact. He may have been wrong to dismiss them so easily. While he still believed that they embellished a story to make it more dramatic, there was no denying that troubadours and peddlers were exceptionally well informed.

"By all the saints above, I know not how they learned that." Alain muttered his displeasure to Charles, who was seated next to him. He spoke softly, so his words wound not find their way into the troubadour's next rhyme.

"Then 'tis true?"

Alain nodded almost imperceptibly. Richard had entrusted him with the information, and until this moment Alain had told no one, not even his brother.

The troubadours continued, entertaining the men with their tales of various knights' exploits. In each case, although the names were disguised, there was no question about the men's identities. And so when they began another intricately rhyming story, Alain listened carefully, wondering what tale the troubadours would spin this time.

It took no more than two stanzas for the story to rivet his attention, for the poet spoke of the fairest lady in the land, a maiden named Iris. Iris, the tale continued, married a knight whose armor never tarnished, a knight who had gained the appellation of the Argent Warrior. But the marriage soon foundered, for when the Argent Warrior left his lady fair, she transferred her affections to her neighboring vassal, the Knight of Azure Water. First Azure Water spent a week at her castle, spending every moment of the night and day with his lady. And when duty forced him to return to his own castle, Iris was so bereft that she cried inconsolably. Finally, true love won, and she fled her castle, dragging her men across the country so that she could return to the arms of Azure Water.

The sound of laughter roared in his ears, louder than the Infidels' battle cry. It was a lie. It had to be. She couldn't have betrayed him. And yet . . . There was no doubt that the troubadours were telling his own story with the names only lightly disguised. Who would not recognize the Argent Warrior as the Silver Knight and the Knight of Azure Water as Henri de Bleufontaine? Even Marguerite's flower name had been transformed into that of another flower.

Anger, far more powerful than he had ever experienced, gripped Alain, and he started to rise. He would kill the troubadour! Never again would that miserable excuse for a man spread his vile tales.

"Stop!" Charles placed a restraining hand on his brother's arm. "Don't fuel the tale with your anger. Besides, the story could be about anyone."

Alain sank back onto the bench. "That is hardly the case," he hissed between tightly clenched teeth. " 'Twas far too pointed a tale. Nay, Charles, the troubadours are saying that my wife has betrayed me."

Reaching for his sword, Alain started to rise again, but Charles kept a grip on him. " 'Tis only a troubadour's song. You know how they take the tiniest grain of truth and embroider on it. Mayhap Henri never visited Mirail. Mayhap he only mentioned he was contemplating a trip. The troubadours invented the rest."

Alain drew in a deep breath and expelled it slowly. It was a technique he had learned when facing the enemy, for it gave a man time to think, to allow his mind to overrule his emotions. The answer was to question the troubadour, to learn from the man himself what had inspired his tale.

But Alain learned nothing, for the troubadour insisted that the story was nothing more than his own creation, that he had seen an iris growing next to a pond of blue water and that he had been so taken with the imagery that he had concocted his tale. 'Twas that and nothing more.

The tone of his voice and the smirk on his face told Alain that the man was lying.

# Chapter Twenty-One

Jean wrinkled his nose in disgust. Even the animals at Mirail lived better than this. Here the air was fetid, rank with rotting mold. That same mold made the stairway so slippery that Jean feared he would lose his footing and tumble headfirst into one of the dungeons. Though his stomach rumbled with hunger, Jean was not certain that even two bowls of soup were enough to pay for this trip.

He followed Cook's directions, continuing ever deeper into the bowels of the house as the corridors twisted like a maze. Whoever this prisoner was, he was secreted far from the Great Hall. Jean was certain he had been walking for at least an hour. No wonder the man was hungry. Who would want to travel this far just to bring a condemned prisoner food? Jean looked down at the bones he carried, tempted to gnaw them clean himself.

"When you see the last iron grate, all you have to do is push the food through," Cook had told him. "No need to dally. That one isn't long for this earth."

Remembering his one night in the Mirail dungeon and the fear he had felt then, Jean felt a momentary kinship toward the unknown prisoner. What could his crime have been? Had he killed one of the barony's deer? Perhaps two? Jean doubted this man had a sister to plead for his life, and from what he had heard, Sir Henri was not one to grant clemency.

"Are you awake?" he asked when he reached the last cell. Though he had not thought it possible, the air was worse here, thick with years of decay and smells whose origins Jean preferred not to consider. "I've brought your food."

Muted groans greeted Jean's words, and he heard the prisoner struggle to his feet, cursing softly at the pain that accompanied the slightest movement.

"What is this? Now they're sending children with my food."

Jean stopped abruptly, the bones tumbling from his arms. Could it be? The voice, sounding as though his vocal cords had been abused, was familiar. Jean felt his heart begin to pound.

"I am not a child!" he protested, reaching down to pick up the food.

The man managed a faint chuckle. "Whoever you are, I vow 'tis good to hear a voice other than my master's."

Jean almost hooted with delight. There was no doubt about it. He would know that voice anywhere. Truly the Fates had been with him, leading him through the narrow hallways toward the unnamed prisoner, never dreaming that the prisoner was also the man he sought.

"You're alive!"

"That I am, no thanks to Sir Henri." Gerard spat out the man's name. "I have not seen the light of day in more weeks than I can count. But tell me, young man, who are you?"

Jean felt a moment of irritation that Gerard had not recognized his voice. After all, he had known his.

"I'm Jean, Louise's brother."

There was a moment of silence, as though Gerard were trying to understand what had happened. "Jean? From Mirail? How did you get here?" he asked at last. "And why did you come?"

"I walked." Jean was not about to tell Gerard about the blisters, the aches and Sheba. A man would not admit to such weaknesses. "I came because my sister would not believe you were dead. She demanded proof."

Another silence. "Why would she think that I was dead?"

Jean's words spilled forth like water that has been released from a dam. As he finished his tale, Gerard began to curse. Jean listened, fascinated. He would have to remember some of those words. They might make Sheba move more quickly.

"Indeed, I am alive," Gerard said. "Henri would not dare to kill me. But your sister and her mistress may not be safe for long. Listen carefully ..."


Why had she done it? The question tortured Alain, inflicting a pain deeper than the worst wound he had endured on a battlefield. Why had she betrayed him? It had been bad enough to watch her infatuation for Charles, but Henri de Bleufontaine, that miserable cur ... how could she have lain in his arms, kissing and caressing him? Had she given that despicable creature all the sweet caresses she had bestowed on him? The thought was like a festering wound that worsened as the hours passed.

His wife had betrayed him.

Alain poured another flagon of ale and drained it, but the pain would not be so easily dismissed. Had she ever loved him? In truth, she had never told him she loved him. It had only been his imagination that had invested their last night together with anything deeper than lust.

What a fool he was! The pain he was feeling today was his own fault. He should have known better. He should have realized that she was no different from all the others. But, no, he had deluded himself, and now he was paying the price for ignoring one of the most painful lessons of his life.

*"If your mother is unhappy, 'tis her own fault. 'Tis naught but retribution for her sins." Philippe stared at the boy who considered himself a man.*

*"My mother is not a sinner."*

*"We are all sinners, your mother more than most."*

*"You lie."*

*Philippe shook his head. " 'Tis not I who lies. 'Tis your mother. She does worse than speak lies. She is living one."*

*Wanting to hear no more, Alain had turned, but Philippe grabbed his arm. "Do you not call it a lie for her to claim Charles is your brother, when he is only your half brother?" As Alain's face whitened with shock, Philippe continued, "Ask your mother if you do not believe me. Ask her who fathered Charles. I assure you, it was not Robert, your own father."*

*When he could not wrench his arm free, Alain had tried to strike Philippe, but the older man had merely tightened his grip. "You think you're a man. Then face a man's truth. 'Tis time you learned that all women are whores who will sell themselves to the highest bidder. For some the price is money; others do it for the pleasure or to spite their husbands. But rest assured that they are all alike. Even your beloved mother."*

Alain winced and filled the flagon yet again. Though it had been many years since that day and the pain had diminished, there were times when it would resurface, breaking through the scar tissue. Times like today.

Why had he been so deluded as to think that this time it would be different, that a woman would love him for himself, not for the glory of his military prowess or his relationship with the duke? He should have known better. But he hadn't.

For that one magical night, Marguerite had been his. He knew her passion had been real, for there was no way she could have counterfeited those responses. But that was all that had been real. Philippe was right. Marguerite was a whore who had given herself to him to satisfy her own needs. She had taken from him and had given nothing in return save a few hours' pleasure.

And then she had gone from his bed to Henri's.

With a cry, Alain flung the flagon onto the floor, denting the finely polished metal.

Never again. He had been a fool to open his heart, to let a woman become part of his life. What a poor warrior he had been, showing a woman the chink in his armor, the hidden gate to his castle.

It would never happen again.

* * *

When she awoke, it was to a sense of profound uneasiness and a queasiness in her stomach. It had been thus every morning since her nightmare had returned. No matter how well she slept, she would waken to a sense that something was wrong. The feeling would diminish as the day passed and she forced herself to think about something, anything other than the fact that Alain was in danger. But each morning would bring a renewed malaise. If only she had some word of him. If only she knew that he was safe.

The sound of two sets of footsteps roused Marguerite from her reverie, and she looked up as Louise flung the door open, barely bothering to knock. Her face flushed but radiant, Louise was smiling for the first time since Marguerite had returned from Bleufontaine. The cause of her renewed happiness stood a pace behind her. His face was more tanned, his clothes had a few more rents and were sorely in need of washing, but otherwise he was unchanged.

"Where were you?" Marguerite's voice was harsh. Though Louise might forgive her brother for the anguish he had caused, Marguerite was no so lenient. "Did you not know your parents and sister would worry about you?"

Jean nodded, but there was nothing of the penitent in his stance. Instead, he appeared far more self-assured than the ten-year-old who had left Mirail only a few weeks earlier.

"It matters not." Louise bestowed a fond smile on her brother. "Oh, Marguerite, I was right. Gerard is alive. Jean saw him and spoke to him."

For an instant Marguerite was silent, considering the implications of Louise's announcement.

"Henri lied to me again." She mused aloud, her anger starting to rise. She had tried to protect Henri's self-esteem, choosing not to shame him in front of the other vassals. And this was how he had repaid her. When Alain returned, she would deal with Henri, and it would be a most public chastisement. The man deserved no less.

Marguerite fixed her gaze on Jean who perched on the edge of the wooden chest. "He put Gerard in the furthest dungeon. It was dark and smelly, and it took hours to walk there."

"That explains why the servants I questioned did not know he was still alive." Henri had obviously planned Gerard's disappearance carefully. What Marguerite did not know was why he had not wanted to forfeit Gerard to her—that made no sense—or why, once he had decided that Gerard was not to leave Bleufontaine, he had kept the serf alive. It would have been easier to kill him.

"Cook knew there was a prisoner in that dungeon, but he didn't know who the man was. Sir Henri told Cook not to talk to the prisoner."

Marguerite nodded her understanding. Gerard's voice was so distinctive that, had anyone spoken to him, they would have discerned his identity immediately.

Henri's disobedience had lasted long enough. No matter what the other vassals believed, it was time for Henri to accept the consequences of his actions. She would not wait for Alain's return.

"I shall summon my men. If we need to, we will storm Bleufontaine to get Gerard released."

Marguerite rose and reached for the bell to summon Bertrand.

"Wait." Louise stretched out a restraining hand. "There is more." She turned to Jean.

He thrust back his shoulders in a conscious imitation of Alain pronouncing judgment. The effect was one of dignity, but it was spoiled as Jean's words tumbled out. "Sir Henri plans to attack Mirail."

Poitiers was a beautiful city. Situated on the banks of the Rivers Clain and Boivre, the grand donjon Maubergeon visible in the distance, the sun gleaming off the city walls, it was a place that inspired minstrels' and troubadours' poetry. Today, however, the men who approached Poitiers were inspired not by architectural beauty but by the prospect of warm food, soft beds and willing women . . . not necessarily in that order.

Richard had told them that the tour would continue, but that for a few weeks they would remain in Poitiers, ostensibly to consult with his mother, in reality, he had confided in Alain, to give the men a respite from the journey. Though they were all warriors, accustomed to spending months astride their horses, that did not mean that they would not welcome creature comforts. The decision had confirmed Alain's belief that Richard was a born leader, one who recognized his men's varied needs, though he himself might not share all of them.

"I thought I would never see you again. You left so hastily the last time, and then I had no word from you." Honore stepped back and let Alain enter her house. Though she smiled, there was a wariness in her expression that Alain did not remember.

"What is important is that I am back." He looked around the room. The same tapestries hung from the wall; the same chair stood in one corner. Nothing had changed, and perhaps Honore herself only seemed somehow different.

"But now you are married." The bitterness in her voice told Alain that was the cause of the wariness he had seen. He felt a flash of irritation. Honore had known from the beginning that they would never marry, and indeed they had never spoken of even a permanent liaison.

"Is this a recent scruple you've developed?" he asked. "Since when have you cared aught for a man's marital state?"

Honore flushed as the barb hit home. "Since the troubadours tell me he loves his wife."

"Troubadours exaggerate." And if there were some truth to the story, it mattered not. What he needed now was the sweet oblivion he could find in her arms. His eyes moved from her face toward the doorway to her sleeping chamber. "I have thought often of my last visit here and how rudely we were interrupted."

"Then you would like to bathe?"

"That would be a good beginning." His grin hinted at delights to come, and as he watched, Honore began to relax. Within minutes of her ringing the bell, servants had filled the tub with steaming water.

"Now, my lord, we have some unfinished business." She lathered the soap between her hands, then began to slowly stroke his body, seeking to stimulate as well as cleanse him. And succeed she did, for under her tender ministrations, Alain's body began to stir.

"Anxious, my lord?" Her voice was husky with passion as she murmured the question, her lips so close that he could feel the softness of her breath teasing the sensitive inner curves of his ear. "Is there something you want?"

He rose, leaving her in no doubt of his wants. "I vow, 'tis not something but someone I want. And that someone is you."

Alain drew Honore into his arms, heedless of the water that still clung to his body. With one swift movement he swept her off her feet and carried her to the bed. Her breath was sweet, her skin was soft; he was needy; she was willing, yet as he lay beside her, Alain found that his passion evaporated as quickly as dew drops in the bright morning sun.

"I'm sorry, my dear," he said when not even Honore's most skilled caresses could arouse him. "It would appear that I am not the man I once was."

The admission was a painful one, for never before had this problem plagued Alain. He had heard other men speak of it in hushed tones, and he had sympathized with them without truly understanding the humiliation it brought.

Honore traced the outline of his lips with her fingertips. "Let it not worry you. 'Tis far more common than you know. I have often seen this happen after a long period of abstinence."

Alain did not contradict her by telling her that abstinence had the opposite effect on him. Instead, he agreed when she offered him a glass of wine, and later that day he suggested they go into the city. They wandered through the streets, stopping to admire the wares in the central marketplace. When Honore's eyes lingered on a piece of emerald silk, Alain purchased it for her. And later when she suggested they visit friends of hers, he agreed. She was displaying him to the city, much as a child does a new toy. At another time, Alain would have been annoyed and would have refused to accompany her, but not today. This was the least he could do for her.

For the next week, Alain and Honore were inseparable. He spent every night at her house, and when Richard did not require his services, he spent the days with Honore. Rumors, long the lifeblood of Poitiers's society, thrived on their renewed relationship, and if there was no truth to the speculation, only Alain and Honore knew it.

Mindful that his knights were warriors and needed to keep their martial skills current, Richard arranged frequent jousts. It was during one of them that Alain bested Bertrand de Villeneuve.

"*Pax.*" Bertrand admitted his defeat. "I cannot compete with you on this or any field. Indeed, you are the envy of every man here."

Alain sheathed his sword. "I have had years of practice, and Neptune is the finest of destriers."

Bertrand stared at him for a moment, seemingly not comprehending Alain's words. Then he shook his head. "You misunderstand. Our envy is not for your martial skills but for your amatory conquests. Honore is the fairest lady in all of Poitou."

"She is indeed, is she not?" Oddly, the other knights' admiration brought Alain no pleasure. He felt as though his life, which had once been eminently satisfying, had a gaping void in it. He was doing the same things he had always done, yet they were no longer enough. Something vital was missing. Unbidden, Marguerite's image danced before him. No, it could not be that he longed for her. There was another reason for his malaise. There had to be.


"I want to talk to you."

Alain looked up from the mail that he was repairing and glared at his brother. "What if I don't want to talk to you?"

For once Charles did not flinch under his sarcasm. "Then don't talk, just listen." He took a step toward Alain. "I thought you were a man of honor."

His words riveted Alain's attention. "Who says I am not?" Had it been anyone other than Charles, Alain would have challenged him for merely making such an accusation.

"You have a strange code of honor, dallying with Honoré when Marguerite is alone at Mirail."

Marguerite. It all came back to her.

"How can you be certain she is alone? Mayhap Azure Water is with her. Mayhap she has found someone else."

Charles flushed. "You know that is not true."

"*Au contraire,* brother of mine, I have every reason to believe it is the truth. Right now she is probably entertaining her latest gallant in our marriage bed." The same bed where she had once tried to refuse Alain his husbandly rights.

"Despite anything you may think, she is still your wife, and she deserves better treatment than this."

Alain laid the mail on the floor and rose to his feet in a fluid gesture. "Save your noble sentiments for someone else. My wife . . ." He spat out the word as though it were a piece of spoiled meat, ". . . does not deserve them."

"You're wrong."

"And you, dear brother, are sadly misguided. I suggest you examine your own thoughts. If you do, you will find they are not as pure as you would like to believe, for it is obvious that you still fancy yourself in love with my wife." Again, Alain's lip curled in disgust as he pronounced the word. "How unfortunate that you can never have her, that you cannot be the next in her string of lovers. But you cannot, because it would be against every law of God and man. You cannot lie with your sister."

Charles's face whitened as though from a blow. "Are you daft? This must be what comes of not wearing a helmet. The rain must have softened your brain."

" 'Tis no laughing matter, Charles. Robert was not your father. Guillaume was."

"You really are crazy." Charles shook his head. "It is no surprise to me that you say Robert was not my father. I have long known that, although everyone pretended otherwise. Still, a man recognizes his father, and I've known that Philippe is mine. We are much alike."

"Philippe is not your father." Alain spoke slowly, enunciating each word carefully as he would for a child who was just learning to speak. "Our mother lusted after Guillaume, and you are the result."

"You are lying! That is not true."

"Think about it. Janelle and Guillaume wanted to marry but could not, so they did the next best thing. They betrothed their children."

"Alain, the rain has obviously addled your brain. You know as well as I do that your betrothal to Marguerite was the result of friendship, a friendship that included Robert."

"That was the story Janelle concocted. In reality, it was nothing so noble. Philippe told me the whole story."

Charles was unconvinced. "Did you ask our mother? Did she confirm it?"

"Would you expect her to admit something so heinous? I did ask her, and she denied everything. The problem is, her words said one thing, her face something very different." Alain paused, hating the words he was uttering. "I saw the way she looked whenever Guillaume's name was mentioned. It was the same expression I saw when I spoke of Janelle to Guillaume. Face the truth, Charles. Marguerite's father was also your father."

Charles shot Alain a look of pure disgust. "You are totally mad. It started when you heard that troubadour's tale, and ever since then you have been overreacting. You keep imagining betrayals where none exist, and now you're even reaching back into the past to find new betrayals. Alain, you're wrong! Absolutely dead wrong. Marguerite has not betrayed you, just as our mother did not betray Robert."

The outburst was so unlike Charles that Alain was silent for a moment. Then he laughed. "You foolish man. You still believe in all those stories, don't you? Damsels in distress and knights who rescue them. Camelot." Alain laughed again, a sound filled with bitterness rather than mirth. "Think about it, Charles. What happened in Camelot? Isn't it true that Guinevere betrayed her husband with his most trusted knight?" When he saw that the blow had hit home, Alain continued. "If you believe those tales, why is it so difficult to believe that Marguerite and Janelle betrayed their husbands?"

Charles had no answer.

# Chapter Twenty-Two

Marguerite stared sightlessly at the book of accounts. Though it was her customary day to enter the barony's receipts, this morning she could not force her eyes to focus on the page or her hand to inscribe the number of eels which Jacques the Fisherman had caught in his net the previous week. She could think of naught but the message the rudely clad man had brought.

"If you love me, come to Jarnac the night of the new moon."

The man had bowed low and tugged on his forelock as he delivered the message, explaining that Alain had had no time to commend his words to parchment but assuring Marguerite that he had not forgotten a single word. The message had come as so many did, transmitted from one traveler to another, each taking it a few miles further until it finally arrived at Mirail. Simplicity rather than eloquence was the author's goal when sending a verbal message, although Marguerite could not fault Alain's eloquence. He had given her a choice, making it a request rather than a command.

But what a choice!

Marguerite dipped her quill into the ink once more. She would complete the accounts before dinner was served.

It should have been such a simple decision with no need for deliberation. Her husband had asked her to join him for another night of the greatest pleasure she had ever experienced. How could she refuse? In truth, she did not want to. And yet, how could she leave Mirail, knowing that Henri planned to attack it?

Marguerite inscribed two numbers on the page, then laid the quill back on the table. It was useless. When her mind was whirling in circles, she could not concentrate on making neat rows of figures.

She wanted to be with Alain. Oh, how she wanted to be with him! But she could not leave Mirail. Her people depended on her to defend them, especially now that her father was dead and Alain was absent. She was their leader. It mattered not that she was not a warrior and that she would not physically lead the men in their defense of the castle walls. She was their symbolic chief, the last in a long line of lords and ladies who had made the welfare of Mirail their primary concern.

From early childhood, her father had instilled in her the knowledge that one day Mirail would be hers. He had groomed her for her role, stressing that the privilege of ruling a barony as rich as Mirail brought with it concomitant responsibilities. Responsibilities that transcended all else, responsibilities that came before any thought of personal pleasure. Guillaume had taught his daughter well. Too well, she realized, for he had left her with no choices. She could not leave her people. They depended on her, and she would not forsake them, not even for the man she loved.

Marguerite closed the ledger, resisting the urge to slam the heavy volume on the table. It was not fair. But no one had promised her that life would be fair. Indeed, her father had stressed that for the nobility, obligation weighed more heavily than aught else. Happiness was an illusion created by poets and troubadours.

Her shoes rang on the stone floor as she walked back to the Great Hall. Alain would understand when she did not come to Jarnac. He must. And yet as she entered the room, a shiver of dread ran down her spine as she remembered her dream. Alain

was in danger. Perhaps that was why he asked her to meet him
in Jarnac. Perhaps he had discovered the threat to his life. In
her dream she had been powerless to help him. Now she was
being given another chance, and she could not let it slip by.
She had to go to Jarnac, if only to assure herself that Alain
was safe. There had to be a way she could do that without
placing her people in danger.

Marguerite closed the heavy oak door behind Diane and
Louise, then waited until she was certain the last of the servants
had descended the stairs.

"I need your help," she told the two women as she outlined
her plan.

Louise was skeptical, her brown eyes reflecting her worries.
"You can't take the risk," she said.

Diane shook her head, dismissing Louise's fears. "It may
work," she conceded.

And so, two days later, dressed in coarse woolen clothes that
showed the signs of too many seasons of wear, mounted on a
mule that appeared far too decrepit to travel more than a dozen
miles and accompanied by only two of her strongest men,
Marguerite left Mirail under cover of darkness. As far as anyone
within the castle walls knew, the mistress had been taken ill.
Louise would say nothing more, but Lady Diane's sober mien
told them she feared the worst. Though no one would voice
the word "pox" for fear of jinxing their lady, there was little
doubt that she had fallen prey to the dread disease.

"Even I did not question Henri when he told me Gerard had
died of the pox," Marguerite had explained. "It is one of the
few ailments that will keep everyone, even Father René, away."
And, most importantly, no word of her departure would reach
Henri. Gerard had not known how soon Henri planned to attack,
but Marguerite was certain that if he knew she had left Mirail
he would attack immediately. This way there was a chance
that she would have returned from Jarnac before Henri's men
arrived.

"My dear, I am delighted to see you." Philippe kissed Marguerite as he helped her dismount from her mule. "But why

are you alone and in those clothes? Surely the fortunes of Mirail have not disappeared.''

Marguerite shook her head, smiling with pure joy at the thought that within hours she would be reunited with Alain. The ride had been a long and hard one, but she had arrived at Jarnac on the day of the new moon. ''I'll explain it all,'' she promised. ''But first I beg you summon the maids. Only the thought of a hot bath has sustained me these last few hours.'' That and the prospect of a night with Alain. It would be unseemly, though, to share that morsel with Philippe.

When she emerged from the chamber she and Alain had shared on their last visit to Jarnac, Marguerite found Philippe waiting. Offering her a goblet of wine, he raised one eyebrow. ''So tell me, my dear, why you have journeyed to Jarnac dressed like a serving woman.''

''To see Alain,'' she replied simply.

''Alain?'' Philippe stared at her, his face reflecting his confusion. ''But he is with Richard.''

''He sent me a message, asking me to meet him here.''

Philippe shook his head. ''You must have been mistaken. Alain would never leave Richard, not while he's ensuring his vassals' loyalty.''

It was Marguerite's turn to shake her head. ''He might. In fact, he did once.''

Philippe drained his wine, then studied Marguerite's face carefully. ''I would never have believed it, but your words have the ring of truth. Perhaps the boy has changed.''

''Alain will be here tonight. I know it.'' Marguerite could not keep from smiling as she thought of the reunion she had planned for them. If he had called her a lusty wench before, after tonight he would have to invent a new term, one filled with superlatives.

Pouring himself another glass of wine, Philippe gestured toward the game board. ''Will you indulge an old man's fancy?'' he asked.

''Only if you cease referring to yourself as an old man. To me you are not old.''

Marguerite took the seat opposite Philippe and arranged the

black pieces on the board. Indeed, a game of dames would be a pleasant way to while away the time until Alain arrived.

"Your flattery is very welcome, my dear Marguerite." Philippe advanced a pawn two squares. "But it is only that, flattery. I am indeed an old man, and one who fears the reckoning that comes with death."

Marguerite looked up from the chessboard. This melancholy was a side of Philippe she had not seen on her last visit to Jarnac. Mayhap it was only the result of a long winter with few visitors to break the tedium.

"Surely you have much to be proud of," she said. "Your sons foremost. There are few men so admired in all of France as Alain, and Charles is the perfect knight."

Philippe waited until Marguerite had captured his pawn with one of hers. "They are what you say," he conceded, "but I cannot take credit for them. I spent very little time with Charles and none at all with Alain." He picked up a bishop, tracing the curves of the piece with his forefinger. "It was probably wrong, but I made Janelle my whole life."

There was such sadness in Philippe's voice that Marguerite felt tears sting her eyes. "You must have loved her very much."

"No one else on earth mattered to me. The only thing I wanted from the first day I met Janelle was to make her happy."

The ache deep in her stomach caught Marguerite by surprise, and she realized it was a combination of longing and jealousy. How odd, to be jealous of a woman who was dead, and yet Marguerite could not deny that she envied Janelle. What woman would not want to be the recipient of a love so strong? It was what she herself had dreamed of all her life. She hoped—oh, how she hoped—that she and Alain would know such a love. But with that hope came the fear that if Janelle's son felt a love so deep, he would never show it.

"She was a very lucky woman to have your love."

Philippe moved his knight forward one square and two to the left, capturing one of Marguerite's pawns. "I doubt Janelle would have agreed with you. It was Robert's love that made her whole. Part of her died the day Robert did, and there was nothing I could do to fill the void."

"But she had Robert's son. Alain was living proof of their love, a part of the man she had lost." Though she refused to think of living without Alain, Marguerite knew that if he were killed and she had his son, she would lavish their child with love.

Leaning back in his chair, Philippe gave Marguerite a long look before he continued. "You might think she would have clung to Alain, but it wasn't that way. Janelle spent no time with Alain once we returned from Outremer. She should have waited until he was seven or eight to send him away for fostering, but instead she prevailed on Guy de Bercé to take him when he was still a small child. Alain never lived here for any length after the crusade."

Marguerite was silent, absorbing the significance of Philippe's statements. She knew that Alain had been only two when his parents had gone on crusade, leaving him in Poitiers with Eleanor of Aquitaine's daughter Marie. What she had not realized was that from that point onward, he had not had a normal childhood. Not only had he been deprived of his father, but it appeared that he had had virtually no care from his mother. And to be fostered with Guy de Bercé. The man was noted for his harsh treatment of squires. What must he have been like with a small child?

A thought assailed her. "Alain must have known Henri de Bleufontaine as a child. Henri was one of Guy de Bercé's squires, and it would have been about the same time." Odd. She had not realized that Alain and Henri had met before that first encounter in the Great Hall of Mirail.

Philippe shrugged. "I have no idea. Alain was rarely here, and even when he came, he did not confide in me."

"Poor Alain." The words slipped out unbidden.

"I doubt he wants your pity."

"It's not pity; it's sympathy." Marguerite spoke more harshly than she had intended. "No one should have a childhood like that."

Philippe studied the chessboard, picking up one piece, then another as though planning his next move.

"You're right, of course," he said at length. "One of the

disadvantages of living so long is that I have had time to reflect on my life and to realize what I should have done differently.'' He moved his queen, capturing Marguerite's bishop. ''I cannot undo my actions, but I can try to make up for some of them. Perhaps that is why God has kept me alive this long.''

Absentmindedly Marguerite moved a pawn, not noticing that she had left her king unprotected. There was wisdom, much wisdom, in Philippe's words. Like him, she had acts in her life, and most particularly in her marriage, that she regretted. While she could not take back the harsh things she had said to Alain, she need not repeat them. From this day forward, she could give Alain the love he had so long been denied.

She glanced at the high window and saw that darkness had fallen. ''Alain should be here soon,'' she said.

''Checkmate.''

Marguerite groaned but agreed when Philippe suggested another game. By the time she had captured Philippe's queen, it was long past midnight.

''I wonder where Alain is.'' The thought had haunted her all evening, and only Philippe's skillful moves had forced her to concentrate on the game board rather than brood on Alain's absence.

Philippe laid his hand on one of hers. ''My dear, Alain is a soldier, and a soldier's life is not his own. Perhaps Richard changed their route, and he is no longer passing close enough to slip away.''

It was a possibility. But as Marguerite reflected on the things she had learned from Philippe, another thought assailed her, sending a shiver of fear down her spine.

''Perhaps you are right,'' she conceded. ''Or perhaps the message was not from Alain at all. Perhaps it was nothing but a ruse to force me to leave Mirail.''

# Chapter Twenty-Three

The attack would come when the castle was least prepared, two hours before dawn. At that time, even the most diligent of watchmen would be dozing, certain that no one else was awake. It was still too early for the cooks to begin preparing the morning meal, and not even the birds had begun to chirp. It was, Henri knew, the perfect time for an attack.

Mirail was silent. Only the occasional mooing of a cow indicated that the castle had not been deserted, for there were no other signs of life, not even the faint light of a fire. Marguerite and her men were most foolishly asleep.

Henri grinned. His plan was masterful. Soon Mirail and all its treasures would be his.

At first he had been annoyed that she had ignored the message he had sent, the invitation that purported to be from her husband. His spies had watched carefully, but she had not left the château. For a few days Henri had thought that mayhap she had come to her senses and had no desire to be with that scourge of humanity she had married. But then the report had come: the mistress of Mirail was dangerously ill.

Henri had waited, delaying his attack. While he did not wish for Marguerite's death—certainly not before he had enjoyed her undeniable charms—by God's will, he would use that sad event for his own advantage. While the people were mourning their loss, the castle would be vulnerable. Only a fool would miss an opportunity like that.

But Marguerite had not died, and so Henri had altered his plan of attack. It was brilliant, truly brilliant. There would be no resistance as he and his men marched into the castle, for sleeping men present no threat to a conquering army. Within minutes they would have subdued the few guards who were not slumbering and would have taken possession of the castle. Then there would be no sleep for at least one inhabitant. No, indeed. Although she would not leave her bed, sweet Marguerite would have no time for sleep. Henri gloated, thinking of the pleasures to come.

What he did not see were the black-cloaked men concealed on the ramparts as they had been every night since Jean had returned to Mirail. From dusk to dawn they remained there, watching and waiting, prepared to give their lives if need be to protect their mistress.

As the enemy drew closer, the men signaled to each other. Not yet. They would wait until Henri's men were directly beneath the walls.

The men from Bleufontaine moved quietly, gathering near the drawbridge which the slovenly watchman had forgotten to raise. So much the better for them. They would have one less barrier to their entry. Their master had been correct in his assessment. Lady Marguerite had no idea they were coming. It would be an easy conquest.

On the ramparts the signals changed as the men reached for their weapons. Tonight they could not use burning pitch to defeat the enemy, for the fire needed to heat the pitch would have alerted Henri's men to the fact that they were awake. Instead, they had gathered piles of stones. For days they had practiced with their ancient weapons, laughing as they became modern-day Davids, ready to slay the enemy with no more than a slingshot and a few stones.

As they watched, a small group of Henri's men broke away,

heading for the rear entrance to Mirail. It took only seconds
for the signal to be sent to the men who guarded the postern.
Lady Marguerite had guessed correctly that Henri would try
to attack on both fronts, and she had ordered men to guard the
entire perimeter. Her finest foot soldiers stood at the postern,
ready to destroy the attackers.

Now!

As the men from Bleufontaine began to file across the drawbridge, Marguerite's men took aim. At first there was no sound
in the still night other than the soft whirling of slings, but then
the sound of stones striking flesh and the groans of wounded
and dying men filled the air. It was only a matter of minutes
before the attackers began to flee, conceding defeat.

Leading the men to the rear gate, Henri grinned again. The
gate was not only unguarded, it was open. Marguerite might
be a delicious morsel, but she was not a wise woman. When
Mirail was his, he would not allow her to make the same
mistake. No, indeed. There would be a guard posted every
night, all night, and woe to the guard who so much as nodded
with sleep during his watch.

Henri pushed open the gate. In just a few moments, the sweet
wench would be his, spreading her legs for him. Oh, how that
would pain the mighty Alain de Jarnac. Henri started to laugh.

The blow caught him unawares. The man had appeared from
out of nowhere, his sword drawn.

"Attack!" Henri shouted the command as he drew his own
sword, but it was too late. His men were surrounded by a large
force of knights, all brandishing swords and spears. They were
good, but he was better. Everyone knew there was no one in
the realm whose skill with a sword could compare to Henri de
Bleufontaine.

He parried the attack, thrust for thrust, but it was no contest.
Though he was the superior warrior, even he was no match
for a dozen men. Henri feinted, then, taking advantage of his
opponents' momentary confusion, slipped between two men.
There was no shame in fleeing. Only a foolish man would fight
a battle he had no chance of winning.

* * *

"Oh, Marguerite, he was so understanding." Louise stood in the solar, her smile belying the tears that streamed down her cheeks. "I did what you suggested, and I talked to Father René, not at confession but as one of his parishioners asking advice. I pleaded with him to release Gerard and me from our penance, telling him that we had paid for our sins. He agreed." Louise's smile was radiant. "He told me that our Lord was merciful. He even said that the payment was appropriate, that today we had saved Mirail, and that compensated for the time you were endangered."

"Then you can see Gerard again?" Marguerite put an arm around Louise's shoulders and hugged the young woman. It was good to see Louise smiling again. The entire barony was rejoicing, celebrating Henri's defeat. And now Louise was one step closer to finding happiness. 'Twas truly a day for celebration.

"Father agreed that was possible, but he forbade me to lie with Gerard again unless we are married."

" 'Tis simple, then. We will find a way for you to marry. Indeed, I have been working to accomplish precisely that." She outlined her demands to Henri, telling Louise that her trip to Bleufontaine had had only one goal: bringing Gerard back to Mirail and that the false reports of his death had saddened Marguerite almost as deeply as they had Louise. " 'Twas not sorrow for Gerard so much as for you," she told Louise. "I could not bear the thought of causing you such pain."

When Louise looked slightly bewildered, Marguerite continued her explanation. "I feared telling you my plan before, because I did not know how long it would take to bring Gerard to Mirail. The worst thing I could have done was to raise your hopes prematurely."

Louise brushed away the last of her tears. "Oh, Marguerite, you know it is my deepest desire to live with Gerard, to be his wife, but I fear that even you cannot make that happen. Gerard will not leave Bleufontaine, and he has forbidden me to go there."

Marguerite raised a questioning brow. "If he loves you, why would he not come to Mirail?"

Her words rushing forth, Louise explained about Henri's threats to Gerard's sister. "Gerard loves his sister, and he will not endanger her."

Marguerite thought quickly, seeking a solution. "Mayhap we could move her to another convent. Would she go, or is she deeply attached to Saint-Lazaire?"

It was a question Louise could not answer. "The only person who can answer that is Gerard. I beg you, Marguerite, let me go to Bleufontaine and speak with him."

Love was a powerful emotion. It turned even sensible women like Louise into foolish girls.

"Absolutely not. Henri is far too dangerous for me to consider letting you near him. No, we will find another way to get Gerard out of Bleufontaine. I fear, though, that we must wait until Alain returns."

"Will that be soon?"

"I hope so." For more reasons than one.


It was difficult to think of her as an old woman, and indeed the years had been kind to her. Though her life had not been easy, the strains had not been written on her face. She was still a beautiful woman. More than that, she was the queen.

Alain knelt before her, waiting for the signal to rise. Eleanor, once Queen of France, Queen of England and still Duchess of Aquitaine, touched him on the shoulder and motioned toward a low stool.

"My son has told me of your bravery and how you fought with him during the ambush. I am grateful for your protection."

Alain shook his head. "Your son needed no protection. He is a valiant warrior and the finest leader I have had the privilege to serve. Of course, that comes as no surprise, knowing his mother." It was not idle flattery. Eleanor would have seen through that and dismissed Alain immediately if she had thought his words false. But they rang of truth, and she accepted them as her due, inclining her head ever so slightly.

''I hope to convince Richard to remain in Poitiers for several months, mayhap through the spring. There is much for us to do, including seeing to Richard's betrothal.''

Alain hoped his face showed none of his skepticism. It was unlikely Richard would be anxious for a betrothal, no matter how comely or how suitable the heiress.

As though sensing his hesitation—or perhaps understanding the reason behind it—Eleanor said, ''I need to surround my son with happy couples so that he may learn from their example.''

Wasn't that what Charles had said, that Diane had had an advantage he and Alain had not, because her parents had been happily married?

'' 'Tis a wise move,'' Alain agreed.

Before he could say more, a tall woman entered the room, her resemblance to the queen leaving no doubt of their relationship.

''Alain!'' The woman's cry of delight was genuine, and she raised her face for his kiss. ''Shame on you. I knew you were in Poitiers, but I have not seen you at my courts of love.'' The beautiful young woman was Marie de Champagne, Eleanor's oldest daughter and Alain's childhood companion. Since her mother had returned to Poitiers and restored the city to its rightful role as the cultural center of France, Marie had instituted what were quickly dubbed courts of love. Though they were the talk of the city and, indeed, all of Poitou, Alain had avoided them, always finding an excuse when Honore suggested they attend. He would tell neither Honore nor Marie that love was one topic he preferred to ignore. That and troubadours' songs.

'' 'Tis not for lack of desire,'' Alain prevaricated. ''It is simply that I have been very busy.''

''So I've heard.'' Marie's smile was arch. ''Honore, it appears, is very happy. I've seen a contented smile on her face almost constantly since you and my brother came back.'' She chuckled. ''Could there perhaps be a causal relationship between your arrival and Honore's happiness?''

It was no surprise that the gossip had reached Marie's ears.

''You always did have sharp eyes,'' he told her. ''Remember when . . .''

* * *

"I knew I kept you alive for a reason." The light of Henri's torch illuminated his face, telling Gerard more clearly than his angry tone that his master was unhappy. Gerard felt a moment of fear. If Henri had attacked Mirail and been repulsed, he might have somehow learned that Gerard had warned Lady Marguerite. In that case, nothing, not even his talisman, would save him.

"On your feet! If I wanted you to grovel, I would have commanded it."

Henri grabbed Gerard's arm and yanked him upright. "Get moving. By all the saints above, this dungeon reeks."

When they reached the inner courtyard, Gerard stumbled. After weeks of total darkness, his eyes were unable to adjust to the bright sunlight, and he closed them involuntarily.

"You dolt!" Henri aimed a blow at Gerard's shoulder. "You're a worthless cur, but you're the only one who can do what I need done. And then we'll see about that sister of yours."

Henri led the way to his small counting chamber. "The castle looked asleep, but there were men on the ramparts," he told Gerard. "It was the oddest thing. They used stones instead of arrows. Imagine, stones. They must have had other attacks and spent all their arrows. Yes, that's it. That would explain why they were on guard." Henri unsheathed his sword and began lunging at Gerard, never quite touching him but coming close enough that Gerard would flinch and move to the side.

"It's understandable. After all, Mirail is a desirable barony, and Marguerite is a desirable wench. Together ..." Henri chuckled. "They will be mine, and then I assure you that no one will breach those walls. Now, listen to me. This is what you must do."

Henri outlined his plan. Gerard was to journey to Mirail and beg admittance. Once there, he was to question Louise until he discovered a way that Henri could enter the castle unseen.

"A simple task," Henri concluded. "And just to ensure that

you do it well, I think I will pay a task to Saint Lazaire. It will be good for my soul to spend some time within holy walls."

His laugh echoed from the walls, making Gerard cringe. Sweet Mary in heaven, he prayed, look after my sister.

"There is someone at the gate." The guard's face mirrored his distress. "It is one of Henri de Bleufontaine's men. Shall I throw him in the dungeon?"

Marguerite frowned. She had thought that after her vassals had repulsed Henri, it would be some time before he returned. She had no doubt that he would try again to capture Mirail, for the man was nothing if not determined. It was only the timing which surprised her. This was sooner than she had expected.

"Bring the prisoner to me," she commanded. Perhaps she could learn something from the man before she consigned him to the dungeon. Moving to the high-backed chair where she administered justice, Marguerite fixed a serene expression on her face. Her father had taught her that a firm but non-threatening look would often elicit more information than the rack.

The man entered the room, his hands bound behind him, his eyes fixed on Marguerite. As he approached her, he needed no bidding from the guard to kneel but dropped immediately to the ground, bending his head in supplication.

"You may rise," she said.

Marguerite looked steadily at the prisoner, trying not to reveal her surprise. This was the one person from Bleufontaine she had not expected to see.

"Why are you here, Gerard?" she asked. Beneath his recent sunburn, his face still showed the pallor of the weeks he had spent in the dungeons. "How did you escape from Bleufontaine?"

His eyes darted to the guard, and she saw the fear on his face. "It is all right," she said. "You can trust him." But she motioned her man to move to the side of the room where he was close enough to defend her but would not overhear her conversation.

"I didn't escape. I was sent here to spy on you." Gerard spoke quickly, the words spilling out. "My master commanded me to learn how he could enter the castle unseen."

Her assumption had been correct; Henri had no intention of admitting defeat. Marguerite bade her guard untie Gerard's hands. When the man had returned to his post, she turned to Gerard.

"He will never capture Mirail," she said confidently, "but he has done me a service by sending you here. Did he tell you that I demanded he forfeit you as payment for his treachery?" Gerard shook his head. "I believe that is why he put you in the dungeon, so I would not find you. But now that you are here, you will remain."

"I cannot." The anguish in Gerard's voice made Marguerite pause.

"I know about your sister," she said gently, trying to alleviate some of his fears. "As soon as Sir Alain returns, we will move her to another convent if she is willing to go. She will be safer there. In the meantime," Marguerite added, "I doubt your master would storm a convent, even though he might threaten it."

"You don't know the treachery he's capable of. Nothing stops that man from reaching his goal, and possessing my sister is something he wants."

Gerard's voice was fierce, and his eyes flashed with anger. Marguerite had no doubt he believed every word he said, but she wondered whether he had somehow misconstrued Henri's intentions.

"If that is true, why hasn't he taken Marie-Claire before this? Surely he has had the opportunity."

Gerard looked around the room, as though assuring himself that no one would overhear his words.

"Sir Henri knows that if anything happens to Marie-Claire or if I should die under suspicious circumstances, he will lose his estates to the Church."

"I fear I do not understand. Why would Sir Henri be punished for your death?"

"Not mine. His brother's."

''But Gilbert was killed by brigands. I remember how sad it was that he was killed on his way to his betrothal.''

Gerard shook his head. ''That is what my master would like the world to believe. The truth is, there were no brigands. Sir Henri lay in wait for him and murdered him, trying to make it look as though brigands had set upon him.''

Marguerite recoiled. Though she had no illusions about her vassal, she had not thought him capable of fratricide.

''Why?'' The answer was simple, once she thought about it. As the second son, Henri had inherited only a small estate. The sole way he could have gained possession of Bleufontaine was for his brother to die before he married and sired a child. No wonder the murder had occurred before he was betrothed. Henri had been running out of time.

''It is still your word against his,'' she told Gerard, ''and though I believe you, I can do nothing without proof.''

''I do have proof. There was a struggle, and Gilbert managed to wrest Henri's sword from him. When he hurled it away, the hilt struck against a large rock, and the great red stone fell out. Afterwards, I found Gilbert with it clenched in his fist.''

Marguerite was silent for a moment, remembering Henri's sword with its jeweled hilt. When she had first visited Bleufontaine after Gilbert's death, she had been surprised that Henri had substituted a sapphire for Gilbert's ruby.

''That still is not proof.''

Gerard nodded. ''Gilbert was alive when I found him. He bade me find him a priest to shrive him, and he told the priest everything that happened. The priest promised Gilbert that he would inscribe his story and give me a copy. I have it,'' Gerard said simply. ''It is the only thing I have that can protect Marie-Claire.''

It was also the reason Henri had not killed Gerard, though he had hidden him in the deepest dungeon. At the time Marguerite had wondered why Henri had bothered to keep a serf alive. Now she knew, and it proved that Henri was vulnerable.

In the midst of the tale of Henri's atrocities, one thing had brought a faint smile to Marguerite's face. Filial love. As an only child, she had had no experience with siblings and the relationships among them, but in the past few months she had seen the deep bonds which could be formed. Jean had risked his own life not once but twice to bring his sister happiness, and Gerard had spent five years protecting his sister. She wondered if her children would forge such strong ties.

"Where are the letter and the stone?" she asked.

"In a safe place." Though he said nothing more, Marguerite heard the unspoken words. Gerard would tell no one, not even her, something that might compromise his sister's safety.

"You can stay here. I will protect you, and I will send men to the convent to keep your sister safe."

Gerard shook his head. "I must return to Bleufontaine."

The proof was hidden somewhere within the walls of Bleufontaine. Gerard's quiet statement convinced Marguerite of that.

"Here is what you must tell Henri." She could no longer call him *sir,* for by his crimes he had broken every rule of chivalrous conduct. "Tell Henri that I am well prepared for another attack, that I have not let my guard down. In the spring, perhaps, I would be less wary."

By spring Alain would be home. He had to be.

Marguerite smiled, thinking of Alain's return. "You must stay at Mirail for several days," she told Gerard. "Tell Henri it was difficult to get the information he needs. And in the meantime, there is a woman here who would like to see you."

"Louise."


"Did you hear it all?" Marguerite turned to Diane. She had heard the other woman enter the small antechamber just before the guard had brought in Gerard. Now Diane joined her, carrying a tray with a jug of wine and two silver goblets.

Diane shuddered as she poured the wine. "It is hard for me to believe that one man can be so evil."

"Mayhap the priests are right and there are devils living on earth. If so, it would appear that Henri is one of them."

Marguerite took a long drink, swirling the wine in her mouth as though to cleanse it. The saints above knew she needed something to take the sour taste away. Breaking his vows of fealty and attacking her had been despicable, but that paled compared to this. Fratricide, threats against a nun. Was there anything so low that Henri would not do it?

"I had thought my men would be able to subdue him," she told Diane, "but now I am not certain."

Diane sipped her wine, her face thoughtful. "When Charles and Alain return, I will summon my men. Together we will defeat that man."

Impulsively Marguerite hugged her. "Thank you."

"What else are sisters for?"

# Chapter Twenty-Four

There was no doubt about it.

Marguerite rinsed her mouth with cool water, trying to chase away the sour taste. She could deny it no longer. The ailment that made her stomach queasy every morning, the same one that caused her to tire more easily than ever before, was not an ailment at all, but rather a wondrous blessing.

She smiled, remembering. Alain had vowed that she would not forget the night he had stolen away from Richard's camp to be with her, and indeed he had not lied. For the perfect night that they had shared had borne fruit.

She was pregnant.

Marguerite placed a protective hand over her still flat stomach and smiled. The rebellious stomach and the constant fatigue were but minor inconveniences. What was important was that ere the year ended she and Alain would have a child. If she was right, the babe would arrive near harvest time. How fitting that would be—a harvest of the sweetest kind—her child and Alain's.

And, oh, how she would love that child. Her baby would never grow up as his father had, not knowing how dearly his parents loved him. No, their child would be cherished from the moment she was born.

Girl or boy. Boy or girl. Maybe one of each. Marguerite grinned.

" 'Tis true! Oh, Marguerite, I'm so happy for you." Diane threw her arms around Marguerite and kissed her cheek.

Marguerite's eyes widened. She had been so caught up in her thoughts that she had not heard Diane enter the room, and so the other woman had seen her touching her stomach. But how had she known? Surely there was more than one reason a woman would place a hand on her midriff.

"I've suspected for a while," Diane continued as though Marguerite had vocalized her thoughts, "but I could not imagine when it happened. After all, I know you did not see Alain when you journeyed to Jarnac."

There was no way around it. Though she had tried to spare Diane the knowledge that Alain had come to Mirail but his brother had not, even though they had been the same distance from the barony, she could not deny the evidence of that night.

"I swore Louise and the watchman to secrecy," Marguerite concluded when she had told Diane about Alain's visit, "because I didn't want to hurt you. I knew you would have wished Charles had come with his brother."

Diane's smile was wistful. "Yes, I would have wished that. And I would have felt a moment or two of sheer envy. I do right now," she confided. "But I also know my husband. Do not misunderstand me. Charles is the most wonderful man on earth, but he's not one who would take a risk like that. Not even for me. Charles is not that kind of man."

Marguerite nodded. Leaving his liege lord was not an act a knight took lightly, and Marguerite did not minimize the courage it had taken, for there was very real danger, had Richard discovered Alain's absence.

"You and Alain are braver than Charles and me," Diane continued. "A person doesn't have to know you two very well to realize that your love is different from mine and Charles's. Yours is more like hills and valleys where the sun is bright but the storms blow. Ours is a gentle plain with pale sunshine. It may not be as beautiful, but our sun is constant.''

Once again Marguerite was struck by Diane's insights. She was right in saying that the two brothers were different, just as she and Diane were different. And their love? If it was indeed that, Diane had characterized it well, for she and Alain had had ups and downs—Diane would call them hills and valleys—from the moment they had met.

Diane gave Marguerite a long serious look before she smiled again. ''It's true that I wish I too were bearing a child. But believe me, there is nothing on earth that would make me trade the love Charles and I share for what you and Alain have. I could not live the way you do, for I cannot believe the peaks are worth the valleys.''

''And I would find the sameness of the plains boring.''

Marguerite remembered the first day she had seen Charles. She had thought him handsome, charming, the perfect knight. All that was true, but it had not taken long to realize that although Charles was a fine man and a good husband for Diane, he was not *her* Lancelot.

''By all the saints above, you had better have a good reason for summoning me.'' Alain glared at the man whom, despite everything, he had never quite learned to hate.

Philippe's message had reached Alain in Poitiers, and there had been such urgency to it that he had realized it was more than a simple command. It was a plea, an impassioned one. For whatever reason, Philippe wanted to see both Alain and Charles, and so they had asked Richard for permission to spend a few days in Jarnac. Now Alain was alone with his stepfather, for Philippe had asked to see each of the men individually.

When they had reached the castle, Alain had been shocked by his stepfather's appearance. Though he had aged over the years, he had remained active, and his trim body had put lie to the years Alain knew he bore. This time, though, there was no ignoring the fact that Philippe was an old man.

Philippe gestured Alain toward a chair. "Sit," he said. "You make me tired looming over me like that."

It was a remarkable admission. Never before had Philippe admitted to weakness in front of Alain.

"Surely you didn't ask me to come here to discuss your fatigue." Though he made no effort to soften his words, Alain took the seat Philippe offered.

Philippe's eyes clouded, and his lips thinned as he spoke. "When the end draws near, a man wants to make peace."

"If that is what you seek, I fear 'tis far too late. At least twenty years too late." Imagine the man's effrontery, thinking he could undo a lifetime of wrongs in a single day.

But Philippe was not to be dissuaded. "So long as the heart beats, it is not too late."

"What would you know about a heart?" Alain demanded. His instinct told him to leave, to spare himself whatever it was Philippe felt compelled to tell him. But something, mayhap a sense of loyalty, kept Alain in his chair. "You have never given any sign of possessing one."

The lines of fatigue etched in the corners of Philippe's mouth deepened. "When did you grow so cynical?"

"Cynical?" Alain leaned back in the chair, feigning indolence. "I would not describe myself that way. What I am is a realist. There's a difference, you know. A realist—and I admit that I am one—sees the world as it is. I pride myself on the fact that I harbor no false illusions, and I've certainly never deluded myself into thinking you cared aught for me. The evidence to the contrary is far too compelling."

Philippe was silent for a moment, the sadness in his brown eyes the only sign that Alain's words had found their mark. "I never thought you were a fool," he said at last, "but now I am not sure. I'm past caring what you think of me, and the good Lord knows I deserve every calumny you wish to heap on me. No, Alain, though you may find this difficult to believe, my concern is for you. You have a chance of happiness with a woman who loves you, and for some reason that makes sense only to your twisted mind, you are throwing it away."

The man might be old, but he had not lost his uncanny ability to rile Alain. Philippe's barbed comments and their power to wound him had been the hallmark of their relationship for as long as Alain could remember.

"I doubt Honore really loves me," he said, forcing himself to remain seated when what he really wanted was to smash his fist into the older man's face. "She loves the thought of me more than the reality."

"Honore?" The confusion on Philippe's face could not be counterfeit. "Who is she? I was talking about Marguerite. You remember your wife, don't you?"

The man's tone, as caustic as it had always been, was all the provocation Alain needed. He sprang to his feet and loomed over Philippe. "Ah, yes ... my wife, the whore of Mirail, Bleufontaine and God knows where else."

In a movement so swift that it belied his age and infirmity, Philippe rose, drew back his hand and slapped Alain, the force of his blow leaving an angry red mark on Alain's cheek.

"Stop it!" he shouted. "I will not listen to this any more. You can insult me all you wish, but I will not allow you to vilify Marguerite."

Alain bared his teeth in a smile that was akin to a snarl. "So she has charmed you, too, has she? I wonder. Is there any limit to the snares my wife sets?" As he had for weeks, Alain imbued the simple word 'wife' with a sarcasm that bordered on hatred.

"I order you to cease! Did I not tell you not to impugn your wife?"

Philippe's voice was hoarse, his face reddened from exertion. Alain stared at him for a moment, his mind assessing the physical changes that the past few months had wrought in his stepfather, his heart refusing to grant him any quarter.

"Over the years you've told me many things, old man," he said, his voice deliberately lowered. "I've listened to you and learned the lessons well. Oh, yes, you've taught me many things, indeed, including the fact that all women are whores. Even my mother."

In less than the blink of an eye, Philippe's face turned from red to white, and he began to sway. Instinctively Alain reached to steady him, but Philippe brushed his hand away. He stood for a moment, visibly trying to calm himself. When at last he managed to speak, his voice was devoid of all emotion.

"I lied."


When Marguerite found her, she was hidden in the small closet she and Gerard had called their own. With the heavy oak door drawn shut and not even the flicker of a candle to betray her, Louise could have remained there undiscovered for days. But as soon as Diane had told Marguerite that no one had seen Louise since morning Mass, Marguerite had thought of the closet. She opened the door slowly, the light from the hall showing her what she had expected: a slender female figure huddled in the corner. What she had not expected was that Louise's shoulders would be shaking from the force of her sobs.

Marguerite knelt and put an arm around Louise. "What is wrong?" she asked, her mind conjuring images of disasters.

" 'Tis naught." Louise's voice was so thickened with tears that her words were barely distinguishable.

"Of course 'tis naught." Marguerite kept her voice light, trying to cajole Louise out of her tears. "You always cry for no reason. Now, tell me, what is wrong?"

Louise shook her head once more, keeping her face averted.

"Did you receive a message from Gerard?"

When Louise shook her head again, Marguerite gripped her chin in her hand and forced Louise to face her. "Is Jean missing again?"

Her eyes still downcast, Louise repeated, " 'Tis naught," and would say no more.

Later that afternoon as she passed through the bailey on her way to gather pinecones for a decoction, Marguerite saw Louise. She was playing tag with three small children, her face alight with happiness, her shouts as joyful as the children's. Marguerite felt her own spirits rise. Whatever had ailed Louise this morning was gone.

"Lady Marguerite." One of the girls crowed with delight

when she saw Marguerite's basket, for she had occasionally carried the basket to the river, receiving a sweetmeat for her pains.

Louise turned. When her eyes met Marguerite's, her face clouded, and even from a distance Marguerite could see her lower lip tremble. Before Marguerite could speak, Louise picked up her skirts and fled toward the castle.

" 'Tis no use pretending." Marguerite's voice was stern. When Louise had avoided meeting her glance throughout the evening meal, Marguerite had resorted to a direct command, summoning Louise to her chamber. "I know something is amiss," she told the dark-haired woman. "You must tell me what it is, or I will continue imagining something far worse than the reality."

For she had spent the afternoon wondering what could have caused Louise such sorrow. Was one of her parents ill? Nay, for she would have asked Marguerite to treat them. Louise had said that neither Gerard nor Jean was in danger. What, then, could have provoked her tears?

"Trust me, my lady. You do not want to know." Louise's eyes filled with tears once again. "There can be nothing worse than this reality," she asserted.

Marguerite's concerns grew, for Louise was not given to exaggeration.

"Let me be the judge." Deliberately Marguerite made her voice harsh, telling Louise she had no choice but to reveal whatever it was that so distressed her.

Louise lowered her head, refusing to meet Marguerite's gaze, and the tears which had threatened spilled down her cheeks. " 'Tis Alain," she said at last. "The peddlers brought word."

Alain! For an instant Marguerite's heart stopped as she remembered her dreams. They had warned her that he was in danger, and now it was true. Her heart began to thud again, crowding her chest with its force.

"He's injured!" She forced the words out, though they hurt as if a knife were being twisted in her stomach.

Louise shook her head, and her sobs resumed. "No . . .

'tis not that.'' She lowered her eyes again, refusing to meet Marguerite's.

"Tell me."

Louise shook her head.

"I insist. I must know the truth."

Louise clenched her hands together, her knuckles whitening from the pressure. "He is in Poitiers and . . . Oh, Marguerite, I cannot speak the words."

"Louise!" Marguerite's tone brooked no opposition. Whatever it was, she had to know. Louise had assured her Alain was not injured . . . or worse. So long as Alain was alive, whatever had caused Louise's tears could not be too serious.

"He's with Honore—his mistress—and the peddlers said he's starting divorce proceedings so he can marry her." Louise blurted out the news as though purging herself.

Peddlers' tales. It was only the sight of Louise's tear-stained face that kept Marguerite from smiling. "Those are rumors, nothing more," she said. " 'Tis naught to concern you."

Louise began to sob again. "That was what I thought when I first heard them. 'Tis why I did not tell you, for I know how you dislike gossip. But then a second peddler brought the same news." Louise brushed the tears from her eyes and faced Marguerite. "Oh, my lady, I fear 'tis true."

" 'Tis nothing more than a vicious lie," Marguerite asserted, "and I will not believe it."

"But what if it is true? What will you do then?"

Marguerite blanched at the prospect. Divorce? Alain wanted to divorce her? He could not! Not now when she had begun to believe their marriage would be a success. Not now when they were to have a child. But, she reminded herself firmly, Alain did not know about the child. As for the night of passion they had shared, mayhap he saw it as lust, nothing more. Mayhap what he felt for Honore was deeper than anything he had shared with Marguerite.

"I will not believe it." She straightened her shoulders and willed herself not to cry out her fear, not to scream her anger. "The only way I will believe those lies is if I hear them from Alain's own lips." And suddenly nothing was more important than seeing Alain, having him hold her close and having him tell her the rumors had no foundation in reality.

"The peddlers say he will not leave Poitiers and Honore."

Marguerite smiled. "If he will not leave, then I will go there!"

# Chapter Twenty-Five

"Repeat that." Alain glowered at Philippe.

"Must you force a man to grovel?" Though Alain remained standing, Philippe sank into his chair as if the force of the blow he had struck had drained the last remaining bit of his strength.

" 'Tis true," he said when he had settled back in the chair. "I lied to you all those years ago. I'm not proud of that, but the alternative was worse. I could not let you know the truth." He leaned forward, placing his forearms on his knees, as though seeking to bridge the distance between himself and Alain. But the distance was more than physical.

"I knew you would never regard me as your father," Philippe continued, "but I wanted you to respect me, and if you'd known the truth, you'd have hated me. So I lied. Saint Genevieve's bones! The truth is I did not want to admit what really happened, not even to myself."

Though Philippe's voice cracked with the effort of his words and though they rang of sincerity, still Alain was wary. The man had admitted to being a liar. Why should he trust him now?

"How do I know you are being honest this time?" he demanded.

Philippe recoiled from the bitterness in Alain's words. "Listen," he said, "and then decide whether a man would invent a story like mine."

Reluctantly Alain took the chair that Philippe offered. The man was talking to him, really talking to him, for the first time in his life, and though Alain did not want to admit it, he needed to hear what Philippe had to say.

"It all goes back to the crusade." Philippe enunciated each word carefully. "You need to imagine what your mother was like then. She seemed the most beautiful woman on earth, making even Queen Eleanor's beauty pale when she was near." Though Philippe labored as he spoke, his eyes softened when he spoke of Janelle. It was the same fatuous look Guillaume had worn when Alain or Charles had mentioned their mother's name.

"Every man on the crusade was more than half in love with her," Philippe continued. "As for Guillaume and me, we suffered through what seemed like hell on earth. We were so close to her. We saw her every day. She laughed with us; she shared meals with us; she'd even mend our clothes. We worshipped her, but she considered us nothing more than friends." Philippe's laugh was a bitter one. "How we envied Robert! He had her in his bed every night while all we had were cold, lonely pallets."

This part of the story was nothing Alain had not heard before or surmised. He drummed his fingers on the arm of the chair, urging Philippe to continue, to tell him something he did not already know.

"In all likelihood we would have gone through the crusade and returned home with nothing changed had it not been for the ambush." Though the memory was decades old, it caused Philippe's face to pale and his lips to tighten. "There are no words to describe the horror of that day. Robert was killed and Guillaume so gravely wounded we feared he would not last the night. My two best friends taken from me in the space of an hour! And I was the only one left to tell Janelle what had happened."

Philippe reached for the jug of wine he had placed near his

right hand, then stopped. "Not again," he said. "I made that mistake once. Facing your mother took more courage than I possessed that night, and so I sought false courage in a jug of ale. I know it was the coward's way, but for a few minutes it deadened the pain enough that I was able to tell her what the day had brought." Philippe's expression was bleak, as though even now the memory of that night had the power to haunt him. "It was worse than I had feared. I had expected tears, not stony silence. It was almost as though Janelle herself had been dealt a death blow along with Robert. Finally she spoke a few words, telling me she could not imagine how she could live without him."

Alain kept his gaze steady, although the old man's obvious anguish set up an oddly responsive chord deep within him. He had known Philippe his entire life, and never before had he seen the man admit to pain.

"My head was muddled by the horror of the day and the ale I had drunk. 'Tis the only excuse I can offer. By the saints above, it seemed to me that her words were the answer to every dream I had had, and so I did what every other man in the king's forces would have done: I begged her to marry me."

Philippe frowned, remembering. "She refused, telling me I was crazy to even entertain the thought. How could I dishonor her husband and my friend in that way? I pleaded, trying to make her understand that I would keep her safe and that Robert would not want her to be alone. I kept on until she finally told me to leave, that the idea sickened her." Philippe raised his eyes to Alain's. "Can you imagine what that felt like? Knowing that the woman I had loved was sickened by the thought of marrying me? An anger like I had never before known swept through me. I grabbed her and . . ."

"And what?"

Philippe swallowed deeply. "I forced her."

No! It could not be. The man was weak—Alain had long known that—but surely he was incapable of such villainy. And yet . . . The image of his mother's tear-stained face flashed before Alain. "You raped my mother?"

The word hung between them, echoing in the room like the death cries of a wounded creature.

Slowly Philippe nodded. "I hate that word, but . . . yes."

Alain lunged to his feet, gripping Philippe's throat between both of his hands. "I'll kill you." He pressed his thumbs into the older man's windpipe. "You animal! That's all you are, an animal. You hurt her in the worst way a man can hurt a woman, and then you tried to make me believe she was a whore." Alain increased the pressure of his thumbs, feeling Philippe's breathing slow. "You deserve to die."

"Listen." Philippe could manage no more than a whisper. "I have not yet finished. No matter what terrible things you are thinking about me, they are no worse than what I have lived with all these years."

Alain released his grip on the older man and shoved him back into his chair.

"Talk," he commanded as he stood over Philippe.

Philippe swallowed noisily, then rubbed his throat. "You can't hate me more than I hated myself the next morning. I would have traded anything to have been able to live that night again and make it end differently. When I was sober, I begged Janelle to forgive me, and I repeated my offer of marriage. She refused. But it was not easy for her being alone. Even Eleanor could not give her the protection a husband could."

Alain heard Philippe's words as if from a distance, for while the man continued to speak, Alain tried to accept what he had been told. This man, this miserable cowering man, had raped his mother. Death was too good for him!

"Then Janelle learned that she was pregnant with my child."

Philippe's statement jolted Alain as little else could have. "Charles is your son?"

"Of course. I thought you knew that. I thought everyone did."

"No. I believed Guillaume to be his father."

"Guillaume? Why on earth would you believe that?"

Alain shook his head impatiently. " 'Tis unimportant. Tell me, how did you finally persuade my mother to marry you?"

"We struck a bargain. She agreed to marriage under two

conditions. The first was that we would raise the child as though he were Robert's posthumous son.'' Alain nodded. That was the reason both Janelle and Philippe had maintained the charade of Charles's parentage.

''And the second condition?''

Philippe flushed. ''Ours was to be a marriage in name only.''

''A what?'' It was an unfamiliar term.

''We shared a chamber and even a bed, but we never lay together as man and wife.'' Tears began to stream down Philippe's face. ''Janelle could not have chosen a more painful punishment. Denying me the right to acknowledge my son was cruel but bearable, but loving her all those years and never once having her return that love . . .'' Philippe rested his head in his hands, as though the weight of his confession was too much to bear.

Though Philippe's thin frame was wracked by sobs, Alain felt nothing but the white heat of anger. ''It was all a lie. Everything you told me was a lie. My mother did *not* betray my father.''

Philippe raised his eyes to meet Alain's. ''I couldn't bear the truth. Janelle never stopped loving Robert, not even for a minute. I would hear her crying in the night, because she missed him and wanted to be with him. Do you have any idea what it was like, knowing there was nothing I could do to comfort her and that I would never have one iota of the love she had given to my best friend?'' Philippe's brown eyes were filled with anguish. ''It was hell, hell on earth.''

There was a long silence as Alain stared at the man he thought he had known all his life, the man who had revealed himself as the worst kind of monster.

''You deserve to die for what you did to my mother.'' Alain forced the words out through clenched teeth. It took every ounce of self-control he possessed to keep from choking Philippe until there was no life left. He drew a deep breath, then exhaled slowly. ''Still, death would be too kind. You spoke the truth when you said that living has been a worse punishment than death would ever be. Let me not be the one who ends your penance.''

Philippe shook the tears from his face. " 'Tis too late to make restitution to Janelle. I only pray it is not too late to undo the damage my lies have wrought on you."

Alain stared at the older man, waiting for him to explain his meaning. Philippe was silent. He met Alain's gaze but would say no more.

Alain closed his eyes for a moment, unable to bear the steady look Philippe was leveling on him. As he did, images began to whirl before him. He saw his mother's tear-stained face the day she had insisted Charles was Robert's son. He saw himself turning from her, rejecting her explanation as the lie he knew it to be. And then he saw the pained expression she had tried to hide when her firstborn had shunned her.

He saw Honore, trying to mask her fear that he would leave and himself unable—or perhaps only unwilling—to reassure her.

Finally he saw Marguerite. She alone had made no attempt to disguise her feelings. No, she had shown her disgust at his crude manners, her dismay when he resorted to violence, her joy when he had displayed tenderness. Marguerite. It all came back to her. She was the one who mattered. She was the woman he loved.

Shaken by the direction his thoughts were taking, Alain gripped the chair so tightly that his fingers bore the imprint of the carved arms. Philippe was right, perhaps more right than he knew. For the thought of his mother's infidelity had colored his entire life, making him mistrust women, causing him to view their every movement through the filter of likely betrayal.

He had expected to find infidelity, and so he had searched for it, perhaps imagining it when it did not exist.

A sense of urgency forced him to his feet. Marguerite. He had to see Marguerite. God willing, she would forgive him. God willing, it would not be too late.

The sun had not yet reached its zenith when Marguerite and Diane approached the ramparts of Poitiers. They rode their white mules, and since this time when she had left Mirail

Marguerite had seen no need for disguise, they were accompanied by a full cortege of men.

"Oh, Marguerite." Diane's face was wreathed in a smile that had grown brighter with each mile they traveled. "This is the most wonderful surprise. Won't Charles and Alain be happy?"

I hope so. Though she would not voice the words, Marguerite could only wonder what kind of reception she would receive. There was no doubt that Charles would be overjoyed at his wife's appearance. Alain, on the other hand, might not be so pleased. If he was indeed enjoying a dalliance with Honore, 'twas likely he would not welcome the intrusion of his lawfully wedded wife. But that was a possibility she had not shared with Diane, for to put it into words would be to grant the monstrous thought credence. It was all a lie. It had to be.

"A wonderful surprise," Diane repeated.

But it was Marguerite who was surprised, for when she and Diane entered the city walls and sought their husbands, they learned that the men had left only two days earlier.

It was irrational. Marguerite knew that. Still she could not dismiss the fear that had assailed her, the fear that—rather than confront her with the truth—Alain and Honore had left Poitiers.

The smile which had illuminated Diane's face faded, and her eyes filled with tears. "We should have sent a message," she said.

Marguerite shook her head slowly. If what she thought was true, her approach had been all the message Alain had needed. And yet that did not explain Charles's absence. Surely he would have wished to see his bride again.

News traveled quickly in Poitiers and by the time Marguerite had been able to secure accommodations for her entourage, the queen had been told of the two women's arrival. "Bring Lady Marguerite to me," she had commanded. And so Marguerite found herself kneeling before the woman her father had once revered. It was difficult to believe she was more than half a century old, for though her once-golden hair was now silvered with age, the queen's face appeared to have escaped the ravages of time.

"So you are Guillaume's daughter and Alain's wife." Eleanor motioned Marguerite to a cushion at her feet. "I bid you welcome to Poitiers. If there is aught I can do to make your visit more enjoyable, you need only tell me."

Marguerite raised one shapely brow. "Mayhap you can help me. I know where my father is," she said, remembering that the queen appreciated humor, "but I fear I have lost my husband."

Eleanor's smile told Marguerite she had judged her mood correctly. The queen murmured a soft command to a servant. "Tell me, my child," she said as Marguerite poured the glass of wine she had requested, "why have you come to Poitiers? Surely 'tis not that you've seen the error of your ways and wish to give your vows of fealty to my son rather than that overly pious man who calls himself the king of France."

Marguerite forbore mentioning that the same 'overly pious man' had once been Eleanor's husband.

"In truth, your majesty," she replied, dodging the second question, "I have come to be with my husband. 'Tis more than forty days that he has been with his lord, and we miss him sorely at Mirail."

It was a thinly veiled reminder that Richard had demanded— and Alain had given—more service than was required under his vows.

Eleanor laughed. "So there are claws under the smooth exterior. I wonder how your husband deals with them."

It was Marguerite's turn to laugh. "He accuses me of having thorns rather than claws, but in either case, he's been unsuccessful in removing them."

"Marie." Eleanor's smile broadened as a beautiful young woman entered the room. "I've found another convert for our court. She needs no instruction, for she's already learned that a woman's position is superior to that of a man. Marie, this is Alain de Jarnac's surprising wife. And this is my daughter Marie, the only good thing to come out of my first marriage."

Involuntarily Marguerite's eyes dropped to her stomach. Would she one day say that this baby was the only good thing to result from her marriage?

The queen turned toward her daughter. "We're trying to find

Marguerite's husband. Richard did not mention that he had left Poitiers. Mayhap did Alain tell you where he was going?''

Taking the chair at her mother's side, Marie arranged her skirts before she spoke, ''Nay, I've heard naught from him, but Honore has not ceased complaining these last two days. She said Alain and his brother went to Jarnac.''

Marguerite blanched at the sound of Honore's name. It appeared that there was some truth to the peddlers' tales that Alain and Honore were intimate friends. And yet there was a ray of hope in Marie's words, for at least Honore had not accompanied Alain.

When she saw Marguerite's reaction, Eleanor placed an admonishing hand on her daughter's arm.

''I'm sorry if I was indiscreet,'' Marie said. ''I thought you knew.''

Marguerite shook her head. ''Do not apologize for speaking the truth. Indeed I have heard the tales.''

The queen questioned her at length about her father, then when the older woman began to tire, she dismissed Marguerite. ''Return tomorrow, I beg you. Marie is holding a court of love then.''

In Marguerite's absence Diane had taken charge of their room, unpacking their trunks and ordering the servants to set up the bed. When she returned, Marguerite found there was little to do.

''Come,'' she suggested, ''let us go to the Great Hall. We can while away some of the time until Alain and Charles return.''

In truth she was plagued by a restlessness that owed more to Alain's absence than to the small chamber she and Diane would share until the Jarnac brothers returned.

It was but a short walk back to the Palais des Comtes. This time rather than being escorted to the queen's private quarters, Marguerite led Diane into the Great Hall. As befitted its role as part of a royal residence, the room was immense, crowded with hundreds of knights, squires and their ladies, all talking at the same time.

''Is this a court of love or chaos?'' Diane asked.

"Both. Neither. It matters not." She looked around the assembly, wondering which of the beautifully dressed women was Honore. Was she the lovely brunette who appeared to be holding her own court, surrounded by no fewer than six knights? Or was she the auburn-haired beauty who stood regally, gesturing at the cherubs carved over the huge triple fireplace? Mayhap she was the blonde who warmed herself by the fire and whose suitors knelt at her feet on the wide stone stairs.

It was only a brief moment that Marguerite and Diane stood alone; apparently unnoticed. Then a knight in a scarlet tunic approached them.

"My lady, 'tis true; you have come to Poitiers to brighten this dull assembly." He dropped to his knees and reached for Marguerite's hand. "The heavens weep, but I rejoice, for a star has fallen from the sky and come to earth. Wise men know the star is named Marguerite."

Her lips twitched. Not since Charles had first come to Mirail had she heard such flattery. Was it only months, or was it a lifetime ago that she had found such phrases romantic? Now she knew them for what they were—empty words, designed to flatter a woman enough that she would grant the would be troubadour access to what he most craved: her bed and her body.

"Alas," she said, " 'tis the earth that weeps, for a hot wind has left the sky, parching all it touches."

The knight laughed and rose to his feet. "My star has wit as well as beauty. Is there nothing she lacks?" He tilted his head to one side, as though seeking the answer to his question. "Ah, yes. She has no dinner companion. May I have the honor of escorting you to dinner today?"

Marguerite shook her head. "I fear the journey has left me fatigued." In truth, she had no desire for his company or that of any knight other than Alain. What she wanted, what she needed, was to see him and learn whether there was any truth in the peddlers' tales.

But the knight seemed unwilling to accept her dismissal. "Then I shall press my suit tomorrow," he told her. "I live for the moment when I see you again."

When the man was far enough away that he could not hear her, Diane turned to Marguerite. "That man has no shame. He knew who you were. He knew you were married."

"Mayhap he's one who finds a forbidden love more appealing." But he had paid no attention to Diane, who was also married. Marguerite had no illusions that she was more beautiful than Diane. No, there had to be another reason the knight had singled her out for his attention.

Wherever the two women went, the scene was repeated. A knight would detach himself from the group and beg for the pleasure of Marguerite's company, totally ignoring Diane. It was almost as though the men thought Marguerite would welcome their attentions, that she sought them.

At first it was mildly entertaining, matching wits with the courtiers, but Marguerite found that their words were so similar, so devoid of any genuine meaning, that the game soon palled.

"I must get out of here," she told Diane. "I need to breathe some fresh air."

Diane looked puzzled. "The air does not seem stale to me."

"'Tis too filled with idle boasts. Come, let us see what Poitiers has to offer the visitor other than preening courtiers."

They walked slowly through the city, marveling at the number of buildings and the sight of so many people gathered in one place.

"Do you want to visit the market?" Marguerite asked.

Diane shook her head. "I should like to see the Roman wall."

"Then the Roman wall it is."

Though Marguerite prided herself on her sense of direction, the streets of Poitiers were narrow and winding, bending in unexpected angles. As they turned one corner, she and Diane found themselves on a street that appeared totally deserted.

"I don't like it," Diane said, her voice quavering slightly.

She started to turn, but Marguerite laid a hand on her arm. "Do you hear it?" she asked. "It sounds like a moan."

Marguerite walked forward, her soft shoes making little noise as she searched for the source of the sound. It was louder now.

"It *is* a moan," she told Diane. "Something is in pain."

She found him slumped in a narrow doorway, his hands gripping one leg as he tried to staunch the blood. This was no serf, for he was well dressed in a brightly colored tunic and hose, though he lacked a knight's finery.

"What happened?" Marguerite dropped to her knees next to the man. When he did not speak, she pried his hands loose, then ripped away the remaining shreds of cloth.

"Thieves. Knives." His voice was ragged with pain.

Marguerite examined the wounds. Though they were numerous and undoubtedly painful, they were not deep enough to threaten his life. She ripped a strip of cloth from her bliaut and began to cleanse the man's leg.

"The bleeding has begun to subside," she told him, imbuing her words with confidence. "I'll fashion a bandage, and then my sister and I will help you return home."

"It wasn't serious, was it?" Diane asked when they had left the man, now singing Marguerite's praises, at his room.

Marguerite shook her head. "Bleeding is always cause for worry, but his wounds were superficial. In three days he'll have no more than scabs to remind him of the thieves."

Since they were close to the Roman wall, the women decided to see it before they returned to their room. The sun was beginning to set, casting a golden glow on the stones as they approached the perimeter of the city. Diane smiled and placed a hand on the hand-hewn stone. "I find it awesome to realize that Julius Caesar might have walked here a thousand years ago."

Marguerite started to nod, then stopped as her eyes moved along the length of the wall. The blood drained from her face, and she reached out, gripping Diane to keep from falling.

"What is it?"

The fear was so great that for a moment Marguerite could not speak. It was all she could do to force herself to breathe.

"The tower!" She closed her eyes, willing it to disappear. But it was no illusion. When she opened her eyes, it was still there.

Marguerite pointed toward the rounded tower at the corner of the wall. "That's the tower from my dream."

# Chapter Twenty-Six

It would be the perfect opportunity.

Henri stroked the fur of his pelisse, reminding himself that of all the inhabitants of Bleufontaine he and only he was entitled to wear it. It was naught but rabbit, but if what he had heard today was any omen—and he was certain it was a portent of the most auspicious kind—he would soon be wearing ermine. Not just on feast days, but every day of the year. Not just trimming his pelisse, but lining it completely. Soon.

The bad luck that had seemed to plague him was gone. Henri crossed himself, then turned an eye skyward and thanked the saints he had implored to intercede on his behalf. Indeed they had served him well. For it had to have been the kindest of fates which had brought the message to him today. Had it been a week later, it would have been too late. But today was perfect.

The whole idea was perfect. Of course, another man might not have realized the significance of the duke's plan. Another man might not have understood the possibilities. Henri was not another man.

It was obvious that in the past he had chosen the wrong approach. Attacking Mirail had brought him naught but the loss of several men. The barony was too well protected for him to succeed that way. But the tournament. Ah, that was a brilliant idea. He would challenge Alain de Jarnac, that miserable cur, to single combat, and unless the man were willing to admit to the world that he was a coward, he would accept the challenge.

It would be the final challenge of the famous Silver Knight's military career. Indeed, it would be the final challenge of his miserable life. For Henri would demand a fight to the death. There was no doubt whatsoever of the outcome, for no one— no one at all—walked away from a contest with Henri de Bleufontaine.

With Alain consigned to the fires of hell, it would be simple to persuade King Louis to award Mirail and the lovely Marguerite to his faithful vassal Henri. In just a few weeks he would be baron of Mirail. The power, the riches and Marguerite would be his.

Henri laughed aloud.


Their horses fairly flew, their powerful hoofs pounding the earth as Alain and Charles urged them forward.

"By all the saints, the good people of Poitiers will surely call us *pieds à poudre* when they see this." Charles grimaced as he looked at the thick coat of grime which covered his mail.

"I've been called worse than a dusty foot," his brother replied. At this point he didn't care what anyone thought, anyone save Marguerite. The very foundations of his world, everything he had believed in for more years than he cared to admit, had been shaken, and Charles expected him to worry about an ounce of dust on his armor. Hardly!

When he had left Philippe and Charles together for the first time as acknowledged father and son, Alain had walked swiftly through the courtyard at Jarnac in the hope that the steady motion of his feet would somehow clear his thoughts.

How could Philippe have done it? The question haunted him as he headed for the old hollow tree. How could he have invented such a heinous lie, calumnifying Janelle rather than admitting his own guilt?

Alain stood in front of the tree that had been his refuge so many years ago. As a small child he had hidden in its hollow base. When he could no longer fit into the trunk, he had climbed onto the largest branch. Today squirrels nested in the hollow, and Alain's branch was gone, the victim of a particularly strong ice storm. Yet the tree remained.

Alain touched the trunk. At least it had not changed. The bark was still as rough as he had remembered, a definite hazard to boys who descended too quickly.

Janelle had always known . . .

Janelle. Alain shuddered, thinking of the pain he had caused her, the way he had rejected even her most tentative gestures of love. He had been so hurt by the years she had virtually ignored him that he had been unable to respond to her overtures. And now it was too late.

He could not make amends for the pain he had caused Janelle, but Philippe was right about one thing. So long as a heart beat, there was still a chance. He would not lose his chance with Marguerite.

As soon as he reached Poitiers he would beg Richard's indulgence, asking his lord to excuse him from the upcoming tournament, pleading the urgent need to return to Mirail. And then he would once again tax Neptune's endurance. God willing, Marguerite would be waiting for him.

"You're riding like a man possessed," Charles told him.

Alain merely shrugged.

When they reached the city walls, Charles's sigh of relief was audible.

"Go ahead. I'll take care of the horses." They had ridden all night, and it was still early morn, too early to approach Richard, but not too early, it appeared, for another knight to be grooming his horse.

As Alain began to rub Neptune's flanks, the other man moved nearer, perching on top of an overturned barrel.

"The city will not soon forget this."

Alain was barely listening. Though Bertrand de Villeneuve was a good knight, he was not a man whose company Alain sought, particularly not this morning. Today all he wanted was Richard's permission to leave Poitiers.

"She's even more beautiful than Honore." The man's voice was warm, as though he smiled at the memory.

"There are many women more beautiful than Honore."

This time Bertrand's smile became a full fledged laugh. "You should know. I must say that I doubt I'd be as liberal-minded as you. I fear I would object to her . . ." He paused, as though searching for the correct word, ". . . friendship . . ." the smile returned, ". . . with other men."

Alain moved to reach Neptune's front legs. "I have no claims on Honore. Indeed, it would be hypocritical to expect her to ignore opportunities with other men, particularly if one of them can offer her marriage. The good Lord knows I cannot." Nor would I want to, Alain realized. Bertrand's words and the thought that Honore had found another protector brought not even a twinge of jealousy. Quite the opposite. He felt a sense of relief. Now he would not have to make awkward explanations to Honore.

" 'Twas not Honore I meant, but your wife."

"Marguerite?"

"Do you have more than one wife?" Bertrand laughed at his own wit. "She's the toast of Poitiers."

Almost involuntarily Alain's head swiveled so that he could see Bertrand's expression. "Marguerite is here?" This was a turn of events he had not considered. Alain frowned. He wanted to see Marguerite, but not here and, if he were being honest, not yet. His emotions were still too raw after Philippe's revelations, and he had had no time to plan his strategy. He needed more time to prepare for what was likely to be the most important encounter of his marriage, perhaps of his life.

Why had Marguerite come to Poitiers? Why now?

Seemingly oblivious to the turmoil his words had created, Bertrand said, "Lady Marguerite arrived three days ago along with your brother's wife. We assumed you had invited them to come for the spring tournament."

"Of course." Alain lied. "She simply arrived sooner than I had expected."

Bertrand leaned back on the barrel, rocking it precariously.

"I can assure you that she has not been lonely. Every knight has sought her company and her favors."

Alain took a deep breath, forcing himself to remain calm. He must not leap to wrong conclusions. The fact that Marguerite had been surrounded by knights did not mean that she had granted favors to them. It did not even mean that she had encouraged them. Their presence was simply the natural reaction of red-blooded men to a beautiful woman. They were drawn to her as bees to a purple thistle.

"That's my Marguerite," he said. "She would not be discourteous to anyone." Somehow he managed to get the words out, and—amazingly—they sounded normal. No one, most especially a man like Bertrand who enjoyed bearing tales, would know how difficult it was to stop, to think and to consider that the flirtation—if it had actually occurred—might not have been initiated by Marguerite.

"I wish I had your luck." Bertrand rose and walked toward the stable door. "When you fight in the tournament, you'll be wearing two women's favors. The rest of us will count ourselves lucky if we can find one."

"Some men have all the luck."

The laugh that accompanied Alain's words was as hollow as the old tree at Jarnac.

The room was crowded with courtiers and ladies, squires and serving maids, the queen's cats and the ever present dogs. The air was so close that on a good day she could scarcely breathe. Today was not a good day.

Marguerite edged toward the door. Though she could not leave without the queen's permission, perhaps there would be a fresh breeze near the entrance. If not . . . she tried not to think of how her stomach might rebel.

'Twas the same every morning. Though she was careful to eat very little, still her stomach threatened to reject even the lightest food. In a few more weeks she should be past this phase, but in the meantime it made attending the queen's morning gatherings most difficult.

The stench grew stronger, and Marguerite's stomach began to churn. No! She could not embarrass herself.

There was a breath of fresh air as the door opened, and Marguerite inhaled deeply.

"Charles!"

Her stomach contracted, and Marguerite clasped a hand over her mouth, willing herself not to be sick. It took only a second, but in her agony she missed the import of Diane's cry. Her face contorted with the effort of subduing her unruly stomach, and she closed her eyes in pain.

"My love!" Marguerite's eyes flew open as Diane forced her way past three courtiers and threw herself into her husband's arms.

He was there, standing at his brother's side, his face more tanned than she remembered, his eyes as blue as ever . . . as cold as ever. Marguerite recoiled. The man she loved was regarding her as if she were a loathsome creature.

"You're safe." She blurted out the words, her eyes moving over his face, then down his body, assuring herself that he had suffered no injury. Though Diane had insisted the tower was not a portent of evil, Marguerite had been unable to dismiss the foreboding that had hung over her since she had seen it. It couldn't have been coincidence that she had dreamed so vividly of the tower and then had discovered it in Poitiers, where the peddlers had claimed Alain wanted to remain. The dreams and the danger they foretold for Alain were far too powerful to ignore. But Alain was back, and it appeared that he bore no wounds, at least none that were visible.

"Are you disappointed?" he asked, one eyebrow raised in the disdainful expression she had seen so many times before.

His words hurt more than a blow. "Of course not. Why would I wish you harm?"

Alain made no move to touch her. Instead he continued to regard her as though she were an unwelcome visitor. "I don't pretend to understand how the female brain works. Why don't you explain it to me?"

From the corner of her eye, Marguerite saw Diane and Charles moving slowly but steadily toward Eleanor. They walked with their arms wrapped around each other, their heads bent together. It was obvious that they sought permission to retire, and no one watching them could misinterpret their plans for the rest of the day.

Alain stood stiffly at Marguerite's side, coldness emanating from him despite the warmth of the room. This was not the man who had stolen away to spend a night with her. This was the stranger she had married, the one she hoped had disappeared forever.

Marguerite took a shallow breath, trying to calm her queasy stomach. Now was not the time to be ill. Something had happened to change Alain back into the icy stranger. Perhaps it was Honore; perhaps it was the memory of all the times she herself had taunted him; perhaps it was something entirely different. It mattered little what the cause was, so long as she could find the remedy.

If only there were an herb to make him love her! But Marguerite knew that Alain needed more than herbs and decoctions. The story Philippe had told of Alain's loveless childhood had haunted her, making her realize that her husband, although outwardly strong, had deep inner needs. Each day she had prayed to Mary and all the saints that she would be able to fill the great voids and make Alain once again whole.

She had to start now. She had to take the first step.

"I've missed you so much," she said, reaching to press a soft kiss on Alain's lips.

If it hadn't been for the warmth of his skin, she would have thought she was kissing one of the statues at Notre-Dame la Grande, for though he did not push her away, Alain's lips remained impassive under hers. He stayed motionless until she stepped away. Then he took her arm and began to lead her toward the queen.

"Have you found rooms here?" he asked, his voice as distant as though she were a casual acquaintance, not his wife.

Marguerite searched his face, seeking the reason for his coldness. Could it be that the unspeakable rumors were true and that he longed to be with Honore? Though it was the last thing she wanted to believe, Marguerite could not help remembering Marie's intimations that Alain and Honore had been living together.

"Yes," she said finally, "but you need not stay there if you would prefer to be somewhere else."

As they approached Eleanor, Alain began to smile. "I would not think of fueling rumors," he told her softly. "We shall go to your rooms as soon as the queen allows."

The thought that he remained with her only to preserve appearances brought Marguerite no comfort.

The chamber that Marguerite shared with his brother's bride was small, little more than an alcove cut into the thick walls, yet somehow she had managed to turn it into a homely place. Alain recognized the thick rug on the floor as one from Mirail, and the furs which covered the bed had once lain on the bed he and Marguerite had shared.

Alain wondered whether the sight of those furs affected Marguerite as it did him. It couldn't, or she would not have brought them to Poitiers, not feeling as she did toward him.

As Alain had expected, Charles and Diane had gone to Charles's room, leaving this one for Alain and Marguerite. It had been a thoughtful gesture on Charles's part, for Alain could scarcely take Marguerite to the place where he normally stayed while in Poitiers. He was not sure who would have been angrier, Marguerite or Honore, but he had no intention of bringing the two women together. He had enough to do coping with the woman who was his lawful wife, the same woman who had been physically repulsed by the sight of him.

Some welcome! Perhaps it was foolish to have expected her to greet him with open arms and a warm kiss as Diane had welcomed Charles, but he had not expected her to grow ill at the mere sight of him. Perhaps this was his punishment for the cruel words he had hurled at Philippe. The man had told him Janelle found herself sickened by the thought of marrying him, and Alain had laughed—yes, laughed—at Philippe's pain. He was laughing no longer, for now the pain was his own. Marguerite, the woman he loved beyond all reason, could barely control her revulsion at him. And still, dear God, he still wanted her. She was the most beautiful, desirable and lovable creature on earth. What would she do if he followed his instincts and threw her onto the bed? If the sight of him created nausea, what damage would his touch wreak?

Alain sought a neutral subject, one that would not further inflame his raging hormones.

"Is Louise not here?" he asked, seeing another servant, one whose name he did not remember, folding Marguerite's clothing.

"I left her at Mirail." Marguerite dismissed the servant. When they were alone, she turned back to Alain. "It is a long story," she said.

"We have all afternoon." And, he told himself, perhaps this story, whatever it is, will keep me from thinking about how soft her skin is and how I've longed to touch it.

"Louise fell in love with one of Henri de Bleufontaine's serfs." As Marguerite began the tale, Alain stretched out on the bed, resting his head on the soft furs, trying not to conjure images of the last night he and Marguerite had spent beneath those furs. He listened while she told of Louise's love, her asking Henri to release Gerard and Henri's refusal.

"Did you go to Bleufontaine?" Alain demanded.

She nodded. "It seemed the only way to get Henri to agree."

Alain closed his eyes for a second, remembering the troubadours' tales. Had this innocent visit been the seed of truth around which they had woven a story of deceit? At the time Charles had told him that he had overreacted, but he had been so predisposed—so damnably predisposed—to believe she was faithless that he had paid no heed to Charles's counsel.

Alain listened carefully, watching his wife's eyes and the way she held her hands. Marguerite was telling the truth; her words had an unmistakable ring of sincerity. And yet there was something she was concealing, for she would occasionally drop her eyes to her hands, as though unwilling to meet his gaze. There was more to the visit than she was admitting.

"I fear that force is the only way to persuade Henri to release Gerard," Marguerite concluded. "Once your tour with Richard is complete and she and Charles have returned to Lilis, Diane has offered to join her men with ours. Surely together we have enough power to obtain Gerard.''

She was different, this wife of his. More assured of herself. Less of an idealist. The Marguerite he had left at Mirail would not have admitted the need for military might. She would have continued to believe that sweet words were all that were required to make a man like Henri capitulate and that using force was a sign of weakness. The new Marguerite had lost those illusions. She was a realist.

''It appears that you and Diane have found the solution to Louise's problem.'' The words came out more coldly than he had intended. Still, it was difficult to reconcile this new Marguerite with the woman he had left behind. She was now the type of woman he had always intended to marry: independent, able to defend his lands while he was at war. His bride had turned into the woman of his dreams. Why, then, did it seem so wrong? Why did he wish she still needed him?

As though she heard the censure in his voice, Marguerite snapped a response. ''I had few choices,'' she reminded him. ''It wasn't as though you added your august presence and sagacity to the decision-making process.''

Alain flushed. What she said was no more than the truth. He had not been there, and so she had had to make every decision alone. She had done well, proving that she did not need him. Mirail was like an army: it needed only one leader, and Marguerite had demonstrated that she was that leader. He was an unnecessary appendage, and so she would cut him away with a surgeon's skill.

One barony. One leader. 'Twas all that was needed. And yet Alain could not forget the time he and Richard had fought together, each serving as the extension of the other. Could a barony be run like that? Could a marriage?

Unable to voice his thoughts and risk having Marguerite reject them—and him—Alain looked out the small window. The sun was lower now.

'' 'Tis time for us to go to the courts of love,'' he told Marguerite. Although Eleanor had willingly released them, she had stipulated that they both attend this afternoon's court.

Marie, she informed Alain, wished to see both him and his wife there. Something in the queen's smile had made Alain wary, but there had been no way to refuse the royal command.

It was agony, pure agony. They walked slowly through the narrow streets of Poitiers, Alain greeting other knights, bowing and smiling when he met ladies. He was the epitome of the *preux chevalier,* the man of her dreams. Why, then, did it all seem so superficial? Why were they sparring, arguing about trivial matters, when they had so many important things to discuss? Why did they seem further apart now than when they were physically separated?

Marguerite fixed a smile on her face. If he could smile, so could she. But, oh, how she longed to hold him in her arms, to soothe away the lines of strain that he could not disguise from her. With all her heart, she wanted to talk to him, to resolve the coldness that kept them apart. And yet she could not, for his expression was so forbidding that she knew he would not allow her to speak of gentler matters. This was neither the time nor the place to press the issue.

Later.

Tonight when they returned to their room, she would insist that he listen.

As they entered the large hall that Marie de Champagne had appropriated for her courts of love, a courtier sprang to his feet.

"Lady Marguerite! The sun has returned to shine on us."

Alain said not a word, but the fierce look he gave the man sent the other knight scurrying to the opposite side of the room.

"I heard a star was falling from the heavens," another said as he approached Marguerite, "and now I have found it."

Again Alain fixed his icy glare on the knight until he, too, fled.

The word spread quickly, and soon the knights and their ladies moved aside, making a path for Alain and Marguerite as they moved toward the front of the hall. When they were seated on the first row of benches, Marguerite turned to her husband.

"Have you been here before?" she asked.

He shook his head. "Marie chided me for not coming. I suspect that is the reason the queen insisted we come today."

"I suppose you were too busy."

A guilty flush was his only answer.

Soon Marie entered the room, taking her place on the intricately carved chair that was placed in the center of the raised platform. She looked around the assembly, smiling when she saw Alain.

"Who brings the first complaint?" she asked.

A woman rose and approached the dais. "My lover promised me poetry and flowers every day, but he has not brought them."

Marie tipped her head to one side, as though considering the accusation. "Then he must forfeit your favors for a fortnight," she announced.

The complaints continued, and with each judgment the women in the audience cheered, for each time Marie ruled in favor of the lady.

Marguerite studied Alain's profile. How could he continue smiling and appearing to be interested? It was all so silly, worrying whether a man had shown the proper respect when he knelt before his lady, whether the poetry he had composed rhymed properly. Did these women have nothing important to occupy their thoughts?

A tall blonde with one of the most beautiful faces Marguerite had ever seen made her way to the dais. As she passed the first row, she turned, her motion wafting the scent of her perfume toward Marguerite. It was sweet, yet musky, unlike any Marguerite had smelled. Sniffing delicately, Marguerite tried to identify the herbs and flowers that formed the base of the woman's perfume.

The beautiful blonde leaned ever so slightly in Marguerite's direction, but her smile—like that of every other woman in the room—was for Alain alone. That was not surprising. The surprise was Alain's response, for the smile he gave the woman in return was a genuine one, as warm as any Marguerite had seen on Alain's lips.

When the woman reached the dais, she bowed her head in

respect, then raised her eyes. "I have a most grievous concern," she told Marie, "and I would beg your counsel."

Marie inclined her head. "Proceed."

"I have sought the wisdom of the ancients but have found no answer. Tell me, you who are the Queen of Love, is it possible for a man and woman to find love within the bounds of marriage?"

Marguerite heard Alain's involuntary gasp, and she turned quickly. But when he met her gaze, his smile was as easy as if the woman had asked for a ruling on the weather.

For a long moment there was silence in the hall, then a soft buzz began as the audience considered the question, speculating on Marie's ruling. If nothing else, the queen's daughter was a skilled entertainer. She paused long enough to generate suspense but did not delay so long that boredom ensued.

Her face grave, Marie leaned forward and touched the blonde's hand. "You have raised a question that has long perplexed me. I, too, have consulted the ancients and those who are not so ancient. I have searched many lands for the answer to this very question." She paused again. "There is no doubt of it." Marie rose. She extended one arm, as though to add more weight to her words. "Hear me, all ye who are gathered here today. Love and marriage cannot coexist. The latter causes the former to dwindle and die." She turned to the blonde. " 'Tis unfortunate but true. You may have one but not the other, my dear Honore."

Honore. So this was the woman rumors linked to Alain. Beautiful, a close friend of Marie, and worried about love in marriage. It appeared there was more truth than Marguerite wanted to believe in the peddlers' tales.

In all likelihood it was no coincidence that Marie had insisted Marguerite and Alain attend the courts this afternoon. She and Honore had undoubtedly planned the question and the response, carefully ensuring that Marguerite was present to hear them.

It was all a formality, for it appeared that everyone in Poitiers believed Marguerite's marriage was ended. Everyone, including Alain.

# Chapter Twenty-Seven

They had reckoned without her tenacity. Though Marguerite had little doubt that the whole afternoon had been planned, that Honore had conspired with Marie to announce to the world that Marguerite and Alain's marriage was doomed, the two women had made a serious error. They had not realized that Marguerite was a fighter. She had not come all the way from Mirail to Poitiers on a mule, enduring morning sickness and the spring rains, to meekly surrender her husband without so much as talking to him. Honore and Marie could make all the pronouncements they wished. Until she heard the words from Alain himself, she would admit not defeat, for it was not just her own happiness that was at stake. She now had the baby to consider.

"Alain." Marguerite turned to face her husband, fixing a smile on her face. "We must talk. There is much that I would tell you." And much, she added silently, that I would ask you.

For a moment she thought he would refuse. He kept his eyes fixed on the dais, and the only sign that he had heard her was the tightening of the muscles next to his mouth. "I agree," he said at length, "but can we not wait until we return to Mirail?"

Marie rose, signaling that the courts were ended. When she

had left the room, Marguerite and Alain joined the crowd that was slowly making its way outdoors.

If she were as perennially optimistic as Diane, Marguerite would have considered Alain's suggestion a positive sign, an indication that he intended to return to Mirail with her. But Marguerite's impatience exceeded her optimism.

"I suppose that we could wait," she conceded, "but what we have to discuss is important enough that I would prefer we not delay."

Alain's eyes darkened with an emotion she could not identify. When he spoke, his reluctance was evident. "As you wish, my lady. We shall find time for a private conversation this evening." His voice bore no warmth, only what sounded like quiet resignation.

"There she is. That's the Silver Knight's wife." The words, which came from a woman only a few feet from Marguerite and Alain, were uttered in a piercing whisper, clearly designed to be heard by everyone who was leaving the Palais des Comtes.

A low chuckle greeted the announcement. "She may be his wife today, but how long do you think she'll stay that way? Honore has never lost a man she wanted, and everyone knows she wants Alain de Jarnac."

It was instinct, pure and simple, that led Marguerite to put her hand on Alain's arm. Though she could not silence the gossips, she had no intention of surrendering so easily. By virtue of law at least, Alain was still her husband.

The murmurs continued, growing more insistent as Marguerite and Alain made their way through the crowd. No one, it seemed, thought it coincidence that Honore had brought her query to the court on the very day Alain appeared with his wife.

If he heard the comments, Alain gave no sign. Instead, he continued speaking softly to Marguerite. "I had hoped that we could leave on the morrow," he told her, "but Richard has asked me to remain for the tournament."

Marguerite blinked in surprise. She had not considered the possibility that Alain would want to leave before the tournament. Tournaments in general displayed a knight's prowess and this—the first since Richard was crowned Duke of Aquitaine—was already being touted as the event of the decade. She wondered why Alain had even considered missing it.

It was not, however, surprising that Richard had refused Alain's petition.

"No doubt the duke wishes his strongest knight to bring glory to his name."

Alain shrugged. "Mayhap. Whatever his reason, he is my liege lord, and I have no desire to displease him. We'll remain in Poitiers until the tournament is ended."

Marguerite lifted her skirt as they started to cross the street, then stepped back at the sound of hoofbeats. Though the street was crowded with courtiers, the armored knight who was approaching paid them no heed. Instead he spurred his massive destrier forward, forcing the crowd to part for him. Reining in in front of Marguerite and Alain, the knight raised his helmet.

"'Tis a pleasure to see you again, Lady Marguerite." Though Henri's words were directed at Marguerite, his voice projected over the crowd's murmurs. "I had heard that you suffered from an ailment."

The audacity of the man! Marguerite kept her voice low and even. Two could play that game. "Mayhap 'twas the same malady that afflicted your man Gerard."

"Mayhap," he agreed smoothly. "Still, I am most pleased to see that you have recovered."

Alain placed a proprietary arm around Marguerite's shoulders. "It was good of you to come to Poitiers, Henri. My wife and I have several issues to discuss with you, and you have saved us the nuisance of journeying to Bleufontaine." His voice was as cold as a winter's wind, his tone leaving no doubt of the contempt he held for Henri.

Those near Alain and Marguerite grew silent, entranced by the spectacle of two powerful knights' obvious hostility. This was even more entertaining than the courts of love.

Henri flushed at the insult. "The only discussion I want to have with you, Jarnac, is at the point of a lance." Raising his voice so that none could ignore him, he announced, "I challenge you to a joust."

His words caused an almost instant silence as the crowd waited for Alain's response. When it came, it drew a gasp from all but the most jaded courtiers.

"I have long known you were a bully and a coward, but this is the first time I realized that you were a fool. Only a fool fights a battle that he has no chance of winning."

Henri's flush deepened, and Marguerite watched him tighten the grip on his reins.

"I am no coward," he cried. " 'Tis you who seek the coward's way out. You don't want to fight me."

Alain's laugh carried as well as Henri's shout had. "You're right that I don't want to fight you, but you're wrong about the reason why. I value my sword, and I'm loath to sully it with your blood."

"Then you need not worry, for it will not be my blood which is shed." Henri raised his spear over his head. "Hear me, one and all. I challenge the man who calls himself the Silver Knight to a *joute à outrance.*"

A collective gasp rose from the crowd. Jousts were normally fought for riches or recognition. A joust to the death was rare unless a mortal insult had occurred.

Henri's laugh sent a chill down Marguerite's spine for she, perhaps more than anyone in Poitiers, knew just how dangerous Henri could be. Her fear grew when he bent his head to address her.

"My lady, I suggest you prepare to be a widow."


She was losing the battle. Though she had tried every trick she knew, her eyelids grew heavier, and she could feel herself drifting into sleep. The thoughts which had been whirling through her brain all evening moved more slowly now, as though they were losing momentum.

Where was Alain? Richard had summoned him hours ago. Surely they should have finished whatever their business was by now. Surely Alain would return at any moment. Though her body cried out for sleep, her mind shouted the need to talk to Alain, to warn him. This was to have been the time she would tell him about the baby, but she was no longer prepared for that announcement. Until she knew the truth about Honore, the child would remain her secret.

Tonight even the babe faded in importance. What mattered was Alain's safety. She knew he was a superb warrior, and in a fair battle he would have no trouble defeating a man like Henri. But Marguerite also knew that Henri would not fight fairly, and so she feared for her husband.

She should have told him about Henri's attacks on both her and Mirail before this. Even if she had not wanted to speak of such unpleasantness on that magical night when Alain had returned to Mirail, she had had another opportunity here in Poitiers when she had told Alain about Louise's love for Gerard. Yet she had not spoken of Henri's perfidy. At the time it had seemed wise not to complicate matters further. She wanted Alain to remain with her because he loved her, not because she needed his protection, and so she had chosen not to tell him of the danger to Mirail.

Now it was too late. If she told him tonight, he would know of Henri's capacity for deceit, but he would also be angry . . . dangerously so. And that was one thing Marguerite could not risk. Her father had taught her that angry men made mistakes. A good warrior, Guillaume had claimed, exploited anger for his benefit. He kept his own fury tightly reined but fueled his opponent's, for in the heat of emotion, a man was apt to make errors. With Alain's life in the balance, Marguerite could do nothing that would destroy his concentration. And yet she had to warn him.

There had to be a solution. She would sleep for just a few minutes, and then she would find the answer.

At the sound of the latch, her eyes flew open. He was back. "I was worried about you." Marguerite sat up and watched as Alain crossed the room. "You were gone a long time."

He stretched his arms over his head and yawned widely, fatigue evident in the slump of his shoulders. "There was no need to worry. 'Twas simply that Richard had much to discuss."

He needed sleep. That much was apparent. Marguerite made a quick decision. She would let Alain sleep, unburdened by thoughts of Henri's potential treachery, and when he woke she would tell him.

Alain undressed quickly, tossing his clothes into a heap at the end of the bed. As he did, a musky scent wafted on the air. Marguerite wrinkled her nose then frowned, not willing to believe her senses. She sniffed again. There was no mistaking that perfume. Only one woman in Poitiers wore it. Marguerite's fingers clenched the sheets. She would say nothing, for now was not the time for recriminations, but it hurt—oh, how it hurt—to know that Alain had been close enough to Honore that his clothing bore her scent.


*She sat huddled in the corner of the room, her knees drawn close to her body, her arms wrapped around them in a desperate attempt to retain some warmth. It was cold, so cold. Even the sun had disappeared, taking the last vestige of warmth from the room. In its place a frigid wind swept through the slit of a window, sending shivers through her body.*

*And yet the shivers owed more to fear than to the cold that permeated the room. She had known fear before, but never had it reached these heights. Though no one had told her, she knew that the end was near, and that knowledge brought with it a foreboding so intense that she could not move, could barely think.*

*She had to go to the window.*

*She could not go to the window.*

*She had to see what was happening.*

*She could not force her eyes open.*

*The wind cried, an unearthly sound that reminded her of animals caught in a hunter's snare. She shivered again, trying to block out the cold, the fear and the dreadful noise.*

*She did not succeed.*

*At length she forced her arms to release their grip on her knees and, moving with the painful gait of an aged woman, she made her way to the window. She knew what she would see. He would be there, that great destrier of his only feet away, grazing peacefully as though unaware of his master's need. Close by but just out of sight would be the other one, the one who wanted to harm him.*

*Though the seasons had changed, the scene had not. She could replay it in her memory, and indeed she did.*

*She stood in the window embrasure, willing herself to open her eyes. Just once more. She would look out just once more.*

*"No!" she cried. It could not be.*

*The horse was gone, and in its place stood the other one.*

*She refused to look at the apparition. Instead she stared at him. He lay crumpled on the ground, his arms and legs bent at unnatural angles. She could feel his labored breathing and the desperation with which he clung to life, a life that was seeping away at an alarming rate.*

*He needed help. He needed it now.*

*The other one moved closer, raising his sword over his head.*

*She clenched her hands and began to pound on the walls, heedless of the blood which stained the cold stone.*

*She had to help him. There had to be a way!*

*The other one laughed as he gripped the hilt of his sword with both hands.*

*"Now!"*

*And the sword plunged downward.*

*She screamed.*

As she had each time, she wakened from the nightmare with tears streaming down her face, her body trembling from the horror she had witnessed. Each time was worse, the danger more explicit, her fear more profound. This time, though, Alain was only inches away. Marguerite slid across the mattress and flung her arms around him, clinging to him as she struggled to control her breathing.

"Don't do it, I beg you. Do not fight Henri." Her words were distorted by the tears that still flowed down her cheeks.

Alain turned and began to stroke her hair. "It was only a dream," he murmured. "You're safe now."

As Marguerite shook her head, her hair tangled around his fingers. "I'm not the one in danger. It's you, my darling. It's you." She gripped his shoulders. "Alain, it was a warning. I know it. It may have been only a dream, but the danger is real. Please don't fight.''

He put his hands on either side of her face and gazed into her eyes. ''I have no choice, my love. I am not a coward, and never will I give any man the chance to call me one. 'Tis my honor that is at stake.''

'' 'Tis your life that is at stake. Henri . . .''

Alain laid a finger across her lips. ''Say no more. I will fight Henri, and I promise you that I will win.''


When she wakened, the bed was empty. Had it not been for the lingering sense of foreboding that was the normal aftermath of her nightmares and the faint masculine scent that clung to the sheets, she might have thought she had imagined Alain's return. But it was not imagination. Alain was in Poitiers, and today he faced a man who had sworn to kill him.

'' 'Tis all anyone can talk about,'' Diane announced as she entered the chamber, her face radiant with happiness.

Marguerite managed a smile. There was nothing to be gained by telling Diane her fears. ''I hadn't realized you and Charles were regaling everyone with tales of how you spent yesterday afternoon.''

Diane blushed. ''As if you and Alain spent it any differently! Everyone knows you came back here and didn't emerge for hours.''

''We were talking.'' Though it was the truth, Marguerite's tone made Diane laugh.

''A likely story.'' She opened the trunk which held her clothing and pulled out a bliaut the color of ripe apricots. ''What did he say when you told him about the baby?''

''I didn't tell him,'' Marguerite admitted. ''He seemed so preoccupied with other things that I decided to wait until we were back at Mirail. You didn't tell Charles, did you?''

Again Diane blushed. ''We didn't talk very much. We were—what was your word?—preoccupied with other things.'' She laughed. ''But today all anyone can discuss is the tournament. The wagers are high, and most people are betting on Alain.''

Marguerite could not suppress a shudder. ''I wish I were that sure. The nightmare came back again last night, and it was worse than ever. This time I saw the other knight trying to kill Alain.''

''It was only a dream.''

''That's what Alain said.''

''He's the best jouster in all of France. You know that.''

It was little consolation. ''That may be true, but I'm afraid Henri will not fight fairly. Alain may be no match against treachery.'' And Lord knew Henri had no compunction about using treachery.

Marguerite helped Diane fasten her girdle, then slipped her arms into her own pale gray silk bliaut. She caught the folds of the skirt in a silver girdle, then reached for the soft bag that she had placed on the bottom of the trunk. She had brought little jewelry with her, but this was one piece she carried wherever she went.

''Charles told me that there has been enmity between Alain and Henri for years.'' Diane began to braid her hair. ''Did you know that they were both fostered with Guy de Bercé?''

Marguerite fingered the silver brooch which had been Alain's wedding gift for an instant before she pinned it on her gown. ''Philippe mentioned that Alain had been with Guy when I was at Jarnac the last time. He didn't know anything about Henri, but I thought they must have known each other there.''

''Charles is not sure what caused it, but one of the other squires told him that Henri had vowed revenge on Alain before they were even knighted.''

Marguerite's hands faltered as they threaded silver ribbons through her hair. Today everything she wore would be silver in honor of the Silver Knight. ''I wonder if 'tis part of the reason Henri seems to want Mirail so badly.''

''It is an almost irresistible combination: you, the riches of Mirail and revenge on Alain all in one package.''

As she remembered the wildness she had seen in Henri's eyes when he had issued the challenge to Alain, a new sense of urgency swept over Marguerite. "Come," she said, tugging on Diane's hand. "I must find Alain. I have not yet given him my favor to wear in the tournament." She reached for another silk ribbon.

The sun was unusually hot for April, causing most of the citizens of Poitiers to stroll slowly toward the lists. As though oblivious to the heat, Marguerite kept urging Diane to quicken her pace. But when they approached the river Clain and the double bell tower of Montierneuf came into view, Marguerite's footsteps lagged. She knew what was waiting around the bend in the road, for there at the confluence of the Clain and the Boivre was the Tour du Cordier, the tower of her nightmare. Diane and Alain could say what they may. Marguerite knew better. It was no coincidence that the tower which had so haunted her was close to the tournament grounds.

With each step, her dread grew, and she remembered the dark knight of her dreams, his sword plunging toward Alain's heart.

"I thought you were in a hurry."

Marguerite stopped. "Oh, Diane, I cannot shake this feeling that something is terribly wrong. Alain must not fight."

Before Diane could answer, a servant wearing the queen's livery approached them. "Lady Marguerite, my mistress bids you follow me. She has reserved seats for you and Lady Diane in her gallery."

It was an honor. More than that, it would make the day far more pleasant, for the queen's galleries were covered with canopies, protecting their occupants from the sun. Marguerite curtsied low, thanking the queen for her kindness. She and Diane walked toward the designated seats, their progress slowed by the ladies who wished Alain's bride well.

"I wonder which danger they consider the greater: Henri or Honore," Marguerite murmured as she and Diane slid into their seats.

Marguerite adjusted her skirt, then sat back. She would have to sit for a few moments, pretending to enjoy the honor the queen had bestowed on her, before she searched for Alain. But she had to reach him. She had to see him before he fought.

Marguerite glanced upward and blanched.

"Oh, Diane!" She gripped the other woman's hand, her fear suddenly becoming a living thing. "I cannot sit here." For while the lists were in full view, so was the tower. It stood there, casting its menacing shadow over the field where Alain would soon fight.

There was no choice, for she would insult the queen by moving. Deliberately Marguerite lowered her eyes so that she did not see the tower. Instead, she focused on the lists and the scores of knights milling around on the grass, as she searched for Alain.

He stood next to Neptune, one hand on the powerful destrier's mane as though somehow soothing the beast. But it was the woman at his side who seemed more in need of soothing. Honore had gripped Alain's right arm with both of her hands, and from the expression on her face, Marguerite knew she was pleading with him. Her lovely features were distorted with fear, yet the look she gave him revealed another far more powerful emotion. Honore loved him.

Marguerite closed her eyes, not wanting to accept what she had seen. It had been easier when she had thought that Honore sought Alain for the power and prestige his company provided. Love? She hadn't reckoned on that. And yet perhaps it was the answer.

A shudder swept through Marguerite's slender frame, and she placed her hand on her stomach, unconsciously guarding the life within. That life was precious, the greatest gift she had been given. But no matter how she valued her unborn child's life, it was no more precious than its father. Marguerite clasped her hands together. She would do anything, anything at all, to protect them both, even if it meant sacrificing her own chance at happiness.

Raising her eyes to the heavens, Marguerite offered a silent prayer. Sweet Mary above, I beg you to keep Alain safe. If you do, I promise I will do anything you ask. If it will bring him joy, I will even give him and our child to Honore. Just keep my love safe.

# Chapter Twenty-Eight

He raised his eyes to the galleries. The hour for the tournament was nigh; surely she would not refuse to attend, no matter how badly shaken she had been by the nightmare. Nightmares. That was one malady from which he did not suffer. There was no need for dreams and chimeras to haunt him when memories were ever ready to disturb his thoughts, both waking and sleeping. The immutable past brought regrets enough; fear of the future and faceless dreams held little power over him.

His eyes moved slowly, scanning the rows of women who had gathered to watch the tournament. There were few men in the galleries save servants, for only those knights so old or infirm that they could not mount a horse would miss the honor of participating in Richard the Lionheart's first tournament.

When he spied her, she was seated several rows below the queen. Alain smiled. Eleanor was ever the consummate politician. While she had given his bride a position of honor by allowing her entrance to the royal galleries, Eleanor had placed Marguerite at a lower level than her most trusted ladies, no doubt because of Guillaume's continued loyalty to King Louis even after Eleanor's divorce. It would have been unseemly, at least in Eleanor's eyes, to ignore such a lapse.

It was the first time he had seen Marguerite wearing gray, and while the somber hue of her bliaut made her stand out from the other ladies in their brightly colored clothing, it was not her gown which caught Alain's eye. Even from a distance he could see that her face was unnaturally pale, and dark circles ringed her eyes. When he had left her, she had been asleep, but it appeared the sleep had had no restorative powers. She was staring into the distance, oblivious to the noisy crowd gathered only yards away from her.

"Jacques." Alain handed Neptune's reins to his squire then made his way quickly to the galleries.

"Good morrow, my lady." His greeting was formal, designed to be overheard by the myriad ladies and their pages. Only when Marguerite had joined him and he could lower his voice would he say what was foremost on his mind.

"How can you call it a good morrow? There's nothing good about it." She descended to the lowest level and approached the wooden wall that separated the viewing stands from the tournament field. Her beautiful face was drawn, almost haggard, though her eyes blazed with emotion.

"Do you see that?" she demanded, pointing at the massive tower which guarded the confluence of the two rivers.

Alain nodded. "They call it the Tour du Cordier. It has been there for as long as I can remember. Some, in fact, would say . . ."

Marguerite gestured impatiently, interrupting him. "That's the tower from my nightmare, the one I keep seeing in my dreams." She turned to face him, her eyes beseeching him to listen. "Other parts of the dream have changed, but two have remained the same: that tower and the danger you face."

Though her voice was low, it was fraught with pain. Alain sought to comfort her. " 'Twas only a dream. You know I put little stock in dreams."

" 'Tis easy enough for you to say that. It wasn't your sleep that was disturbed. It wasn't your days that were haunted by the horrors of those dreams." She shook her head. "It was a warning. Alain, that tower means you are in danger. I beg you, do not fight today." She gripped his arm. "Stay with me."

The trumpet sounded, signaling the beginning of the tournament, and the crowd began to move restively. This was the reason they had gathered under the hot sun, to see knights display their martial skills.

"Henri de Bleufontaine challenges Alain de Jarnac."

It was time for him to prepare for the joust, yet he could not leave Marguerite. Not yet. Not until he had somehow managed to wipe that haunted expression from her face. She needed reassurances.

"Every knight who jousts or is part of the melee is in danger," he told her. "I've done this hundreds of times before, and I've always been the victor. Today will be no different."

It was not what she wanted to hear. She gripped his arm so tightly that her knuckles turned white. "Don't try to placate me, Alain de Jarnac. This is serious, and you are simply too stubborn to admit it."

At least she was not so pale. Anger had colored her cheeks, and the fierce expression on her face reminded Alain of the early days of their marriage. He tried a new tactic.

"Stubborn, you say? Then I'm in good company.

> A savage-creating stubborn-pulling fellow,
> Uncurbed, unfettered, uncontrolled of speech,
> Unperiphrastic, bombastiloquent."

He had thought to bring a smile to her face, reminding her of the way they had once traded classical quotations, each trying to outdo the other in finding obscure lines to prove their points.

He failed.

"Stop it!" The emotion blazing from her eyes was easy to identify. His bride was angry. "How dare you quote Aristophanes at a time like this? Can't you see how serious this is?" She reached out to touch his face. "Alain, I'm terrified that you'll be killed. Please, I beseech you, do not fight today."

Tears welled in her eyes, and for an instant Alain wavered. He had never seen Marguerite so distraught. Even when her father had died, she had been composed and had handled her sorrow with dignity. Yet this was different. She was frightened—to use her word, terrified. Amazingly, her fear was for him. She cared about him. An unfamiliar warmth began to spread through Alain.

When he spoke, it was gently. "I must fight. You know that."

The trumpets sounded again, calling Alain and Henri to the lists.

Marguerite's tears overflowed, coursing down her cheeks. For a long moment she did naught but stare at him, as though memorizing the lines of his face. Her eyes were somber, her cheeks stained with tears, and yet her face seemed lit by a powerful emotion.

Alain caught his breath. Could it be? The warmth that had begun as a tingling began to blaze.

Seemingly unaware of the tumult she was causing, Marguerite reached for the silk ribbon that decorated her sleeve. "I beg you, wear my favor." Her fingers began to untie the ribbon, then paused. She bent her head and quickly unfastened the brooch from the center of her gown.

Alain smiled. She was wearing his wedding gift. He had noticed something shiny before but had paid it little attention.

Holding the silver rose in her palm, Marguerite raised her eyes to meet his. "When you gave me this, you said the rose and its thorns reminded you of me. Today I beg you remember only the sweet scent of the rose, not its thorns."

Alain's heart began to pound. What she was giving him was far more valuable than a mere piece of silver, no matter how beautiful the workmanship. She was offering him something no woman had ever before given him.

Marguerite reached over the wall and pinned the brooch onto his shoulder. "Wear it, my love, as a part of me. Take it into battle, and God willing, it will keep you safe."

She leaned forward and pressed a kiss on his lips. The fire became an inferno, threatening to consume him. Alain had never liked fires, but this was different. This was a cleansing fire, destroying the shell he had so carefully erected, turning his fears into ashes, leaving only the pure kernel behind. For a moment Alain stood bemused. She loved him! No matter what happened today, no one could take that from him. Marguerite loved him.

"I'll win this joust for you," he vowed and dropped to his knees in the traditional gesture of submission. As Alain walked back onto the field, his step was light.

When she returned to her seat next to Diane, Marguerite closed her eyes in a silent prayer that Alain would remain unharmed. He would never know how difficult it had been to let him return to the lists when all she had wanted to do was hold him close and prevent him from fighting.

"He'll win." Diane patted her hand as she murmured the reassuring words.

Marguerite wished she shared Diane and Alain's optimism.

The crowd grew silent with anticipation as Alain entered the lists. Though there were a dozen other jousts scheduled, this was the one that had captured their interest. By rights it should have been the last contest, but it appeared that Richard was as anxious as they to have the outcome decided. 'Twould be a battle royal with two of the most skilled knights in France fighting to the death. In truth, none believed that Richard would actually allow either man to kill the other. Still, there was always the possibility of seeing blood spilled. Accidents did happen, particularly when the contest was based on deep-seated enmity. The tale that the two men had been foes since childhood had spread quickly, the rivalry growing more intense with each retelling.

As Alain crossed the grassy expanse to reach Neptune, the crowd began to murmur. Henri was already mounted on his golden destrier Zeus, waiting at the opposite end of the field for the joust to begin.

"Look!" Marguerite heard the shout but kept her eyes fixed on Alain, willing him to be safe. She could not stop him from fighting. All she could do was pray and hope that the strength of her pleas would protect him.

"He's coming." A hoarse cry sounded above the murmuring. Alain started to mount.

Marguerite heard the sound of hoofbeats, and the crowd's murmurs became a roar.

"Sweet Mary above! Look at that! He didn't wait."

Though the queen had not given the signal, Henri was charging toward Alain.

Alain paused, his foot poised to leap onto Neptune's back. At the last moment, he turned, his eyes moving to the galleries. When his gaze met Marguerite's, he flashed her a smile.

The delay was infinitesimal, but it was all Henri needed. Spurring Zeus, he raced across the ground, his lance lowered, attacking before Alain could mount.

Marguerite gasped, her eyes moving involuntarily to the tower. The dreams had been more than a premonition. They had been accurate predictors of danger. Her heart stopped, and the blood drained from her face as she saw her nightmare come to life. It was all so clear now. Henri was the other knight, the one who sought to kill Alain. This was how he would do it. He had taken unfair advantage, and now Alain would die, for a knight on foot, no matter how skilled, was no match for one on horseback.

With the instincts that had made him such a formidable enemy, Alain moved swiftly to protect himself. It was too late. Henri had the superior position, and he used it to full advantage. Drawing back his lance, he aimed carefully and struck Alain's right shoulder. The crowd roared with displeasure as blood stained Alain's tunic.

Marguerite leaped to her feet. She had to reach Alain. But Diane placed a restraining hand on her arm, reminding her that until the queen called a halt, no one could interfere with the joust.

Marguerite turned imploring eyes toward the queen. There was no need, for Eleanor had already risen.

"Stop!" Her cry silenced the onlookers, and even Henri reined in his horse. "The joust is forfeit, for Sir Henri has broken a fundamental rule of chivalry. No honorable knight would attack one who is unmounted."

Marguerite's heart thudded as she stared at Alain, trying to assess the seriousness of his wound. Dear God, please don't let it be deep. Diane wrapped her arm around Marguerite's waist, wordlessly giving comfort. Then Marguerite's eyes moved to Henri. Though he had raised his helmet and inclined his head in a gesture of deference to the queen, she saw no sign of remorse in his posture. His shoulders were squared, and the set of his lips made him appear insouciant, some might say insolent.

"It is over." Eleanor repeated her judgment.

Thank God! Alain would be safe. Marguerite's pulse began to slow.

Alain shook his head. "It is apparent that Henri wishes a fight," he said, his voice carrying to the furthest corner of the field. "It will be my pleasure to give him one . . . a fair fight."

There was a long pause as the queen appeared to consider Alain's request. No! The word resonated within Marguerite's head though she made no sound. The queen could not allow this foolishness to continue.

At length Eleanor smiled at Alain. As the queen nodded her assent, he sprang onto Neptune's back. The joust had begun.

The two men rode to opposite sides of the field, then turned and faced each other, waiting as the crowd did for Eleanor's signal. She stood, her bearing regal, and looked from one opponent to the other. Marguerite could almost feel her silent command that the men behave as true chevaliers. Not that a command, spoken or not, would have much effect on Henri. Marguerite had no illusions where her vassal was concerned. The queen, however, had no way of knowing how typical his unchivalrous behavior had been. If she had, Marguerite was certain she would never have allowed the contest to continue.

Eleanor paused, then slowly raised her arm. The men lowered their helmets and adjusted their shields. As the queen released a golden scarf, signaling the start of the contest, the crowd roared. This was why they had come.

Spurring their horses, the two men raced toward each other, their lances lowered. Marguerite knew that while the first blow was rarely decisive, the knight who struck it had a psychological advantage over his opponent. Henri had achieved not only the first blow but the first blood letting. Marguerite could only pray that that would be the extent of his dominance.

Both men leaned forward, choosing the position that gave the most power to their strokes. The crowd was silent once again, the only noise the pounding of the horses' hooves and the drumming of Marguerite's heart. She watched as, seemingly in unison, the two men drew back their lances. They were good, almost perfectly matched, but Alain was a fraction of an instant faster. Though Marguerite knew that his arm must ache from the wound to his shoulder, he did not falter. His lance struck Henri's shield at dead center, connecting with such force that Henri rocked backward, his own lance pointing harmlessly into the air.

The crowd laughed.

It took only a second for Henri to recover from the punishing blow. By the time the destriers had wheeled around and the men faced each other again, Henri was once more firmly seated on his horse.

He had made a mistake, but Marguerite knew there would be no more, for if there was one thing Henri hated, it was laughter. He would not risk being the butt of the courtiers' jokes.

As their horses met a second time, Henri seized the offensive. He kept his lance held parallel to the ground, pointed directly at Alain's shield. Then, at the last moment, he lowered the lance, trying to slip it beneath Alain's shield. It was a bold move and one which was used so infrequently that it rarely failed, but Alain deflected the blow easily, almost as though he expected it. Marguerite expelled a sigh of relief. Her warrior was still safe.

On the next round, Henri dealt Alain a sharp blow to the head. Alain responded by piercing the mail on Henri's right side, causing blood to stain his tabard and to drip onto his horse's flanks.

The crowd roared, thinking the end was near. But they had reckoned without the men's skill and determination, for the fight continued, each man parrying the other's thrusts.

It was as though they anticipated each other's moves, Marguerite thought, as though they were following a script they had already played a dozen times. Perhaps it was the result of their training together under Guy de Bercé's tutelage. This time there was a vital difference. When they had trained it would have been to prepare them to battle the enemy, not each other. After they had gained their silver spurs, the two men had gone in different directions, Alain to distinguish himself fighting in the Holy Land, Henri to master the arts of cruelty and treachery. And now they were facing each other again, fighting in the shadow of the tower to settle some age-old score.

The tower. It drew her eyes as surely as a magnet. Though she tried to ignore it, she could not, and the sight chilled her blood, negating the warmth of the morning sun. The tower remained, a visible reminder of her nightmares. With it hovering on the periphery of her sight, Marguerite could not shake the fear that Henri would find a chink in Alain's armor, some way to defeat him.

More than an hour had passed, and still the men battled. Marguerite could see the sweat pouring from beneath Alain's helmet, and the blood still leaked from his shoulder. He was tiring, he had to be, and yet he continued to fight. For his part, Henri seemed indefatigable, possessed with a superhuman strength. It had to be an illusion, for he was naught but an ordinary man, but he fought as though the passage of time had had no effect on his strength.

The crowd grew restive. It had been far too long since fresh blood was spilled. This was becoming boring.

The men were at opposite ends of the field, their lances poised for yet another joust. There was no longer any need to spur the horses, for Neptune and Zeus knew what was expected of them. They raced forward, covering the distance almost as quickly as they had the first time.

Alain and Henri drew back their lances, aiming at each other's shields. But at the last instant Henri lowered his arm, thrusting the unblunted point into Neptune's soft underbelly.

The destrier whinnied and reared onto his hind legs as blood poured onto the ground.

Marguerite saw what few others did, the momentary tightening of Alain's shoulders. He was angry now, far angrier than he had been when Henri had wounded him. Alain leaned forward slightly, soothing the horse.

When the men faced each other for the next joust, Marguerite watched Henri straighten his shoulders then point his lance at Neptune's bleeding belly as if saluting the wounded animal. The man was confident of victory.

If Alain saw the gesture, he gave no sign. Instead, he and Neptune charged forward as though neither had been injured.

The crowd roared its approval.

Henri leaned forward, openly aiming his lance at Neptune's unprotected belly.

The crowd booed.

Alain continued forward, apparently oblivious to Henri's threat and the crowd's roars. He kept his lance pointed at the center of Henri's shield as he had a hundred times before. Then, at the last second, Alain shifted his weight to the right. His arm thrust forward in a movement so swift that it was over before Henri realized what had happened. Alain had taken Henri's own maneuver and used it against him, for he had slid his lance beneath his opponent's shield, knocking him from his horse.

Marguerite threw her arms around Diane. Alain was safe!

The crowd leapt to its feet and shouted its pleasure.

Dropping his lance, Alain jumped from Neptune's back and unsheathed his sword. Before Henri could move, Alain stood over him, the point of his sword pressed to Henri's throat.

"I'm not ready to die." Henri blubbered.

Alain pressed harder. "Any man who deliberately wounds my horse deserves to die," he said, his voice carrying clearly across the field. "You are less than a human being, and the earth would be well rid of your scum."

A murmur of approval rose from the crowd.

"Fortunately for you, I have no desire to sully my sword with your cowardly blood." Keeping his sword pressed firmly on Henri's throat, Alain turned to Eleanor, silently seeking her assent. When she nodded, he continued. "Are you willing to trade your worthless life for something of value?"

"Anything." Spittle gathered at the corner of Henri's mouth. "Take my armor, my horse, anything."

This time Alain's eyes sought Marguerite's. She smiled, knowing her face reflected her relief that he was safe and joy that he had not killed a man, no matter how heinous his act.

As Alain paused, deliberating the judgment, Henri squirmed.

"For losing the battle, you will forfeit your armor and your horse," Alain announced. It was the traditional penalty. "Zeus is too fine an animal to be ridden by scum like you."

Alain looked at Marguerite again, and this time he winked. Turning his attention back to Henri, he said, "You have shown yourself unworthy to be a knight, and so you must pay. For your unchivalrous behavior, I demand your man Gerard. He will become Lady Marguerite's servant."

Alain silenced Henri's moan of protest with the tip of his sword. "As insurance that Gerard has safe passage to Mirail, I ask Queen Eleanor to keep you imprisoned here until I notify her that the man has reached Lady Marguerite's castle."

For the first time that day, the tears which filled Marguerite's eyes were tears of joy. Her prayers had been answered. Alain was safe. The world had seen Henri for what he truly was, a dangerous coward. And in one stroke Alain had accomplished what she had sought to do for months. He had guaranteed Louise's happiness.

Raising her eyes to the tower, Marguerite smiled. Perhaps now the nightmares would end.

# Chapter Twenty-Nine

There was no doubt about it. By the end of the day, Marguerite was certain there was some cosmic conspiracy designed to keep her and Alain from having a moment alone together. At the end of the joust, the queen had summoned both Alain and Marguerite to her side while she presented Alain with the scarf she had used to signal the beginning of the joust. It was, Marguerite knew, an honor, but at the same time that she was mindful of the favoritism Eleanor was showing her husband, she was fuming inwardly. Surely the queen should have seen that the man was still bleeding from his wounds.

Though the blood was no longer streaming, the red patch on Alain's shoulder continued to spread. With a healer's insight, Marguerite knew that Alain needed care, and he needed it soon. No one, not even the Silver Knight, could continue to lose blood without paying the consequences.

"My lady," she said quietly as she curtseyed to the queen, "I beg your indulgence to care for my lord. I fear his injuries are more serious than he would have us believe."

Giving Alain a shrewd glance that took in the pallor beneath his normally bronzed face, Eleanor nodded and dismissed them

with the admonition that she did not want to see them again
until the evening feast.

But even then there had been no privacy, for Charles had
disengaged himself from the group of men who clustered around
Richard and had accompanied Marguerite and Alain back to
their rooms.

"You gave us all a fright," Charles admitted as Marguerite
unpinned the silver rose from Alain's shoulder, then helped
him remove his mail chemise. She laid both on the carved
wooden chest. "I have never seen a man fight the way Henri
did."

"I have." Alain's words were tinged with humor. "Remember that he and I trained together. We know each other's tactics.
And I had one advantage that he did not."

"Experience fighting against the Saracens." His brother
completed the sentence.

Alain shook his head. "A reason to win." And, though
Charles pressed him for further explanations, Alain would say
no more.

While Marguerite cleansed the wound and stitched the ragged
pieces of skin together, Charles continued to talk to his brother,
recounting the praise that the other knights had bestowed on
him. "It will be a long time before anyone forgets this battle,"
he concluded. "There's speculation that Richard will ask you
to remain with him permanently."

That was a possibility Marguerite did not want to consider.
Still, when they reached the banquet hall that evening and were
directed to the head table, it was apparent to anyone watching
that Alain was the royal favorite. He wore the golden scarf that
Eleanor had given him, but even without that tangible reminder
of his victory, Alain was clearly an honored guest. He was
seated in the center at Richard's right hand, while Marguerite
had been placed at the end of the table next to Maurice de
Bernis, one of Richard's most trusted knights.

Though her companion was congenial, Marguerite found the
meal endless. She had little desire for the succulent dishes
which the pages offered, and the wine, though of an excellent
vintage, tasted sour. When would it all end? The only thing

she wanted was an hour alone with Alain, an hour when they could talk.

It had been a day fraught with emotion: fear, loathing, then almost ineffable joy. And yet it was not over, for she had not spoken with Alain. She still did not know whether the rumors were true, whether he returned Honore's love and wished to marry her.

There had been no sign of Honore since the end of the tournament, but that signified little. Mayhap she had returned to her rooms and was preparing for Alain's visit.

When the pages brought the sweetmeats that signaled the final course, Richard rose. Holding his silver goblet aloft, he began to speak of the tournament. "I thank you all for being here with me at my first grand tournament. Today was a day that will long be remembered. It was a day for brave men, and the bravest of them was Alain de Jarnac, the man many of you know as the Silver Knight. Let us drink a cup of wine in his honor."

As the last of the cheers subsided, Richard turned to Alain, bidding him rise. "You fought when others would have stopped, and in doing so you taught us all the meaning of courage. I thank you, and to show my gratitude, I offer you anything you wish." Richard paused for a second. "Within reason, of course."

The crowd laughed.

Marguerite caught her breath. This was the opportunity Alain needed. She knew he would do naught without his lord's approval. Instead of riches or other tangible rewards, would he ask for permission to divorce her and marry Honore?

Alain bent his head, acknowledging the duke's offer. "I am deeply indebted to you, my lord, for it was you who set the example of courage. I have but followed in your steps."

The crowd murmured its approval of Alain's graceful words.

"It is most generous of you to offer me a reward for doing no more than my knightly duty. On another day I might have refused your offer. But today I cannot, for there is one thing I desire above all else." Alain paused then turned to face Richard. Matching the duke's slightly humorous tone, he said, "You need not fear that I seek to empty your coffers. What I ask has no price and yet is priceless to me. I beg your leave to return to Mirail. My bride and I have matters to attend to.''

Richard laughed, clapping Alain on the shoulder. "I can guess what sort of matters you have in mind.''

The crowd roared.

"It appears your husband is anxious to be alone with you,'' Maurice de Bernis said to Marguerite.

"And I with him.'' It was true, oh so true, but while the crowd assumed that Alain wished to be with her because he loved her, Marguerite was not so certain. 'Twas still possible that Alain wished to see her safely back in Mirail before he returned to Poitiers and a life with Honore. Only if she and Alain were alone would she be able to learn the truth. And learn the truth she must.

The meal was only the beginning of the evening, for Richard had arranged for jugglers, dancers and troubadours to entertain his guests. They were skillful, the best in the country, and yet not even the most talented could hold Marguerite's attention. She watched them, applauding at the proper times, while her mind kept whirling, wondering what Alain would say when they were alone.

As the third troubadour approached the high table, Marguerite turned from Maurice. Something about the man tugged at her memory.

"I bring a tale of the kindest lady in the land,'' the man told his audience. He strummed his lute, punctuating the verses of his song with a delicate melody as he wove the tale of a woman whose soft hands and warm smile had won his heart, a woman whose generosity knew no bounds, a woman who had given him life's greatest gift, a woman named Marguerite.

At the sound of her name, Marguerite stared at the man, recognition flooding over her. But she had no time to even smile at the troubadour, for a large hand gripped her shoulder.

"Come!''

Alain glared at her, his eyes dark with emotion, his lips thinned with anger.

Maurice de Bernis laughed. "A bit anxious, are you?''

Alain did not deign to reply. Instead, he placed both hands on Marguerite's shoulders and lifted her off the bench. Grasping her hand, he began to march toward the door, dragging Marguerite behind him. It was only when they reached the privacy of their room that he spoke.

"I've tried to be trusting. God knows I have," Alain said as he closed the door and latched it. "But this must stop." He loomed over Marguerite, his clenched hands and the tension in his voice the only sign of his tightly controlled emotions. "If we're going to have any kind of future worth having, you must—you must," he repeated, "stop encouraging every man in the kingdom. First Charles, then Henri, now the troubadour. Who's next in your bed?"

Marguerite stared at him, aghast. "In the name of all the saints, what are you talking about?"

"Then you don't deny it?" His voice was low but fierce.

*He* was accusing *her?* Marguerite saw the anger on his face and felt an answering anger rise deep within her. He spoke of trust, when it was clear the man had no understanding of the word.

Marguerite met his gaze then shook her head. "This time you've gone too far. I will neither deny nor confirm anything," she told him. "If you think about it, Alain, you'll realize how absurd it is that you of all men dare to accuse me of anything. You're the one who's broken his marriage vows. You're the one who's proven himself unworthy to be the father of my child."

The words tumbled out unplanned. It was only when they hung between them that she gasped, realizing what she had done.

Alain's eyes widened, and his face turned white then red. "Child?" There was a sense of wonder in his voice. "You are with child?"

But Marguerite was not to be sidetracked. "Our child is not the issue," she said shortly. "Our marriage is. I didn't have to go to the courts of love to learn about Honore. It was bad enough that the peddlers brought the tale to Mirail, but once I came to Poitiers, I couldn't take two steps without hearing her name coupled with yours.''

As a cool breeze swept through the open window, Marguerite shivered. The heat of her anger had dissipated, only to be replaced with a deep sadness. She had vowed that she would do anything, even release Alain from his marriage vows, to keep him safe. But now that the moment had come, it was far more difficult, far more painful, than she had dreamed. She loved him, and God forgive her for her selfishness, she wanted him with her. But she had made a vow, and though it might tear her apart, she must keep it.

''Honore loves you. That much is obvious to even a casual observer.'' Somehow her voice was even and did not betray the anguish she felt. She would not disgrace herself by crying and begging for his love. If it was to have any value, it must be freely given. ''I know Honore loves you. What I don't know is how you feel. If you love her, now is the time to admit it. I promise you, Alain, that I will not be a barrier to your happiness.''

It was as though he had not heard her question. He was silent for a moment, and when he spoke his voice was low, almost reverent. ''Why didn't you tell me about the baby sooner?''

The baby. That miracle that had resulted from their night of love. How could she bear to give up both Alain and the child? Marguerite put a protective hand on her stomach. ''I wanted to tell you, but the time never seemed right. It was a dilemma, because I was afraid you would guess and be angry about learning the news that way.''

She let her hand drop to her side while Alain stared at her body, searching for visible signs of her pregnancy. ''I thought you might have guessed, for I'm still in the early stages where I suffer from morning malady, and that's impossible to hide. I was having a particularly difficult bout of it yesterday morning.''

A smile of wonder crossed his face. ''Then you weren't sick at the sight of me?''

Marguerite reacted as though he'd struck her. ''Of course not! How could you think that?'' Then she remembered how her stomach had been roiling when Alain and Charles entered the queen's chambers. Her voice was gentle as she continued, "You would never sicken me. It was simply that our child was making his presence known in a most unpleasant manner." As Alain smiled again, Marguerite thought about his question. If he had truly believed she was so unhappy that he had returned that she had been physically repulsed by him, it was little wonder he had been cold toward her. No wonder he had not responded to her kisses. No wonder he had sought Honore's company rather than her own last night.

"I had planned to tell you about the baby last night," she continued, "but after the courts of love, I could not." Though she did not mention Alain's own behavior, the memory hung between them. "I could not use the child to bind you to me."

"And you believe I love Honore?"

Marguerite tried to read his expression, but once again it was shuttered. "I don't know what the truth is, other than that I cannot continue living in ignorance. Alain, we must be honest with each other."

He took both of her hands in his, waiting until she met his gaze before he spoke. "I have never loved Honore. In truth, I was sure that I could never love anyone. I thought I was lacking some key component that allowed other men to love and be loved." There was no smile on Alain's face, and his eyes reflected the pain that admission brought. "I'd be less than honest if I didn't say that I enjoyed Honore's company, for I did. And, yes, she was once my mistress, but that ended the day I met you."

Marguerite wanted to believe it. Oh, how she wanted to believe it. If she could believe it, it would be the answer to all of her prayers, save one. And yet . . . "I heard you were living in her house here in Poitiers."

" 'Tis true. Not only have I lived there, but I've let everyone believe we were once again lovers. I'm not proud of that, but I was so hurt by the tales of your infidelity that I took whatever revenge I could find. It was petty and, like most acts of revenge, brought me no joy."

Alain touched the silver rose which she had pinned on her

shoulder. Tonight she wore a deep blue bliaut, and the brooch shimmered against the dark background. "Marguerite, you're the only woman I want, thorns and all." His eyes darkened again, and his voice resonated with emotion. "I know very little of love, and so for a long time I did not realize that what I felt for you was love. All I knew was that I had a dull ache, an emptiness when we were apart."

Marguerite smiled, for Alain was describing the way she felt when he was gone.

"You smile, but 'twas no laughing matter. I never realized that love could hurt so much. No one warned me that the stories of your infatuation with other men would be more painful than the worst wound I'd ever had."

He loved her! Marguerite's heart began to sing with joy.

"Oh, Alain, there have been no other men."

"What about Charles? You kept his poem as if you treasured it."

Marguerite blushed at the memory. "That was childish foolishness. 'Twould seem we both have things we're not very proud of, for that's one thing I'm ashamed of. You said you knew little of love. I'm afraid I knew even less. I believed the troubadours' stories and the tales of the ancient heroes. They made me think that Charles was the perfect knight." She paused for a second. "It took me a while to realize that he is the perfect knight . . . for Diane, but not for me. As for the poem, if you had read it before you tossed it into the fire, you would have seen that it was Charles's farewell to me. In it, he told me that he had discovered the love of his life and that he realized what he had felt for me was only a passing fancy. In truth, I kept it as a reminder of my own foolishness."

"Then what inspired the troubadour to claim you had given him the greatest gift? I vow there was not a man in the hall who did not believe you had bestowed your favors on him."

"Surely you know troubadours exaggerate. All I did was staunch his bleeding." She explained how she and Diane had found the man slumped in an alley and how she had treated his wounds.

"Then the gift you gave him was life, not love."

Marguerite shrugged. "Even that was hyperbole. The man was not dying." Her face darkened. "You said you had heard rumors that I encouraged Henri. That is a very different situation from Charles and the troubadour. Henri is far from harmless, and what he wants is not a simple flirtation. That's why I was so worried about the joust." As Marguerite told Alain of Henri's attack on her and then on Mirail, she watched his face darken.

"I'll kill him." It was a statement of fact, not an idle threat. "No man attacks my wife and lives."

Marguerite put a restraining hand on his arm. " 'Tis for exactly that reason that I did not want to tell you about Henri the night you came to Mirail. I knew you could not leave Richard's entourage, and I feared the devastation of war."

"We must take action, Marguerite. We cannot allow him to continue unpunished."

She nodded. Although she had been willing to overlook Henri's transgressions against herself and her people, she could not ignore the fact that he had tried to kill Alain. For that he deserved to be punished.

"Will you trust me to resolve this without bringing war to Mirail?" Alain asked.

Marguerite's eyes were bright with joy. "I love you, Alain," she said simply. "I trust you with everything I hold most dear."

Alain was silent for a moment as he gazed at Marguerite, his eyes reflecting in turn his own vulnerability and the joy that her words had wrought. When he spoke, his voice was husky with unshed tears.

"I never dreamed there could be anyone like you, and the saints above know I've done naught to deserve you. But, oh, Marguerite, I cannot believe the good fortune that brought you into my life. You've given me everything a man could want—your love and your trust—while I've given you nothing in return."

She placed her hands on both sides of his face, studying the hard planes of his cheeks and the softness of his lips, committing to memory the features she had feared were lost to her forever.

"No, my love," she said with a sweet smile, "you're wrong.

You've given me something no one else could. You've shown me what real love is.''

''Then let me show you once again.'' Alain drew her into his arms and proceeded to do just that.

# Epilogue

"Oh, that feels good." Marguerite leaned back against the soft grass, enjoying the warmth of the late summer sun. It had been weeks since she had left Mirail, and though prudence had dictated that she remain within the barony's walls until the child was born, her restlessness had overweighed prudence, and she had convinced Alain to bring her to a small pond only a few miles outside Mirail.

"Your son wanted to escape," she told Alain, patting her now huge stomach. If her calculations were correct, the child would make its appearance within a week.

"Your *daughter* is like her mother, never satisfied to sit still." He laid his hand next to hers, feeling the child within kick. "That felt like a hand," he said. Marguerite smiled. No matter how often Alain felt the babe within her womb, his voice never lost that note of wonder when he spoke of the child. "Do you suppose she wants to pick flowers and herbs?"

"She may," Marguerite said, "but today all I want to do is rest and enjoy having you to myself."

The months since they had returned from Poitiers had passed quickly, filled with the normal activity of the summer and the aftermath of the tournament. Within weeks of Marguerite's return, Gerard had come to Mirail, and the barony had celebrated his marriage to Louise. There had been no question of allowing Henri to continue as a vassal. Together Marguerite and Alain had publicly disenfranchised him. And the other vassals, far from condemning the action, had applauded it, for Henri's behavior during the tournament had destroyed any illusions of his chivalry.

"The summer would be perfect, if only Diane were with child," Marguerite mused. She closed her eyes, reveling in the warmth of the sun on her face.

"If I know my brother, he's doing everything he can to make that happen." There was a new easiness in Alain's voice when he spoke of his brother. Though Marguerite had not asked what had transpired between them, she was pleased by the camaraderie and open affection which they now shared.

Alain stretched out next to her, propped on one elbow. "Speaking of babies, do you think it's too soon to start working on this one's brother?" His breath fanned her lips as he moved to kiss her.

"Enjoy it, Jarnac, for it will be the last time you kiss her."

"Henri!" Marguerite's eyes flew open. He had moved so stealthily through the soft grass that she had not heard his approach. Now he was standing over them, his sword pointed at Alain's throat.

Instinctively Alain rolled away from Marguerite and leaped to his feet, keeping Henri's attention and the lethal sword aimed at him.

"What happened, Henri?" Alain's tone was deliberately taunting. "Did you get tired of living under a rock and decide to come out for some sun?"

Henri waved the sword in Alain's direction. "That's right. I wanted some sun. I'm not going to live in your shadow any longer." He turned the hilt in his hands, as though testing its weight. "You should have died in the tournament, but you were lucky that day. This time will be different. Your luck has run out, Jarnac. Without a sword you have no chance." Alain's sword glinted in the sunlight, yards away from him.

Alain raised one brow, mocking Henri. "Is that so? I understand that my wife . . ." Alain emphasized the word, ". . . a mere woman fended off your attack with no more than a common knife. It proves you quite the warrior, doesn't it, Henri?"

He was deliberately goading Henri. Another man would have sought to placate the man. Not Alain. Instead with each taunt, he moved another step to the left, drawing Henri further from Marguerite. It was a masterful ploy; unfortunately, it also took Alain further from his own sword.

Marguerite's brain began to whirl. There had to be a way she could help Alain. She moved cautiously, shifting her body mere inches at a time lest Henri be aware of her movements.

Henri lunged toward Alain. "That's enough! You've made people laugh at me all my life, but you'll never do it again. Never. Do you hear me?" He swung the sword in an arc. "It started when we were squires for Guy de Bercé. You fooled everyone there. They thought you were the best warrior, and they wouldn't look at me."

Marguerite slid another few inches closer to Alain's sword. If only he could keep Henri talking. She needed to slide the sword out of its sheath, then distract Henri enough that Alain could reach his weapon.

"When I challenged you, you just laughed and refused to fight me. Everyone else laughed, too. Those fools! They called me Harmless Henri."

Marguerite's eyes widened. Was this the reason Henri had vowed to kill Alain, a simple childhood nickname? The man must have been unbalanced his entire life. But there was no time to pity Henri, for Alain's life was at stake. She stretched her fingers and touched the sword's hilt.

"No one calls me Harmless Henri any longer."

"Indeed not." In the instant before she spoke, Marguerite hurled the now unsheathed sword toward Alain. "Today they'll call you . . ."

"Hapless Henri." Alain completed the sentence as he seized the sword and aimed it at the other man. "If you want to fight, I'll fight you. This time, though, I will show no mercy." Alain balanced on the balls of his feet, ready to attack.

"Those are bold words, Jarnac, but you'll be the one who's

begging for mercy. You thought you were so brave, taking away my lands. Today I'll get them back . . . and more.'' Henri swiveled his head to look at Marguerite. ''This very night I'll have your sweet wife in my bed. As for that devil's spawn she has in her belly.'' Henri laughed. ''There will be an unfortunate accident. Mark my words, Jarnac. There will be no trace of you left on this earth when I'm done.''

He gripped his sword tighter and lunged. Alain moved swiftly to the side, missing the blow.

''You coward! You're afraid to meet my blade.''

It was an unfair contest, for Henri was wearing mail while Alain's body was unprotected. Marguerite scrambled to her feet, seeking a way she could help Alain.

He kept his eyes fixed on Henri, his sword seeming to move effortlessly as he parried the other man's thrusts. When Henri aimed for his right shoulder, hoping to reopen the wound he had inflicted in the tournament and disable Alain's sword arm, Alain stepped deftly to the side, his own sword moving at the last moment to deflect the blow.

Henri's yowl sounded more like an animal's cry than a man's. ''You die!'' he shouted, lowering his head and charging at Alain, his sword aimed directly at Alain's heart.

It was ended almost before it had begun. In one of those movements that had ensured his reputation as a skilled warrior, Alain shifted his weight, thrusting his sword forward and impaling Henri. As the man crumpled to the ground, Alain dropped his sword and ran to Marguerite.

''It's over,'' he murmured and drew her into his arms. ''He'll never again hurt you.''

She was trembling from fear and relief as she fit her body to Alain's, drawing strength from his nearness. ''Just hold me, my love,'' she whispered.

With tender hands, Alain smoothed her hair, then tipped her face toward his. At first his lips were gentle, seeking only to comfort, but the fire that his touch ignited could not be denied.

As they embraced under the late summer sun, Marguerite felt the horror of the day disappear, replaced by the certainty that she had found her destiny. This was why she had been placed on earth, to share her life with this man, to be held in his arms, to bear his children. She would never have the life she had once dreamed of, a quiet existence with a knight who spent his days composing poetry. What she would have was far better: a life with Alain, a man who—like her—had his thorns; a life that would never be boring; a life that would be filled with love.

Her fingers traced the familiar planes of his face, and she smiled as Alain's eyes met hers, their deep blue depths reflecting the love she knew shone from hers.

"I never dreamed that love could be so wondrous," she said softly.

" 'Tis no dream," he murmured, his lips capturing and caressing her fingertips. "What we share is real and far more lasting than a dream. But 'tis true that it is wondrous, this thing we call love. For love you I do, my sweet Marguerite, and love you I will for all eternity."

And then there was no need for words.

Dear Reader,

I think every writer has a story that grips her imagination and simply won't let go, a story that demands to be told. For me, *Silver Thorns* was that kind of story.

It started when my husband was stationed in Germany with the Army. We had no money and, at the time, no car. (Our ancient sixth-handed Volkswagen had decided it preferred life in a junkyard to traveling with us and had left us stranded miles from the closest train station with two huge duffel bags . . . but that's another story.) Suffice it to say that we soon discovered the German pastime of walking.

We lived in a small farming village in southern Germany, midway between Stuttgart and Munich. Not only was the village delightful in its own right, but it was surrounded by forests that were crisscrossed with logging roads. It was while we were exploring one of these roads that we discovered a ruined castle. I have to admit that under normal circumstances ruins hold little appeal for me, but there was something about this castle that beckoned me to come closer, and so I did.

Do you believe in déjà vu or reincarnation? I never did . . . until that day. But once inside the castle walls, I knew—yes, I knew—I had been there before. I tried to ignore the story of the people who had once lived in that castle, and for a while I was successful. But at the oddest times, their voices would intrude, reminding me of the Second Crusade and the people who survived the dreadful ambush. Insomnia is not a pleasant malady, and so finally I agreed to tell one of the stories, if only they'd let me sleep. *Silver Thorns* is the result.

But, you're saying, *Silver Thorns* takes place in France, not Germany. That's right, and that means that I've won only a temporary reprieve. I still owe Catherine her story. Lady Catherine, you see, was the woman who lived in the castle when it was first built. But Catherine will have to wait, because right now Amelia is demanding all of my time. Amelia's a doctor in Gold Landing, Alaska at the turn of the century and, oh, the problems she faces, not the least of which is an arrogant mine owner who has no use for doctors of any sort. As for female doctors . . .

Be sure to watch for my next book, *Midnight Sun,* the story of those two stubborn people and the problems they create because neither is willing to admit to love.

Until we meet again, I wish you love, laughter and many happy hours reading.

*Amanda Harte*

## About the Author

For as long as she can remember, Amanda Harte has wanted to be a writer. Her dream came true in 1981 with the publication of her first romance. Since then, she has sold six other books and has published dozens of articles in technical journals.

Amanda is a graduate of Syracuse University with a degree in French literature. She counts herself fortunate to have studied in Poitiers and credits that stay, as well as living in Germany compliments of the U.S. Army, with the background for *Silver Thorns*. When she is not writing, Amanda manages information technology projects for a major manufacturing company. She lives in New Jersey with her husband.